Keeper of the Lambs

by

Dr. Sue Clifton

Sisters of the Way, Book 2

Keeper of the Lambs

Cover Art by *Kim Mendoza*

The Wild Rose Press, Inc.
PO Box 708
Adams Basin, NY 14410-0708
Visit us at www.thewildrosepress.com

Publishing History
First Mainstream Paranormal Rose Edition, 2019
Print ISBN 978-1-5092-2661-0
Digital ISBN 978-1-5092-2662-7

Sisters of the Way, Book 2
Published in the United States of America

The blades on the two oversized fans hanging on either end of the ceiling stopped abruptly and then turned the opposite direction, whirring louder and louder, threatening to chop up whatever or whoever was beneath them if they fell. Charlie covered his eyes and rocked forward and backward. Harri and Teesh hugged him, putting their bodies tight against him to shelter him from the terrifying happenings. The camcorder flew off Harri's lap and landed at her feet, but she made no attempt to retrieve it.

Hank stopped playing and grabbed Cayce in a bear hug to prevent her from being cast off the bench as it vibrated and then levitated, rising at least five feet off the floor.

What happened next proved to be the shocking conclusion to the horrific scene. A large, dark fog appeared on the walkway that looked down from the second story. It moved stealthily toward the stairs, making its own whirring sound like a mass of huge, nasty, black flies beating their wings in rapid succession. Then the beating turned to deep bass, drumming more like a cave full of bats than tiny flies as the black mass moved down the stairs and approached the dazed onlookers.

Books by Dr. Sue Clifton
Available from The Wild Rose Press, Inc.

Sisters of the Way Series
THE BREATH OF SPANISH OAKS
KEEPER OF THE LAMBS

~

Daughters of Parrish Oaks Series
THE GULLY PATH
UNDER NORTHERN LIGHTS
HEART OF THE BEARTOOTHS
MOUNTAIN MISTS
WINGS ON MOUNTAIN BREEZES

Dedication

TO NYOKA,

my real-life sister and researcher who traveled with me to haunted hotels, ghost towns, and even cemeteries, looking for the perfect ghostly settings and material for this "Sisters of the Way" series.

I never apologized to you for chasing you through the house with that butcher knife when we were nine and ten years old—you know, retaliation for the numerous times you jumped out from behind doors and scared the "bajiggers" out of me? WELL, DON'T HOLD YOUR BREATH! APOLOGY NOT FORTHCOMING!

Just remember—that line in *Keeper of the Lambs* is true! I WAS the one who crawled "under the house when we were kids, during snake season, to drag out the stray dog's puppies," one of whom (the prettiest one) you claimed immediately!

Ditto to the words written on my favorite Hallmark cup you gave me, the one that has been sitting on my desk for decades: "When I think back on the way I treated you when we were young, the mindless jokes, the cruel taunts—IT CHEERS ME RIGHT UP!"

I need new material and settings for future books! Pack your bags, Sista!

~Sue

Acknowledgments

My thanks to the Cole family, owners of the Thomas House, Red Boiling Springs, Tennessee, who introduced me to little ghost girl Sara many years ago. Everything Sara does in *Keeper of the Lambs* is something I, and others, have witnessed at the Thomas House. Whether you believe or not is your choice, but Sara is real!

I also would like to thank Montana and Texas artist Janet Olson for explaining and demonstrating the *Plein-Air* technique and for acting as my consultant answering any questions about Piper's painting scenes. Any mistakes made in these descriptions are mine alone and are due to my total lack of artistic ability.

~Dr. Sue

Prologue

Bar None, Idaho
1928

The bent, frail woman circled the cemetery, choosing not to take the short path to the grave she visited every day, even under a scorching summer sun, through mudslides brought by spring or fall drizzles, or in blizzards that threatened to bury her. As the woman walked, she kept her head hung low, her chin buried in her stiff, high-necked, black bodice. She knew in this position she would be unable to see the small transparent figure of a young woman dressed in a white lace dress who paced around the grave of her own baby, her voice crying in delicate, restrained sobs so soft they were barely audible.

The older woman's eyes stared down through the dark veil at her black lace-up shoes that crunched with every step like the rhythm of the deep bass of a church hymn sung solo with no melody, no joy—a somber reminder of her many sins. Trying to clear her mind, she trudged on. The snow fell thicker as she neared the spot up the valley where her little treasure, Sara, lay resting, free of the stomach aches plaguing her short seven years of life.

The mourner refused to look up at the monolithic Jesus she had custom ordered from San Francisco and paid an additional ten prices to get transported across desert and mountains. The statue was an afterthought to the unnamed children buried in its shadows in a common grave. All this was for show, a bribe to convince God not to take Sara. But the bribe had gone unacknowledged, and Sara had been taken from her.

Jesus' outstretched arms embraced a throng of marble children, all with slanted eyes, who looked out of place in the mostly Anglo cemetery. Words from Mark 10:4, dialogue spoken by Jesus, were written along the statue base. The lady in black shortened the verse, locking one phrase in her mind and on her lips as if the repetition might somehow relieve her own suffering:

"Suffer the little children to come unto me…Suffer the little children to come unto me."

She whispered the words to the breeze playing through the surrounding forest—gloomy background music, harp chords strummed in a minor key. Her conscience primed her search for justification and forgiveness for past transgressions. Over and over the same sermon, "seek forgiveness," played in her mind like the few old worn-out hymns sung by the miners' women in the small rustic log chapel. He, the man she had always loved, had built it so his precious young wife would have a place to kneel and pray after she accepted his God. He stopped attending the church after his wife died and refused to pay for its upkeep—his effort to punish God for taking his wife.

The woman in black had promised to rebuild the church now standing as blackened, burned timbers—another attempt to bargain for Sara's life, but she never carried out the promise. After God took her baby, the woman severed all contributions to any church and shunned the one remaining church, refusing it as a site for Sara's final goodbye. Sara's service was held in the hotel parlor instead. Now the woman realized her only hope of seeing her Sara again was in the afterlife rejected along with any belief in God.

I need to go to heaven and be with my baby again. Please, God, don't punish me more! I swear I believe! I'm even talking to You!

As the woman slowed and glanced toward the transparent figure that hovered over the grave of her own child, she momentarily forgot the pure thoughts she was pretending in case the Heavenly Being was watching.

I love him more than she did!

She wrung her hands, not to aid circulation in the frigid temperature, but in the gesture that had become habit, her symbol of validation replacing her remorse for past transgressions.

I took care of him—still take care of him, like I took care of Sara.

She turned her gaze from the small figure. Her thoughts softened as she neared her destination, and purity of thought returned to overpower her contempt for the small white shadow.

Suffer the little children…Suffer the little children.

She mouthed her thoughts in rhythm to the wringing of her hands. Her footsteps quickened, turning to strides as she came in sight of the precious mound of dirt lying just out of His shadowy reach.

"Haven't I paid my penance by taking care of him all these years?" She lifted her gaze and screamed the words at the gray heavens and then at the figure of

Jesus. Then, as if afraid He would move His gaze from the babies buried beneath His shadow to her, she dropped her eyes to the ground again and altered her stride to a quick but quiet gait the rest of the way to the child's grave.

Dropping to her knees below the pure white angel tombstone she had added just for her own little angel, she brushed away the white as if afraid the child would be chilled by the first snowfall. As she swept the flakes, she cried, tears forming icy paths to her quivering, downturned mouth. Unable to keep up with the thickening flurries, she spread her body across the grave and wailed—a long, mournful sound that reverberated through the cabins and buildings mostly empty now. The sound had been heard for so long the townspeople, what few remained, had grown immune, if they had ever cared at all.

"My baby! Child of my child!" Raising her gaze from the grassless knoll, she screamed at Jesus, who continued to gaze down, ignoring the ravings of the crazy woman.

"When will my suffering end?" Again, her tears poured, springs of human misery.

"Suffer the little children…Suffer the little children," she repeated, attempting to redirect her thoughts. Then she buried her face in the grave. Pounding the snow-flecked mound with her gloved fists, she moaned a cry not human, the last replay of this daily ritual. She glanced up from the ice patch formed by her tears and rose to her hands and knees, hastily retreating backward on all fours in a tangle of black satin and lace. Hordes of blue, rotating circles approached from the mass unmarked gravesite, the spot where Jesus cast His protective shadow on clear days.

The mourner's eyes reflected terror, but she could not move; her escape route was blocked! Her back was pressed tight against a nearby tombstone crudely chipped out of sandstone for some person of insignificance—her description of everyone in the cemetery with the exception of Sara. As the blue orbs swarmed around her, she swatted at them as if surrounded by bees. Then she recognized the tiny slanted eyes in each nucleus, all enraged. The woman covered her face with her arms, her scream replaced by one last gasp for air as she curled into fetal position.

****

Idaho, the Present

He whistled in short shallow breaths in an attempt to restrain his crazed excitement. Then, unable to contain his exhilaration any longer, he leapt across the rocky terrain as surefooted as a mountain goat. His adrenaline pushed him back toward the long, black SUV, a vehicle much too similar to a hearse.

Onward, Christian soldiers, marching as to war, with the cross of Jesus going on before.

The lyrics danced through his head, threatening to escape his lips and bombard the serene mountain setting.

Spurts of air burst from his lips as if from a freed, untied balloon, always the same tune whistled after the fulfillment of a mission; his breathing followed the animation of his body as he lifted his arms toward heaven. His jubilation never waned; his rush peaked as he tore loose the top two buttons on his shirt using only his thumbs, being careful not to soil his shirt with his red-stained, dirty hands.

He opened the door behind the driver's seat and, with one sweeping motion, thrust in the tool that had buried a wealth of sin and sinners, careful not to hit the prized cargo bound in the back. Again, he lifted his arms to heaven and laughed the laugh of a madman proud of the blood on his hands as he both hummed and whistled another stanza of his battle hymn. Then, lowering his arms, he slid into the driver's seat, never losing his momentum.

"At the sign of triumph, Satan's host doeth flee; on then, Christian soldiers, on to victory." His melodic tenor filled the night as he stretched his arms to the vehicle's ceiling and belted out his song of war and victory.

Resuming his humming of loud, sharp notes, he pulled down the sun visor and stared into the mirror behind it. With the certainty of one who had accomplished this task many times before, the killer opened his shirt and outlined the diamond shape that contained a thick cross. He colored in the empty spaces of the tattoo with the rest of the victim's blood before wiping the excess on his shirt. Staring with wild eyes, mesmerized by his own reflection, he finished his solo aloud.

"With the cross of Jesus go…ing…on…be…fore!"

The killer held the final note longer, waving his hands in the air as if directing an unseen choir of angels…or demons, and then clasped his hands together on the wheel and lowered his head into them.

With eyes closed, he whispered the words in hushed, reverent tones, and when finished, clutched the wheel for a few more seconds before lifting his eyes.

He stared at himself in the mirror as if seeking additional reassurance and smiled with the satisfaction of a job well done. The killer repeated aloud the same words as he looked past his reflection toward the back of the vehicle.

"A necessary waste…a justified killing for the sake of the lambs. Not murder, which would imply innocence. Others must be eliminated. I am the Keeper, armed with truth and the sword."

****

"What's happening? Where am I?"

The questions screaming in the girl's mind were audible only as a deep-throated moan.

The scarf, soggy with her tears, was tied so tightly it felt as though her eyeballs were being buried in their sockets. Her nose was running rivers, and her mouth was sealed shut with duct tape. Her whole body—arms, legs, torso—and even her head were bound tightly to the gurney-like bed. The girl could only swallow her sobs of anguish and fear as she listened in the darkness from the back of a vehicle she knew must be a van or a large SUV.

The girl—all five feet, four inches of her—lay flat on her back. She stretched her fingers to search for Johnny, but she could only reach out an inch or two. Without the use of her senses of sight and touch, she resorted to using "Grammar Sense."

Her favorite grandmother had been an English teacher. Hence, the clever grandmother name. Grammar had gone blind at the age of fifty, but being an optimist, said her blindness only heightened her other senses. The two often played the girl's favorite game, "Grammar Sense," in which she would blindfold herself

7

and describe everything she was experiencing, matching her sensations to her grandmother's real-life ones. Her Grammar had died a few months ago, but she was always in her granddaughter's thoughts.

Grammar, are you with me? I'm scared.

In her mind, the girl could hear her Grammar's reply: *I'm with you, Billie. You are strong, smart, and brave. You're a survivor. Never forget this. Use your strengths, Granddaughter.*

Billie swallowed the sob trapped in her throat and pretended she and Grammar were being driven to an undisclosed location by Billie's dad, who often shared in the game with his daughter and his mother. Billie could feel her grandmother's fingers entwined with her bound ones as they began their imaginary move, hand in hand, through the secret location, using the senses available to them.

"Use the senses you have, Billie. What do you hear? What do you smell?"

Billie listened. She heard the hum of the car's motor—a heavy, powerful sound. *"It's an SUV, not a van; it's one of the big ones like a Suburban."*

Billie sensed smooth pavement as they traveled along, not speeding, but not going too slowly.

A main road, then.

Something rattled beside her, like an unbalanced tool was hitting against the side of the vehicle. The driver was silent...a good thing, she hoped.

She opened her nostrils a little and took a shallow breath. Her surroundings reminded her of her dad's garage where he worked on the vintage truck he was restoring.

"Older vehicle...no new car smells. Oily...dirty...

definitely a working man's vehicle...dirty work. Pine scent but not real pine...one of those cheap, smelly pretend tree things that hangs from a mirror...one bought recently because it smells strong, masking other smells. Light smell of diesel like a lot of ranchers burn in their vehicles."

Sniffing again, she caught the faint scent of Johnny's cologne, the brand she had bought him for his birthday. Billie made herself think back to that happy time. It seemed a forever ago, although it was only a few months. She needed to think good thoughts.

What will I get Johnny? What will he like? What will he want? What will he even use?

She remembered how she had agonized over what to get this gorgeous guy who had everything, this guy she had just met but who she already knew was the one. She had decided on cologne, a safe gift, and picked out her favorite scent. It was a sweet yet hardy smell, warm and electrifying—manly, but not macho. She could see herself wrapping it in a black box with a blue bow and attaching a silly, sweet card, and then remembered the moment when Johnny had anxiously unwrapped the present. How she'd wished she had come up with something more original.

Cologne! What was I thinking?

But it proved to be the perfect gift. Johnny had smiled when he saw the bottle. He'd sprayed it, breathed in the aroma, and closed his eyes as if being transported to another time and place. It was the same cologne his mom had bought his dad for a wedding anniversary gift. His dad had loved it and wore it to work, church, dinners, football games, and everywhere he went. The pleasant scent brought back his father, who had died when Johnny was fifteen. Johnny told her how safe and happy he'd felt with his dad, the way he wanted Billie to feel when she was with him. She remembered his sweet kiss as he thanked her for the gift. Johnny wore the cologne every day after that.

Billie breathed deeper, the only way she could be close to Johnny as she lay unable to move, unable to reach out to him. It was the scent of the man she hoped to spend the rest of her life with—the loving, protective Johnny. She could only hope Johnny would be able to save them both.

Her good thoughts fell prey to the present as she returned to how this terrifying ordeal had begun.

They had sped along on his Harley across Montana and Idaho, feeling alive and free—a false illusion. The last she remembered was using the outhouse at one of the campgrounds in the wilderness section of Idaho. When she came out of the outhouse, someone had grabbed her from behind and put a bad-smelling cloth over her mouth and nose, instantly suffocating her. When she awoke, she was captive to pitch black terror.

Her heart pumped violently; the veins in her neck felt as if they would explode as the vehicle slowed to a creep. The road changed from smooth pavement to a bumpy road that spit gravel under the wheels. She was being taken deeper into the isolated wilderness.

I won't think of it!

Her mind commanded, but she was not convinced.

I'm not going to be raped or murdered! Johnny will save me!

More sobs were absorbed by the duct tape.

After a few jarring minutes, the vehicle stopped. The driver exited and opened the door behind his seat, putting Billie on high alert. The groans and heavy breathing of the man fueled more fear in her as he pulled and lifted something from the back. The scent of Johnny permeated her surroundings, heightening her sense of smell. But his cologne became overpowered by a different smell.

Metal…iron, maybe.

The scent wafted through the air and into her nostrils; a strong smell that found its way into the back of her mouth, giving her a taste she did not want to experience.

Blood!

The vibrato of the man's whistle was interrupted by the burden of what he lifted. Even though she recognized the tune as one she had often sung in church, she found no comfort in it and began to sob and tremble. Her thoughts turned from the head-game she played to the worst possible scenario. Then she heard the heavy object being dragged away from the vehicle, and the whistling was replaced with more heavy breathing.

Dull terror sharpened to fierce realization as she heard the unique ring tone of Johnny's cell phone, the distinct base rumble of a Harley starting up followed by Steppenwolf bellowing out "Born to be Wild." The words faded, becoming less and less distinguishable as if the cell phone had been hurled away from the scene. They ended short seconds later in a shatter followed by silence. She strained her ears but could not discern the new sounds she heard behind the labored breathing of the kidnapper.

Then came sounds of small rocks avalanching down a cliff or embankment, and she heard the footfalls coming closer. Her heart somersaulted as the back door opened at her feet. She tensed, sure she was about to be dragged out like Johnny, and began to gasp and cry behind the duct tape, but he did not move her. He took out something from beside her that gave a deep scraping noise and then a ping as it hit the vehicle bumper. The door slammed shut, and footfalls crunching gravel moved away from the vehicle.

A long time passed before the man returned to the vehicle where Billie lay drifting in and out of exhausted sleep. She had lost all track of time. He whistled the tune that seemed to dominate his thoughts as he opened the door behind the driver's seat and threw something into the backseat that hit the opposite door with the same pinging sound she had heard earlier. Whistling gave way to jubilant singing of words of praise as the man took his seat in the SUV.

New tears soaked the blindfold as Billie realized the truth.

Johnny would not rescue her. She could only pray death would not follow her and the small life forming in her body, all that was left of Johnny, the life Johnny had demanded they end. She closed her eyes as the drug- and terror-induced drowsiness took control.

Chapter One

Montana, A Few Weeks Later

"I can't believe we're riding in eighty-degree weather with no air conditioning. You have gone completely insane this time, Cayce. Actually, I've gone insane to be riding with you in this old truck. What year did you say it is?"

"It's a fifty-two, too near our age to criticize, I'm afraid." Cayce smiled, then gave Harri a quick glance. "And we're still going strong."

"Easy for you to say, dear sister. You run a ranch and throw fifty-pound bags of horse feed over your shoulder. I run The Teacake, a very genteel teahouse, keep the air conditioner set on sixty-eight degrees, prefer silk to denim, and don't lift anything heavier than my make-up bag." The truck hit a pothole and knocked her against the door. With a deep sigh, she stared at the side of Cayce's grinning face. "Take a lesson—you're a woman first, a cowpoke second, or make that last."

"Yes, but not a weak damsel. One of us has to be strong, considering the messes we get ourselves into. Actually, it's our connection with the living dead that gets us into messes." The sisters' father had been the giver of their "Gift" that often landed them in trouble.

"Speaking of messes, what mess is it your lover boy is getting us into?"

"Joshua is a best friend—you being first best as well as sister—and he is lover boy second, although that identity could move up if he's ever available. Anyway, he wants us to check out this ghost town in Idaho he has purchased. He's restoring it, making it into a place where lovers of the Old West can come and relive history."

"And that involves us how?" Harri gave her sister the questioning sideways stare, her eyebrows wrinkled.

"Joshua has had workers up there for months restoring three of the old buildings, but the crew has run into a few problems of the paranormal variety." Cayce pulled her sunglasses down her nose and gave Harri the look that yelled, "Here we go again!"

"Before you even begin to tell me what's going on there, what's the name of this ghost town, and what's the history? I can probably surmise who is lingering from that."

"The name of the ghost town is Bar None. Catchy, huh?" Cayce lifted her eyebrows, matching Harri's cynical look. "Actually, I've got a document from the County Historical Society that pretty much covers the history, but since I know you hate to read while riding—especially in a bumpy old truck—I'll hit the highlights for you."

As if Cayce needed justification for her statement, she swerved the old truck, but not soon enough to prevent hitting another pothole in the highway.

Harri clenched her lips and held a death grip on the seat and door.

"Dear Lord! I don't know if my bladder can adapt to this." Harri lifted herself to sit with one leg under her. "Keep quiet while I count. If I start the Kegel now, maybe I can make it for two weeks, or however long we're out here." She counted while Cayce shook her head and laughed. "Twenty-eight, twenty-nine, thirty. How about we stop and rent a nice SUV? I'll spring for it." Harri put on her best begging look, hoping her sister would run with it.

"My trip, my choice, and you already know what the answer is. Besides, Hawk, here, has taken me on much worse trips than this and made it just fine." Cayce rubbed her hand across the dashboard as if caressing the old truck.

"You named your truck after Hawk, the hero from your favorite romance novel? Sounds just like you."

"You need a different adventure, Harri. Something other than all the comforts of home such as riding around in a BMW convertible." Cayce kept her eyes on the road and hesitated before continuing, "And, while we're on the subject of comfort, I need to tell you Joshua specifically wanted you along because there is a cooking element only you can handle."

"Putting cooking and 'other than all the comforts of home' in the same context has me really worried." Harri kept her eyes straight ahead as apprehension circled head to stomach.

"You are so right. As in cooking on a fireplace, a wood stove, and even over a campfire—pioneer cooking, so to speak. In fact, Joshua wants to keep the experience as close to the nineteenth century as possible for those brave enough to come."

"Stop right there! If there is no air conditioning and no indoor plumbing, I'm on the next plane out of here. I didn't sign on for roughin' it." Harri set her jaw, struggling not to yell expletives at her sister for coercing her into this craziness. "And the mention of campfire cooking sounds like roughin' it to me."

"Oh, don't be such a sissy, Harri." Cayce dismissed Harri's argument with a wave of her non-driving hand. "The work crew has already installed indoor plumbing of the communal type, with shared showers and toilets on the top floor of the hotel. However, there are cabins that have outhouses in case some tourists want a true historical experience. And before you ask, we have rooms in the upstairs of the hotel."

"That doesn't explain campfire cooking." Harri folded her arms and shook her head, disliking the potential hardship suggested. "I'm not sure I want to hear this."

"Okay. I might as well get this over with. Joshua is coming out in a few days, and he has a guy lined up to take us on a wagon train trip, something he will include in the guest package. He wants you to come up with the meal plan." Cayce kept her eyes straight ahead and sped up.

"Whoa, Cayce! Turn this thing around and take me back to the airport. I don't do dirt, insects, or hanging your butt over a felled tree limb to do your business. And I will not afflict my nice makeup bag with a small handheld spade for burying such business." She couldn't believe Cayce had planned something so extreme without giving any initial warning of what all it entailed. Panic formed a hard ball in Harri's throat, leaving her feeling sick.

Cayce refused to look at her.

"I mean it, Cayce, I'm not doing this!" She shouted to bring home her point.

"Don't get your thongs…or whatever…in a tiny,

lacy knot. There will be some really nice streams to bathe in, and I've already purchased you a battery-operated blow dryer and curling iron. As for the business, there'll be plenty of outhouses for that, except maybe when you're between outhouses." Cayce smiled her mischievous smile.

"That is so disgusting!" Infuriated, Harri shuddered and turned away, looking out the side window with her arms crossed. Dollar signs replaced her angry thoughts. "What's in this for me? He's bound to have something in mind, or he knows I wouldn't consider this."

"I knew I could count on you, and Joshua did, too. He wants you to do a cookbook for the ghost town. He'll pay you to do it, and you'll be able to sell it other places for profit." Cayce risked looking at her sister, knowing the cookbook idea would cause a change of attitude.

Harri stared straight ahead, her elbow rested on the other arm crossed over her waist while she tapped an index finger against her top lip. This pose always meant deep financial contemplation.

"Hmmm. You know, I did do a campfire-cooking lesson for a troop of girl scouts in Germantown, Tennessee one time. I just need to find a nineteenth-century substitute for aluminum foil." Harri's lip tapping returned, and Cayce knew she could count on her sister regardless of her earlier misgivings. Cayce remained quiet, ready for Harri's brainstorms.

"We need to stop at some antique shops. I need to buy a couple of Dutch ovens and some cast iron cookware. Maybe I'll luck up and find some frontier cookbooks, too."

"We'll wait until we get closer to Bar None. Joshua

told me when the word was out that Bar None had been sold, someone went in and ransacked the buildings, taking everything that might be of value. Joshua hired Steve, a man who owns one of the old cabins in Bar None, to watch over the town. Steve is the only full-time resident there."

"It's time to fill me in on the history and the paranormal activity at the town. I might as well know who or what we're up against." Harri turned her whole body toward her sister, settling her shoulder into the seat.

"Okay. Here goes." Cayce leaned back in her seat and lifted her left leg to rest her foot on the edge of the driver's seat. She moved her hands to the bottom of the huge old steering wheel, her "long haul position," as her sister called it, her storytelling position or "plotting" position.

"Bar None sprang up in 1867 with the discovery of gold. By 1900, it was a fairly large town, though remote, with close to nine hundred people living in it. A railroad was built with part of it running right through the middle of town, but only one piece of track remains, a track going nowhere. Most of the railroad ties probably now outline flowerbeds in the yards of local lovers of antiquities. Make that pilferers." Cayce glanced at Harri to make sure she was listening and saw she had her sister's full attention.

"In the early nineteen hundreds, most of the town burned, and by then, the vein of gold was running out, so Bar None was never rebuilt. All that remains of the town is a hotel and the building that once housed the town newspaper, *The Bar None Sentry*, plus a few small, rundown—or make that falling-down—cabins and homes, and a large two-story building called The Nugget, with a saloon on the bottom floor and a famed house of ill repute in the back and upstairs sections. The Nugget provided entertainment for the mostly male population of Bar None. The local clientele called it by a different name—the cat house."

"Sounds appropriate." Harri gave a one-syllable mini laugh.

"Madam Belle's girls made her wealthier than any of the miners, the exception being Absalom Duluth, the owner of the Duluth Mining Company, the largest and last gold mining company in the area." Cayce stretched over the huge steering wheel and stared ahead, making sure no surprise potholes were in her path. "The company dissolved in 1935 with the death of Absalom Duluth, who had no known heirs. The gold vein had run out way before then, anyway." Cayce stopped and drank from the bottled water she'd propped between her thighs.

"Okay, now get to the good part. Does Absalom still reside at Bar None, and what other used-to-be residents are thought to be roaming about wreaking havoc on the construction project?" Harri loosened her chest strap, switched legs under her, and leaned against the truck door, facing her sister, ready for the ghost stories.

"The construction boss for the project is a guy named Hank Coulter. He's had a heck of a time keeping workers, especially the night crew, because of the activity there. Men have been knocked off ladders by black mists or shadowy figures and hit with flying objects. They've heard a phantom train approaching with its horn blowing, and saloon music at night."

"Holy crap! This is going to be exciting." Harri rubbed her hands together as if in anticipation. "Any apparitions?"

"Oh, yes, especially in the cemetery. The figure seen most often is a beautiful young Chinese woman thought to be Yu, the wife of Absalom. Her full name was Yu Lin. That means 'beautiful jade' in Chinese. She mostly walks the cemetery, wringing her hands and whimpering. She's distraught over the loss of her baby girl Tamara. Yu is buried between her husband and their child."

"So Absalom Duluth had an heir for a short time."

"Yes, and that is the most tragic story of all. Absalom Duluth was a light-skinned African American who came to Bar None when he was very young, in his early twenties. No one knew anything about him other than he was a mechanical genius, especially when it came to mining, and he was exceptionally adept at supervising workers and making money. Even though the Civil War had ended only a decade earlier, the whole town respected Absalom without prejudice. Absalom fell in love with Yu Lin, who was one of Madam Belle's girls, and made Belle a deal she couldn't refuse in order to buy Yu's freedom."

"Wait a minute." Harri held up her hand. "What do you mean 'buy Yu's freedom'? Slavery ended with the Emancipation Proclamation. There was no slavery after the Civil War."

"Yes and no. It seems Madam Belle, like many, practiced her own form of slavery. She paid off the debts of young women, lured them with promises of a better life, and then refused to release them. They were slaves to prostitution. But Yu's story was different.

Belle hired an old client from San Francisco, where her business was before moving to Bar None, to buy Yu Lin and other Chinese girls from a Chinese agent who is said to have kidnapped the girls to sell on the slave market." Cayce shook her head at the thought of having a child, especially a daughter, stolen and placed into prostitution in a foreign land.

"I can't imagine anything worse than having your daughter stolen." Harri spoke her sister's thoughts aloud.

"And most of Belle's girls were Chinese; probably easier to control since they did not speak English and were too far from family to be rescued. But Yu was luckier than most of the girls. Once Absalom saw Yu, he fell madly in love and told Belle to name her price for Yu's freedom. When Belle refused, Absalom offered her half interest in Duluth Mining Company. Belle took the offer. It's a classic love story." Cayce knew she'd captivated her sister with the tale, since Harri never took her eyes off her.

"So what happened to the child? Did he or she die a tragic death?"

"I know what you're thinking, but this is different than Chloe at Spanish Oaks." Cayce took a quick glance toward Harri. "However, this is where the love story becomes a tragedy. While Absalom was away on a business trip, Yu went into early labor. Belle took care of Yu in Absalom's absence, but the baby died before Yu was well enough, or conscious enough, to see her. The birth was just too hard for the petite Yu." Cayce paused for a few seconds and glanced at the landscape surrounding them, wondering how such a beautiful place could be the setting for so much heartache and cruelty. She took another sip from her water bottle and then continued.

"Belle sat by Yu's bedside for days thinking Yu, too, would have to be buried before Absalom returned to Bar None. Yu survived the birth, but was so distraught over losing Tamara, the name Absalom had chosen for a baby girl, she never spoke again. When Absalom returned, he cared for Yu, refusing to leave her side. Belle had to run the mining operation in Absalom's absence. Unable to tolerate her loss, Yu refused food and water and literally starved to death out of grief a few weeks later."

"How awful for Absalom, first his child and then his wife." Harri changed her position, leaning against the door again with her left knee up on the seat. "What happened next?"

"After Absalom buried his beautiful wife, he drowned his sorrows in whiskey and continued to neglect his mining business. Belle kept control and ran the company for both of them. To Absalom's regret, he managed to live a long sorrowful life and never remarried. Madam Belle took care of him until she died in 1928. I'm not sure what 'took care of him' meant. Absalom lived a few years longer than Belle, and he, too, is buried in the cemetery at Bar None. The tale was Belle had always had her eye on Absalom from the first day he rode into town in 1875."

"So what about Absalom? Is he also walking the cemetery mourning for Yu and the child?"

"No, not that anyone has been able to identify, but there are shadows, and Belle has appeared. Oh, yes, and there's one more real character seen around town. Her name is Peg, not short for Peggy, but a nickname due to her having a peg leg. She supposedly got drunk one night at the saloon after winning big at poker…an unusual pastime for a woman…woman being a stretch since Peg wore only men's clothes and kept her hair bobbed off. She is said to be a scary character, with deep scars covering one side of her face and both hands. Peg, whose real name was Annie, passed out by the railroad track on her way back to her cabin. Story goes when she fell, one of her legs lay across the track. I figure you can guess what happened next."

"Ouch! That must have hurt." Harri shuddered and made a face.

"Probably no worse than when the saloon keeper lost the toss and had to saw her mangled leg off. There was no doctor in the town at the time. Supposedly, Annie guzzled whiskey until she passed out again. The saying goes 'she went to sleep Annie and woke up Peg.' "

Harri laughed at the inference. "I can hardly wait for this. What does Peg do?"

"There's no mistaking Peg Leg Annie. She's mostly seen in the saloon, usually at the one poker table not stolen because it, like Peg, was missing a leg. She is pretty much always seen sitting, but the place she frequents most is the entrance to the old boarded-up mineshaft. There are signs all around it reading, 'Danger! No trespassing!' Up until she lost her leg, Peg was the only female miner in Bar None, and no man dared cross her. Since she couldn't go down in the mine like she once did, she sold whiskey."

"Sold whiskey? You've got to be kidding! Did she make it herself?"

"Probably so. It was obviously a lucrative business.

She'd sit in her rocker with her rifle across her lap and her whiskey bottles lined up in front of her. Needless to say, she was never robbed. Her cabin is the only one still standing, partially anyway, close to the remains of the old railroad tracks. Supposedly when the phantom train blows its whistle, Peg can be heard cursing it and is seen as a wispy, dark mist with fist shaking at the train."

"I wonder how much farther to Bar None?" Harri reached under the seat for the atlas.

"Oh, probably five or six hours yet. We haven't been in Idaho very long. We have to drive the last fifteen miles on gravel. Right now, we need to find a gas station. Hawk's tummy is growling."

Cayce pulled off at the next exit and stopped at a small café-gas station combination. Harri went inside while Cayce filled up the truck. When Cayce came out of the restroom a few minutes later, Harri was paying for two big cups of coffee to go. Before leaving the cash register, Harri pointed out a poster taped to the back of it and a stack of leaflets with the same picture and information on the end of the counter. The picture showed a young couple on a motorcycle.

MISSING! REWARD OFFERED!
Johnny Stinson and Billie Townsley
Last seen in Butte, Montana on May 18. If you have any information on the whereabouts of these young people, please call 406-327-9002 or any law enforcement agency.

"Look at this. What a nice-looking young couple." Harri handed one of the leaflets to Cayce, who absorbed every detail.

She was reminded of a Hollywood poster that always caught her eye in her favorite hair salon where Susan, her hairstylist, worked a magical disappearing act on her client's gray streaks.

In the Hollywood picture, James Dean sat astride a motorcycle with Marilyn Monroe cuddled to his back, a seductive look plastered on her flawless face. The similarities between the two males were amazing. Johnny and James both had thick, longer hair combed straight back, outlining serious, posed faces. Both were dressed in jeans, distressed leather jackets, and cowboy boots, and were obviously proud of their biker chicks. But there the similarity ended. Billie was not cuddled to Johnny like Marilyn was to James Dean. Billie looked young, full of life, athletic and fit, and very sure of herself, possibly even a little aloof as she stood smiling, leaned against Johnny's bike.

"May we take one of these?" Harri held up the leaflet. "We have a good bit of traveling ahead of us. You never know. We might just spot them."

"Please do. The sheriff's office brings a new stack by every week." The girl came from behind the cash register where she could talk to Harri and Cayce better.

"This is getting pretty scary. We don't have much crime around here, but in the last ten months, three girls have disappeared. My parents hate that I work here by myself during the day. Sometimes, my dad comes and just sits with me like a guardian angel."

"I don't blame your parents," Cayce remarked as she looked at the poster Harri was holding. "I have a daughter, Piper, and I'd be frantic if something like this happened to her." Cayce took the poster and read it silently. "It says they've been missing for over a month

25

now. That's a long time. I hope they're just runaways and no harm has come to them."

"Unfortunately, that's probably not the case. The deputy that brought this stack in said they found the motorcycle the other day. It had been pushed off into a stream near a public outhouse in a national forest in our state. They found some old blood outside the outhouse, but I haven't heard if the DNA matched either of the two on the poster. Law enforcement is looking in both Montana and Idaho." The girl reached behind the counter and pulled out a newspaper. "Here, you can have this. There's a big article in it about the disappearance. I'm done reading it anyway."

****

Cayce drank her coffee and drove in silence, waiting for Harri to finish reading the article. Coincidences just were not in the scheme of things where the sisters were concerned. Cayce remembered the philosophy of their father, a philosophy that always proved true: "Keep an open mind and an open path, and the Way will find you."

The Way had found them time after time, and Cayce wondered whether this gas station and this poster had found them, rather than the other way around. She hoped Johnny and Billie would not show themselves to her. Cayce's visions were with those who were no longer alive, but she had to come in contact with some personal item or be in a place where they had been in order to connect. Harri, on the other hand, could often sense the emotions felt by those in question, and needed only to be in close proximity with an item or place familiar to the person.

"Are you ready for this information? I'm having

one of those feelings, and I know you are, too." Harri folded the paper and laid it on her lap.

"I'm ready. I just hope we're not too late to help. Give me the details."

"The two were from southeastern Montana, from Hardin. They had been gone for three days, on a motorcycle trip across Montana with no particular destination in mind. The parents of the girl, Billie, tried to talk her out of making the trip. There was some family disagreement over her being with Johnny, who is twenty-two. Billie is only eighteen, a recent high school graduate. The two never contacted their parents by phone, but Billie texted her mother periodically. The last text she received was from Butte, the same place they were last seen buying gas at an Exxon station. The picture on the poster was texted to Billie's mother from the station."

"Too bad Billie never called her parents. Texting is so impersonal. I'm always glad to hear from Piper, but I've told her to please call more than text. So far, she hasn't let me down. Now that she's in Europe, communication is even more important. I'll be glad when she's back in the States." Cayce tightened her hands on the steering wheel. "I know studying art in Europe is a dream come true for her, but I'm so ready to see her. The last time I talked to her, she sounded like something was bothering her, like she had something she needed to tell me. When I asked her if anything was wrong, she said no, but I couldn't shake the feeling."

"Piper will be fine. She's from good stock." Harri gave a reassuring smile before unfolding the newspaper to read more of the article and then began speaking again without looking up. "Maybe Piper's met someone. Maybe she'll show up on the arm of Jacques Pierre with a big ol' diamond on her left hand."

"She wouldn't tell me if she had. Piper is so independent, but it would be just like her to show up with a fiancé, or maybe even a husband. She's thirty years old, so I guess she's old enough to make her own decisions. As long as Cody keeps paying for her to study abroad, or whatever idea she comes up with, I'm sure that's what she'll do."

"You were lucky you married Cody, even if you two did divorce. I've never seen a daddy dote on his daughter like Cody does Piper."

"I agree. Our sharing Piper has kept Cody and me friends. I'll always value his opinion where Piper is concerned." Cayce thought back to the loving farewell Cody had given Piper the day she left for Europe and knew he had called Piper almost every day since she'd been gone.

Harri went back to reading the news article. "Here's the bad part. Two days ago, a hiker came across the motorcycle in the stream near the outhouse at Meteor Lake National Park. Sheriff's office deputies combed the area and found old blood near the back of the outhouse. DNA results are not back from the lab yet, but the sheriff's office is treating this as a criminal investigation."

"The girl in the gas station mentioned two other disappearances. Does it say anything about those?"

"Yes. One was a nineteen-year-old girl named Lisa Perkins, from Billings, who disappeared six months ago, and the other was twenty-five-year-old Denise Mansfield, from northern Utah. Denise disappeared about ten months ago. It looks like she was the first reported missing. Denise was pregnant and unmarried. Her parents became alarmed when they were unable to reach her by cell phone and she never showed up at the cousin's house where she was going. They had argued because Denise wanted an abortion, something against their faith, but Denise told them she was going to have an abortion with or without their support."

"What about Billie and Lisa? Does it say if they were pregnant or not? Did they have boyfriends not endeared to parents?"

"It doesn't say. Do you have a hunch? Surely, you're not getting vibes already, Cayce." Harri folded the paper and put it on the seat.

"No, no vibes. I'm just trying to see if there are any patterns. Look on the map and see where they found the motorcycle." Cayce grabbed the atlas from under the seat and handed it to Harri.

Harri flipped pages until she found Idaho. Cayce glanced over and saw her running her finger along the page.

"Here it is." Harri poked the page. "It'll take us longer to get to Bar None if you want to go by this location. You're not thinking of finding this outhouse, are you?"

Cayce heard disapproval in her sister's voice, but said nothing, keeping her eyes focused on the road.

"Of course you are. Why am I bothering to ask?"

Cayce peeked over as Harri redirected her gaze to the atlas. "Let's see. We'll have to turn at Idaho Falls. We probably won't make it to Bar None tonight. Is that a problem?"

An hour later, the old red truck turned off the

interstate, heading to Meteor Lake.

Cayce drove along the two-lane highway with her hands gripping the steering wheel. As they began seeing signs directing them to Meteor Lake, she became more tense. They passed two gravel roads that led to the park, and at each one, Cayce stopped and rolled down her window as if getting a sense of each road. At the third road, she repeated her actions, but this time turned and drove slowly.

A few miles down the road, they turned again, onto an even bumpier road. Harri would have hit the top of the truck if it hadn't been for her seatbelt.

"About that outhouse!" Harri crossed her legs, but got no reply from Cayce, who seemed intent on driving the narrow road.

Then they saw it. Yellow crime-scene tape surrounded the outhouse and the parking lot, most of it sagging or lying on the ground.

Chapter Two

Cayce parked in front of the yellow tape and got out. Looking around and seeing no one, she ducked under the tape and walked toward the outhouse. Harri held back a few seconds before moving.

"Isn't this illegal?" Harri ducked under the tape and followed. Cayce stopped in front of the outhouse and turned her head in every direction, trying to alert her senses.

"Are you getting anything, Harri? Any feelings of fear or anything?" Cayce scanned the area but saw and sensed nothing at this point.

"No, and that is really strange. Surely, if they were abducted here, I'd get some emotional sense." Harri stopped every few steps, as if trying to get her Gift to work.

Cayce walked to the rear of the structure.

"Here's the bloodstain." They both approached the back wall. "Anything now, Harri?" Cayce turned and saw Harri holding her head.

"Pain, a lot of pain. One of the worst headaches ever."

Harri walked away from the site as Cayce moved closer. She stood inches from the blood and stared at it, deciding whether or not she wanted to touch it. Finally turning away from it, she walked several yards to the back and looked down the steep embankment.

"Here's more yellow tape at the bottom, down by the stream. I guess this is where they found the motorcycle." Cayce headed back toward the outhouse. "Do you think you can drive the truck, Harri? You know, just in case I'm weak after what I'm about to do."

"Straight shift, huh! How much do you like your transmission?" Harri began making shifting motions with her hand. "Reverse, first, second, third. Is there a fourth gear?"

"Never mind. We'll just sit here until I can drive, if need be. That transmission cost a fortune to restore." Cayce walked to the bloodstain and put her fingers to it.

Instantly, mist enveloped her. A handsome young man leaned against the wall looking as if he had not a care in the world. Hearing something behind him, he turned just in time to see a hand holding what looked like a tool used to change a tire come down on him. The young man dropped to his knees, blood spurting from his head on impact before beginning its trail of death through his thick hair, down his neck, and saturating his collar before leaping onto the shiny leather jacket and running down. A hand reached down from inside a heavy navy sleeve, and the attacker knelt beside the victim and placed two fingers to the young man's throat.

Cayce's eyes followed the navy sleeve upward to the face barely visible from within the jacket's hood covering the side profile of the attacker's face. Hints of red-and-black plaid peeked from the neck of the hooded jacket only partially zipped and from its sleeve closest to Cayce.

As the mist moved back in, Cayce heard a girl's voice calling, "Johnny, I'm ready." The scene faded, leaving Cayce straining to get more details and to see the girl moving into the scene. Neither the mist nor the vision cooperated further.

Returning to the present, Cayce found herself sitting at a picnic table between the outhouse and the end of the parking lot. A bottle of water was opened and placed in front of her.

"Here. Drink this! This is not a good sign. What did you see?" Harri stared at her sister from across the picnic table.

Cayce took a long drink of water and then poured some on her hand to wash away the effect of the dried blood she had touched. "I think the boy is dead. Someone hit him over the head with a tire tool. I heard the girl calling him and telling him she was ready to go. She didn't sound alarmed, so she didn't know what had happened to him."

"You mean Johnny, the biker boy? Do you want to call the sheriff's office? I think our cell phones work here." Harri checked her cell phone for signal.

"No use. They wouldn't believe us anyway. You know how most law enforcement refuses to believe in our kind of Gifts. Besides, I didn't get a good look at whoever hit Johnny. The attacker wore all navy, except for red plaid showing under his jacket." Cayce gulped another drink of water. "I do believe Billie is still alive. I got no vibes from her. What about you, Harri? Did you get any sensations?"

"After I walked away because of the headache that was probably what Johnny felt, I stopped at the front of the building but felt nothing other than extreme drowsiness, probably the aftermath of Johnny's headache." Harri rubbed her temple between her fingertips.

"Or the girl could have been abducted and hit on the head like Johnny. Maybe you felt her headache instead of the boy's." Cayce considered this for a moment. "If you feel nothing, Billie probably never knew what happened. If I feel and see nothing about the girl, it probably means Billie is either still alive or was not killed at this site. Let's hope the first part is right, but my senses tell me Johnny is no longer with us."

"Strange, isn't it? We go looking for the past and somehow get involved in an ominous present. Sometimes I wish the Way wasn't so good at finding us." Harri linked her fingers and put them under her chin. This was a trait Cayce remembered from childhood, something her sister did when she was worried.

****

The next morning, Cayce and Harri remained quiet as they drove, each absorbed in her own experience at the outhouse the day before. Harri picked up the poster and looked at it again, then folded it and stuck it in her purse.

Cayce sensed Harri's concern for the young couple, but was absorbed in her own fears. Somehow, she didn't think Johnny was killed instantly. Just before the mist cleared away, she'd sensed movement and heard the sounds of something or someone being dragged. She didn't think Johnny survived long, because no other vision had materialized.

"What little towns are up ahead? You need to be on the lookout for antique shops if you're going to get ready to do some pioneer-style cooking." Cayce broke the morbid silence and got back to the reason they were in Idaho. As soon as she got it out of her mouth, Harri pointed and yelled.

"Look! That sign! There's an antique shop at milepost sixty-seven at a place called Sluice Town." Harri picked up the atlas, searching for the town. "It looks like it's only about twenty-five miles from Bar None. It's not far from where you turn onto the gravel road."

"Sluice Town, huh? Sluice is a mining term. Most of these gold mining ghost towns started out with placer mining that used long sluices, wooden structures like troughs, to separate gold from sand and rock with a river-washing process. Bar None started out as a placer mine, a surface mine operation, until the gold from the stream was washed out. No pun intended. That's when Absalom Duluth used the wealth he had made from mining in Montana to start a lode operation, where they dig mineshafts and mine gold from the rich underground gold veins." Cayce noticed Harri's questioning look at her mining knowledge. "I had a nice long visit with my good friend Google."

"Can gold still be found in the river where Bar None is located?" Harri's dollar-sign twinkle returned to her eyes.

"It's actually a big creek—Rocky Creek, to be exact. Joshua said diehards still turn up a little gold while panning on the stream, but no major-sized nuggets have been found in years. Panning for gold is strictly for the hobbyist nowadays. You can't make a living at it, although the price of gold per ounce is out of sight."

"No, but I'll have to try my luck while we're there. A nice nugget ring or pendant would be a good souvenir of this trip. I better look for a gold pan when we get to the antique shop."

Cayce and Harri found themselves going deeper into the Sawtooth Mountains. Both were completely absorbed in the scenery.

"This reminds me of the Beartooth Mountains. I think Joshua has bought himself a jewel. How far are we from Sluice Town, Harri?" Cayce pushed the atlas across the seat to Harri.

"Let's see." Harri once again traced her finger along the page. "Not that far. Maybe twenty miles or so. Depending on how good the antique shop is, we should be at Bar None plenty early."

A few minutes later, Harri pointed to a building just ahead that sat a good piece off the road, with gorgeous mountains as a backdrop. The tall cupcake mountain's white icing had been mostly licked off by the warm summer sun. The range was so close it looked as if the shop was built right into it.

The shop, an old log cabin, must have been chinked and re-chinked many times. A large addition on the back had been covered with weathered boards, and a new out-of-place red metal roof spoke to its seeming success even though its location was isolated. A large sign across the front read Gold Pan Antiques.

"I think you might just find what you need to wash up that big nugget." Cayce parked the truck in front of one of several hitching posts.

As Harri pulled the screen door open, a bell jingled to announce their arrival.

"Come in, ladies. Make yourselves at home and

have a mug of coffee. Name's Lester, and I'll be glad to answer any questions."

The shopkeeper appeared to be in his late seventies or early eighties and could have been left over from the pioneer days. His shoulder-length thin gray hair and stubble outlined a face that looked like one of those Ozark Mountain dolls with its face made out of a dried apple. In Cayce's cowboy terminology, he looked like he'd been "rode hard and put up wet." The faded bandana around his neck was the perfect complement to his coffee-stained shirt, faded jeans, and worn-out cowboy boots.

"Oh, my! You certainly do have a lot of stuff." Cayce scanned the antiques consisting of about eighty-percent junk. Things hung from the ceiling and were propped in every wall, nook, and corner. She'd need to blaze a trail to get through, and wondered how they would ever find anything of real value.

"There's a roomful in the back, too. It's a little more organized. My granddaughter has the back room, but she's not here today. Janie's gone buying. She's got it all priced, so if you see anything you want, make an offer. Antiquing ain't no fun 'less you dicker a little."

"This could be dangerous," Harri whispered to Cayce, looking up as she followed in Cayce's steps heading to the back room.

Cayce turned back in time to watch Harri swerve as pitchforks, wagon wheels, and all kinds of rusted, dangerous-looking iron tools seemed suspended in midair over their heads. Seeing the alarm on Harri's face, Cayce let her sister pass.

Just before stepping down into the back room, Harri picked up a dented pan with holes in the bottom.

"Rocky Creek, here I come." She stuffed the pan under her arm and stepped down into a large room the opposite of the front of the shop.

"Talk about deceiving. This looks more like Natchez than the mountains of Idaho." Cayce stood with her hands on her hips and did a quick survey of the antique furniture, china, and everything imaginable. "This is going to be fun."

"I'm doing a quick walk-through before I begin to focus. I want to know what all is here."

"Good idea, Harri. I'll follow you."

Harri took off, but as usual, Cayce could not keep up with her sister, who walked like a short-legged racehorse. Cayce immediately got caught up in one section filled with primitive pieces. One step-back cupboard, painted with blue buttermilk base paint, looked more southern than western.

Cayce had no idea where her sister went until she heard her calling from the back of the room. Cayce hated to speed past all the wonderful pieces between them, but she could tell Harri was excited by some find. Harri stood in a section set up like a pioneer kitchen.

Sitting in a rocker, Harri looked up from a cookbook and immediately held it out to her sister.

"Look at this, Cayce. I have to have this for my cookbook collection and for Joshua's little project. It's a Mormon cookbook from the early twentieth century, a collection of recipes handed down from the first Mormon pioneers who settled in this valley. They were handcart pioneers. Can you imagine pushing handcarts over and through these mountains?" Harri turned the pages one at a time, and Cayce knew her sister would be held captive to this spot for a long time.

"That's great, Harri, but I think I'll just keep browsing. You know I don't have much interest in cooking, but I'll be happy to taste-test any recipes you try from it." Noticing several old cookbooks lined up on the wooden table beside her sister, she knew it was time to wander off before Harri began reading aloud to her.

As Cayce meandered through the building, she came across a scction that really caught her eye. An old, slightly faded photograph of a mining town hung on a makeshift wall. Close scrutiny revealed it to be Bar None in 1880. She ran her fingers over the old town scene and smiled at the thought of what lay ahead for her and Harri. Removing the picture from the wall, she tucked it under her arm.

In the next section, she saw an oversized dough bowl hollowed out from a log. Knowing this was something Harri would be interested in, she headed back to where she had left her sister. Harri was engrossed in another old cookbook.

"Harri, there's a huge dough bowl up here you have to see. It's the largest one I've ever come across. It would look great in The Teacake."

"Really? That is so strange. I just found a recipe for sourdough biscuits that sounds great. But from the amounts of ingredients listed, the cook must have been cooking for an army. You have to have a starter dough for it. I've never had much luck with starters, but it might be fun to try again. Look here." Harri held the book where Cayce could see it. "Here's an old picture of a woman kneading bread in a big dough bowl. The caption under it says the woman's name was Sally Bender, and she made huge quantities of sourdough biscuits for the miners in this old gold mine. She must have eaten a fair share of her own cooking, too. She looks like a short, round gourd doll wearing an apron and a bandana headscarf."

"Oh, my gosh, Harri! That looks just like the dough bowl I found. Bring the book and I'll show you." Cayce led the way after Harri stuck her finger in the book to mark her place.

"You're right. It does look like the same bowl, but I imagine there were a lot of dough bowls that looked like this." Harri put the picture beside the dough bowl, and they began to compare the two.

"Look here, Harri. Do you see this long streak of dark grain ending in this knot? It is exactly the same." Cayce outlined the grain with her finger as they compared it to the picture.

"You're right, Cayce. It is the same dough bowl. I think I've got to have it. What's the price on it?"

Cayce searched the sides, but could find no price tag. "This sucker is heavy." Cayce lifted one end. "Pick up that end, Harri, and let's turn it over. The price must be on the bottom."

"Two hundred fifty dollars. That's cheap, Harri. You need this. Maybe we can disinfect it and you can make sourdough biscuits in it." Cayce leaned down to look closer at the bottom. "Look here. There's something carved in the bottom."

"For Sally, the best cook ever! Bar None, March 1879," Cayce read aloud.

"Hmmm. I don't think I can beat Sally in the biscuit-making department. Besides, that's a butt-load of biscuits, even if you're using Sally's butt for measurement. You think 'Bar None' means something more than just a compliment to the cook?" Harri set the dough bowl back on its bottom.

"Let's ask the shopkeeper and see if he knows anything about the dough bowl—especially where it came from." Cayce put the picture inside and moved to pick up one end of the wooden bowl. "We might as well start hauling it up to the front."

Harri put Sally's cookbook and the gold pan inside the dough bowl and moved to her end to help carry the heavy piece.

"I'll make another trip back and pick up the Dutch ovens I found." Harri was huffing and puffing her way to the front. "So what's the picture, Cayce?" Harri asked after they placed the dough bowl on the counter.

Cayce turned the picture so Harri could see it. "It's Bar None in its glory days."

"That's great. I can't wait to see how this picture compares with Bar None in the present, but I've got a hunch you'll be seeing it in the past on your own."

The old man's dried-apple face wrinkled more with his big happy smile and could be interpreted as "sale in progress" as he approached the counter where the sisters had placed their treasures.

"Well, I see you found the mother lode, ladies. My Janie said she'd give this old biscuit maker a week, and if it didn't sell, she was gonna take it home for her own collection. She needs to make a sale, but I think she'll be disappointed it's gone."

"Well, if it's any consolation, tell her it will be much treasured. I'll take good care of it." Harri stroked the bowl before taking the items from it. "Let's see now. How about you add this all up and take maybe ten percent off the top. How does that sound, Lester?"

"Sounds like a deal to me." Lester began listing

each item in a ledger and then added it all up on his calculator. "Will that be check or cash? We don't take credit cards."

"It's an out-of-state check. Is that all right?" asked Harri, hoping not to have to use that much cash so early in the trip.

"Reckon so. I ain't been bit but once. Got a trustin' nature." Lester took the check and put it in a metal cash box. "I'll carry these treasures to your vehicle."

To Cayce's surprise, the older man picked the dough bowl up like it was nothing. Cayce thought this old cowboy must have lifted a lot of hay and bags of horse feed in his day, not to mention heavy antiques.

"You can just put it in the back next to the cab. I'm not driving too fast, so it should be all right."

"A fifty-two, huh? She's a beauty."

Cayce did not bother to tell Lester Hawk was a "he," and allowed the admirer to continue looking the truck over.

"Had one like it myself, once upon a time, but it was green." Lester walked around Hawk, eyeing every detail. "I did have an old Ford one time I got painted candy-apple red after a girl I'd taken a hankering to, named Candy."

Lester smiled, and Cayce didn't know if the smile was for the truck or Candy. She did not ask.

"Well, my sister's truck is painted viper red—after her ex-husband." Harri never cracked a smile as she opened Hawk's door and climbed up into it.

"How far did you drive it?" Lester either paid no attention to Harri or didn't get her joke. He rubbed Hawk's hood as if the old truck was a potential horse for sale. Harri wondered if the old man would raise the hood to check Hawk's teeth.

"From Montana. I've had a lot of work done on it, but the motor is original. I even have to add lead when I fill up with gas." Cayce set the Dutch ovens in next to the dough bowl.

"Ain't that something? You must be a lover of antiquities. Where you two headin'?" Lester looked up, still rubbing the hood.

"To Bar None. A friend of mine bought the old town. I'm sorry. I should introduce myself. I'm Cayce McCallister, and this is my sister, Harri Wellington." Cayce pointed to Harri, who waved from the truck but did not get out.

"Pleased to meet you both. I'm Lester Scott." Lester gave Cayce a good firm handshake. "We heard the old town is gettin' rebuilt. You know, Janie bought that dough bowl and some other items from a family that had kinfolk that lived in Bar None in the old days. We're just spittin' distance from there as the eagle flies. Kinda over the mountain, but there's no road that connects us."

"Speaking of how Bar None was in the beginning, do you know anyone who knows the history of the town? Joshua Devaux, the new owner, wants us to find out as much about its history as possible." Cayce kept her eyes on Lester, hoping for the right answer.

"Sure do. That would be Teesh. Lives in a cabin up the gravel road going to Bar None, about a half-mile or so from the old town. Teesh's old like me, but she and her family have lived in the area forever. Her grandfather was one of the first residents of Bar None. I better warn you, though. If you get her started talkin' about the old town, she'll talk your ears off. She likes company but hates tourists."

Lester snapped his fingers. "Wait a minute. I know just what you need to get old Teesh to be real friendly." Lester went back inside and came out a minute later with a small white box. "This here is huckleberry fudge. It's Teesh's favorite. Janie makes it to sell in the shop. You're in luck. This is our last box." Lester handed the box to Harri through her open window. "Don't forget to tell her I sent you, now."

"Thank you, Lester, but we'd be happy to pay you for the fudge." Harri reached for her wallet.

"No, no. Just promise you'll each try one. That way, you're guaranteed to come back. Nobody can resist Janie's fudge." Lester started walking back to the shop but turned before he opened the door. "You ladies come again—I know Janie'll want to meet you—and be real careful. Watch for Difficult Road on your right, 'bout ten miles ahead."

"You mean like a steep and winding road? Or bumpy?" Harri asked.

"No. That's the name of it—Difficult Road."

Cayce and Harri both burst out laughing as they pulled away from the antique shop.

"Difficult Road, huh? About that bladder problem, Harri. Maybe we better stop when we turn on the gravel and let you squat behind a tree." Cayce looked straight ahead, still laughing.

"I can't help it if my bladder has early onset leakage. I'm older than you, you know. Just stop at the next quick-stop, and I'll be ready…might even buy some Depends. Just don't tell anybody."

"Kegel not working for you, Sister?" Cayce shot

Harri a questioning glance. "I hope you're joking about the Depends. You're less than a year older than I am, and I'm way too young for that."

"Yes, I am joking, but a restroom would be nice. I'm not going to squat behind a tree. I know they have rattlesnakes out here, and other creepy, crawly things. Besides, Harriet Wellington does not drip dry or bare her butt in the wilderness."

"Changing the subject…talk about a productive stop at Lester's! Funny how things always seem to fall in place." As soon as Harri made the remark, they looked at each other and laughed.

"Yep, just one more of a million coincidences in our lives." Cayce settled into her favorite driving position—left foot on tip of seat, hands at bottom of steering wheel. "Now, on to Bar None and whatever awaits us. Lester said it isn't far to the gravel road where we turn. He also said we need to be careful. I assume he was talking about the road."

Cayce found a service station for Harri just before they turned onto Difficult Road. She got the exact mileage from the cashier and asked about the missing bikers when she saw the same flyer taped to the counter.

"Nope. We never saw 'em, but everybody's talking about it. It's still on the news. They're dead, for sure." The cashier, a young pimple-faced guy with a black T-shirt embossed with a skimpily clad, buxom blonde and the words "Bronc riders do it with spurs" written underneath, made the remark matter-of-factly with no sign of concern.

Cayce left the station shaking her head at the dispassionate attitude of the young man. "Either his daddy owns the station, or cheap labor is mighty hard to come by in the wilderness."

A few minutes later, Cayce knew how Difficult Road got its name. She could hardly hold the wheel on the bumpy gravel road, and it became even more winding and narrow the farther they got.

"Holy Tallahatchie! This is as curvy as a 'toe sack full of chicken snakes,' as granddaddy Zeke used to say. What do we do if we meet someone?" Harri held tight to the door handle and the seat, and Cayce could tell her sister had her brakes on.

"Be careful, Harri. You know this floorboard is pretty old. You might just push a foot right through to the gravel."

As soon as Cayce got the words out of her mouth, she had to hug the nonexistent shoulder to keep from hitting a bright-yellow pickup truck that blasted around the curve. The man at the wheel grimaced when he saw them.

"Remember that truck. If that's one of Joshua's work crew, I'm giving him a what-for when I see him." Cayce looked at Harri, who had turned around to get a good look at the pickup.

Harri bit her lower lip. "The color would make forgetting it impossible. I think it's a Dodge, newer model. It's covered in dust, so it's hard to tell. Should be easy to spot; he has "Cowboy Up" in big dusty letters across his back window."

"Could be worse. My ex had "Kick Ass" on his back window. Another reason the viper is an ex."

Cayce made no attempt to pull onto the road. "I'm shaking so bad I can hardly hold on to the steering wheel. I think I'll just sit here a minute until I can hear over my heartbeat."

"We need chocolate!" Harri held up the white box and smiled, what their pop would have referred to as a shit-eatin' grin. "But I think you better at least move up to that little pull-off, in case some other idiot comes along."

"Oh, my gosh! Harri, you have to get this recipe." Cayce pulled over and became lost in the fudge. She took small bites and chewed slowly, savoring the yin/yang of rich, dark chocolate and sweet, tart huckleberries.

"Umm," was Harri's only comment as she hurriedly finished off her piece and reached for another.

Cayce slapped her hand and grabbed the box away from her. "We each get one. Remember? This is our bribe to get Teesh to talk to us." She pulled back onto the road.

Harri pretended to pout. "Well, she better have something good to tell us for this sacrifice. I wonder when Janie will make more."

"I don't know, but I think I see Teesh's cabin ahead."

Chapter Three

Billie awoke startled and sat up in pitch black. Disoriented, she suffered the same terrifying nightmare as every night. But it was not a nightmare; it was reality. She pulled up her legs and rested her head on her knees while hugging them tight. As a reflex, she brushed her finger over her ear as if getting her hair out of her face, something she had done all her life until now. She rubbed her scalp, feeling the prickly beginnings of new growth. The sore spot on the back of her head had finally healed with the aid of the salve the Keeper had provided each day for the first week, but she could feel ridges and knew there would be scars.

The first day of her captivity, she had awakened from her drowsy state to the sound of loud buzzing. She swatted at bees she dreamed were swarming around her head as she rode on the back of Johnny's Harley. When she finally regained full consciousness, she realized the buzzing had been her head being shaved. From the bad sore spot on her head, it appeared she had been cut in the process. Her screaming had been interrupted by a synthesized voice.

"And when thou art spoiled, what wilt thou do? Though thou clothest thyself with crimson, though thou deckest thee with ornaments of gold, though thou rentest thy face with painting, in vain shalt thou make thyself fair. Repent of your vanity, Billie. Thirst after righteousness, or ye will burn in hell. I am the Keeper. Heed my words."

The sermons continued every morning, followed by organ music blasting over some type of speaker system with surround sound. Billie always covered her ears with her hands and rolled into fetal position on her mattress as soon as the sermon ended, in anticipation of the music that threatened to burst her eardrums.

Her prison cell was large compared to her small bedroom at home, and it seemed to be a scantily furnished cave with rock walls on three sides. The floor was concrete, and the only wall not part of the cave was made from concrete blocks. A heavy door, the only way out, was always locked. The room smelled a little musty, but not as unbearable as a regular cave with no heat. A row of fluorescent lights attached to a high ceiling provided the only source of light.

Billie longed for home—the home she'd hated when she left it over a month ago. Then, all she'd thought about was getting as far away from her parents as possible. Being with Johnny was all that had been important to her—something her parents opposed. She had just graduated from high school and was a free adult until the home pregnancy test jolted her back to reality. Now, she had the added responsibility of her unborn child.

Billie's mind replayed over and over the circumstances surrounding her being here, until she thought she would go insane. She'd tried to convince Johnny they should move away and become the perfect little family, but her plan never materialized. Instead of going to a justice of the peace or to one of those romantic, quaint little chapels set up for quick weddings, like she had seen in Red Lodge, Johnny drove the Harley across Montana into Idaho, pulling up at an abortion clinic two days after they left Hardin.

Billie thought back to their argument that day when she realized where they were. In the end, Johnny had convinced her to at least see what the clinic offered. The doctor there told her she was only eight weeks pregnant, a good, safe time for terminating a pregnancy. They gave her a packet of information to read over and told her to consider her options before making a decision.

She left the clinic more confused than comforted. Yes, it would be easier to go on with her life without a baby—especially since she had not told her parents, or anyone, she was pregnant—but Billie loved Johnny and wanted to do what was right for their baby. She wondered if she and a child could settle Johnny down. Deep down, Billie knew if she had to make a choice, she would choose her baby over Johnny. It was the moral and responsible choice. Johnny was too independent, a wanderer who had drifted into her life the last semester of high school. He lived in a fancy RV on the Big Horn River, spending days fly fishing and nights at the local bars and casinos, except for the time he spent with her.

Billie lay on the mattress, remembering Johnny. She wanted to cry, but her tears had dried up with the realization Johnny was gone. The first few days, she'd been traumatized, and refused the healthy food offered three times a day. She would not speak and tried not to listen to the horrifying voice of the Keeper. He always used a synthesizer to preach to her about her sins, demanding repentance and warning her of hell. The voice reminded her of the horror movies she'd once loved, rather than of Mrs. Wilson, her favorite Sunday school teacher.

Billie knew how long she had been held captive. Once she had come to her senses, she used the Bible, her only source of entertainment allowed for passing time, to keep up with her days in captivity. She started with Genesis four after estimating the number of days she had passed in a zombie-like state, and read a chapter each day, with little comprehension of the verses she read aloud. What was important to her was the chapter number. For forty-five days, she had been a captive.

Billie was smart, valedictorian of her class, and was physically fit because of being a competitive cheerleader and a track star for four years of high school. Soon she realized what she had to do to save herself and the unborn child she had refused to abort at the clinic.

It seems an eternity ago when I told Johnny I needed time to think, to figure out what was the right thing for me to do.

Johnny had given her until the end of the week, but the end of the week never came for Johnny. Now her world was a mattress in a cave prison where her only pleasure was feeling the baby growing inside her.

I've got to pee again. It's the worst part of being pregnant.

Billie lifted herself from the floor and touched the rough stone wall, feeling her way through the dark by holding rock outcroppings in order to get to the strange, stainless steel toilet standing in the corner. As she inched along in the dark, she hummed a lullaby her mother had sung to her as a young child. She convinced herself she hummed it for her unborn child, but in reality, she hummed to comfort herself, to lessen the terror.

No seat or handle was attached to the strange toilet, and no holding tank could be found. It automatically flushed twice a day, leaving only a trace of antiseptic liquid in its bowl.

Damn cold steel!

Billie stopped her humming long enough to silently curse the toilet, but then started again, humming louder. Shivering, she hummed in staccato and pulled her thin dress up over her arms trying to get warm. The dress was thick gray paper, hard to tear but possible. This was the only clothing she was given; no shoes, socks, or even panties were given to her. She received a new, clean paper dress every other day when the automatic shower by the toilet turned on for about three minutes. She ate her food with her hands. Not even plastic eating utensils were allowed. Billie's logic told her the Keeper was afraid she would find a way to commit suicide if given any tools to assist—a thought that had come to her many times.

It was warm enough in her prison—a good thing, because she had no cover on her bed. Her furnishings consisted of a mattress on the floor, a small stainless steel chair made from one piece of steel, and a small one-person table made the same way.

Her urine sounded like a torrential downpour as it hit the sides of the empty stainless steel bowl.

What does he think? That I'll drown myself in toilet bowl water?

She would have laughed, but humor could not be

used to describe her situation. As she tore off a few sections of the toilet paper, rationed each day, she thought she heard a voice—a female voice so soft the words were not intelligible. Billie looked around the dark room, trying to figure out where it came from, and realized it was beneath her. She rose from the toilet and held up her dress. Kneeling beside the toilet, she lowered her head as far down inside as possible without touching the liquid. The smell of Pine Sol and urine threatened to suffocate her, so she pulled her loose dress up over her shoulders and covered her nose and mouth. With her head only an inch from the liquid, she listened.

"Help me! Is anyone there?"

The sound was muted, like someone speaking under water. The voice was so soft Billie could hardly make out the words. She had been blessed with very sensitive ears—something bothersome at Fourth of July celebrations and birthday parties with balloons popping, but now she counted it as a blessing.

I'm not alone.

Billie pulled her dress completely off, covered her mouth and nose with her hand, and stuck her face even farther into the toilet bowl. She covered her head and the toilet with her dress to muffle the sounds she was about to make.

"I'm here. Can you hear me?" Billie spoke just above a whisper, as loud as she dared, and prayed for a reply.

No reply came. Billie glanced from under her sound shield to make sure the red camera light was still off, as it was every night, and then put her head down in the toilet again. This time, she included one hand.

"Ew!" Billie thought as she poked her finger through the lukewarm liquid on the steel bottom. She jerked, surprised as the flap opened. All the liquid ran out.

Whoever she is, her voice is being carried through the pipes. We must share the same pipes, and she must have this flap open. Billie lowered her head to only an inch from the flap.

"I am Billie. Who are you?" She spoke tersely, trying to be understood.

"Lisa. My name is Lisa. I hurt. I think my baby is coming early." The girl began to sob and moan softly.

"How long have you been here, Lisa?"

"Months. Don't know. I'm scared. Can you help me?" The girl begged, but Billie could do nothing.

"I can't get out. Scream for help, Lisa. The Keeper will come."

"No!" The distraught girl yelled the quick reply. "He will kill me after my baby is born...like he did the other girl."

"What?" When Billie whipped her head up, the flap snapped closed. She opened it again and asked, "How do you know?"

"...told me...cursed him...go to hell." Not all of the girl's words could be understood. She was crying hard now.

"Who told you that, Lisa?" Billie spoke too loud and knew she had to control her voice.

"The Keeper. Oh!" The girl's muffled moans grew louder.

"Be brave, Lisa!" Billie's head dipped so close her nose touched the stainless steel. Then she heard the girl scream, a high-pitched cry shortened by a snap. Lisa had let go of the flap, ending all conversation.

"Lisa! Lisa!" Billie whispered as loud as she dared, but no answer came.

Billie shook so hard she could barely pull on her dress, and then she backed away.

My cell and Lisa's must share common water and drain pipes. Lisa must be just behind this wall.

Billie frantically felt all over the wall of stone behind the toilet, running her fingers over every inch of the rocky outcrops from the ground up as high as she could reach, but she could distinguish no possible opening. She put her ear to the wall every few inches, but heard nothing. It was useless. She couldn't get to Lisa.

Billie retraced her steps, allowing her body to fall onto the mattress. Once again, she curled into fetal position, numbed by the magnitude of what Lisa told her and numbed with fears of what lay ahead for her. The young woman was so distraught she popped her thumb into her mouth, succumbing to the self-soothing she'd used as a child, a habit she had been forced to break when she entered first grade.

After several minutes of trembling, Billie left the mattress, felt her way across the concrete floor, and lifted the steel chair up over her head. She continued what had become her nightly routine until her arms and hands grew shaky. Then she jogged in place while counting slowly to one hundred, concentrating hard not to lose count. Following this would be crunches, side bends, stretching movements, jumping jacks, and many other exercises she needed to increase her strength and stamina. She exercised for what seemed hours, stopping to rest every few minutes. She wanted to become exhausted so she could sleep through the next long, endless day. In her mind, she could hear her Grammar's voice.

Good girl, Billie! You can do this. Don't give up.

With motivation born of a new sense of urgency, Billie decided to add to her exercise ritual. Feeling along and up the wall as far as she could reach, she pinpointed each narrow rock ledge in her mind, used the lowest stones for footholds, and began climbing. The ceiling in the room was high, but she would not go too high for fear of falling and hurting herself and her baby. The goal was to strengthen her grip, something that would come in handy with the escape attempt she knew would come. Reaching, feeling along each side and higher, she moved her hands and feet until her arms and legs trembled. Fearing she would cramp up, she retraced her climbing path downward.

Exhausted, Billie lay back on her mattress. She gently rubbed her belly and mentally made an oath to herself and her child.

We may die, Baby, but not without fighting to live!

Eyes watched and ears listened until the girl slept. Then the watcher replaced the loose stone in the hole and backed away into darkness.

Chapter Four

Cayce slowed, turning into the dirt trail leading to a quaint log cabin trimmed in red. The flowerbeds in the front were outlined with old, weathered railroad ties, and Cayce figured these were likely leftovers from the railroad track to nowhere.

"Looks like Teesh still lives in the old days. This should be fun." Harri picked up the box of candies and followed Cayce to the porch slanted with age and ground-settling. A huge black cat materialized from nowhere and stopped them on the steps. Her body sprawled out full-length on the second step, blocking their path as if she was the old lady's personal guardian.

Harri reached down to pet the cat, but it proved to be anything but friendly. Hissing, it raised one paw and scratched in the air at Harri. Harri jerked her hand back.

"Well, Missy, I guess you don't know my sister here is a real animal lover. You be nice, you hear?" Cayce put her hands on her hips and stared down at the cat. "Where's your mama? We really want to see her. Lester sent us, so I promise we're okay."

As if understanding every word Cayce said, the cat rose and arched her back into an elongated stretch so she looked like she needed to be sitting on the tail end of a broom. She ambled toward the front door and scratched, making the screen door bump with each swipe. Footfalls could be heard inside the cabin, and within seconds, the wooden front door creaked open just enough to open the screen door and let the cat in.

"Come on in, Jez. Quick, now, before you let a fly in." The old lady's voice was so faint the visitors hardly heard her.

"Hello. We're looking for Teesh." Cayce had followed the cat to the screen door, but the wooden door behind it was nearly closed. She knew she had to say something while the main door was partially open.

"Oh, my goodness! You gave me a fright." The old lady opened the door and stuck her head out. "I didn't know anyone else was out here except Jezebel." The lady's high-pitched voice crackled with age.

"Lester Scott sent us," Cayce explained before introducing herself and Harri. "My name is Cayce McCallister, and this is my sister, Harri Wellington. We're on our way to Bar None to spend a couple of weeks helping our friend, the new owner."

"Oh! Lester sent you this." Harri held out the box toward the lady, who took it and smelled it without opening it.

"My goodness. That Lester knows how to guarantee entry into my cabin. Well, come on in, and let's see if he's a good judge of character. Jez let you past the steps, so you've already passed her test."

Teesh held the door open for her guests, who waited for their host just inside the door. Teesh was a petite lady, very striking for her age, the quintessential western pioneer woman with her long gray hair braided into one thin braid that hung over her shoulder and almost to her waist. Her wrinkled face was outlined with character and joy in living, her laugh lines predominant around eyes and mouth. Her dress—faded blue jeans, old brown cowboy boots with pointed toes, and a gray Yellowstone sweatshirt, somewhat faded with wear—was not atypical for the West. She exuded pleasantness, and her first impression on the sisters was positive.

The inside of the cabin appeared clean but cluttered. At one end of the room, floor-to-ceiling shelves held what might have been every *National Geographic* and *Reader's Digest* ever published.

Realizing she was staring, Cayce attempted to justify her bad manners. "That is quite a collection of magazines. I love *National Geographic* myself. I also collect antiques, and you have some wonderful pieces." She didn't know how to address the old lady. "I'm sorry, but Lester didn't tell us what your last name is. He just said 'Teesh.' "

"My last name is Johnson, but you can call me Teesh. Everybody does."

"Is that short for Patricia or Laticia?" Harri asked.

Teesh laughed. "No, but that's what everyone thinks when I meet them for the first time. I was a teacher and taught on the Shoshone-Bannock Reservation when I was a lot younger. The kids started out calling me 'Teacher,' but somehow it got shortened to Teesh, with the c-h sounding more like s-h. I liked it, so I just sort of started calling myself that. My real name is Virginia, but nobody has called me that since I was twenty, the year I started teaching." Teesh headed for the kitchen area and motioned for the sisters to follow.

"I'm very informal. I like to sit at the kitchen table when I have company. How about a glass of sweet sun tea made with spring water?" Without waiting for an answer, Teesh reached into the cabinet and took down three old, brightly colored aluminum glasses from the same era as the rest of her kitchen.

Harri seemed fascinated with Teesh's appliances, all from the nineteen-forties or earlier, but most of all, Harri loved the old rounded Frigidaire refrigerator with its old-timey aluminum ice trays that demanded a bit of a beating to get the ice cubes to release. She noticed Teesh held the tray with a dishtowel to keep the frosty aluminum from sticking to her fingers.

"This kitchen is like our grandmother's. It brings back a lot of good memories. Doesn't it, Cayce?"

"Yes, it does." A tall antique oak bed, with a primitive table beside it, sat in one corner of the large main room. Cayce knew a room like this, containing a complete house in it, was called a keeping room. A beautiful hand-stitched quilt was spread across the bed.

"What a gorgeous bed and quilt. Log cabin pattern, isn't it? Did you make it?" Cayce loved the design and wanted to run her fingers across the beautiful stitching. She remembered the pattern from one of her grandmother's quilts. Cayce turned to Teesh, waiting for the old woman's response.

"No, I'm not very crafty. My grandmother made it for me when I turned sixteen. My stuff is old, but I like it. I see no reason to change it out. It's good enough for a ninety-two-year-old." Teesh opened the box of candy and offered each of the sisters a piece.

"Oh, no. We've had the one Lester told us we could have, and that was just to get us back to the shop for more. It is delicious." Harri eyed the fudge left in the box and had to turn her gaze away to keep from taking Teesh up on the offer.

"We're fine, Teesh, but you go ahead and have a piece. I know you're dying for it. It's the best fudge I've ever eaten." Cayce followed Harri's lead and looked around the room.

"Well, if you insist. While I devour this, why don't you girls tell me why you wanted to visit with this old-timer so bad?" Teesh broke one of the candies in half and stuffed it into her mouth. "Mmm! That is good."

Harri looked at Cayce and gave her the nod to begin.

"Our good friend Joshua Devaux bought Bar None a few months ago and has begun to restore the old buildings. He wants to make it a place where people can bring their families and relive the history of the gold mining era. Joshua loves history."

"And let me guess. Your Mr. Devaux is having unforeseen difficulty with his restoration project." Teesh picked up another small piece of fudge and popped the whole thing into her mouth, chewing slowly, savoring it.

"You are so right. I'm sure the stories abound in the old town. They don't call them ghost towns for nothing." Harri sipped her tea, keeping her eyes on Teesh, awaiting her response.

"Stories? No, these are not stories. These are facts. I've seen and heard enough in Bar None to field several seasons of those reality paranormal shows." The old lady took a sip of tea. Her eyes smiled, as if amused at the surprised look on Harri's face, and Cayce knew her own face must have reflected something similar.

"Yes, I have satellite TV and watch all those ghost-hunting shows, but TAPS was my favorite until Grant left. Grant was like the grandson I never had. I was an old maid schoolteacher, or schoolmarm, you know."

"Joshua is really beginning to have problems." Cayce chose to ignore Teesh's description of herself and return to the main topic. "He's having a hard time finding construction workers to finish the project. They keep getting scared off. Can you tell us about your experiences? Anything you know about the resident spirits that might help us put them to rest, so to speak?"

Cayce folded her hands on the table and was surprised when Teesh stood and left the keeping room. Harri and Cayce looked at each other. Cayce wondered if she had offended the elderly woman. In a few seconds, though, she returned, struggling to carry a very large, heavy book.

"Let me help you with that, Teesh." Harri jumped up, took the book, and brought it to the table.

"This is just one of dozens of volumes I have—every newspaper ever printed in Bar None. These will tell you everything you want or need to know about the town from 1879 'til 1937. I had it in the back room where I do most of my reading. The light is better back there." Teesh pushed the volume across to Harri, who began turning pages.

"My grandfather, Proctor Henry Johnson, established the newspaper, *The Bar None Sentry*. He came to Bar None in 1875, a young man seeking adventure in the Wild West and hoping for a quick fortune. He panned the streams but didn't like the hard labor it demanded. Then he worked in the mine for a couple of years—more hard labor.

"Grandpa Proctor was the son of a schoolteacher and a Presbyterian minister, and was quite literate—self-educated—but never liked getting dirty. After he finished his schooling, he apprenticed as a typesetter and a reporter at a newspaper in Springfield, Missouri, the town where he grew up, before getting gold fever and heading west. He managed to save enough of his earnings from working gold to open the newspaper, and he kept it running until 1937, although it changed to a much smaller operation, a weekly county paper, in 1915. My father worked with Grandpa Proctor but couldn't keep the paper going. *The Sentry* died with the town. My father moved us to Idaho Falls but kept the family cabin. I inherited it and moved back forty years ago and never left again."

"So if you are ninety-two, you remember some of the first pioneers in Bar None, like Belle and Absalom Duluth?" Cayce's interest was piqued, and she could see by the way Harri looked up from the volume that her interest heightened, as well.

"Well, I don't know that I actually remember so much as I know the stories passed down and the ones from my own perusing of these old newspapers. But I do remember Absalom—Uncle Ab to my sister and me. He was Pa Proctor's best friend. They came to Bar None on the same day in 1875. My grandpa caught a ride with Uncle Ab from the train station in Boise." Teesh paused and sipped her tea before continuing. She spoke slowly, savoring her memories as she had each bite of Janie's fudge.

"Absalom was a quiet man who smelled of sweet cigars and liquor. But that didn't matter to my family. He was especially fond of Irene and me, although Irene was only three years old when Uncle Ab died, and she never remembered him. He always made us wood carvings of animals, or made us wood toys that could move in all sorts of ways. Pa Proctor said Absalom was a mechanical genius, probably why he was so good at mining."

"What about Belle? Do you remember her?" Harri asked.

"Oh, yes. But mostly I just remember seeing her. She was a floozy, as my mother called her. Mama and the church women didn't like her, but they prayed for her, mostly for her forgiveness, I reckon." Teesh leaned in and spoke barely above a whisper. "I think the women mostly prayed their husbands wouldn't fall prey to Belle and her girls' spells." Teesh chuckled, hiding her laugh behind her hand, and then sat up straight to finish her explanation.

"I was not allowed to go past the porch of Cole Springs Hotel. That was the name of the hotel Belle owned, but Belle also owned The Nugget, a saloon and bordello. In her mind, Mother could not separate Belle's hotel from her other business endeavors, and I could only go onto the hotel porch if Uncle Absalom was sitting out there. Uncle Ab sat on the porch every day, whittling. I didn't understand why we were forced to stay on the porch until I got older.

"Well, I'm really running off at the mouth. I know Lester warned you that would happen when I get started talking about Bar None."

"Oh, please, Teesh, promise you'll always run off at the mouth. Hearing you talk is even better than going through your newspapers, but they are a treasure." Cayce pulled open the volume in front of her to get a quick glance inside.

"I'm surprised some museum hasn't bought them off you. What a treasure! Irreplaceable!" Cayce caressed the old book as she closed it.

"Oh, I could have sold the lot a dozen or more times, but I won't. What do I need with more money? I even have nursing home insurance, but hopefully I won't ever have to use it. I've seen enough of those while visiting my friends and my sister Irene." Teesh left the kitchen and returned with a picture in her hand. "This is Little Sister, poor dear." Teesh handed the picture to Harri. Cayce moved closer so she could see the woman.

"My, she is beautiful! Look at that thick white hair." Harri pointed to Irene's hair, which was pulled away from her face and loosely held back with an antique pearl-embossed comb.

Cayce nodded and handed the picture back to Teesh. "You look alike," Cayce added.

"Thank you both. I'd love for you to meet her, but she doesn't know anyone anymore. Irene is only eighty, but her mind left her a long time ago. She was in an institution for a long time, but I had her moved to the nursing home a few years ago."

"I am so glad Lester told us to come see you, Teesh. It has been a pleasure visiting with you. Having someone who remembers the town founders is invaluable. Do you mind if we come back to see you and take a look at the newspapers sometime? We need to get to Bar None right now, but I know we'll have many questions after we get there." Harri picked up the book as she stood. "Now, where can I put this for you?"

"Just go through the main room. The door beside the bed will take you right out to my spare bedroom and the back porch. It's been glassed in so it's more like a sunroom. That's where the good light is for reading."

Cayce picked up the tea glasses and put them in the sink while waiting for Harri to return.

"Thank you for the tea, Teesh, and especially for taking us back in time in Bar None. I really hope we can visit you again, and we hope you'll come visit us while we're at Bar None."

"I would love the company. Come spend as much time as you want in my old musty cellar."

Cayce and Harri waved at Teesh, who stood with her arms full of Jezebel as they pulled out of her driveway. Cayce knew they would be back. She could hardly wait to begin searching through the written history of Bar None.

****

Hawk bumped along on the gravel road, which seemed to have more potholes the closer the sisters got to the old town. Cayce hugged the shoulder, afraid of another near miss on the narrow road. Then the gravel turned to packed dirt.

"We should be close. Maybe just over this next hill." Harri leaned up in her seat, probably eager to start panning for gold in the stream running beside the road.

"Here we are, Harri." Cayce pulled onto the shoulder and stopped at the top of the hill so they could gaze down into the valley that held the remains of Bar None. She walked to the front of the truck. "Oh, my gosh! This is much more beautiful than Joshua described it. Would you look at those mountains?"

Harri climbed out of the truck and walked over by Cayce, who added, "I can see why no ghost in his or her right mind would want to leave here."

Harri leaned closer to Cayce. "Ghost in his or her right mind?" Harri cupped her hands over her eyes.

"Your words make me uneasy, but the view is breathtaking!"

The sun reflecting off the scene below made the town look as if gold dust had been sprinkled over it, adding brilliance to the natural hues of the landscape. Several cabins and buildings were nothing but shells of their former selves, but three big buildings in the middle of the town looked as if they had been bypassed by Father Time. The Nugget, Belle's saloon and brothel, stood in the center, not acknowledging any sign of repugnance for the lives the girls who worked there were forced to live. Antique wicker chairs and lounges, symbols of a more genteel population, adorned its front porch.

"Can't you just see Belle's girls, dressed in their finest Victorian outfits, their parasols twirling over their shoulders as they stand on the edge of the porch soliciting clients?" Harri, with her flair for fashion romanticized the era, temporarily forgetting the agony and distress the young Asian prostitutes were forced to endure.

Cayce moved several steps and shielded her eyes with one hand. "Actually, I don't see the girls, but I think I just caught a glimpse of Belle looking up at us, her lace glove covering her eyes just as I'm doing right now. But she wasn't decked out in bright-colored silk with a plumed hat and a parasol. She was dressed in black, a veil over her face…a dark puff of air, here one second and gone the next."

Cayce dropped her hand from her face and turned to Harri. "Well, sister, are you ready to start this adventure? Looks like the residents of Bar None await us."

She headed for the driver's side of the old truck while Harri crawled back into the passenger seat.

Chapter Five

Cayce parked at the hotel just in front of a long hitching post. To the right of them was a narrow alleyway, and The Nugget stood next to it. There was no sign of Belle or of any of the construction crew, although several ladders were propped against the building and piles of lumber and material covered the grounds.

"Well, it looks like Joshua might be recruiting workers again." Cayce pulled out her cell phone and moved in a circle, holding her phone out checking for a signal. "Nothing. Can you believe that, Harri?" She put her phone back in the truck.

"Of course. We're between mountain peaks in a secluded valley. Unless Joshua puts in a cell tower or has telephone lines run, there will be no communication with the outside world." Harri walked to the entrance of the hotel and tried the door. When it clicked, she pushed it open. "After you." Harri rolled her hand down, bowing, and gestured Cayce in ahead of her.

"Oh, my! This is amazing." Cayce walked in and did another complete circle, soaking in the elegance of the Victorian establishment. "Joshua will be pleasantly surprised, should he ever get his workers back to finish, that is. Joshua didn't tell me he already had it furnished, with the exception of our bedrooms. He had an antique dealer from Boise find period pieces for all the bedrooms." Cayce headed for the stairs, with Harri on her heels.

When they reached the top of the stairs, Cayce stopped abruptly, and Harri plowed into her. Cayce motioned for Harri to be quiet and pointed down the hallway that overlooked the lobby. Ten doors opened onto the balcony, but all were closed.

Cayce and Harri directed their gazes toward the seven rooms to the right at the top of the stairs. A creaking sound came from one of the rooms, the sound of either footsteps or a rocking chair in motion. Cayce led the way as the two tiptoed past every door, stopping to listen at each one. At the next to the last door, Cayce stopped and pointed. She and Harri put their ears close to the door. The noise continued. Cayce began her game of charades with her sister, a game they often played when confronted with the unexplained.

She held up her fingers to signify counting and motioned they would both push with their shoulders on the count of three. As she placed her hand on the doorknob, she held her breath, hoping it would be easy to open and not damaged by their shoving through.

One, two, three! Cayce lip-synced while gesturing with her fingers. On three, they both rammed their shoulders against the door, but the door was no longer there. It opened before Cayce turned the knob, and Harri and Cayce fell into the room in a heap. The rocking chair scooted slightly as it continued to rock as if someone had jumped out of it in a hurry.

"Ouch!" Harri rubbed her arm where Cayce fell on it.

"Ditto!" Cayce rubbed her upper right arm. "Did you see anything?" She nodded toward the rocker now slowing down.

"All I saw was you landing on top of me. You're a lot heavier than you look."

"Sorry about that. I guess maybe the door was ajar." Cayce stood and gave her sister a hand.

"Or not." Harri stood and crossed her arms, staring at the rocker as it creaked to an abrupt halt as if someone had put a hand on it to stop it.

Cayce moved to a large, ornate wardrobe and threw open both its doors, jumping back, expecting another surprise. Nothing happened.

"This is a beautiful room, even with the ghost."

Cayce turned and saw Harri on all fours looking under the antique bed that stood tall and gave plenty of room for anything to hide under it.

"See anything?"

"Nope. But just to block any future argument, this room is yours, not mine. Should it be a choice, that is." Harri walked to the other side of the room and stared at a door for a moment. She started to open it but then stopped. "Since it's your room, Cayce, you do the honors and see what's in your closet."

"You are such a sissy. You must get that from Mother's side of the family. And yes, I know, you are about to remind me of crawling under the house when we were kids during snake season to drag out the stray dog's puppies. Honestly, Harri..." Cayce jerked the door open, still talking and looking back at her sister while shaking her head.

Harri screamed and took off for the other door, almost giving Cayce a heart attack. She ran after Harri without turning to see what frightening thing lurked behind Door Number Two.

Chapter Six

When they reached the stairs, they both stopped, hearing a man's deep voice behind them.

"Whoa, you two! I ain't no spook!"

The sisters turned at the same time and saw a tall man with long white hair tied back in a low ponytail. His hair matched a white beard. The man stood staring at them from the doorway of the room they had just left. He wore overalls and a black-and-white-striped railroad cap.

"I'm Steve, the caretaker Joshua Devaux hired to watch over this place." The man held out his hand as he walked toward them. Cayce shook his hand with apprehension, and Harri followed suit, giving a half-hearted wimpy shake, not her usual.

"So you two must be the fearless sisters, Cayce and Harri. Joshua told me you were coming to sort out our ghost problem." Steve chuckled as he combed his beard with his hand. When he saw the sisters not laughing, he cleared his throat and started over.

"Sorry about scaring you. I thought sure you heard me call when I came in the front door. I thought I heard you in the other room 'til I got in there. Guess I'm a little spooky-looking, if you're not expecting me to be standing behind the door you're opening."

"So the door goes to the next bedroom and not to a closet?" Cayce asked, trying to cover her embarrassment and lack of bravery.

"Yep. No closets here," he answered and then added, "but lots of skeletons." He cocked his head at Harri and smiled, and then winked at Cayce. "Just kiddin', ladies."

"You're a real funny guy, Steve. Just don't do it again, or you might find yourself being beaten over the head by Louis Vuitton." Harri smiled, but Cayce knew her sister was serious. Harri was petite but could be really dangerous when carrying her big, heavy purse—especially when she packed her Glock, which she always did when they traveled.

"Louie who?" Steve cocked his head again. "Is that your boyfriend?"

"Just ignore my sister, Steve. By the way, I'm Cayce McCallister, and this is my fearless sister, Harri Wellington."

"Pleasure to meet you both. Now, let's get your luggage to your rooms, and I'll make us a pot of coffee." Steve passed the two and headed down the stairs past them. "Guess I owe you for scarin' you like that."

Harri's mouth flew open when she saw the kitchen in the hotel. The modern appliances were either camouflaged by wooden doors or were reproductions of the early 1900s but with modern mechanisms. A huge walk-in freezer and a pantry were stocked with everything imaginable for the gourmet chef. Harri found packages of frozen huckleberries as well as dried and canned ones in the pantry.

"Oh, boy! Your interest in these huckleberries must mean you're going to figure out Janie's huckleberry fudge recipe." Cayce rubbed her hands together as she reached for a package of gourmet coffee. "Here you go, Steve. You do owe us for scaring the bajiggers out of us, so you make the coffee." Cayce handed the coffee to their bearded host.

Harri came out of the pantry holding flour, baking powder, and a can of huckleberries.

"I've got something else in mind. Huckleberry scones. My own recipe, but I'll replace raspberries, my used-to-be favorite, with huckleberries. It will take a few minutes, so save some coffee."

A short time later, the three were munching away on scones.

"Well, here's the first item for your cookbook. Reckon you can make these in a Dutch oven over a campfire?" Cayce looked at Harri and cocked her head sideways like Steve had done earlier.

"Don't remind me of the camping thing. I'm still wondering where I'll take a bath and find a potty." Harri put her last bite back on her plate. "That's it. I'm stuffed. By the way, Cayce, that was dinner."

"You don't have to worry about a restroom, Harri. Joshua has taken care of all of that. In fact, most of the workers have been on the wagon trail for the last few days, building outhouses and doing some special landscaping around the hot springs. I hope you brought your swimming suits. Don't reckon you'll want to skinny dip like the locals." Steve did not give one little glance at the sisters as he left the table. "More coffee?" He filled his cup and then topped off Cayce's, with Harri declining.

"Hot springs?" Cayce and Harri asked in unison.

"That must be the reason Joshua told me to bring a swimsuit. The stinker. I guess he wanted to surprise me.

He knows how I love Chico Hot Springs in Montana."
Cayce smiled over her coffee cup, remembering the last
trip she'd made to Chico with Joshua. She also
remembered the encounter with the resident ghost,
Percy, at the old hotel there.

"You didn't know 'bout the springs?" Steve looked
at Cayce. "Well, there are mineral springs all in these
mountains. Some of 'em are red, but the ones on the
land Joshua bought are all crystal clear."

"You mean mineral springs like the ones famous
for their medicinal benefits?" Harri asked.

"I bet you're thinking about our favorite Victorian
inn in Tennessee, the Thomas House, aren't you?"
Cayce directed her question to Harri and then turned
back toward Steve to explain further. "The original
hotel, named the Cloyd Hotel, was built in 1890 at Red
Boiling Springs for clients seeking the healing powers
of the red mineral springs' water. The Thomas House
also has paranormal activity." Not waiting for Steve to
comment, Cayce asked, "So how far to these mineral
springs? I might want to check them out before we go
on the trail with Joshua." She looked at Harri to gauge
her interest.

"Yeah. I wouldn't mind taking a dip…wearing my
swimming suit, mind you. I've read that mineral springs
are like a fountain of youth for the aging." Harri rubbed
the crows' feet around her eyes, and Cayce remembered
Harri had mentioned working on those little lines with
some extremely expensive creams.

"Oh, you don't have to go that far. There's a
bathhouse right out back. The mineral springs at Bar
None are called Cole Springs, after the old pioneer who
found 'em. That's where Belle got the name for the

hotel. She was businesswoman enough to know not to name a hotel after herself, since she was hopin' to establish a different kind of clientele from the cat house. Cole Springs backs right up to the hotel and supplies water for the bathhouse. The mineral springs were a real drawing card before and after the mine shut down. Bartholomew Cole, the old trapper that discovered 'em, claimed the hot water cured him of the Arthur-i-tis, as he called it." Steve chuckled.

"And yes, it's clean and safe, so don't worry about that. The crew updated it, and the health department for the county checked it when they inspected the rest of the water before any construction started. Joshua Devaux's a good businessman. Can't wait to meet him. I was gone when he came here not long ago. Only talked to him on the phone." Steve took his dishes to the sink, rinsed them off, and put them in the oversized commercial dishwasher before heading to the door.

"You mean you have a phone, or a cell phone that works here? Mine is as dead as road kill." Cayce was anxious to talk to Joshua and give him a report.

"No. Cell phones don't work here, but Hank Coulter gave me a satellite phone so Joshua could contact me. You're welcome to use it." Steve stopped at the door. "'Preciate the vittles. Them scones was mighty good, Miss Harri. Anything else I can do for you ladies?"

"No, we're good. And thank you for bringing up our luggage. So your cabin is right out back in case we need anything?" Harri pushed back the curtain and looked out the window at the fast-approaching dark.

"It's actually a little farther than that…over at the edge of the woods. Don't worry. There ain't nothin' here that'll hurt you." He opened the door to walk out but then stopped. "But they might make you hurt yourself." Steve laughed loudly as he closed the door behind him.

"I can't decide if I like him or not. Just when I think he's okay, he makes a smartass comment and laughs. The audacity!" Harri took the rest of the dishes to the sink and rinsed them before putting them in the dishwasher. "I guarantee you we've had many more experiences than he has. Hurt yourselves! Indeed!" She rubbed her bruised arm.

"And just to prove we're not scared, let's get our swimsuits on, get our flashlights, soap, and towels, and check out the bathhouse. Okay, Harri?" Cayce got up from the table, but waited for her sister's reaction.

"You bet. Let's hit it." Harri left the kitchen and headed up the stairs without hesitation.

Chapter Seven

"You think rattlesnakes are out?" As they stepped off the porch, Harri tiptoed, hurrying to catch up with Cacye, and felt more at ease when Cayce slowed to allow her to catch up.

Cayce noticed her sister's recurring fear as they headed around the hotel into the alley. It was pitch-black dark, but the full moon helped to light their way. Cayce kept her flashlight on for backup and saw the bathhouse just ahead, camouflaged on the outside with logs but with a big carved bear holding a sign to identify it. The door was unlocked, and Cayce found the light switch just inside the door.

"Holy Tallahatchie! That man of yours does not miss a trick! Would you look at this? I may never leave." Harri must have retrieved her bravery as she walked to the huge bath, which looked like a small pool, outlined and lined inside with river rocks. She stuck her fingertips into the steaming water. "Perfect!"

Cayce zeroed in on the furniture made from logs with comfortable-looking, fat leather cushions on oversized lounge chairs—way too inviting not to pounce on.

"I knew it. Filled with kapok just like at his house in Mississippi. You just sink right into it." She put her head back and closed her eyes. "Heavenly!" Hearing

Harri splash into the steamy bath, she opened her eyes and left her spot.

"No. This is heavenly. I can feel my crows' feet tightening already. I hope these minerals will lift everything that's sagging." Harri used both hands to push up her breasts as she looked down at them. "All we need is background music."

As if on cue, surround sound music began to play and the lights dimmed, making it twilight in the magical bathhouse. Cayce loved the easy listening music; it was like what she always carried when away from her own mountains. She always said music helped her "envision mountain streams cascading over giant river rocks, all beneath snowcapped mountains." But Bar None was the reality of now. Native flute accompanied the orchestra, giving the music a surreal, almost eerie resonance.

"Nice!" Harri waltzed herself over to the edge where Cayce stood. "You found the right switch."

"Actually, I didn't. Joshua must have the lights and music on some kind of a timer. I didn't touch anything."

Cayce added her sweats to Harri's pile and slipped into the bath.

"Oh, you are so right. This is heaven." Cayce looked around and noticed a big sign they had missed when first entering the bathhouse.

"Uh-oh! We were supposed to shower before we got in. See the open showers over in the corner? Right now, they look like little trickles coming out of a stone cave wall. How beautiful!"

"I'll shower before we leave. I'm not moving for at least an hour. My body is still aching from the ride here in Hawk." Harri laid her head back on the towel she had rolled up on the edge of the river rock ledge.

"The sign also recommends you not stay over twenty minutes or risk shriveling away to nothing." Cayce rolled her towel like her sister's and laid her head back. "Shriveling off five pounds would be pretty nice, though."

The sisters lay quiet. Harri's eyes were closed, but Cayce enjoyed looking up at the skylight. The lights dimmed even more, allowing the moon and the stars shining through the skylight to take over as the cabin's main sources of light. Within minutes, Harri was snoring softly.

Just as Cayce was reminded again of why she always demanded her own room when they traveled, a shadow drifted across the water, bringing her to full alert.

Must have been a limb moving with the breeze in the moonlight.

Cayce laid her head back again, but did not close her eyes. Thinking she heard a noise, she glanced toward the window without moving her head. Again she saw the silhouette of the mountain in the moonlight, but a shadow moved outside the window, distorting the silhouette. She slid closer to her sister and poked Harri until she gave another loud snort and opened her eyes.

"Harri. Keep looking at me, and don't panic."

"What?" Harri jerked her head off the towel, flailing the water as she tried to stand without leaning.

"I said, *don't panic*. Now just pretend we're having a cozy conversation. Someone is outside the window watching us. I see his silhouette with the moonlight behind him."

"Has to be that weirdo Steve. I told you I didn't

like him." Harri moved to get out, but Cayce grabbed her arm.

"No, I want you to stay here as though nothing is happening," Cayce whispered. "I'm going to slip out of the water on the other side where it's darker and go out the back door. I'm not letting some creep put a damper on our trip. What I see is a Peeping Tom, not a ghost." She left the bath as quietly as possible.

"Wait! I'm coming with you..." But before Harri could get out of the water, Cayce was gingerly sneaking out the back door.

Harri sat back against the river rock, frozen in place, her eyes locked on the shadow at the window.

"Where are Louie and Glock when I need them?" she whispered.

Cayce flattened her body against the outside log wall and inched toward the side where she had seen the Peeping Tom. She stopped to pick up a short piece of two-by-four left by the construction crew, and when she got to the corner, stuck her head around the wall just enough to see if the intruder was still at his post. He stood there with his hands shielding his eyes against the window, obviously trying to get a better look. The silhouette appeared no taller than Cayce and looked like a male, dressed in dark clothes with the brim of his hat pulled down tight on his head.

Cayce dodged around the corner of the log building yelling at the top of her lungs, holding the board up and ready to swing. "Hey, you! What the heck do you think you're doing?"

The figure got one quick glance at her, gave a clipped yelp, and fled toward the woods like a grizzly was chasing him.

Cayce ran after him but was no match with bare feet. She stopped at the edge of the woods and bent over to remove pine needles stuck to her foot.

Harri ran to her side. "Did you get a good look at him? Was it Steve?"

"I didn't see his face, but he did not have a long, white beard and hair." Cayce held her side as she panted. "I would have seen a beard and long hair for sure. And he was short. That leaves out Steve." Cayce finished catching her breath.

"I say bath time is over. Let's get our stuff and go back to the hotel. We can look for tracks in the morning."

As they re-entered the bathhouse, Cayce looked around for the switches that dimmed the lights and turned on the music. "Here are both switches, if you can call them that." Cayce was on the opposite side of the room from the main light switch where they'd entered. She put her fingers on the buttons that were lit up and pushed on each, causing the lights to dim and the music to turn on and off. "These big buttons are so sensitive, you just barely touch them, and they turn lights and music on and off."

"I see what you mean." Harri touched the buttons, copying Cayce's moves. "Question is, who pressed the buttons, if it wasn't you? I don't think Boo Radley could have sneaked in here without us seeing him."

"Good question. If the lights hadn't dimmed, I wouldn't have known anyone was outside the window. Since they don't seem to be on a timer, then someone…or something…wanted to help us. Let's hope all the spirits here are this protective."

Chapter Eight

Before they had coffee the next morning, Cayce and Harri practiced sleuthing outside the bathhouse, looking for tracks under the window.

"Look here!" Harri followed tracks from the window to the woods. "No way those are Steve's. They're not much bigger than mine." Harri placed her foot next to the track to compare. "Could have been a woman, albeit a woman who didn't care much for fashion, since this sole shows some serious wear." Harri was bent over with her finger in the holes shown in the dirt. "Not to mention the tracks look like they were made by work boots."

"I don't think it was a woman. The yell I heard sounded male." Cayce went to the back of the window and found more tracks, but they came toward the bathhouse, not away from it. "Let's follow these and see where he came from."

They followed for a few minutes, but lost the tracks again at the woods. Noticing a path a few yards away, Cayce walked toward it.

"Where do you think this goes, Harri?"

"Only one way to find out."

The two headed up the path and soon came to a small cabin that looked just like the ones not yet restored in Bar None, but this one had been refurbished somewhat, although not professionally. Built of wood, but not log, it had a red metal roof. The windows were all trimmed in red like Teesh's, and two red straight chairs sat on the porch. Cayce thought the owner of this cabin and Teesh must have shared a gallon of red paint.

As Cayce and Harri approached, they saw the curtain move at the window. In a matter of seconds, the door opened and Steve stuck his head out.

"Howdy, ladies. See you made it through the night."

"Did you think we wouldn't?" Harri asked with attitude.

"Nope. Didn't doubt you for a minute. Had coffee yet? I just made a fresh pot." Steve opened the door, and Harri and Cayce entered.

The cabin was surprisingly clean, for a bachelor's domain, but was furnished sparsely. A crudely constructed table with three straight chairs separated the kitchen area from the living room-slash-bedroom, another keeping room like Teesh's but with no extra room attached. The main part of the room was furnished with a worn recliner, a platform rocker, a rustic pine log bed with a sunken spot in the middle, and a table that held a fat, old-timey twenty-inch TV with a video player and several stacks of videos—no DVDs.

"No satellite TV out here? Guess I won't be watching my shows for a couple of weeks. That will be a real hardship." Harri shifted her gaze from the TV back to Steve, who held the coffeepot while taking stained coffee mugs from the cabinet.

"Thanks, Steve, but we've got the coffeepot set up and ready to brew when we get back to the hotel. We need to head back pretty quick. We're just out tracking." Cayce decided to tell Steve about the Peeping Tom and gauge his reaction. She was disappointed to get no reaction at all.

"Well, that could be Charlie. He's a recluse that lives up the valley. He comes to Bar None a lot, mostly at night. Charlie's a real night owl. I would have warned you about Charlie in due time. Kinda keeps watch over the town. I'm sure he didn't mean no harm. Just a curious sort. Checkin' you out to make sure you're not intrudin'." Steve took a sip of his coffee while directing his gaze at the sisters.

"Intruding? I'd say it's the other way around." Harri sat in one of the straight chairs at Steve's table, obviously wanting to hear more.

Cayce pulled out a chair and sat across from her. Wanting to be polite and to get information, she decided to take Steve's offer. "Actually, I'll take a coffee, Steve, but just half a cup. It smells good." She knew Harri would not drink any. She was far too germ-conscious to risk drinking from one of Steve's cups, especially with no sign of running water in the cabin.

Steve handed Cayce a cup with a spoon and put sugar and cream in front of her.

"You sure you don't want coffee, Harri?" Steve asked, still holding the pot.

"No, thank you. I'm fine. But I do want to know about Charlie. I'm not particularly fond of peepers, especially if I'm the peepee." Harri crinkled her brows together and gasped. "Wait a minute. That didn't come out exactly right."

Cayce and Steve laughed.

"Don't know much to tell about Charlie. He don't talk hardly at all. I've never got him to carry on a conversation as such. Just comes and goes as he pleases." Steve sat at the table. "Every once in a while, he'll come 'round and buy some of my flour, coffee, rice, and oatmeal—necessary supplies like that—but he mostly keeps to himself. He picks berries and catches trout, but that's about it. A real animal lover, that one, and won't even keep trout for himself, but he'll catch 'em for me and Teesh."

"He sounds like an interesting character. And it sounds like you and Teesh are his best friends." Cayce smiled and looked at Harri to see if she was looking more at ease as she learned more about her Boo Radley, the character from Harri and Cayce's favorite book of all time, *To Kill a Mockingbird.*

"I like Charlie, but he and Teesh are like family to each other. I think Teesh keeps him in clothes and anything else he needs to survive. Charlie's kind of childlike. He's probably forty or so years old, but his mind is like about a five- or six-year-old in most ways. He's a little feller. Wears an old brown hat that's seen better days. Keeps it pulled way down on his head and makes his ears stick straight out, kind of elfish-looking. Tough as a pine knot and fit as an athlete. He's here one second and gone the next. That little guy can run like the wind."

"You don't know anything about him?" Harri asked after taking a drink of her coffee.

Steve shook his head. "I've never asked. He leaves me alone, and I leave him alone. Every once in a while, I'll find some fresh fish or a bucket of berries he's left for me on the front porch. He's a pretty good neighbor that way."

"About that satellite phone, Steve. Do you think we

could borrow it and check in with Joshua? I'm hoping he'll send me one by Hank Coulter. If I ever see Mr. Coulter, that is."

"Sure. You can keep it. I don't have no need of it. It's a pain in the ass to remember to charge it, anyway. I don't have electricity, but Joshua says he's gonna hook me up pretty soon. Some guy who thought he wanted to buy a ghost town come up here one summer and parked his fancy RV up by the spring. He had a big ol' heavy generator that ran off diesel and didn't want to take it with him when he got his belly full of ghost town living. He give it to me. I keep it full of diesel but don't use it 'cept to watch John Wayne or Jeremiah Johnson ever' once in a while. Now I have to run it to keep that dadgum satellite phone charged. If I need to tell Joshua anything, I'll just tell Hank. Tell Joshua I give it to you, so he won't be calling me."

"What kind of vehicle does Hank drive?" Harri must have been thinking about the yellow Dodge truck that almost ran them off the road.

"Drives a new yellow truck. He was here yesterday with a couple of workers but left in kind of a hurry. I was panning down on the creek and saw him pass just a-flyin', like the devil was chasin' him."

Harri straightened at the mention of "panning."

"So do you get much gold out of this creek?"

"Enough to survive. Don't look to make a fortune."

"Do you mind if I watch you sometime? I bought myself a pan at the antique shop and would sure like to give it a go."

"Not at all. It's pretty easy. Even Charlie can do it. He pays me in gold when he needs groceries and don't have nothin' to barter."

When Cayce and Harri got back to the hotel, Hank's dirty yellow truck was "cowboy'd up" in front of the hitching post next to Hawk.

"Be nice, Cayce. He might have had a good reason to have been speeding down that road yesterday."

"Aren't I always nice?" Cayce opened the door to the hotel and stomped in, gunning for the driver. He was in the kitchen pouring coffee, his back to the door.

"So I guess it's you I have to thank for almost giving me a heart attack yesterday. Where'd you learn to drive, Mister? Nascar?"

The man turned around, and Cayce almost wished she had taken Harri's advice. Hank Coulter was every bit as good-looking as Joshua, but in even more of a cowboy way. He was tall and had thick, prematurely gray hair that hung a little long over his ears. His blue chambray shirt was laundered to perfection with heavy starch and fit him tightly, showing off muscular arms and chest. His Wranglers, molded to his trim physique, fit him "real good," as cowgirls would say, with heavily starched creases that glistened under the hotel lights and ran the full length of his muscular legs from boots to pockets, like track lights to heaven. Like on all true cowboys, his jeans hung long over his boots, dragging the floor a little. The day-old scruff of a beard outlined a rugged but handsome face.

"Oops!" The cowboy looked sheepish and held out the mug of coffee he had just poured to Cayce.

"Oops! Is that all you've got to say for yourself? You could have killed us, and all you can say is oops? Is that your way of apologizing?" Cayce stepped closer and folded her arms, staring at him.

"Take the coffee, and I'll explain, but I need a cup

myself." He forced the cup into Cayce's hands and turned to Harri. "How about you, ma'am? Coffee?"

"Yes, but I'll get it. You appease my little sister." Harri reached in the cupboard for a mug and poured herself a cup of coffee, stalling with the cream and sugar.

"All right." Cayce sat at the table with her hands wrapped around the mug of coffee. "I'm ready. Let's hear it."

"First of all, I'm Hank Coulter. You two must be Cayce and Harri. I trust from the description Joshua gave me you would be Cayce." The cowboy sat across the table and smiled at Cayce.

"True. But I want to know why you ran me off the road." Cayce took too big a sip of her coffee and put her cup down fast, spilling it on the table. She frantically waved her hand at her mouth. "Oh! That's hot."

"Coffee generally is. Sorry! Should have put a warning label on it like they do at MacDonald's." Hank didn't laugh, but the twinkle in his eyes gave him away.

"It's not funny!" Cayce yelled at Hank as she wiped tears from her eyes.

"Is she always like this?" Hank turned to Harri.

"Only on her good days." Harri brought her coffee to the table and sat between Hank and Cayce. "You really don't want to be around her when she's having a bad day."

"Okay. I call a ceasefire. Let me explain about yesterday." Hank put his cup down. "We were finishing up the roof on the back side of the cat house. My main roofer was up on the steepest part and, like a fool, did not tie himself off. Next thing I know, he yelled and came rolling off, right over the ladder. He grabbed hold of the ladder, and it broke his fall just enough to keep from killing him. Anyway, it was obvious his leg and his arm were broken, so I headed out with him to the hospital. I had a helicopter meet me at the service station and fly him to Idaho Falls. I've been there most of the night."

"Oh." Cayce dropped her gaze, feeling sheepish. "Sorry for jumping on you like that, Hank. I should've known something was wrong." She took another sip of her coffee, being careful not to burn her lips again. "Will your roofer be okay?"

"Yeah. But he's finished with me. I can't have my people ignoring safety codes like that. He scared me to death. I thought sure I was going to have to break some really bad news to his young wife. Not that a broken leg and arm aren't bad enough."

"So what happened on the roof?" Harri asked.

"I don't know. Will—that's the roofer—won't talk about it. He said nobody would believe him and we'd think he was crazy, so he was keeping his mouth shut." Hank took another sip of coffee.

"That's not the first thing that's happened while we've been working on the cat house. We started restoring that building first, but so much stuff happened I was afraid I'd lose all my crew. I moved to Cole Springs Hotel, and the paranormal happenings—at least the bad activity—pretty much stopped." Hank left the table and headed back to the coffeepot. Without asking, he topped off his and Cayce's cups.

"Oh, we've seen shadow figures," he continued, "and the lady in black peeking at us from upstairs, but it was nothing trying to harm us." Before Hank sat back down, he backed up to the counter, propping his hands behind him. "You wanta know what's really strange?"

Cayce and Harri gave Hank their full attention without nodding, and Hank went on.

"As long as we were working on Belle's living quarters—you know, the addition behind the hotel—well, everything was fine. But as soon as we started on The Nugget, the saloon or cat house, whichever you prefer to call it, all hell broke loose."

"How so, Hank?" Harri asked.

"The men would nail boards on the walls or ceiling, and sometimes they'd pop loose and fly at them, barely missing them most of the time. One time, a carpenter got hit…cut a little gash in his forehead. Fortunately, Bill is a mean cuss, tough as nails. He just picked that board up without saying so much as 'dadgum' and sailed it right back at the wall it came from. Bill is as big as a bull and just as strong. He broke two boards in the wall when he slung that board, and they had to be replaced."

"He didn't quit?" Cayce asked.

"Or curse?" Harri added.

"No, Bill doesn't curse, but he can sure bellow. These are his exact words—probably heard in the cemetery he yelled so loud—'There ain't a ha'nt or a demon alive that can scare ole Bill off.' " Hank laughed at the idea of a ha'nt being alive. "And Bill's still here. In fact, if any of the guys get scared working in the cathouse, they just send for Bill, and he calms everything down. I think Belle has taken a shine to him. Must like the rough and unruly type. Bill, with his big muscles, must be good-looking to Belle and whoever else of the feminine variety still hangs out here. Just to keep the project going, I made Bill foreman. Bill was not here yesterday when Will fell off the roof. I think Belle was trying to tell me she missed Bill."

"I guess Joshua told you why he wanted Harri and me to come to Bar None." Cayce rubbed her thumb over the side of her coffee mug, not looking up.

"Yeah, he did. Three months ago, I would have said, 'Hogwash,' to the whole ghost thing, but not now. I am a full-scale believer in all things paranormal. Joshua says you ladies have a gift of some sort."

"Yes, from our father's side of the family. We don't publicize it, but it's real. I just hope we can figure out what's going on here and help Joshua and you," Harri explained as she added more cream to the strong cowboy coffee.

"I told Joshua he ought to leave the ghosts here, since that seems to be the trend nowadays. There have been all kinds of ghost-hunting groups wanting to be the first to stay here. I've had to run some groups off, and Steve has, too. Joshua is afraid somebody will get hurt and he'll be sued. That's another trend in today's society." Hank took another sip of his coffee.

"So what's on your agenda today, Hank? Do you have a crew coming out?"

"No. They're all working on the trail. I'm bringing horses over later in the week and riding up. You wanta come along? Joshua says you're a real cowgirl, a Montana rancher and all. You're welcome, too, Harri."

"Maybe you could get back to me about that. Harri and I are planning to check Bar None out pretty thoroughly." Cayce glanced at Harri over her coffee cup and saw a twinkle in her eye. She knew what her sister was thinking.

"Don't get back to me, Hank. I don't straddle horses. I tried it once and couldn't walk for three days." Harri looked at Cayce, who snickered. She had taken a picture of Harri on the short, fat horse named Roscoe, and her short legs stuck straight out. Harri's feet had dangled out in midair most of the way up the mountain trail on that trip so long ago. She could not keep them in the stirrups that curved with the horse's fat belly.

"And, for future information, I'm not looking forward to this wagon trip I hear Joshua is taking us on. I'll put the trail off as long as possible." Harri took another sip of coffee, grimaced, and pushed it back. "That has to be the strongest coffee I have ever tried to drink. No offense, Hank, but it tastes a little like bug spray."

"None taken. I forgot one of you is a delicate city girl when I added extra coffee to your setup. Is my brew okay for you, Cayce, other than being a little bit too hot?" Hank looked at Cayce and smiled.

"No, it's good. I like strong coffee." Cayce took another small sip. "So you have had some paranormal experiences at Bar None too?"

"If you want, I can show you two around," Hank offered. "Show you the 'hot spots.' I think that's what they call it on TV." He left the table and put his cup in the dishwasher. "I have to run to town and pick up some supplies, but I'll be back after lunch."

"We'll probably start without you but would like for you to tell us what you've seen and heard and show us where it happened, when you get back. If you're sure you can spare the time, that is." Cayce looked at Harri again. She was grinning.

"Sure. I'd be happy to. Believe it or not, I've had

more happen right here in this hotel than anywhere." Hank walked to the corner under the open staircase.

"You see this old table here? We have repaired this leg four times, and it's still loose." Hank leaned over and moved the table, and it wobbled like it was ready to collapse.

"Let me guess. That must be Peg's table." Harri walked over and shook the table.

"You did your homework, Harri. This *is* Peg's table. It was originally in the saloon, but Joshua had us bring it up here to fix it. It'll go back to the saloon after we restore it." Hank left the table and walked to the baby grand piano.

"I'm not going to tell you what happens here. I'm staying here the rest of the week to finish up the roof of the cat house, so I'll show you, but you have to get up about two-thirty a.m. It's the most unbelievable thing I've ever seen. But I'm not telling you anything more."

"The witching hour," Cayce said as she sat down on the piano bench.

"The what?" Hank asked as he ran his fingers across the keys without playing any notes.

"From two-thirty to three-thirty a.m. is the witching hour. They do show up at other times, but those early morning hours seem to be the best time for contacting spirits," Cayce explained.

"More like spirits contacting you," Harri added.

"Our dad had a saying that Harri and I live by, 'Keep an open mind and an open path, and the Way will find you.' It seems to always prove true."

"Nice play on words. I bet your dad was a character." Hank sat beside Cayce on the bench and leaned over with his elbows propped on his knees and his hands clasped.

"Definitely! We miss Pop, but a lot of the time we think he's still with us. Not in the ghost sense but in the protective daddy sense." Harri smiled, thinking of Pop.

"I tell you what, Hank." Cayce stood and placed a hand on Hank's shoulder, trying to show she could be friendly. "Harri and I will put our talents to use here, and we'll come back to the table with you later and compare experiences. That way, we won't be establishing any kind of a mindset." Cayce did not want to be rude, especially since she had been so rude already, but she liked to experience the paranormal firsthand without any preconceived knowledge.

"That makes sense." Hank glanced at Cayce and also stood without moving away from the bench. "I need to hit the road anyway. I really just came to meet you two and to apologize for yesterday. Joshua told me you would be driving a vintage truck, so I figured it had to be you." Hank headed to the door, stopped, and turned back toward Cayce. "Hawk, is it? He's a beaut', by the way."

As soon as Hank backed his truck out and waved goodbye, Harri started. "I guess you noticed Hank was not wearing a wedding band." Harri's eyes had a permanent twinkle.

"No, I did not notice. Anyway, that doesn't mean anything. A lot of construction people don't wear rings because of safety codes." Cayce walked into the pantry and came out with a box of cereal. "Want some?"

"No. I hid a leftover scone from last night." Harri dug the scone out of the back of the refrigerator and put it in the microwave to heat. "Now back to Cowboy Hank."

"He is definitely a cowboy, and a fine specimen of one, but my interest is still in Joshua; that is, if he ever decides to come around again." Cayce poured milk over her cereal and began crunching. "Doesn't mean I can't look, though, especially when the scenery is so awesome." Cayce spoke through a mouthful as she sat on a stool at the island.

"Changing the subject. What do you think about Boo Radley?" Harri pulled off a piece of scone and popped it in her mouth.

"Charlie? Not a clue. I just hope he's as harmless as Steve says. We'll have to remember to ask Teesh the next time we visit. I bet she can give us his life history." Cayce put her empty bowl and spoon in the dishwasher and turned to Harri. "Well, it's show time. Where do you want to start?"

As if on cue, a huge thud came from one of the bedrooms upstairs. They looked at each other and headed toward the stairs.

Chapter Nine

Billie ate the oatmeal and fruit, something she was told she had to do for the health of her baby. How the Keeper knew she was pregnant remained a puzzle to Billie. The food he gave her was always tasty and healthy. "As close to the way God created it as possible" was how the Keeper described it, but today the oatmeal had a funny taste to it.

As soon as she put the Styrofoam tray in the depository where she always had to put the disposable dishes, the shower came on. Quickly, she headed to the corner, undressed, and got under the warm water. She had learned to lather fast with the rationed soap so she would have time to rinse thoroughly. The first time she had not been quick enough and had to wear soap until the next shower. When the shower turned off, she dried with paper towels and put her dirty dress back on. She placed the wet paper products on the depository.

"I'm ready for my clean dress," she called. The door opened a few minutes later, and she retrieved her clean paper dress. She walked to the back corner again, under the camera where she had been told she could dress without being seen. The Keeper assured her he "respected the modesty of women." What he really meant was he insisted upon it.

As always, the small door automatically shut, and she heard someone remove the items off the revolving shelf. A second later, the door opened, and she took out her rationed toilet paper and drinking water that had to last all day.

Billie dressed quickly, still embarrassed by the thought someone might be watching even though she was beneath the camera. The real reprieve from being watched came at night when it was so dark she could not see her own hand in front of her face. She'd been afraid of the dark before. Now, it was her only friend.

Billie went to her mattress and lay down. Feeling exceptionally sleepy made her wonder if she had exercised too much the night before.

Soon, she was sound asleep, dreaming she was floating along, almost flying, her feet not touching the ground. When she stopped, she tried to open her eyes, but could only manage a peek. Two people dressed in white stood over her. Their faces were covered with masks, and their mumbling was incomprehensible. She felt something cold on her belly. Round and round the cold thing moved. When she shivered, the shorter person, a female, patted her arm without saying a word.

Am I in heaven? Will I get to see my Grammar? Is my baby here with me?

Billie tried to open her eyes, but they would not open.

Where's the light? Everyone says there's a light. I want to go to the light.

But no light came. She felt something else cold. This time it was between her legs, pushing up inside her. She tried to press her legs together, but could not move. Again she shivered, but this time a woman patted her arm and whispered in her ear.

"It will be all right, Billie."

"No! Do not speak to her!" The voice did not come from the man who stood over her but from across the room. The voice, loud and sharp, was not spoken through a synthesizer.

Billie could hear her Grammar's voice.

Whistling!
Singing!
Remember, Billie! Remember!
Run!
Get up!
Run!

Then her own voice took control.

Falling! Falling!
Clouds!
Mom! Dad! Grammar!

Blackness.

Billie awoke on her mattress. It had been a strange nightmare, so real. It was as if she had been transported somewhere, somewhere away from the cell. She felt wet between her legs and tried to get up to go to the toilet, but she was too groggy. She fell back onto the mattress. Her dress was stuck to her belly and the upper part of her legs. She tried to get up again, and this time stumbled to the toilet.

She peed, but it hurt a little this time. When she wiped, she saw tiny specks of blood and something else thick and sticky. She pulled her dress away from where it was stuck to her belly. Reaching under, she felt small drops of something dried to her skin.

She recognized the little bit of gel that had been left on her stomach. It was from a sonogram like the doctor had given her at sixteen, when they'd thought she had appendicitis. She remembered the cold from her dream on her stomach and between her legs.

It was not a nightmare. The Keeper drugged me. The oatmeal!

He drugged me and took me somewhere.

I've been examined!

Billie closed her eyes, wrapped her arms around her knees in a fetal position, and rocked herself to sleep.

Chapter Ten

The sisters stopped at Cayce's room first. The door was still closed, and no sound came from inside. Slowly, Cayce turned the doorknob.

Everything looked just like she had left it. Her suitcase lay open on the floor under the window, and her bed was still unmade, something she planned to remedy after they completed the tracking.

"Nothing amiss here. Let's check your room, Harri."

Cayce walked to the door leading directly into Harri's room. Harri had insisted the door stay open when they finally went to bed, uneasy with the Charlie episode, but Cayce had closed it in the night when the noise of Harri's snoring, abnormal but not paranormal, became too much for her. She would have to get some earplugs the next time they were in town.

Gingerly, Cayce opened the door, remembering the last time, when she'd opened it only to discover a tall, bearded, and very scary stranger behind it.

Cayce and Harri squeezed through the door together.

"A little messy in your old age, aren't you, Harri? Did you forget your upbringing?"

Harri's suitcase had been emptied, her makeup and jewelry strewn all over the floor. Her lipstick and compact lay open on the dresser as if someone had been using them.

"If I didn't know better, I'd say a little girl has been in here playing with my makeup." Harri picked up the lipstick that was out of the tube full-length and turned it to get it back down in its case. "And where's the top to my lipstick case?" Harri looked under the dressing table and on the floor. "Now, this beats all. This is an expensive lipstick case, has mother-of-pearl on the top. Help me look for it, Cayce."

Cayce helped search for the top. "Yep. Looks just like what you used to do with our mother's makeup when you were little."

"I remember you playing with Mom's lipstick, too. You used it for war paint when you played like an Indian on the warpath in your barn loft hideout." Harri was still on her hands and knees looking under every piece of furniture. Suddenly, Harri stopped and looked at Cayce.

"Did you hear something?" Cayce stood and wiped the dust off her hands.

"Was that a giggle?" Harri, too, stood and looked around.

"It certainly sounded like a giggle. I think we have company. It sounded like a little girl's giggle. I just wish we knew her name." Cayce sat on the bed, and then spoke. "We heard you giggle, and I think you have had fun with my sister's makeup. My name is Cayce, and my sister is Harri. What's your name?" She sat quiet, hoping for an answer.

Harri sat on the stool in front of the dressing table and reached for her purse where it sat on the bed. Slowly, with as little movement as possible, she pulled out a small digital recorder, turned it on, and laid it on one end of the bed.

"Do you like playing dress up? I did when I was a little girl. I played with my mother's makeup, too." Harri picked up the lipstick. "My favorite color for lipstick is pink, like this. What's yours?"

Still no answer, and the room seemed eerily quiet.

"Come over here and stand by me, and I'll show you how I put my lipstick on." Harri hesitated a few seconds as if giving the little girl time to get beside her before she faced the mirror again.

"First, I take out my lipstick brush." Harri reached into her makeup bag and pulled out a container holding a short brush. "Then I outline my top lip, like this." She dabbed the brush on the lipstick until the bristles were thoroughly covered, then carefully followed the contour of her top lip, leaving a dark pink outline. "I do the same thing to my bottom lip, like this. Are you here?" Harri glanced to each side in the mirror as she completed the outlining.

"Once I've done that, I take my tube of lipstick and color inside the line on my lip, my top lip first and then my bottom lip. Be careful and stay inside the lines just like you do in your coloring book…or I think you would have called it your painting book." Harri carefully filled inside the lines with hot pink lipstick.

"The last thing I do is take a little piece of tissue and put it between my lips and press my lips together. That gets the extra lipstick off so it doesn't smear. Well, how do I look?" Harri looked straight ahead in the mirror, and Cayce figured it was because Harri did not know on which side of her the little girl might be standing.

"So that's how you get your lips to look like that?"

Cayce had been watching, mesmerized with her sister's demonstration and had forgotten about the real audience. Cayce knew Harri saw her watching, too, and held up her hand to stop Harri from speaking. "No, I don't want you to show me how to do my makeup. If it takes more than two minutes, I'm not up for it."

"Cayce is my little sister. She's a tomboy and likes to play with cowboys and ride horses. But don't mind her. Sometimes she's fun." Harri kept her eyes on the mirror. "I'd really like the top to my lipstick case back. It was a gift from my husband and is very special. He died a few years ago, and I really miss him." She paused a few seconds as if giving the little spirit time to think about what she had said. "If you happen to find it, would you put it on the dressing table? I would really appreciate it."

Harri picked up the recorder and headed toward the door. Cayce followed her. Just as they got to the door, they heard a noise like something had been dropped. They both turned toward the dressing table and saw the lipstick case top rolling toward the edge and to the floor. Harri walked over, picked it up, and put it back on the lipstick.

"Thank you so much. I'll leave my makeup out so you can play with it some more. I know you will be really careful and put it back in the bag when you finish." With these words, Harri left the room, followed by Cayce.

The sisters said nothing until they got to the kitchen.

"Oh, my gosh! That was fantastic!" Harri was so excited she almost dropped the digital recorder. Cayce took the recorder from her sister's hand.

"Here, let me do it." Cayce punched rewind and then play, and held the recorder up between her and Harri's ears. Harri's whole demonstration played, and both smiled.

"I do the same thing to my bottom lip like this. Are you here?" The recorder repeated what Harri had said as she'd looked into the mirror, trying to gauge where the little ghost girl was. In the few seconds of silence following Harri's question, a sweet, faint voice responded.

"I'm right beside you." The little girl giggled.

Harri and Cayce gasped at the same time and began to jump up and down in excitement. They'd caught an electronic voice phenomenon, an EVP, just like many they had caught over the years, but none as sweet-sounding as this little girl.

Chapter Eleven

"The best way to find out who our little friend is will be to visit the cemetery. Steve said it's up yonder, whatever that means. Let's head up the valley." Harri picked up her daypack and walked into the kitchen. "I'll get us some water bottles and granola bars."

"Better throw this in, too." Cayce walked out of the pantry with a can of bear spray. "I assume there's a reason why they keep this here."

"Maybe it's for Boo." Harri took the bear spray and placed it in a side pocket for easy access. "I'm still not convinced a Peeping Tom can be harmless."

Cayce and Harri followed the railroad track for the short distance it led out of Bar None, going into the mountains. The scenery was spectacular once they got past the last of the falling-down cabins and charred remains of buildings, not enough left to distinguish what the buildings had been originally. Cayce knew these would be bulldozed away eventually, and she could not help but feel sad at the prospect of losing some of the history of this wonderful old town.

"I wonder if Hank knows what cabin belonged to whom. If he doesn't, he should get Teesh to tell him what she remembers."

"Speaking of Hank, did he say he was staying at the hotel? I wonder if Joshua thinks we need protecting." Harri's eyes twinkled. "The way Hank looks at you, I'd say Joshua messed up if he ordered the good-looking cowboy to stay."

"Oh, Harri. Give it up."

Cayce intentionally out-walked Harri to put a stop to the conversation. She had not gone far when she saw what looked like an old mineshaft up the hill. Old timbers outlined piles of huge stones blocking the entrance. Hanging from several of the timbers were signs announcing Danger! No Trespassing!

Turning toward the mine, she climbed to the top of the hill and sat on one of the boulders waiting for Harri. "I'm up here." Cayce motioned for her sister to climb up the hill. "Look what I found." Just as she got the words out of her mouth, she caught a glimpse through her peripheral vision of an apparition sitting a few feet away on another boulder.

She did not look at the apparition for fear of losing the sighting. The figure was looking down, watching Harri as she scrambled up the hill. Then, in a flash, the apparition disappeared.

"I see. The old mineshaft." Harri huffed her way up to sit beside Cayce, and then took a bottle of water from her daypack, handing another one to Cayce.

"No. I'm not talking about the mine. Look." Cayce pointed to the ground in front of her.

"Oh, my gosh!" Harri got up to get a closer look. "Tracks! Strange tracks! Like someone with one boot and a peg leg."

"Yep. Reminds me of that line from *The Man From Snowy River* where Clancy says 'Spur leaves tracks like a sea drill,' or something like that. Look at the deep holes left by Peg's wooden leg. I think Peg is a little on the heavy side." Cayce glanced to her left, remembering the apparition she had just seen and knew it was probably Peg, and she was still listening and watching.

"So you think these were made by Peg, huh?" Harri looked around.

"Well, story goes, Peg guards the entrance to the mine. Her tracks are everywhere." Cayce followed the tracks. "They're coming from down the opposite side of the path we traveled, down by the railroad tracks." Cayce bent over and looked closer. "This is strange. There are plenty of boot tracks coming up to the mine, but I don't see any going away from the mine."

Harri left her stone perch and began looking for tracks. "You're right. Hmm! Peg is lingering at the mine." Harri stood still, in her thinking mode. "You know, it could be Peg is trying to keep others from going into the mine, protecting would-be trespassers rather than trying to scare them. Did you think about that? Everyone has a story, and everyone has some good in them, or most everyone."

"Ever the optimist, Sister. No, I didn't think of that, but you could be right. The best way to keep people away is by being a scary bad-ass. You just might have figured the old girl out." Cayce noticed the apparition was back and hoped it was Peg's way of acknowledging Harri was right about her. Peg left a few seconds after she appeared, but not before glancing up at the sisters from under her old, worn, black hat.

"We'll have to follow the tracks and see where she's coming from. We know one of those falling-down cabins was hers. We'll have to get Hank to show us which one. Maybe Peg will make contact with us."

Harri and Cayce left the mine and headed down the

trail. Once, Cayce sensed a presence behind them and glanced back discreetly, not wanting to alarm her sister. Nothing was there except for boot tracks, or rather one boot and one peg, but they were going the same direction as the sisters, away from the mine. Just around the next curve, they saw what was left of a rusted iron fence surrounding what must have been a hundred or more tombstones.

"I didn't expect it to be so big. Did you?" Harri stood wide-eyed, staring.

"Well, if you think about the history, Bar None was a boom town at one time. A lot of people lived here; a lot of people died here. Problem is I don't know where to start looking for our little girl. Any ideas?"

The sisters saw it at the same time—a huge statue of Jesus with outstretched arms on the far side of the cemetery. They headed in that direction.

"I love old cemeteries but hate that I don't know if I'm stepping on a grave or not. These old homemade tombstones are so crumbly, and it looks like many have fallen and formed little piles like red sand. See all the piles of sandstone? What a shame." Harri, focusing on the stacks of sandstone, tripped over a piece of tombstone half-buried in the ground. She tried to stop her fall by catching hold of another tombstone, but it crumbled into a pile of red dirt with her weight.

"Oh, no! I am so sorry…whoever you are…were." Harri worked at stacking the fallen stones that remained intact, but some of these crumbled to dust.

Cayce took Harri's pack and dug out the water and snacks. "Let's eat a granola bar and have the rest of our water before we start our search."

"Here. Let's sit right here beneath Jesus and eat."

Cayce took a seat on the wide base of the statue. "We should probably say the blessing." Harri lifted her granola bar up toward Jesus. "Bless this food, Lord, and help us to find our little girl." Both sisters said, "Amen," at the same time.

"Eating in a cemetery reminds me of when Grandpa Zeke used to take a quart jar of sweet iced tea and a pimento cheese sandwich and eat at the cemetery with Granny Lou every Wednesday at lunch when it wasn't raining."

"Yep. Now that was true love." Harri chomped on her granola bar as she talked. "This statue is in remarkable shape. It looks as if it has been cleaned recently. There's hardly any black from aging, and it doesn't have a chip on it. I wonder what its significance is, other than the obvious, of course." Harri shaded her eyes and looked up at the statue standing fifteen or more feet high. "It's really quite beautiful, don't you think?"

"Yes, I do. I bet there is a heck of a story behind it, too. Do you notice anything about the children clinging to His robe?" Cayce stood on the base, where she was eye level with the children. Harri climbed up beside Cayce and stood on her tiptoes to get a good look.

"Oh, my gosh! They're all Asian! Look at their eyes. How sad!" Harri tenderly stroked the face of one little girl as if comforting her. "I'm going to take some pictures of the statue with my camcorder—some still shots, and then I'll zoom around for movie footage. I want it from different angles." Harri moved to several locations and began taking pictures.

"I'll start searching away from you so I won't contaminate any sounds you might pick up. Remember the EVP you caught that time in the old cemetery down in Natchez?"

"How could I forget? It was the scariest thing I've ever recorded. That deep man's voice in my left ear saying 'Go away!' scared the bajiggers, as you say, out of me. I think I had stepped on him and some of his brothers that died in the Civil War." Harri shivered. "I hate you reminded me. That tombstone I just killed will probably have something to say."

Five minutes later, Cayce called, "Over here. I think I found her." Cayce motioned from behind a large tombstone with an angel on top. It, too, sparkled white like the statue of Jesus. As Cayce watched her sister walk toward her, she noticed Harri was not alone. A dark shadow moved right behind her. Then, as if the shadow saw Cayce watching, it faded into the background. Harri was not cognizant of the shadow behind her, and Cayce once again decided not to tell her.

"Oh, my gosh! Just look at that. It even had her picture on it, but it's too faded to tell anything about her now." Harri knelt down to get a closer look at the picture and read the engraving aloud: "Sara Elise Ezell, born August 3, 1918, died September 5, 1925. A beautiful gift too shortly given; Forever, she dances with the angels in heaven."

As soon as she finished reading, a giant shadow fell over the grave like a man with outstretched arms trying to grab her. Harri screamed and fell back on her butt. Cayce laughed. She heard another deeper laugh beside her and turned in that direction but saw nothing.

"You got a problem with the Lord trying to protect you? Look." Cayce pointed to the statue of Jesus. The sun was directly behind it, causing him to cast his shadow over the little girl's grave. The shadow of his left arm seemed to encompass the grave as if comforting Sara.

Harri stood and brushed off the seat of her pants.

"No, I don't. I just wish I had known it was Jesus. Keep it up, Lord. I think we're going to need you in Bar None."

"Well, check this out." Cayce moved to the grave next to Sara's, one with only a small plain headstone, no angel. "Now we know who Sara was. Belle's grave is right next to hers, and look at the name. Isabelle 'Belle' Ezell, born February 12, 1850, died November 3, 1928. But if Belle was seventy-eight when she died, Sara could not have been her daughter. Maybe there's no connection. But the last name Ezell would imply otherwise." Cayce continued to read. "May God have mercy on her soul."

"A fitting cliché, I'd say. I wonder if that is what Belle wanted, or if the women of the church had that put on for the 'floozy.'" Harri looked from Sara's grave to Belle's. "Maybe Sara was a granddaughter. Of course, that would mean Belle had a son, since the last name is the same as Belle's."

"Think about that—about Belle's career choice. If she had a daughter that took after her in career preference, it was likely there was no father's last name." Cayce shaded her eyes and looked directly into the sun. "Look, Harri. The shadow stops at Sara's grave. It's like Jesus doesn't want to touch Belle's grave. So much for mercy." Cayce turned away from Belle's grave. "Let's find the rest of the story, so to speak—Absalom, Yu, and the baby, and maybe Peg."

Cayce and Harri separated, wandering the cemetery and looking at tombstones. A cloud covered the sun for a minute, giving the cemetery an eerie look and feel. No breeze stirred; it was deathly silent.

Cayce broke the silence. "We should look for other little girls buried here. Our little spirit might not be Sara, but it seems logical that only a child connected to Belle would linger in a hotel owned by the madam. Remember, Teesh said she and her sister were not allowed past the porch. I'm sure the other ladies of the town felt the same way as Teesh's mother."

"Wait a minute," Harri yelled from several yards away. "I've already been in that area. Here, let's make a grid and mark each one so we won't overlap." Harri handed the camcorder to Cayce and went to the edge of the woods surrounding the cemetery on three sides. She began dragging in fallen limbs. Cayce realized what Harri was doing and walked over to help with a big log.

"I've got it, Cayce. For some reason, this thing is light even though it isn't rotten."

Cayce stood back and realized why the log seemed so light to her weak city sister. The black mist behind Harri held up the log. Cayce turned the camcorder on record as Harri and her friend moved the log with ease and then walked to the edge of the woods to get another. Cayce stopped recording and went after logs of her own. Soon, the back of the cemetery was cordoned off, with each sister taking a section.

"Here's Absalom!" Cayce called fifteen minutes later.

Harri joined her, and they both leaned down to read the blackened tombstone.

"All I can read is his first name. I can feel the

indentions of the rest of the letters, but can't decipher them." Cayce left Absalom and ran her fingers over the gravestones closest to his. "These are probably Yu's and Tamara's, but I can't read them at all."

"We could visit Teesh. Or we could just Google LDS Genealogy or Archives, or Ancestry.com and look up the information. I'm sure even Bar None had census takers, and the *Bar None Sentry* had to be full of obituaries."

"No cell phones, no Internet, so we can forget Mr. Google," Harri reminded Cayce. "Teesh is a better idea for the obituaries in the newspaper. We need to find Peg's grave, too, but we don't even know her last name. And would she be Annie or Peg? Can you imagine how many Annies are in this cemetery? I've seen several already."

Harri must have sensed the shadow behind her, because she turned and looked behind her.

"What's wrong? Did you see something, Harri?"

"Not so much see as feel. Must be restless spirits, or my very vivid imagination."

Harri and Cayce talked little as they walked down the road from the cemetery. Cayce suspected Harri was thinking about the same thing she was—the little spirit they thought was a seven-year-old girl named Sara. How could they help her?

Harri knew someone or something had watched them the whole time they had wandered through the cemetery. In fact, she felt she and Cayce had been watched ever since they left the mine. She kept turning around, expecting to see a mannish woman with a scarred face and hands and hear a not-too-feminine laugh. She also expected to see tracks right on their heels, tracks consisting of a boot and a wooden peg leg. The tracks were there, and she knew Cayce had seen them. Cayce never missed a trick when they were on the paranormal trail.

I guess my sister thinks I'll freak out too early if I know Peg is with me, but she's wrong, as usual.

Cayce noticed her sister looking back, but chose to ignore it. She also did not tell Harri about the apparition of Peg at the mine and at the cemetery, even if she had only seen it for a split second each time. Peg showed great interest in Harri, but Cayce did not know what the interest was. Her sister and Peg were miles apart in physical and mental characteristics, not to mention they existed in two different worlds.

As they reached the first of the cabins, Harri stopped and stared, first at the piece of railroad track just across the road in front of the cabin. The track ran a little piece up into the valley and stopped at the cabin remains.

"I feel so sad right now, like I could sit on what's left of that porch and cry my eyes out." Harri walked toward the porch.

"Do you think we should maybe try to pick through the rubble?" Cayce caught a glimpse of a shadow just inside the front room, the same shadow traveling wherever Harri went.

"Yes. I think I'm supposed to go into this cabin. I just know it belonged to Peg."

The walls were still standing, but most of the roof was gone. The inside was strewn with broken dishes, pottery, and whiskey bottles and garbage left by curiosity seekers who had no respect for the departed. In one corner of the front wall, someone had built a fire, possibly young people trying to conjure up ghosts on a cold night. Cayce kicked at the piles of garbage carefully, afraid of disrupting the nap of a snake or rat. Harri moved to the second room. A coiled, rusted bedspring was all that was left to signify the room had been used for resting.

"The table with one leg might have been used as a bedside table here rather than in the saloon or hotel. And no, I'm not having visions like you do. It's just a feeling."

"I guess I could try to touch things and see if Peg will appear to me." Cayce scanned around the room, looking for objects she could hold.

"Why? Haven't you seen Peg enough?" Harri smiled, letting Cayce know her sister was not born yesterday, as their dad always said. "Surely, you don't think you are the only one that saw her. I knew she was behind me the whole time, and yes, I saw her tracks in the dust. I just can't figure out why she attached herself to me."

Harri stood in the middle of the back room and spoke without raising her voice. "Peg, now listen carefully. If you need a friend, or even better, a fashion consultant, I'm here for you, but if you have any other notion under that ugly black hat of yours, get it out of your head. I was a happily married woman with a husband I adored. Get it?" Harri walked back into the front room, leaving Cayce stunned.

Beside the fireplace, Cayce saw a stack of boards that looked as if they had fallen from the wall or had been pulled up from the floor. At the same instant, the sun shot a ray of light directly on that section of the room, setting off sparks somewhere deep down in the pile of decaying lumber.

"I think I've found something. Come help me." Cayce began moving the pile, board by board. Harri soon joined in the effort.

"I see something under there, but I'm not reaching my hand in and tickling a rattlesnake's belly." Harri took two steps back as she spoke.

"Come on. Let's move this lumber, and then we can get to the bottom."

Cayce and Harri moved the boards, one piece at a time, until they reached the objects they had seen.

"Oh, my gosh, would you look at this?" Harri picked up what was left of a hairbrush. The handle and frame holding only a few bristles were extremely ornate, and though tarnished, looked like real gold. "This is beautiful! Do you think Peg wants me to take it?" Harri looked from Cayce to the ornate brush in her hand. "I can clean and polish it and then give it to Hank to display in the hotel, or maybe return it to Peg's cabin when it is restored."

"I think Peg meant for you to find it. Besides, if you leave it here, it will end up in the wrong hands, hanging beside rusty hoes or frayed leather horse collars on Lester's wall, or with another antique dealer in the area. This brush is way too personal not to be saved by someone who knows its human value is more important than its monetary value." Cayce reached down and brought up the other item lying face down. "Well, would you look at this?" Cayce wiped the face of the object on her sleeve and handed it to Harri.

"What a beautiful family portrait! Can you believe this glass isn't even cracked? What's up with that?" Harri examined the frame, which was not ornate like the hairbrush, but was also gold. "We know this is not Peg's family. This young woman is beautiful. Her lacy blouse really sets off her pretty face. And those tantalizing dark eyes!" Harri shook her head in awe and held the picture so Cayce could look at it with her.

"Look at the way her long brown curls drape over her shoulder and hang almost to her waist. Her husband is handsome, too, although I'm not a lover of handlebar mustaches."

"And these children look like angels." Cayce took the picture to get a closer look. "The little girl is so pretty and looks so sweet with her hand on her daddy's shoulder. She looks like a little copy of her mom. But this little boy sitting on his daddy's lap is my favorite. I love a blond child, and look at his dimples."

"Usually, everyone is somber in these old family pictures, but this little guy looks like he couldn't be anything but happy. He looks about three years old." Cayce handed the picture to Harri. "Here, I think you need to take this with the hairbrush. I know Peg wants you to have it. She led you here. This man and these beautiful children were important to her, and eventually, she will let you know why."

When Cayce and Harri got back to the hotel, Harri replayed the footage she had taken in the cemetery, and they watched on the camcorder screen. As Harri scanned the cemetery in the first shots, the camcorder caught a very light, wispy shadow at the graves of Absalom's family. She and Cayce knew it had to be Yu pacing, mourning the loss of Tamara. But the best evidence caught was not the video; it was the sound coming from the front of the Jesus monument, the faint sound of a small child humming "Jesus Loves Me."

Cayce laughed with her own recorded laugh when the picture went wild, shooting up into the sky as Harri fell on her butt at Sara's grave. Harri shushed Cayce and told her to listen, and she rewound the footage. This time, two voices could be heard laughing, but it was not just Cayce's voice. It was her laugh plus a deeper sound, the raspy chuckle of Peg.

The best video footage was the one where Cayce recorded Harri dragging the log. A dark, almost transparent figure wearing a black hat and clothes could be seen limping behind Harri, helping her carry the heavy log.

Chapter Twelve

The next day, Harri and Cayce pulled up in front of Teesh's cabin and found her rocking on the front porch with Jezebel in her lap. The cat kept her eyes closed, probably hoping her owner would not leave the rocker.

"Well, hello, sisters. I was in need of company today. If I sit on the porch long enough, somebody passing will stop and visit. It's usually a local stopping at the spring to get water, but I'm glad it's you this time. I like talking 'bout the old days and Bar None." Teesh motioned toward two other rockers. "Pull a chair over and tell me what brings you."

Cayce and Harri pulled the rockers over close. Cayce spoke first.

"We seem to have a little spirit with us in the hotel where we're staying. We feel sure it's a little girl, because she likes playing with Harri's makeup."

"And we heard her giggle," Harri added. "We found a grave in the cemetery, beside Belle's grave, belonging to a seven-year-old girl named Sara. Can you tell us anything about Sara, Teesh? Could she be our little spirit?" Cayce and Harri leaned forward in their chairs, ready to hear Teesh.

"Oh, yes. That would be Sara, Belle's granddaughter. I hoped she would be the first spirit you would encounter. Belle gave birth to Salina, her daughter, at the age of forty, very unusual for those times and for a woman like Belle." Teesh paused as she often did when giving a long narrative.

"Salina hated her mother, and when the girl was only sixteen, she caught a wagon train coming through bound for San Francisco. She ran away but chose the same career path as her mother. Belle was devastated, not wanting her daughter to be a prostitute, and went after her, but Salina refused to return to Bar None. Belle never saw her daughter again until Salina was thirty years old."

"Guess Belle got a taste of her own medicine," Harri remarked. "But it is sad for Salina. Please continue, Teesh."

"Salina came back to Belle unmarried and ready to give birth. Supposedly, she had a fiancé who had promised to marry her when he returned to San Francisco, but of course, he never returned. After Sara was born, Salina ran away again, back to San Francisco."

"What happened to Sara? How did she die?" Harri asked.

Teesh rubbed the cat and got a somber look on her face and stopped rocking.

"Sara was always sickly. We were about the same age. She came to my house a couple of times, but my mother would not let me visit her in Belle's house even though she had living quarters completely separate from the bordello after Sara was born. Sara was my best friend. We played together around town. Belle stopped letting Sara play at my house when she realized my mother would not let me come to her house." Teesh paused, collecting her thoughts for a few seconds, and rubbed Jezebel.

"Sara had bad stomach aches. We'd be playing, usually on the porch of the hotel where Uncle Ab sat watching us, and Sara would double over in pain and start crying. Uncle Ab would pick her up and take her back to Belle's quarters in the hotel."

"What was wrong with Sara?" Cayce asked.

"Belle never found out. She paid doctors from all over to come to Bar None, but the doctors could not figure out what was wrong." Teesh shook her head, remembering her childhood friend.

"I'll never forget the day Sara died. It was the only time my mother let me go to her house, but Mother accompanied me. Belle had begged my mother to let me come because Sara wanted to see me. The poor thing was so weak, she could hardly sit up, but she was still so pleasant. I took my china tea set, and we played as best we could. Before I left, Uncle Ab came in and picked Sara up. My mother went into the hotel parlor and played the piano, a lively tune Sara liked, and Uncle Ab held her tight and danced her around the room." Teesh covered her mouth to hide the quivering in the corners. Her eyes shone transparent with moisture caused by remembering.

"Sara loved to dance and was always twirling when she heard music, especially when we were on the porch with Uncle Ab. He would clap and laugh as Sara danced. Uncle Ab loved Sara, and she loved him. We played like there was no tomorrow. And there weren't many tomorrows."

"That is so sad." Harri wiped a tear from own her eye.

"Sara died in her sleep that night, after Mother took me to visit her," Teesh continued. "Belle never got over losing Sara and went crazy, or I should say crazier. Belle was always a little off-balance, or maybe she was just heartless. She went to the cemetery every day, and you could hear her loud crying all the way into town. Belle shut down the brothel a few months later and sent all her girls off to San Francisco with one-way tickets on the stagecoach and a hundred dollars each. Mother's friends remarked Belle was trying to buy her way into heaven so she could be with Sara."

Harri and Cayce looked at each other. Cayce thought about the shadow of Jesus not reaching Belle's grave and knew Harri was thinking the same thing. She also recalled the words etched on Belle's tombstone.

"When we were at the cemetery, we saw the huge statue of Jesus." Cayce leaned closer, resting her elbows on her crossed leg. "It looked really out of place in the rundown cemetery. Who put that up, and why?"

"Yes, and we noticed it looks brand new. So white and unmarked, it doesn't have a chip on it anywhere," Harri added.

Teesh smiled. "That statue was brought from San Francisco by Belle after Sara got so sick she was bedridden. Sara loved Jesus. Uncle Ab told her Bible stories, something Belle did not do. She was not a churchgoer." Teesh leaned toward her visitors as if about to disclose a secret and spoke even softer.

"This was speculation from the town's women, but they thought Belle bought the monument trying to bribe God into making her granddaughter well, as well as to compensate for her own sins." Teesh stopped rocking for a few seconds and smiled as if thinking of a good memory.

"It's a beautiful statue, isn't it? No telling what

Belle paid for it. Townspeople said it took months to get it over the mountains on a wagon specially made to carry such a huge statue. Everybody turned out the day it was placed in the cemetery. It took a lot of men and horses to set it in place."

"What is the symbolism of the Asian children tugging at Jesus' robe? Cayce and I looked closely at the children's faces and did not see any Anglo children."

"Once again I'll give you town speculation, but Mother said it was true. Mother was not one for gossip. She heard the story from her mother, who had a friend who worked as a cook for the hotel and the brothel," Teesh whispered as if what she told was a secret.

"Supposedly, when the girls, most of whom were Chinese, became pregnant, Belle would make them abort their babies. Mother never talked about how. Women just did not talk about that sort of thing back then. A couple of the girls died after their abortions, or so Mother's source told her. The fetuses were buried in a mass grave at the cemetery, a plot Belle had sectioned off way back when she first opened The Nugget, but there was no monument to mark the mass grave. A lot of shallow grave diggings took place at night. Just another of Belle's cruelties."

Teesh started rocking again and stroked Jezebel, keeping time with her rocking. "Belle had the statue placed in her private plot, but she and Sara were not buried anywhere near it. Very unusual, considering the expense Belle went to in getting the statue." Teesh folded her hands in her lap. "I guess Belle thought the unborn children of her girls were beneath Sara. Not something sweet Sara would have ever thought. Sara loved everyone, and everyone in the town loved little Sara, regardless of her grandmother's career."

"So the statue has been standing more than ninety years, but it looks brand new." Cayce was anxious to hear Teesh's explanation.

"That would be Charlie." Teesh smiled at the mention of his name, and the sisters knew immediately the old woman was very fond of the little Peeping Tom. Cayce and Harri read each other's minds and knew not to say anything negative about him.

"Oh, you'll be seeing Charlie around, mostly after dark. Charlie is fragile mentally, but strong as an ox and fit as a fiddle. He might talk to you, but chances are he won't, at least not at first. He's real shy, but awfully curious when strangers show up. Charlie loves Jesus and thinks the statue is really Him. He keeps it pure white, climbs to the top of it like a monkey to keep it looking ageless. Good thing he's a little feller. He's not any bigger than you, Harri." Teesh chuckled again. "He takes care of Sara's angel tombstone, too. Jesus and the angel—Charlie loves them both."

"We actually did get a glimpse of Charlie last night, but mostly we just saw his hat heading into the woods." Harri was careful not to give away her previous feelings about the peeper.

"So has Charlie always lived on his own like that?" Cayce asked.

"Pretty much. Charlie is forty-three years old. His daddy was a forest ranger in the area and took good care of Charlie—taught him how to be self-sufficient even with his mental limitations. Charlie has some unique talents. He never forgets anything, almost savant-like when it comes to remembering things he's seen or heard. Good thing Charlie was able to learn from his dad, 'cause his dad died when Charlie was just sixteen." Teesh became quiet and began rocking again as if giving herself time to think.

"Surprisingly, Charlie has done okay living on his own. He has a little cabin he and his dad lived in, up the valley, and Charlie has other secret places he goes to, or so he tells me. His daddy left him a trust fund, but he hardly ever uses money. His legal guardian brings money to me to buy things for Charlie, and I keep him in shoes and clothes, but he feeds himself, barters for staples in groceries, and lives off the gold dust and nuggets he gets panning. Charlie is a true mountain man, though 'man' is used loosely."

"You might need to get him some new shoes, Teesh. We saw his tracks, and it looks like one of his boots is worn pretty bad." Cayce was hesitant to disclose this, but felt it was in Charlie's best interest to tell Teesh.

"I appreciate that information. Charlie is due by any day now. I'll make sure I go to the mercantile and get him a pair of summer work boots, although it's hard to get him to wear new boots. His boots have to practically lose the sole before he'll break in a new pair. He needs a new hat, too, but he won't give up that old beaver felt hat. It was his dad's old forest ranger hat.

"I saved Charlie a couple of pieces of Janie's fudge, knowing he'd be by soon. He loves it like I do. Janie brings Charlie a care package by, every so often, and it always has fudge in it."

"Are Lester and Janie related to Charlie?" Cayce asked.

"Lester was related to Charlie's mother, something

Lester won't talk about, and Lester is Charlie's legal guardian, although he never visits Charlie. I don't think he and Charlie like each other much. They avoid contact. I'm the go-between—for Charlie, not Lester. Truth is, Lester and I just tolerate each other."

"How do you contact Charlie when you have something for him?" Cayce asked.

"Oh, that's easy. I just get out my old Studebaker and drive to the cemetery." Teesh pointed to the outbuilding used as a garage, where the rear end of a very old car was barely visible.

"I hang a red bandana around one of the children's necks on the statue, and within a day or two, Charlie shows up at my back door. We've been communicating like that for about thirty years now. I look forward to Charlie's visits. But most times, he just shows up without my signaling him. Charlie just seems to know when I want him to visit me."

Teesh continued to rock, but Jezebel became restless. She stood in her owner's lap, stretched her back, and then leapt down and headed to the side of the porch, where she jumped down to the ground. Cayce watched Jezebel until she disappeared and then saw the tip of a brown hat peeking out from behind the cabin. Teesh glanced around and stopped rocking. A smile came across her face.

"Charlie, come on out. I see you over there. Jezebel gave you away." More of the hat brim appeared, but Charlie did not come around.

"I've got some new friends I want you to meet. They are not strangers. They saw you last night and want to meet you." Teesh motioned with her hand. "Come on, Charlie. Cayce and Harri won't hurt you."

Charlie came around where he could be seen, but stopped at the far end of the porch.

"Hi, Charlie. I like your hat." Cayce spoke softly so she would not scare Charlie. "My name is Cayce, and this is my sister Harri."

"Hi, Charlie. Steve says you are a good fisherman. Maybe I could get you to catch me some trout. I'm a real good cook, and I know how to fry fish really well. You can eat some of it. How about it, Charlie?" Harri smiled.

All three of them looked toward the end of the porch where Charlie still hid in the shadow. Teesh turned back to Cayce and Harri, winked, and motioned for them to turn their attention away from Charlie.

"Yes, Charlie is a great fisherman, Harri. He brings me trout sometimes, and I either fry them or bake them, not that it matters to Charlie. He will eat a few bites just to say "thank you" to me for cooking for him, and then he fills up on biscuits, potatoes, and whatever else I cook. He especially likes vegetables of any sort, so I keep a bunch of bags of frozen ones just to cook for Charlie."

All three of them kept looking away from the side of the cabin. Cayce could see Charlie through her peripheral vision inching his way around.

"Harri makes great desserts, too. I really have a sweet tooth, myself."

"Oh, I do, too, Cayce. That's why I was so pleased you brought me Janie's huckleberry fudge yesterday. I've got a couple of pieces left, you know." As soon as Teesh got these words out of her mouth, Charlie eased around and sat on the front end of the porch as far away from Cayce and Harri as possible. He had his felt hat pulled tight down just above his eyes, making his ears turn down and stick out like bird wings.

"Charlie like Janie fudge real good, Teesh. You save Charlie some?" Charlie spoke softly, looking straight ahead toward the road, and inched down closer to Teesh's rocker.

"Now, you know old Teesh would save Charlie some of Janie's fudge. You want me to go in the cabin and get it for you?"

Charlie shook his head and inched away from the group again. Cayce feared he would run. She noticed Harri watching Charlie closely.

"He means 'no.'" Cayce turned her head slightly as she whispered to Harri, barely moving her lips. "He's afraid of being left alone with strangers."

"Ahhh, gotcha. I'll have to get used to 'Charlie talk.'" Harri mimicked her sister's style of speaking.

"It's okay, Charlie. I'll get it for you in a few minutes. You just sit here with us a little while." Jezebel jumped up on the porch, arched her back, and rubbed it against Charlie's arm.

"Jezebel is wanting a good rubbing from you. She's been missing you."

Charlie reached behind him and took the cat into his lap. He touched the cat gently and rubbed his cheek to her head.

"Charlie found Jezzie as a stray kitten in Bar None and brought her to me. I named the old girl Jezebel, since she's kind of a wayward woman like Belle." Teesh chuckled.

"Charlie miss Jezzie. Jezzie catch a chipmunk today?" Charlie talked baby talk to the cat, but still refused to look at anyone as he spoke barely above a whisper. His voice was unusually deep for such a little man. As if answering for herself, Jezebel reached up and licked Charlie in the face.

"Charlie take bath in creek this morning. Him not need face wash." Charlie gave a heehaw kind of laugh that went on several seconds, and Cayce, Harri, and Teesh all laughed with him. His laugh was infectious. Cayce could tell by her sister's smile that she no longer saw Charlie as a threat. He was an innocent soul with a curious nature, just as Steve and Teesh had suggested. As they all laughed with Charlie, he moved a couple of feet closer but kept his seat on the edge of the porch.

"Charlie like chocolate pie, too. You make chocolate pie, Harri? Charlie like ever'thang chocolate. Teesh read *Charlie Chocolate Factory*. Charlie Chocolate." The little man pointed at himself with his thumb and hit himself in the chest, gave another cheerful guffaw, and puffed his chest out with pride. He glanced under his hat brim at Harri, waiting for her answer.

"Oh, boy, can I make a chocolate pie. You like thick meringue, Charlie, or whipped cream on your chocolate pie?" Harri now directed her attention to Charlie and smiled.

"Charlie like m'rang." He gave Harri a crooked smile, looking up at her in quick glances and then back down toward Jezebel, who had curled up in his lap. "Charlie like chocolate cake, chocolate puddin', chocolate candy, chocolate cookies, hot chocolate, cold chocolate, chocolate, chocolate, chocolate." Charlie guffawed again, keeping his gaze downward.

"I bet I know something chocolate you've never had, and my sister makes the best ever. You eat it with biscuits." Cayce smiled at Charlie, and he gave her a quick glance. His light-colored eyes danced with excitement, and he looked at her again, holding his gaze a little longer this time. Once again, Charlie scooted closer.

"Charlie know ever'thang 'bout chocolate." Charlie bobbed his head up and down as he spoke, fully animated about his favorite topic.

Cayce was reminded of Bubba in the movie *Forest Gump* and his expertise in shrimp. Charlie was the "Bubba" of chocolate.

"How about chocolate gravy?" Harri whispered, leaning toward Charlie. He did not move away. "Have you ever tasted that, Charlie?"

"Chocolate gravy?" Charlie laughed. "Charlie not know chocolate gravy. Teesh know chocolate gravy?" Charlie looked at Teesh and cocked his head.

"Nope. That's a new one on me, too. Maybe Harri will cook us some trout and some biscuits and chocolate gravy sometime." Teesh looked toward Harri.

"Just as soon as Charlie brings me the trout, you will both be invited for dinner."

"Charlie eat on porch with Sara. Charlie not come inside with ghost-es." Charlie vehemently shook his head.

"You know Sara, Charlie?" Cayce asked.

"Charlie know ever'body at Bar None, but him not like black Belle or Peg. Peg scare Charlie. Charlie not like black fog, neither. No, him not." Charlie gave his head an exaggerated shake. His hat was pulled so far down on his ears it never budged.

"Charlie get fudge, Teesh. Him go catch trout. Charlie eat chocolate gravy."

Teesh got up from her rocker and looked toward Charlie to see if he was comfortable with her leaving. Charlie did not move from his spot.

"I'll be right back with your fudge, dear. You visit with Harri and Cayce. They're your new friends now."

Charlie looked a little hesitant, but did not move. He stared toward the road and did not speak.

"Harri and I are so glad to meet you, Charlie. I'm glad you're our new friend."

"Charlie see you in water last night. You like?"

"Yes, we do like it, Charlie. Next time you see us, come in and say hello."

Cayce knew Harri hoped Charlie would not sneak up on them anymore.

"You didn't know who we were, did you?"

Charlie shook his head and continued looking down at Jezebel.

"Steve tell Charlie you good and not peek. Charlie not try scare. Charlie run like wind." Charlie made a fast-moving motion with his hand in the air.

"You are a fast runner, but I won't run after you anymore. You come see us whenever you want." Cayce hesitated for a few seconds before changing the subject. "We saw Jesus today. You take good care of Jesus. I bet Sara likes that." Cayce hoped to get Charlie to talk about the little spirit again.

"Sara sing 'Jesus love me, dis I know.' Sara dance when I give Jesus bath. Charlie like Sara, but Charlie not like black Belle. Not like black fog neither, but him like blue bubbles."

Teesh came out of the cabin with Charlie's fudge wrapped in foil.

"Here are some more plastic bags for you to use for

the trout you're getting for Harri. Clean them good like you do for Teesh, and put 'em in cold water and then in the bag. Zip it tight." Teesh zipped and unzipped a bag to show Charlie.

"Charlie clean good. Charlie not come in. Charlie not like black Belle."

As soon as Charlie got the fudge, he pulled his hat down, even though it appeared impossible to get it any tighter, and put Jezebel on the porch. He gave the cat one quick pat on the head and walked back toward the side of the cabin.

"Come back in a couple of days, Charlie, and I'll have you some new boots."

"Bye, Charlie," Cayce called.

"Come visit us soon," Harri added.

Charlie threw one hand up in a half-wave and disappeared around the corner of the cabin.

Chapter Thirteen

Piper boarded the small plane in Salt Lake City, dreading the window seat she had been assigned. The flight was full to Idaho Falls.

Thank goodness there are only two seats on each side, or I couldn't stand it. I'll die if some big fat man or woman sits beside me and hangs over onto my seat.

Piper knew she would not be a burden to whoever sat beside her, with running three or four miles every day, lifting weights three days a week, and watching what she ate. Piper was physically fit and trim, taller than her mom by two inches or so but with her mom's build otherwise. Dressed for comfort, something very important after hours of flying from France to New York City, she wore her usual faded jeans, a fitted green T-shirt, and hiking boots. Piper was glad for the afternoon flight to Idaho Falls and had slept late that morning, hoping to ward off jet lag before reaching the ghost town where she planned to surprise her mother and aunt.

Piper's long, curly blonde hair was pulled back in a ponytail reaching halfway down her back. She had further contained the thick mass of curls under the bright-yellow fly fishing cap her mom had sent her. "Winston Rods" was written across the cap. Her mom had sent her a five-weight Joan Wulff Winston fly rod for Piper's thirtieth birthday along with the cap, but she had been so busy studying art in Europe and visiting all the great art museums she'd never found the time to use her new rod.

Nine, ten, eleven...thirteen...oh, there's row fourteen.

Piper checked to see where seat D was. A man was putting his pack in the overhead bin with his back to her.

Thank goodness! If that's my seatmate, I'm in luck. He's tall, but trim. No hangovers.

Piper continued to stare, noticing the guy's faded but nicely creased Wranglers, roper boots, and thick, black, slightly wavy hair that hung over his jacket collar in the back. He took off his jacket and stuffed it on top of his pack.

Not bad from the back. Cute butt and awesome physique. If he looks that good from the front, this could be an interesting flight...maybe even too short.

Impressed with the muscles in his upper arms showing from under the short-sleeved tight-fitting gray T-shirt, Piper also noticed a black cowboy hat beside his pack.

He turned and started to sit in the aisle seat when he noticed Piper and did a double-take, teetering on the armrest of his seat. He immediately stood back up in the aisle and faced her.

"You might want to wait a second. That's my seat by the window." Piper smiled at the guy and was further impressed by his extremely handsome face. His hair was parted in the middle and hung over a dark-complexioned face with high cheekbones. He smiled, showing two deep dimples that somehow did not fit the high cheekbones. He moved out of her way in the aisle.

Piper took her pack off her back and reached to place it in the overhead.

"Here, let me help you with that." He took her pack, scooted his down, and placed hers directly over the seats.

"Oh, I'm sorry. I forgot to get something out of my pack," Piper apologized. She had been too intent on staring and had completely forgotten about her sketchpad.

"Not a problem." He handed the pack back to her.

Piper took her sketchpad and pencils out of the pack and handed it back to the young man. "Sorry about that, but I need entertainment. Never can sleep on a plane."

"I know what you mean. I can't either. I've got some work to do myself."

Piper slid into her window seat and placed her sketchpad in the seat pocket in front of her. After putting on her seatbelt, she turned to the young man.

"My name is Piper McCallister." Piper held out her hand to the good-looking stranger.

"I'm Zachary Rockaby." Zachary took Piper's hand, gave it a firm squeeze, and held on to it while staring into her face. Then suddenly, as if he just realized he still held her hand, he dropped it. "Sorry…I uh…"

Piper noticed he was embarrassed and decided to start a conversation. "So you must be a BYU fan." Piper nodded toward Zachary's T-shirt.

Zach looked down at his shirt. "Well, yes, I am." He hesitated before continuing. "But I also work at BYU."

"Oh, really?" Piper replied. "What do you do

there?"

"I teach psychology and history." He paused before continuing, "And yes, I know it's an odd combination, but I have degrees in both. BYU needed a part-time professor in each department, so I lucked up and got the job."

"Pardon me for saying it, but you don't look like any of the professors I had in college." Piper smiled. "So are you *Doctor* Zachary Rockaby?"

"You're not the first person to be surprised by my profession." Zachary smiled in return. "But please call me Zach. That's actually what most of my students call me, and no, I don't have my doctorate yet. I am close, though. ABD, as those with doctorates like to call it."

Noticing the questioning look on Piper's face, he explained the acronym. "All But Dissertation. I'm having a hard time narrowing down my topic." He rubbed a hand through his hair that had fallen across one eye. "So what do you do, Miss McCallister...or is it Mrs. McCallister?" Zach looked at Piper's ring finger and saw a large solitaire diamond on a wide gold band inlaid with crushed turquoise.

"No. I'm not married," Piper answered a little too quickly. Embarrassed, she continued, "This was my mom's wedding ring. She gave it to me when she and Dad divorced." Piper straightened the diamond. "I should probably wear it on my right hand, but it has actually saved me from creeps a few times over the years. Not that you're a creep or anything...far from it." Again, her cheeks heated, and she decided to change the topic. "Actually, I'm just returning from Europe, where I've been studying art. But I'm not famous—at least, not yet. I have a degree in art and probably will teach at some point, but right now, I'm a starving, unemployed artist."

"Well, I'm somewhat unemployed myself. I'm on sabbatical while I finish writing a book. I need to be published in order to make full professor, and I have a publisher lined up already—a university press, so I probably won't make the bestseller list. I just need to finish it." Zach reached for the zip notebook under the seat in front of him. "And this is my entertainment for the trip."

"What's your book about? I'm guessing it's nonfiction, of course." Piper was enjoying the conversation with the handsome professor. She hoped they would talk all the way to Idaho Falls so she could continue to look into those tantalizing dark eyes.

"I'm researching ghost towns of Idaho, and I'm thinking about extending my research to Montana. I know it has nothing to do with what I teach, but I've always been fascinated by them. I'm hoping I can connect my interest to my fields at some point, but right now, I just need to get published."

Zach seemed to also enjoy looking into Piper's eyes, and he smiled considerably, as if the pleasure was all his. "You have the most beautiful green eyes I've ever seen. They're like light-colored emeralds—real ones, not the dark green like the manmade ones." Zach continued staring until her face heated even more with embarrassment. He cleared his throat and looked away for a second, like maybe he realized what he'd done to her, and then turned back. "You ever been to a ghost town?"

Piper could not believe what she was hearing. If she was anyone other than Cayce McCallister's daughter, she might actually believe in coincidences, but her mother had told her many times, "Coincidences and luck do not exist in our family," a philosophy Piper was trying to come to terms with, along with the Gift her mother and aunt had, the one she insisted she did not have. Yet here it was again, one of those nonexistent coincidences happening way too much lately. Piper looked away from Zach to fidget with her sketchbook, not wanting to continue the conversation. Zach, however, would not let her reaction go unnoticed.

"Is something wrong, Piper?" Zach cocked his head, lowered it, and looked up into Piper's face. "I'm sorry if I embarrassed you with the beautiful-eyes remark. I meant it as a compliment, and I swear it isn't a pick-up line."

"Oh, no. I'm not embarrassed." Piper stopped fidgeting, placed the sketchbook in her lap, and crossed her hands on top of it. "I mean, thank you. I did take it as a compliment." She smiled at Zach. "Uh, what was it you asked me?" Piper attempted to give herself time to think, afraid of what was coming next.

"I asked if you had ever been to a ghost town."

"No. But my mother and aunt are staying in one as we speak, and I'm headed to visit them." With reluctance Piper asked the next question. "Where are you headed?" As soon as the words left her mouth, Piper threw up one hand to stop Zach before he could answer. "No, wait! Don't tell me." Piper tore off a corner of an unwanted page in her sketchbook, tore the scratch paper in half, and handed one piece to Zach.

"Okay. This is a little experiment, so bear with me. Don't let me see what you write but write the name of the place where you're going. I'm going to write down

139

the name of the place where I'm going to visit my mother, but I won't let you see it, either." Piper took a pencil from the spirals of her sketchbook while Zach took a pen out of his notebook pocket.

"Okay. I like games." Zach leaned over into the aisle, hiding his paper from Piper. Piper turned her back to the window and did the same. They each folded their papers twice.

"All right. On the count of three, we exchange papers," Piper instructed. "One, two, three." Quickly, the two exchanged scraps, and each unfolded at the same time.

"I cannot believe this! Is this for real?" Zach looked puzzled after reading Piper's scrap of paper.

"I'm afraid so. I had a feeling you were going to Bar None. Coincidences have a way of finding me, and it is becoming a little disconcerting." She wadded the scrap of paper up and put it in the seat pocket.

"ESP? Can you predict the future?" Zach looked serious, but had a little bit of a twinkle in his eye. Piper eyed him suspiciously. "But then, you couldn't have planned this. Hmmm. Very interesting." Zach rubbed his chin and smiled at her. "Care to explain why you turned this into a game?"

"Like I said, it's something that has been happening to me a lot in the past few months, mostly since I've been away from Mom." Piper looked at Zach. "And no, I had no idea we would be heading to the same place. I can't explain the coincidences or the things that have been happening to me, and I can't explain why we just happened to be seated beside each other. I guess we can just call it fate." She shrugged her shoulders and gave a half-hearted smile.

"You know, the word 'fate' can have negative connotation. I just can't seem to feel anything negative about this encounter. Feels pretty darn lucky to me." Zach winked at Piper and gave her hand a squeeze, but then let go of her hand and rested it on his notebook in his lap.

"If you want to talk about these...uh, coincidences...I'm a pretty good listener. Remember, I had a double major in undergrad and grad school, and psychology is a main area of interest. I promise not to psychoanalyze you." Zach crossed his heart. "Promise."

Their conversation was interrupted by, "Please use the card in the seat back pocket and follow along with our safety instructions."

Piper was relieved the flight attendant started the pre-flight instructions. She was not sure she wanted to confide in her new friend about all the experiences and mixed feelings from the past six months in Europe. Part of her wanted to tell someone, and the other part still wanted to pretend it wasn't happening. She was glad for the few minutes to think about it as their plane took off.

While Zach looked at the safety card, Piper flipped through her sketchbook and stopped at a page containing scenes from a frontier town that seemed to be alive and thriving. Buildings covered both sides of the street, with snow-capped mountains forming the perfect backdrop. On one side of the town ran a meandering stream with big boulders beside it, and on the other side was a railroad track, part of which ran right through the middle of town. Piper was so intent on staring at the scene she didn't notice Zach looking over her shoulder.

"I thought you said you've never been to a ghost town."

"I haven't." Piper closed the sketchbook.

"Wait a minute." Zach flipped through his notebook. "Here it is." He pulled the rings open and took a sheet out of his notebook. "Check this out." Zach handed the sheet of paper to Piper and almost butted heads with her as they both looked at the picture. It was almost identical to the sketch Piper had drawn.

"Let me guess. This is Bar None before it died." Piper turned back to her sketch and held the picture beside it. She looked at Zach, disbelieving and more than a little spooked.

"It's Bar None in about 1880," Zach explained. "You're sure you've never seen a picture of the old town before? Maybe your mom sent you a picture and you forgot about it."

Piper was not buying it and shook her head. "Zach, I dreamed it. I woke up at two-thirty a.m. a couple of days ago, like I do almost every night, and the picture appeared in my mind, so vivid I spent the rest of the night sketching it." Piper handed the picture back to Zach and closed her sketchbook. "This just can't be happening to me again." She leaned her head against the window, folded her arms, and closed her eyes with no intention of sleeping.

"This really bothers you, doesn't it?" Zach hesitated, but got no response. "You said, 'again.' Have you had other dreams? Do they all come true?" Zach put the picture back in his notebook and zipped it closed, giving her all his attention.

Piper opened her eyes but looked straight ahead, not knowing whether to continue discussing her fears with this stranger or not. "I just met you, Zach, but for some reason, I don't want to scare you away. But if I tell you everything and you're as smart as I think you are, you'll ask to change your seat." She looked at Zach, who was regarding her with concern.

"I don't scare easily, and to be quite honest, I'm thrilled we are going to the same place. I would like nothing better than to get to know you, Piper McCallister." To Piper's surprise, Zach reached over and put his hand over hers. "Now, tell me as much as you feel comfortable with telling me."

Piper had no idea why she trusted this complete stranger, other than his awesome good looks, but she did feel comfortable with him. Before she knew it, words flowed from her mouth about her family's Gift, that came from her grandfather's side of the family, and how it affected her mother and her aunt Harri. She also told him she did not want to have paranormal powers and had tried not to acknowledge what was happening to her but could not ignore it any longer. Before she knew what was happening, tears puddled in her eyes.

Zach still had her hand covered with his and now locked his fingers through hers. "Piper, I wish I could help you with this. I don't have any kind of powers, so I have no firsthand knowledge of how you feel, but I do have Native American ancestors. They were all spiritualists. My grandfather was Shoshone-Bannock, and though not a shaman himself, he believed in the power of the shaman, and that included the power of dreams. So I'm not foreign to the subject; I just don't have any powers of my own."

"Native American ancestors? Well, that explains your dark hair and eyes and high cheekbones. I'm not sure if it explains the wavy hair and the dimples, though." Piper looked into Zach's face, scrutinizing his features. "And there's something about your eyes that is not quite Native American."

"Yeah, well, I'm kind of a mixture in the bloodline department, but I've been told I look like my grandfather." Zach ran his left hand through his thick hair again.

Piper was feeling power from Zach as he continued to hold her hand, but it was not paranormal. She had not experienced a romantic relationship since she'd been in Europe. She'd had plenty of offers but was just getting over a relationship that had lasted over a year—until she found out Jonathan was leading a double life, as in having a wife in Colorado. She'd been so hurt by his duplicity she'd sworn off men indefinitely. This was another reason she had wanted to study abroad. But here she was feeling something like complete trust, along with another kind of sensation that had nothing to do with trust and everything to do with physical attraction.

As if realizing he was moving way too fast, Zach let go of Piper's hand and pulled his notebook from under the seat again. Piper also, under the same impression, began flipping through her sketchbook. She stopped at an unfinished sketch of two little girls in Victorian dress having a pretend tea party.

"You are very talented, Piper. Even with a pencil drawing, there's so much realism to your work. What do you do with it once you've sketched it?"

Piper could not believe how comfortable she was with Zach watching her sketch. Usually, she put herself in a corner of the room at the back in her art classes, where no one could see her sketching or painting.

"I usually turn the sketches into oil paintings if I have one that particularly strikes my fancy, but my passion is a technique called *plein-air*. I mostly paint with oils, but I've used water colors, as well."

"Oh, you mean you paint outside while looking at what you're painting…like Claude Monet. I'd love to see your sketches. That is, if you don't mind." Zach reached for her sketchbook. "May I?"

Piper, who usually hesitated to share her sketchbook, surprised herself by closing the book and handing it to Zach. "So do you have other old pictures of Bar None?" She reached for Zach's notebook. "May I?" She put emphasis on the word "I."

"I have a few, all in black-and-white, of course. They're old pictures, but I do have a few recent ones, in color, that I got off the Internet." Zach handed his notebook to Piper. "You're welcome to look. Don't mind my scribbled notes."

Piper unzipped the notebook and perused, glad she was a speed reader and could read the notes Zach had scribbled for each picture. They were numbered to correspond with his notes, allowing her to focus on relevant ones. She absorbed the picture of the town Zach had shown her, remembering details from her dream.

The picture came alive on the page as she compared it to her dream. She could see the people dressed in period clothing bustling in and out of the buildings. Her focus centered on The Nugget, and in her mind, she saw the two young lavishly dressed Oriental ladies standing on the porch. Piper leaned toward Zach, who was totally engaged in her sketchbook, and held the picture in front of him.

"Zach, what is The Nugget? Is it what I think it is?"

Zach took on a serious look. "If you think it's a brothel, or a bordello, you would be correct. It was also the local saloon—saloon downstairs, bordello upstairs and in the back. Aren't those young Chinese ladies beautiful? They look like China dolls. And I bet they are as fragile as they look. What a shame."

"But why Chinese girls? They can't be more than teenagers...or in their early twenties, maybe. And their dress is so wrong. They should be covered in beautiful Asian prints, like petite China dolls, and not be forced to look like...like what they obviously are. Even geishas, who I know were Japanese and not Chinese, exhibited beauty and an almost purity, and never gaudiness."

"That was the point. The madam, Isabelle Ezell, supposedly bought the girls from a dealer, or I should say a kidnapper, from San Francisco. The young girls were stolen from their homes in China, or possibly bought outright from their parents, who obviously did not love their daughters. The girls did not speak English and had no family or friends to save them. They were at the mercy of the madam."

"That is so awful, so painfully sad!"

Piper put the picture back in her lap. Her thoughts returned to her dream. She remembered the emptiness in the young girls' eyes. As if they were robots, going about their work without feeling or emotion, forcing smiles as men approached the porch where they stood poised. One of the girls, in particular, had caught

Piper's eye in another recurring dream, and she had meant to sketch the girl by herself but had not.

Once she had completed her sketch of the town scene, the dreams stopped. Wanting the dreams to stop, Piper usually sketched the scenes lingering in her subconscious as soon as possible. But this tiny beautiful China doll still invaded her dreams, even in Salt Lake City the night before, and Piper knew she would sketch her as soon as she got to Bar None and could talk to her mother. For some reason, she did not want the dream to stop. She needed to see and know more about the girl. Her haunting eyes came to mind again as Piper shut the notebook and closed her eyes, leaning her head against the window.

Mom will understand. She'll help me deal with this.

Zach continued looking through the sketchbook, marveling at the talent of his newfound friend, wondering whether it truly was fate he and Piper shared side-by-side seats and headed to the same exact location in this small plane. He couldn't understand the strong feelings he had for Piper but found them comforting, as if he had found the soulmate he had been searching for the last few years. He thought he had found such a person not long ago, but it was a false illusion, one with dire consequences that still haunted him.

Zach shook himself out of his thoughts and glanced over at Piper, whose eyes were closed. He took advantage of the situation to stare at her. He wanted to pull her to him and rest her head on his shoulder, all the time kissing the eyelids covering those tantalizing emerald eyes. But he knew his wishes were premature, and the timing was not the best. But then, timing was not something that could be planned.

Piper opened her eyes and smiled. "I'm not asleep. Just thinking about those poor girls and about my dreams."

"Dreams? You've had more than one dream about Bar None?" Zach closed Piper's sketchbook.

"Yes." Piper hesitated, afraid disclosing her dream would sound like a fairy tale—a fairy tale that might have Zach running away from her. "I know this will sound preposterous, Zach, but I've seen that tiny girl in more than one dream. I need to talk to Mom. She'll help me come to grips with all of this. She knows how I've fought any possibility of having the Gift she and my aunt have."

"Do you plan to sketch the girl?"

"No. If I sketch her, she won't visit me in my dreams anymore." Piper looked at Zach, wondering if he thought she was crazy. "But I do plan to paint her. This will be like *plein-air* with my eyes closed." Piper gave a little laugh. "I may be inventing a new technique—painting from a recurring memory. But we have to get to Bar None first." Piper smiled with the knowledge they were going to the same place.

"Speaking of which…I'm renting a Jeep for the trip. The roads are pretty rough going in. Why don't you ride with me?" Zach paused. "That is, if no one else is picking you up at the airport."

Piper smiled. "That is very kind of you to offer, but I, too, have a Jeep reserved." Piper looked away a second before returning her gaze to Zach. "Besides, how do I know you're not some hardened criminal? You know, Ted Bundy was a fine-looking specimen of a man, too."

"Thank you…I think." Zach frowned at Piper,

reached into his back pocket for his wallet, and took out two pieces of identification. "Here." He handed his driver's license to her. "Do you see I am who I say I am?" He pointed to the other ID. "And here's my BYU faculty ID, as well."

Piper looked at the picture ID and back at Zach as if doing a mental comparison.

"Well, I guess it will be okay." She smiled. "I plan to call Harri, my aunt, when I get to Idaho Falls, and let her in on my surprise visit. I just hope she answers the satellite phone they're using, and not Mom. Cell phones don't work there. Harri usually answers since she talks to her staff often in her business back in Tennessee. I'll make sure to tell her I'm riding with you...just as a precaution." Piper grinned and handed the two ID cards back to Zach. "We can make it to Bar None tonight, but it will be late."

Chapter Fourteen

Harri could not contain herself after talking to her niece. This would be a difficult secret to keep from her sister, but she could not wait to see the look of surprise when Piper showed up at the front door of Cole Springs Hotel later that night. She began scheming ways to keep Cayce up late.

Cayce had just started watching the rest of the footage from Harri's videoing at the cemetery when there was a knock at the back door. She opened it to discover Charlie holding two Ziploc bags bulging with fresh, cleaned trout.

"Woo, Charlie! Those are some beautiful trout…just right for pan-frying." Cayce backed up for Charlie to come in, but he didn't move.

"Cayce give to Harri. Tell her Charlie Chocolate catch." Charlie held the bag out to Cayce, but made no move to come inside.

"You can give them to her yourself, Charlie. She's in the kitchen, and from the smells coming from there, you came at just the right time." Cayce stood to the side, but Charlie still did not step forward. He peeked around the doorframe and looked inside the hotel.

"Charlie not like black Belle. Charlie not like black fog neither."

"The room is clear, Charlie. We haven't seen Belle or the fog, and we've been here a couple of days."

Cayce motioned for Charlie to come in. "Don't be scared. You'll be safe here with Harri and me."

Reluctantly, Charlie stepped across the threshold, holding tight to the bags. He glanced around before taking another step and repeated this maneuver as he inched his way toward the kitchen. Taking one last look behind him, he raced ahead, high-stepping all the way to the kitchen. Harri was bent over, taking something from the huge oven.

"Charlie catch trout. Harri make chocolate gravy?" Charlie held out the bags to the still-bent-over Harri. She stood up and turned around in full smile.

"Oh, my!" Harri took the bags of clean trout. "These are wonderful! There are enough trout here for a crowd of people." She put the bags in the refrigerator. "You bet, we're gonna have chocolate gravy, and fried trout, and Nanny's French fries, and big, fluffy biscuits. How does that sound?"

"Charlie like ever'thang chocolate. Charlie like biscuits and fry taters." Charlie lifted his head and sniffed. "Charlie smell chocolate?"

Harri got her cooking mitts on and turned back to the oven, taking a pan out. "Granny Lou's brownies!" she announced as she turned around.

Charlie clapped and gave his wonderfully goofy laugh. Harri and Cayce laughed with him, with Harri giving one of her wholehearted snorts like she did when she was really tickled.

"Charlie like brownies, Harri." Charlie circled the counter and put his nose close to the pan of brownies and gave a big sniff. "Charlie eat now?"

"We need to let them set for just a few minutes, and then we'll have some sweet tea and a brownie."

Harri motioned toward Charlie's head. "You want to take your hat off? It will be a few minutes before we can eat brownies." Harri held out her hand for Charlie's hat.

Charlie cut his focus up at the hat's brim, looking cross-eyed. He held his gaze on the brim for a few seconds and looked back at Harri. Then he repeated the look before reaching up and prying the hat off his head using two hands.

"Charlie hold hat." Charlie held it to his chest like a golden treasure.

Cayce was surprised at how thick Charlie's hair was. She'd figured it would be thin because he always wore the old felt hat, especially the way he kept it tight on his head. His hair was brown with hints of gray and was cut short over his ears.

"Who cuts your hair, Charlie?" Cayce asked, figuring Charlie would say Teesh.

"Secret." Charlie whispered the word and put his finger to his lips. "Charlie eat brownie now, Harri? Him got good blower." Charlie made blowing sounds with his lips, making Cayce laugh and Harri snort.

"Okay, Charlie. Let me get the iced tea ready. You can go in the bathroom and wash your hands. Do you know where it is?" Harri pointed back through the parlor.

Charlie acted nervous, and Harri knew Charlie was scared to leave the kitchen.

"I tell you what." Harri turned the faucet on in the sink. "You can wash your hands in the kitchen sink."

Charlie rushed to the sink as if afraid Harri would change her mind. He stuck his hat under his arm and clasped it tight against his body before he held his hands under the spigot, rubbing them together and even cleaning under his nails, which were already clean. Harri got a towel out of the drawer and placed it beside the sink, while Cayce took out three glasses and filled them with ice.

"Let's sit here at the bar and eat our brownies." Harri put a brownie on each of three dessert plates and set them on the bar. Charlie climbed onto the stool in the middle. His short legs dangled under the bar, and he swung them as he stared big-eyed at the brownie.

Cayce picked up her brownie and started to take a bite, but Charlie stopped her by folding his hands under his chin, ready to say a prayer. Cayce and Harri bowed their heads and closed their eyes like their guest.

"Charlie thank Jesus for brownies. Charlie like chocolate. Amen."

Cayce and Harri repeated "Amen" through their smiles.

Before any of the three could take a bite, they heard the front door slam and footsteps coming toward the kitchen. Charlie became nervous, stuffed the whole brownie in his mouth, and headed for the back of the kitchen, pulling his hat tight over his ears again.

"Wait, Charlie!" Cayce headed to the back corner to stand by Charlie. "It's probably someone we know."

"Anybody home?" Hank yelled before entering the kitchen. "Something smells good."

"Come on in, Hank. We're having brownies and sweet tea with Charlie," Harri called. She motioned for Charlie to come back to the bar, but he wouldn't budge.

"Hank, have you met Charlie?" Cayce had Charlie's arm and led him back toward his stool.

"No, I haven't officially met Charlie, but I think

I've seen him at the edge of the woods. I'm Hank. Pleased to meet you, Charlie." Hank held out his hand to Charlie, who ran past him to the counter and gulped iced tea while fanning his mouth. He wiped his tearing eyes on his shirtsleeve and then backed up next to Harri.

Harri took Charlie by the arm and redirected him to stand in front of Hank.

"Shake hands with Hank, Charlie, like the man you were taught to be."

Reluctantly, Charlie shook hands with Hank, pulling his hand back after one quick, firm shake.

"It's okay, Charlie. I'm a friend." Hank tried to put Charlie at ease. "You were watching the day my worker fell off the roof, weren't you?"

Charlie stood by his stool and reached for the second brownie Harri had just put on his plate. He took a small bite this time, but he chewed fast when he discovered it was only slightly warm. Before he finished, he spoke through a mouthful. "Charlie see black fog on roof. Charlie not like black fog. Charlie not like black Belle, neither. Black fog make man fall." Charlie covered his eyes with his hands. "Charlie cover eyes so black fog not see him."

"You saw the black fog make my worker fall?"

"Charlie see." Charlie cocked his head and looked from under his hat brim at Hank. "Man die?"

"No, he will be fine, but it gave him and me a good scare." Hank looked at Cayce and Harri. "What did the fog look like, Charlie?"

"Charlie not look. Charlie not like black fog. Charlie not like black Belle, neither. Fog go round and round man like this." Charlie stood and twirled around with his arms out. "Charlie cover eyes so black fog not see." Charlie pointed to the other brownies on the plate. "Charlie take brownie to Teesh now?"

"Of course you can. I'll wrap up enough for you and Teesh." Harri took the brownies from the bar and placed them on the counter.

"Whoa! Aren't you forgetting someone, Harri?" Hank reached for the biggest brownie on the plate. "Now you can wrap them up." Hank ate the brownie in two bites.

"Charlie, I'm going to send a letter to Teesh. I'll cook the trout tonight, and I want Teesh to come. Will you take the letter to her?" Harri reached into the drawer and pulled out a writing pad and began writing.

"Charlie take letter. Charlie and Teesh eat chocolate gravy and biscuits." Charlie nodded his head. "Charlie like chocolate. Charlie Chocolate." Charlie pointed to himself and began laughing, and the others followed his lead.

Harri put the letter in an envelope and handed it with the baggie of brownies to Charlie, who moved gingerly toward the door. He stopped, peeked around the door facing, and made a fast dart to the back door. He was outside before anyone could say goodbye.

"Fascinating little dude, and likeable. He'd watch us for hours, but wouldn't come near the work site. I'm glad I finally got close enough to introduce myself."

"And now you know what your worker saw just before he fell," Cayce added.

"Yes, and that's a good thing." Hank looked toward Harri and smiled. "Did I hear something about trout and, if I heard right, chocolate gravy, whatever that is?" Hank smiled even bigger, hoping for an invitation.

"Are you staying tonight, Hank?" Cayce asked before Harri could answer Hank, and then wished she could take back the question when she saw Harri's mischievous grin.

"Yes. I'll be here for a while. My crew is coming off the trail tonight and will start back to finishing up The Nugget tomorrow. Should stir up some activity for you, but I hope nobody gets hurt this time." Hank left the stool and fixed himself a glass of tea.

"Where will they stay?" Harri asked the question Cayce wanted answered. Neither of the sisters wanted to share the communal bathroom with strangers—especially men.

"Don't worry, Harri. They're setting up camp in the valley, between town and the cemetery." Hank took a big gulp of tea. "That is, if Peg will let them. It's pretty near her old cabin." Hank looked at the sisters as if gauging their reaction. "They're okay with the saloon music that sometimes echoes through the canyon, but they're just a little afraid of Peg."

"Well, you're welcome to eat with us, Hank. There just won't be enough for the whole crew."

"Thanks, Harri. I look forward to it. The crew fends for themselves anyway. The only one not camping is Bill. He has a place somewhere close enough to come and go. You'll meet him tomorrow." Hank headed for the door. "And don't you two worry about having to share the showers with me. There's a finished bathroom in Belle's living quarters. I'll use it. I would stay there, but the bedroom isn't furnished yet. I think Joshua wants you ladies to help with the finishing touches of that, including choosing the wallpaper."

"We don't mind sharing the bathroom with you, as long as you knock before entering," Cayce said. "But suit yourself."

Later that afternoon, after being run out of the kitchen by Harri, Cayce and Hank sat on the front porch of the hotel drinking iced tea when Teesh drove up in her 1966 Studebaker. It was olive green and looked as new as the day she had bought it in 1966, the chrome shining as if it had just been polished. Hank stood up, planning to help Teesh out of the car, but Charlie, who rode shotgun with Teesh, jumped out and ran around the front of the car to open Teesh's door. Charlie gave Teesh his hand just like the gentleman he had been taught to be.

"Thank you, Charlie," Teesh said. Carrying her big black purse, Teesh walked briskly up the path to the hotel. Hank remained standing, prepared to help Teesh up the steps, but she climbed the steps as fast as Charlie, and without assistance. Cayce watched in amazement and just hoped she could be that agile at ninety-two years of age.

"That is a beautiful Studebaker, Teesh," Cayce commented. "What model is it?"

"It's a nineteen sixty-six. I bought it brand new and have never had a minute's trouble with it. It's just like the one Aunt Bea had, in real life. You know…from the *Andy Griffith Show*. I saw it on TV, and I had to have one the same olive-green color, just like Bea's. Charlie loves my old car. He keeps it polished for me."

"Good work, Charlie." Hank gave the little man a thumbs-up.

"Charlie has done nothing but talk about chocolate gravy all afternoon. Thank goodness it's almost time to taste it. I imagine I'll be getting Harri's recipe," Teesh remarked as she sat in the rocker Hank had pulled closer for her.

"Charlie Chocolate gravy." Charlie laughed, nodding to indicate he was ready for dessert, and as always, everyone caught the laughing bug.

Harri's trout tasted delicious, and she had to explain in detail to Teesh and Hank just how she had cooked it. But the real hit was buttered biscuits dabbed in chocolate gravy. Charlie only ate one big bite of fish, just to be polite, and a pile of Granny Lou's French fries, as Harri called them. Charlie said he was saving room for chocolate gravy. Charlie's mouth was covered with chocolate when he finally pushed back from the table. Teesh wet her napkin and offered it to Charlie, pointing out spots he needed to wash. Charlie had been so excited about the gravy he'd completely forgotten about being afraid to come into the hotel, at least until the meal was over and everyone moved into the parlor.

Charlie sat as close to Teesh as he could get without sitting in her lap. He held his hat close and sat up on the edge of the antique velvet sofa as if ready to bolt at a moment's notice.

"How about some music?" Hank asked, and to everyone's surprise, the big cowboy left his chair and headed for the piano. He scooted the bench back to give his long legs plenty of room to reach the piano pedals and played "Claire De Lune" by Debussy. He sounded and looked like an accomplished classical pianist, complete with hand and body movements. At one point, he even closed his eyes, moving his head, clearly feeling the music as he played. When he finished, he held his hands up, allowing the last notes to linger.

Everyone clapped.

"That was a real treat, not to mention a surprise," Cayce remarked, still clapping. "How in the world did you learn to play like that, Hank?"

Hank turned on the piano bench and faced his audience.

"My mother, in addition to being my father's partner in the hard labor it takes to run a ranch, was a classical pianist, born and raised in New York City. She insisted my brother and I be allowed to learn to play. My dad was always afraid his delicate little wife would tire of the ranch life and was so pleased she loved it he never fought her on the piano issue. My brother didn't take to the piano like I did, but I loved it and still do, especially classical music. But it's not all I can play."

Hank swung his legs back around and pounded on the piano keys, playing music befitting a western frontier saloon. It was the saloon rendition of "The Old Mill Stream" with a faster beat. Harri sang along with Hank's music, and soon Teesh stood and had Charlie by the hand. The two danced around the floor, with Charlie laughing at the top of his lungs. Cayce and Harri clapped as they danced. When Hank stopped, Teesh practically fell onto the sofa but was not nearly as winded as a woman her age should have been.

"Charlie like dance. Charlie dance with Sara and blue bubbles for Jesus."

Cayce and Harri looked at each other.

"You dance with Sara, Charlie?" Harri asked. "In the cemetery?"

"Sara like dance. Right, Teesh?"

"Who is Sara?" Hank asked as he turned to face the group.

Cayce and Harri filled Hank in on their experience with the little girl ghost, Sara, and Teesh told him how she and Sara had been friends in life. Hank gave them his undivided attention, sitting on the edge of the bench so he could hear the soft-spoken Teesh give her account of Sara as she knew her.

"So Sara loved to dance? Well, that explains it." Hank paused and rubbed his chin. "Remember how I told you I had an experience here in the hotel that would shock you?" Hank directed his question to Cayce and Harri, both of whom nodded.

"Well, I couldn't sleep one night, and I decided to come down and play the piano." Hank looked at Cayce. "I believe you refer to it as the witching hour, two-thirty to three-thirty a.m. Anyway, I played this piece by Bach, 'Minuet in G,' and things started happening. Blue circles—orbs, I believed they're called—encircled me, but kept a distance of about five or six feet from me, and they were pulsating, keeping time to the music. It scared me to death, so I stopped playing, ready to bolt out of the room. But when I stopped, they circled closer to me. I thought I was being attacked, so I closed my eyes and played again. They moved away from me, but again danced to the music. I played until my fingers were getting numb, and then I heard it."

Hank had everyone's attention, even Charlie's. Cayce and Harri both leaned forward in their chairs.

"I heard a child giggling, sounded like a little girl, and it was like she sat beside me on the piano bench. The next thing I knew, two keys started playing on the end of the piano where the giggle was coming from. She didn't bang on the piano, but played two notes complementary to the chords and notes I was playing. It was like she wanted to play a duet with me."

"Did you stop playing?" Harri asked.

"No. I got over my fear because the little girl sounded so happy. I caught myself just smiling away at the empty spot beside me—the spot I knew was not really empty. The next thing I knew, the blue orbs had left me, but were swirling around the room nearby like a blue dust devil. I thought I could see eyes in the middle of the circles, but I didn't want to look too close for fear they would get in attack mode again. I continued to play and finally got up the nerve to look in the direction of the blue swirl, and there she was…"

"Sara," Teesh answered for Hank and smiled into her fingertips, remembering her little friend.

"I assume so, after hearing your stories about her. She was dressed in a white lace dress and had a wide blue ribbon around her waist, tied in a big bow in the back, and the same kind of blue ribbon was in her hair. She danced in white, shiny, lace-up shoes and had on white stockings and those long white ruffly things under her dress. Her whole attire was from the early nineteen hundreds."

"That would be pantaloons," Teesh added. "We all wore those in the old days, but Sara's always had rows and rows of ruffles on the bottom, and her dresses always had lace and ribbons. Her favorite color was blue—especially aqua blue like the ocean."

"I couldn't see her facial features, but she had the most beautiful dark curls that hung almost to her waist. She twirled inside the blue swirl, keeping perfect time to my music. She tried dancing on her tiptoes like a ballerina, giggling all around the room. The blue orbs stayed the same exact distance away from her, completely encircling like they were protecting her, except for when she stretched her arms out toward me. I think she was telling the blue circles she wanted me to see her dance, and they spread out so I could watch. The more she danced, the more I smiled, and the happier I played. The keys literally danced under my fingers. I honestly think the piano would have played by itself if I had let it."

"Keep playing, Hank. Maybe Sara and the blue orbs, or bubbles as Charlie calls them, will come out and dance." Cayce looked toward Charlie to make sure he wasn't afraid, and he was smiling. She looked back at Hank and nodded in the direction Charlie was staring. Hank grinned and turned back facing the piano keys.

Chapter Fifteen

Zach took Piper's bags from her and put them in the back seat of the Jeep while Piper placed her art bag behind her seat. The Jeep was a Wrangler, complete with ragtop. Before leaving the airport, they removed the doors to get the full effect of the fresh mountain air. The small back seat bulged after propping the doors behind the seats, but Piper was comfortable, especially with her newfound friendship, and Zach seemed the same. Piper and Zach talked the whole way, and when they weren't talking, they were casting glances at each other, each glance followed by a big smile.

Soon after they started their trip toward Bar None, Zach reached for Piper's hand and entwined his fingers in hers. She did not object and reveled in the vibes. Even after they had been traveling several hours, Zach held Piper's hand, with the exception of a couple of short moments. She wondered if those times were to give her a little reprieve she did not require.

"Oh, look, Zach!" Piper yelled so loud Zach jumped. She pointed to a small sign on the side of the road. "There's an antique shop ahead."

"You're into antiques, huh?" Zach smiled as if he approved. "Being a history buff, I cannot object. It's not far ahead. I think if I push this Jeep a little, we can make it before they close. I bet they stay open late. Tourist season, you know." With this, Zach sped up, glancing in his rearview mirror for any state troopers. "Are you looking for anything in particular?"

"My mother loves primitive antiques. I want to take her something. I left France in such a hurry I didn't have time to shop." Piper looked at her watch. "It will be close to six o'clock when we get there. I hope you're right about tourist season."

An hour later, they pulled the Jeep in by the same hitching post where Cayce had parked Hawk just a few days before. An elderly cowboy sat in a straight chair, tilted back, balancing on the chair's two back legs worn to a slant from many years of leaning. When he saw the couple get out of the Jeep, he set the chair down and rose to greet them.

"Howdy! You're just in time. Another ten minutes, and I would be closing. Anything in particular you're looking for?"

"Oh, I don't mean to hold you. I'm looking for a gift for my mom. She loves primitives. Do you have any?"

The man held the door open, and Piper went through, followed by Zach.

"I got all kinds of primitive tools and such, but if you're looking for real good primitives, you need to head on to the back section. My granddaughter Janie has a right smart selection of stuff back there I think you'll like." He showed them to the back but did not go into the huge back room. "I'll let you look for yourself. And don't be in no hurry. I got nothin' pulling me home."

"Thank you. I'll look as quickly as I can." Piper set out in a hurry, wanting to make sure she got a quick look at everything. She stopped at the same blue, buttermilk-base-painted, step-back cupboard her mom had spotted and ran her hand over it.

"Uh, Piper, that's a beautiful cupboard, but I don't think it'll fit in the Jeep."

Piper smiled at Zach. "I know. Just couldn't pass this beauty up without a little love-stroking." Piper headed off again. "I'm looking for something a lot smaller." Piper showed Zach a size with her hands. "Maybe a small crock or something."

"Oh, my! Look at this section, Zach!" Piper stood in the kitchen section where Harri had consumed a great deal of time looking at cookbooks. "Not only can I look for a crock for Mom here, but I can pick up a cookbook for Harri. My aunt has a teashop in Tennessee, and is quite the cook and the collector of cookbooks."

"I think I'll wander over to that fly fishing section on the other side while you browse. Do you mind?"

"Fly fishing section?" Piper looked past Zach with excitement. "Do you fly fish?"

"Well, yes, I do, as a matter of fact, but I forgot my fly fishing gear. Left it sitting by the front door. I've been wanting some vintage equipment for a while, and there's a ton of it in that section over there." Zach pointed. "And yes, I noticed your Winston cap, so I know you must be a diehard fly fisher yourself. Winston rods don't come cheap."

"I'll just be here a second, and then I'll be over there. Actually, I think I'll look there for something for Mom. She collects antique creels and would like that much better than a crock. I'll just grab a cookbook for Harri." Piper began scanning the cookbooks, anxious to get to the fly fishing section. She saw just what she was looking for up on the top shelf, *Mormon Pioneer Cooking*, and it was written by an Idaho pioneer woman. "Yep, this will be perfect."

When Piper got to Zach, he had already found a treasure.

"Check this out, Piper. It's a Hardy bamboo rod in perfect condition, and it has a Hardy reel with it." Zach had it out of its canvas cloth sleeve and was putting the three-piece rod together. He moved to the aisle, where he would have more room, and whipped it gently. "This sucker is beautiful but heavy. The flex is something I would have to get used to, but I'm buying it." He took the rod apart and placed each section carefully back in the old faded sleeve. "And look at this reel, Piper. What a gem!"

"It's a beauty, all right. My mom will want to try that out, I'm sure. I bet there are some high mountain lakes around Bar None, not to mention streams, and they would have to be full of rainbows and cutthroats. She has to take a break from ghost hunting at some point." Piper walked through the section and spotted two vintage creels hanging on a wall.

"There! I want that creel, Zach, the one with the dark leather trim on the front. Can you get it down for me?"

Zach only had to reach a little to get the creels down. "Now you can look at both of them and see which one you want." He handed her the one she'd asked for and inspected the other one. "And I'll warn you—I'm getting whichever one you don't want. Gotta have a place to put the trout we'll catch, just in case we decide not to be catch-and-release anglers." Zach put his finger to his lips and whispered. "Shhh! Don't tell anyone I said that."

Zach and Piper headed back to the front with their treasures. Just as they got to the cash register, the front door opened.

"Hi, Janie. You're just in time. You got some new customers here, and it looks like they're fishermen... er, fisherman and fisherwoman."

Piper turned around, ready to introduce herself. The woman smiled, but her smile faded quickly as she got a good look at Piper. Then she began backing toward the door.

"No!" Janie continued to back up, dropped her purse, and held her hands up.

"Janie, you done gone crazy? What's the matter with you, girl? You act like you seen a ghost." The man moved from behind the counter and walked toward his granddaughter.

Janie, realizing her behavior was too strange, shook herself out of whatever trance she was in. Piper moved toward her and stuck her hand out.

"I'm Piper McCallister, and this is Zach Rockaby. We love your shop, and we found some great buys."

Janie smiled, but still seemed reluctant to take Piper's hand, giving it a wimpy shake after forcing herself to move closer.

"I am so sorry. You look so much like someone I know it startled me." Janie still acted nervous but moved behind the counter to finish the transaction. She had on sunglasses and did not take them off, something Piper thought unusual.

"You're not from around here, are you?" Janie asked while wrapping the creels.

"No, I'm from Montana, and Zach is from Utah."

"Are you planning to fly fish while you're in Idaho?" Janie did not look up as she continued to wrap and tape the items.

"Probably. If we can find some good streams or lakes, that is. Do you fly fish?"

"No. I'm too uncoordinated for it. Besides, my eyes are very sensitive to the light, and so is my skin. I stay out of the sunshine as much as possible. I don't need any more freckles."

"Truth is my granddaughter is not much of an outdoors girl." Her grandfather wrapped the cookbook. "I like to fish, though, but I'm more the worms-in-a-can, spinning-rod kind of fisherman. But I like to watch fly fishermen—and fisherwomen—cast a fly rod. Kind of an art to it, ain't it? Or at least that's what they say on television."

"Where are you two headed? I know just about every stream around has trout." Janie finally looked up and made eye contact with Piper through transition lenses that were beginning to lighten up.

"My mom and aunt are at Bar None. A friend of theirs is restoring the old ghost town."

"Wait a minute. Is your mom's name Kati? No, that's not it." The man scratched his chin to help him remember. "Cayce! That's it. Unusual spelling. I remember from her check. She stopped by with her sister a few days ago. Nice ladies. Bought some good stuff."

"That's my mom, and her sister is Harri. I should've known they couldn't pass up an antique shop."

"Cayce and her sister bought your old biscuit maker, Janie. I told you about that."

"Yes, I remember, Papa." Janie handed Piper and Zach the creels and the reel. "Do you want the rod wrapped?"

Janie finally seemed at ease. Piper noticed how pretty she was, with medium-length dark-brown hair, a beautiful complexion with a few freckles across her nose, and she was about Harri's size, very petite. But it wasn't her hair or freckles that caused Piper to study Janie closer. It was her eyes. Through the slow-changing lenses of her glasses, Piper saw they were light in color, like her own, but blue instead of green. When Janie wasn't nervous, she was pleasant-looking.

Something about her is familiar to me, but there's no way I've ever met her. This is my first time in this area.

Piper quickly looked away so Janie wouldn't notice her stares and moved her attention back to Zach and the transactions going on.

"Nope. It'll be fine just like this." Zach picked up the rod and the wrapped reel. "I'm glad you made me stop, Piper. I've been wanting a Hardy rod for years."

Janie followed them out to the porch.

"Thank you for your purchases, and tell your mom, or your aunt, I hope she enjoys the dough bowl." Janie hesitated. "And I'm really sorry for the way I acted. I hope you'll come back."

"I'm sure we will. Thank you, Janie." Piper gave a quick wave to Janie from the Jeep as they drove away.

"Very odd. I wonder who she thought I was. And I know I've never met her, but she did look familiar."

"Yep. She was a little strange. Didn't seem like she ever was totally comfortable." Zach turned his attention back to Piper. "Okay. Get your GPS on your phone while we've still got a signal, and get us some directions to Bar None."

Chapter Sixteen

In the far corner of the room, bubbles swirled in a thin blue mist as if they were trying to move undetected. Inside the mass of blue, a smaller white circle of motion spun faster than the blue bubbles. Cayce looked at Harri and pointed. Then she moved to the piano bench and sat beside Hank.

"I think Bach's 'Minuet in G' is working, Hank," she whispered, tipping her head toward the corner. Hank took a quick glance and continued playing with his right hand. With the other, he patted the left side of the bench, reminding Cayce she was sitting in Sara's spot.

Harri picked up her camcorder, aimed it at the blue swirl, and pressed record. The blue bubbles became more visible, moving toward the piano. As Hank played with light, playful strokes, the mist moved closer until only a foot or two away from the piano.

Cayce could do nothing but stare in amazement as the blue engulfed her and Hank. She hoped Harri was capturing this fantasy. If so, it would be the most dazzling piece of paranormal footage she and her sister had ever recorded. Without thinking, she put her arm through Hank's left arm. He tightened on her arm to signal he was there for her. Turning her head in every direction, she could not help but smile. In the midst of a swirling sea of aqua, they were surrounded by what seemed like hundreds of spherical fish with slanted eyes and tiny mouths, each bubble fish keeping time to Hank's playful notes. In the middle of the sea, a tiny ripple of white twirled like the ballerinas that once stood on top of the music boxes she and Harri had as children, special gifts their dad had given each girl.

Harri looked at Teesh and saw tender, pleasant joy in her wrinkled face. Teesh had her hands over her open mouth, her eyes twinkling behind the moistness that was testament to her experiencing a childhood friend. Sara was trapped between memory and reality, a replay few people experience.

Then it happened.

First, the bubbles began moving about erratically as if disturbed. The slants of their tiny eyes darted in every direction, and Harri was sure the eyes were circling around their little heads, or was it the bubbles completely circling in an effort to see behind, in front, and to each side? They encompassed the little white mist, keeping her in the center so tightly she could no longer twirl, even as they spun out of control. Their swirling became more violent, like a severe tornado. The whole room shook; the chandelier swung so hard a few crystal prisms popped off and landed on the floor. One fell in Teesh's lap, making her jump.

The blades on the two oversized fans hanging on either end of the ceiling stopped abruptly and then turned the opposite direction, whirring louder and louder, threatening to chop up whatever or whoever was beneath them if they fell. Charlie covered his eyes and rocked forward and backward. Harri and Teesh hugged him, putting their bodies tight against him to shelter him from the terrifying happenings. The camcorder flew off Harri's lap and landed at her feet, but she made no attempt to retrieve it.

Hank stopped playing and grabbed Cayce in a bear hug to prevent her from being cast off the bench as it vibrated and then levitated, rising at least five feet off the floor.

What happened next proved to be the shocking conclusion to the horrific scene. A large, dark fog appeared on the walkway that looked down from the second story. It moved stealthily toward the stairs, making its own whirring sound like a mass of huge, nasty, black flies beating their wings in rapid succession. Then the beating turned to deep bass, drumming more like a cave full of bats than tiny flies as the black mass moved down the stairs and approached the dazed onlookers.

The blue tornado moved in front of the piano as if seeking Hank's protection, but Hank and Cayce remained afloat on the bench. Harri saw Hank look behind him, and she caught a glimpse of Sara's face in the midst of the slanted dark eyes surrounding her. Her eyes, her only feature showing, were crystal blue, surrounded by flopping dark curls and an aqua blue bow; the little girl was being tossed about in the protective funnel like a rag doll caught in a hurricane.

Charlie peeked through his fingers and then covered his eyes again. He tried to escape from his protectors, but Harri and Teesh held him tight.

"Charlie not like black fog!" he shrieked. "Charlie not like black fog!" The little man continued to yell, getting louder and louder as if building up his immunity and his bravery.

The black mass gave off a deep, sadistic laugh, the

laugh of a devil, as it drew closer and closer to the piano. But it wasn't Hank and Cayce it was after. It headed for the blue bubbles and Sara. The bubbles darted away from the piano toward the door.

"Charlie not like black fog!" Charlie bellowed, a deep-throated bellow of a person highly agitated. He was easily heard over the roar of the devil twister, causing Harri to shake and lose her grip.

Charlie broke free and darted for the door ahead of the bubbles. He threw open the door, but did not run through. Instead, he allowed Sara and her protectors to rush through the door. Charlie slammed the door shut behind them and stood in front of it, arms folded, blocking the demon's path.

Hank jumped from the elevated bench, clutching Cayce, letting go only after she stood securely on the floor. He ran toward Charlie to help him, both to protect Charlie and to keep the fog from going after Sara. But just before Hank reached Charlie, the little man pulled a small bag from his pocket, opened it, and slung the contents into the black mass hovering near him. The drumming stopped, and a deep, booming voice howled and faded away, gradually slipping into nothingness and ending as a whisper of mist like the breath of a man who steps into freezing night air. Then it disappeared.

The fan blades slowed, the chandelier steadied, the room stopped shaking, and the piano bench fell to the floor, breaking a leg off as it landed with a thud. The floor in front of the door was covered with a fine mist of glitter.

"Gold dust!" Cayce blurted out.

No one spoke for what seemed an eternity. Teesh hugged her purse for comfort and stared at Charlie, the hero of the hour. Hank walked over to Cayce and put his arm around her even though she no longer appeared frightened. Charlie walked slowly, as if nothing had happened, back to the sofa and took his place between Teesh and Harri, giving his protectors a reassuring smile. Everything was calm until…

Rap! Rap! Rap! Rap! Rap!

Chapter Seventeen

Teesh gasped, Harri jumped, and Charlie shrieked, putting his hands over his eyes again.

"I'll get it. All of you stay put." Hank moved toward the door but hesitated to open it. He looked back at the others in the room and was reaching to open it when…

Creeeeeeeeak! The door slowly opened.

"Anybody home?" A female voice called cheerily from the cracked opening.

"Piper?" Cayce rushed to the door and embraced her daughter.

Cayce's first thought when Piper introduced them to Zach a few minutes later was that she had been right. She immediately looked at her daughter's left hand to see if Piper wore a big diamond on her finger, but Cayce only saw her own old wedding band and diamond. Piper saw her mom looking and immediately pulled Cayce into the kitchen, where Harri was heating up leftovers.

"Mom, I just met Zach today. We sat together on the plane from Salt Lake," she whispered, eyeing her mother and frowning. "And yes, I know I got in a car with an almost stranger, but I checked his credentials, and I called Harri to tell her I was coming with Zach."

Cayce looked at her sister and frowned. Harri, overhearing the conversation, just smiled, shrugged her shoulders, and walked back to the refrigerator to fix iced tea for her niece and her very handsome friend.

When the second meal—complete with more reheated chocolate gravy and biscuits for Charlie—was finished, the group went back into the front parlor.

"Okay. Now it's time to explain what happened here," Piper said when she saw Hank sweeping the gold dust into a pan. "You all looked like you were expecting Frankenstein's monster when I opened the front door." Piper sat by Zach on a short Victorian loveseat. Charlie squeezed in between Teesh and Harri on the sofa again, clearly liking the security they offered, and Cayce helped Hank hammer the broken leg back onto the piano bench after the gold dust was back in Charlie's bag.

"There. That seems pretty steady now." Hank shook the bench, to make sure it would stand without wobbling, before he sat on it. Cayce took her place again by Hank and hoped this time it would not take them on a magic bench ride.

"Well, after scanning through this camcorder footage, I think it's movie time. No explanation will be necessary after you watch this, Piper." Harri left the sofa and set the camcorder on a small table she had set in the center of the room. She then moved a couple of chairs and directed everyone's attention to the back wall by the kitchen door.

"My camcorder has a built-in projector, so we can watch it straight from the camera. I'll warn you, though. You might have to turn your head upside down for some of it, or I can turn the camera, which might be easier. The camcorder flew off my lap at one point and was recording from its side."

"Would you get the lights, Hank?" Harri glanced at Charlie, who already had his hands over his eyes.

"Oh, Charlie, you don't have us fooled anymore. You are one brave little man, yes, you are." Charlie slid his hands down and gave his hearty laugh to show he liked Harri calling him brave. But when he saw the scene replaying on the wall, he lost his nerve again and covered his eyes. What had seemed like hours was only ten minutes, according to the camcorder, but it was the longest ten minutes anyone in the group had experienced.

"Oh, my gosh! I cannot believe that happened! Mom, is that what you and Harri deal with all the time?"

"It isn't all negative or this scary, Piper. Sara is the most endearing little spirit we've ever contacted. If you could have heard her giggling when she was playing with my makeup..." Harri smiled, remembering their first encounter with the little spirit.

"And you should see how happy she is when she dances—in person, that is. Right, Charlie?" Hank directed his remark to his new friend.

"Charlie love Sara and Jesus. Sara dance with Charlie and sing Jesus love me, dis I know."

Piper looked at Cayce with questions written on her face.

"I'll take you to the cemetery tomorrow, and you will meet Jesus in person, and if we're lucky, Sara will dance for you." Cayce saw worry written all over Piper's face. "Is there something bothering you? Other than the worst scary movie you ever watched?" Cayce noticed Piper held tight to her new friend's hand.

Piper dropped Zach's hand, and went to her art

bag. She pulled out her sketchbook and flipped to the page of Bar None and handed it to her mother. Harri left the sofa and looked over Cayce's shoulder, and both sisters stared at Piper.

"I knew something was wrong with you the last few times we've talked on the phone. Spill it, Piper. How did you come to sketch a ghost town you've never seen? This looks exactly like the picture I bought in Lester's antique shop." Cayce paused. "And when exactly did you sketch this?"

"I sketched the one of Bar None a couple of days ago."

"The same day I bought the picture. I bet if we figured out the times you were sketching this, or perhaps dreaming it, it'd turn out to be the same time I was looking at it on Lester's wall. Interesting!"

Piper told about the recurring dreams of the beautiful Chinese girl and said there had been other dreams, as well, some she had not sketched.

"Oh, Piper, I know how you have fought the possibility of having the Gift, but it is really not something to be feared." Cayce saw the disturbed look on Piper's face and knew her daughter needed reassurance. "But we'll talk later, before bed. You can show me your sketches and tell me about your dreams—especially the ones that have come true so far."

Wanting to lighten up the atmosphere after the movie footage and after Piper's disclosure, Cayce turned to Zach.

"Well, Zachary, you seem like a nice young man, and I like your connection with history. But tell me—do you wish you had not been chosen to sit by my

179

daughter on that flight from Salt Lake City?"

"I like the sound of that, Ms. McCallister. Being 'chosen' to sit by Piper would mean there is much Piper-and-Zach ahead." Zach squeezed Piper's hand and smiled at her. "I don't have any paranormal gifts that I know of, but like I told Piper, I do have Native American ancestors—a grandfather, to be more exact. So I am intrigued, to put it mildly, with the world of spirits. Experiencing them would be a real adventure, but hopefully, not the black cloud—or fog, as Charlie calls it. That is pretty terrifying. Right, Charlie?"

Zach looked at Charlie and smiled. Charlie had taken right to Zach from the first introduction. Charlie had told Zach about his hat and how it was his dad's. He'd even taken it off and handed it to Zach so he could get a closer look at a "real forest ranger hat." After that, Charlie pulled out a pocketknife and showed it to Zach, telling him it, too, had been his father's. Cayce was impressed with this, feeling Charlie was a good judge of character.

After Teesh and Charlie left, Hank showed Zach to his room on the opposite end of the hall from the ladies' and right beside his room, and then helped him put his gear inside.

"Is that a Hardy rod, Zach?" Hank reached for the rod Zach was about to put down.

"Yep. Found it in the antique shop and couldn't resist it." Zach handed the rod to Hank, who began putting it together. "It's heavy, and the flex will take some getting used to, but any diehard fly fisher like myself needs at least one in his collection."

"I see what you mean about the flex." Hank flexed the rod a few times and then took it back apart to place in the sleeve. "I love to fly fish but haven't had much time for it lately. Maybe we'll get to wet a fly while you're here."

"Hope so, and I know Piper and her mom are hoping so, too." Zach leaned the rod against the wall. "Guess we better check in with the ladies, huh?" Zach headed out the door behind Hank.

On the opposite end of the hall, Cayce chose the room next to hers for her daughter. This room was beautiful, and Cayce had imagined her daughter sleeping on the tall Victorian bed. Now she knew why. Cayce was always tuned in to Piper, either as a result of the Gift or having a close mother/daughter relationship. She felt at ease where her daughter was concerned for the first time in months, even in a haunted ghost town in Idaho.

Cayce listened intently as Piper told her about some of her dreams, of places she'd painted before she ever saw them, and about her very first dream nine months ago, the dream of Jonathan with another woman. The woman she had sketched and finally showed to Jonathan turned out to be his wife, and he could do nothing but confess when he saw it. Her dreaming had stopped with her despair from the breakup, but it had resurfaced a few days after she reached Europe.

As their conversation wound down, Cayce reassured Piper. "Your Gift is a true Gift if you use it for the good of those communicating with you, be they alive or be they dead. I know you, my daughter. You will use it to save, never to harm, and you will not ignore it."

Piper thought about the sketch in her new

sketchpad, but decided not to show her mom right now for fear of ruining the most perfect day either of them had experienced in months. Neither had she shown the sketch to Zach or anyone else. It was the scene of the most frightening nightmare of all. She had forced herself to sketch it hurriedly when she woke up in the night, hoping to make it go away forever. She wanted to show her mom and get her take on it, but it frightened her so much she could not bring herself to look at it even once after she had drawn it. Piper put the dream out of her mind for fear of conjuring it up in her sleep again.

I'll save it for another time, if there is another time, and just hope the dream won't reoccur. If it leaves me alone, I will continue to leave it alone. Maybe I'll even destroy the sketch.

It had been a good day. Piper felt at peace for the first time in months, having finally accepted the Gift as a blessing and not a curse. She could now look forward to her dreams, and would sketch them as soon as she had enough vision to accomplish the task. Sometimes she would need to wait for repetition, like she had with the dreams of Yu. The sketch had to be realistic and perfect.

Despite her mother's surprise when she'd arrived at Bar None that night, especially being accompanied by Zach, Piper somehow had a second sense her mom had expected her.

After taking a long, hot shower in the communal bathroom, Piper buried herself in the crisp sheets and soft down comforter of the beautiful Victorian bed. She loved the intricate angel carved in the tall headboard and knew now why her mother had told her this was her room. As a child, Piper's bed always had a picture of a guardian angel over it, protecting her from bad dreams and childhood fears. Now here she was again, thirty years old but still seeking the protection only a mother and an angel could offer.

Piper's head sank into the supple down pillow, and she placed her hands under it, giving her head extra support. She shook briefly, not from being chilled, but with the feeling of complete contentment and warmth that security can bring. She knew it would be the best night's sleep she had gotten in six months, the length of time she had been dreaming these unexplainable dreams.

Piper smiled with the anticipation of her dreams tonight being replays of the tiny China doll standing on the porch of The Nugget. Her mom had convinced her it was Yu, and Piper knew she would begin painting the lovely girl tomorrow without the aid of a sketch, her own form of *plein-air* where she would close her eyes and see Yu in her subconscious, a mental field sketch. Yu would be a live model posing for the artist even though she had died ninety years ago.

Piper woke with a start and glanced at her travel clock. Still early, but her dream loomed in her mind. It was not the tiny Yu who had consumed her short night, and it was not a scene of pleasantry. Piper left the comfort of her bed, retrieved her sketchpad and pencil, and moved to the table by the window. When she opened the curtain, rays of sunlight poured through the wavy old salvaged and reused glass, every curvature casting distorted energy onto her page as if lending a different time to her artistic interpretation.

Slightly to the right of the page, she sketched an

old, hand-hewed, black-singed cabin from another era. Then she surrounded the cabin with burned timbers, giving it a sinister appearance. Once the sketch was transformed into oil, the only semi-bright hues to be cast on the scene would be the moon casting its glow over dripping snow piles, leftovers from winter's high mountain winter pack. The snow would disappear fast now with summer's daily warmth, only to be frozen again into crusty ice with nightfall's cold. The off-white berm dripped onto a dirt path, outlining it, directing the eye of the beholder to the blackened, ill-omened door.

Piper closed her eyes every few minutes, recalling even the smallest detail. When she finished, she propped the sketch on the other chair, moved several feet away from it, and stared, mesmerized. The picture, ominous and disturbing, gave the artist a sense of foreboding. For some reason, she felt an urgency to reproduce the landscape in oil as soon as possible.

Yu will have to wait. Mom told me to always trust my instincts.

Piper unpacked her canvases and set up her easel where the sun could cast its rays across the developing scene. She chose a medium-sized canvas and prepared her palette with mostly black and white with just a hint of yellow for the moon's soft glow, an intruder on the otherwise austere scene.

Piper forced a smile—not what she was feeling— realizing she was not the picture- perfect artist. She still had on her T-shirt and short pajama bottoms and stood in bare feet. Her mop of long, blonde curls hung across one eye, forcing her to contain as much as possible in a messy loose ponytail before beginning.

She chose a long-handled brush with thick bristles

to give her interpretation the depth it needed to convey the mood of the landscape. Holding her brush at the end, she gave in to long brush strokes embedding her dream's image on canvas.

She worked with no thought of time, each stroke evoking a scene of danger and apprehension, a premonition of something yet to be experienced, at least by the artist. She continued painting when she heard a soft rap on her bedroom door.

"It's open," she called through locked teeth holding an extra brush, a new brush she had stuck there trying to save precious seconds, knowing she would need it soon. Not giving any thought to which visitor it might be, her mom or her aunt, she continued to paint, concentrating on her canvas.

Zach stood in the doorway, mesmerized by the scene before him. Piper stood completely entranced in her painting, her back partially to the door. She was lost in her work and never turned toward him. The sunlight completely enveloped her, giving a halo effect around her whole body. Even in her disheveled state, she was the most beautiful woman he had ever seen.

Piper McCallister was pure magic! Her long, lean figure, clad in T-shirt and short pajamas and standing barefoot, needed no pose to stir every masculine desire in his body. He stood for several minutes watching her without moving or speaking, never even glancing at her painting. Finally, he could restrain himself no longer. He closed the door behind him and walked to her.

"Piper?" he spoke softly, not wanting to startle her, but loudly enough to bring her out of her pensive state.

Piper stopped her brush in mid-stroke and turned to face him, her eyes smiling at him over the brush still clenched between her teeth. He moved closer, reached down to take the brush from her teeth, and dropped it on the easel's ledge. She watched, her gaze never leaving his face as he pushed a lock of curls from her eye and tucked it behind her ear. Zach continued to stare into her alluring green eyes.

She moved into him, requiring him to enfold her in a tight embrace. As his mouth covered her lips, they parted in an invitation for more. She put her arms around his neck, entangling his hair in her fingers, and allowed him to savor their kiss as she prolonged it.

He finally pulled back to look into her eyes again, trying to gauge whether her thoughts and desires mirrored his own; he slid her hands down from his neck.

Piper could feel his hard, muscular chest through his T-shirt. When she placed the toes of her left foot on top of his bare foot, skin against skin sent a jolt up her leg, pausing mid body. She lifted her mouth to his face, demanding another, deeper kiss. His lips locked against hers, Zach lifted Piper into his arms and carried her to the bed. Piper shivered with excitement, losing all bad memories of love gone wrong, anger, and fear. It was Zach and her, and that was all that mattered.

Chapter Eighteen

Piper and Zach sat beside each other drinking coffee and eating the huckleberry muffins and bacon Harri had left for them on the counter. They smiled often, and Piper thought about the turn of events in their already speedy romantic relationship.

"So what now?" Piper asked.

"Don't know." Zach took a sip of coffee and smiled.

"Do you think we're moving a little too fast, Zach?" Now it was Piper's turn to take a sip of coffee.

"Well, let's see. You're thirty, and I'm thirty-two, both of us still single and unattached, as far as I know—not that it matters at this point—an obvious attraction between us from the first moment we locked eyes." Zach hesitated. "I guess I'd better clarify that. You had me from the first moment my eyes locked on yours. I can only hope you felt the same way."

"Obviously so, considering we just made love after knowing each other for not quite twenty-four hours." Piper smiled as she pinched off another bite of muffin. "So much for giving up on men." She pushed her plate away and pulled her coffee mug in front of her. "So how did you know Mom and Harri were gone and we were all alone?"

Zach left the counter to get more coffee. "Truth?" He gave Piper an impish grin over his shoulder.

"You stinker!" Piper tried unsuccessfully to look serious. "You didn't know, did you?" She held her cup out for a refill.

"Well, I didn't know for sure, but I came down to the kitchen and saw the muffins and the note from Harri that said, *Help yourself.*" Zach raised and lowered his eyebrows and gave her his biggest grin, his dimples as big as the Grand Canyon, second only to the smile he'd given her after they'd made love.

"So…I helped myself—to you." Zach put his cup down and stood beside Piper's stool at the counter. He twirled her around to face him and bent down to kiss her—a long, hard kiss. Holding her chin in his hand, he looked into her eyes. "Would it have mattered?"

"Well, yes. I would not have let myself give in if my mother and aunt were here, and I'm pretty sure Harri was talking about the muffins when she said to help yourself."

"Oh!" Zach had a twinkle in his eye. Then he took a step back, eying her seriously. "Did you say, 'give in'?" He cocked his head and frowned at her.

"Okay. It wasn't as if I was forced into making love." Piper reached out and pulled Zach to her, giving him a quick kiss and her most innocent look. "You caught me off guard. I was really into my painting and didn't have time to even think where my mother was."

"Well, even if you might not have been smitten with me, I was totally enamored with you and had a very hard time sleeping knowing you were just down the hall in that big bed all alone. You know, I can dream, too." Zach sat back at the counter, popped the last of his muffin into his mouth, and then picked up both plates and loaded them into the dishwasher.

"Now. What's on your agenda, my love of almost a day?" Zach walked back and pulled Piper to him in a bear hug. He released her and looked at his watch. "Let's see. We boarded yesterday about one o'clock. So… What can we do to celebrate our anniversary in two more hours?"

Piper opened her mouth to react to the statement, but Zach pulled her back to him and covered her lips with his, stopping all further conversation and potentially sarcastic remarks. She pushed away when she heard the front door open.

"Well, it's about time you two got up and at 'em. Your mom and I have visited the cemetery again and have just met Hank's construction crew. They'll all be here shortly to start back working on the saloon—the cat house—or The Nugget, as it is formally known." Harri went to the fridge and took out a bottle of water.

"Did you sleep well?" She smiled sheepishly behind her plastic bottle as she drank, like she knew what had happened after she and Cayce left.

"Where's Mom?" Piper looked toward the parlor, ignoring her aunt's question.

"Oh, she's with Cowboy Number Two. If Joshua knows what's good for him, he'll get his tail out to his ghost town before Hank steals his woman, if it hasn't already happened." Harri took another big gulp. "I think I hear them on the porch now."

Piper hurried into the parlor in time to meet her mom and Hank as they entered. Cayce was all smiles at the sight of her daughter, and walked straight over and hugged her.

"This has turned into a great trip, thanks to my daughter, even with the invasion of the black fog."

Cayce looked past Piper to Zach, who had settled on the loveseat. "I'm glad you're here, too, Zach. I need another protector for Piper."

"Mom, I don't need protecting. I'm thirty years old, you know."

The way Piper crossed her arms and tapped her foot gave Cayce a flashback of her as a little girl even though she was taller than her mother.

"You say that only because you weren't here to experience the black fog firsthand. It lost some of its terror in Harri's camcorder footage."

"I'm a pretty big guy, Piper, and I'll be the first to admit I was scared to death," Hank confessed as he left the front window where he had been looking out. He now headed for the front door. "Here comes Bill, my foreman. I want you guys to meet him," he called over his shoulder as he reached for the door. "Now, here's a protector. Come on in, Bill. I want you to meet everyone."

Bill was so tall, he had to duck under the top of the doorway, most likely a habit. His muscular body filled out his frame.

"I've just got a minute, Hank. You know the boys won't stay in the cat house without me."

"You mean they're scared?" Piper asked.

"Yes, ma'am." Bill took off his cap and held it like a gentleman with old-time manners. "And they have a right to be, after what they've been through. A couple of them are on the verge of quitting after spending the night in the camp up the valley. I think they might move closer to town, but I'm not sure that's a better idea. Heard you had a little activity last night in the hotel." Bill's eyes gave away his joy in knowing Hank and the group had been scared.

"Before you start telling your tale, Bill—and I know you've piqued everyone's interest—I want to introduce everybody."

Hank made the introductions and asked Bill if he wanted coffee, then headed into the kitchen to get himself a cup after Bill declined his offer.

"So what happened in the camp, Bill?" Cayce took a seat on the sofa.

"Oh, Peg really showed out. She didn't like the men being so close to her cabin or the mine. She sent that doggone train, or the sound of it, right through the middle of camp about every two hours and just howled every time the men came running out in their long-johns. When they finally did get settled and thought the train was done, the saloon music started. It echoed in the canyon all the way from here." Hank gave a low chuckle. "I've heard a couple of them whistling and humming 'Down by the Old Mill Stream' all morning. Can't seem to get it out of their heads."

"Would that be Peg Leg Annie's train?" Zach asked.

"That would be the one," Bill answered. "Well, nice to meet you all, but I better get back over to the house before Belle…or whoever…starts slinging boards. If your black fog appears, I'll be heading to Idaho Falls or wherever to hunt up a new crew." Bill replaced his cap and walked out.

"That is a big man. I expected him to have a big old booming voice, but it wasn't any deeper than Hank's. Still, if the black fog comes back, I want to be next to Bill." Piper looked at Zach and gave him an impish grin.

"Wait a minute. I'm not exactly a runt, you know." Zach looked serious.

Piper walked over and sat in Zach's lap, putting her arm around his shoulder. "Yes, I've noticed that." Piper felt Zach's biceps, which he immediately flexed to show off for her.

Cayce stared at them. "And you two met when?" she asked with a suspicious grin coupled with a slight frown.

Piper blushed.

Zach looked a little uncomfortable. "Piper, you should show your mom and Harri the painting you did this morning."

"A painting?" Cayce cocked her head to one side. "Not a sketch? That was fast. Have another dream, Piper?"

"Yes, and you won't believe the outcome. I've got some details to finish, but you can get the gist of it." Piper left the settee and moved toward the stairs, where she stopped and turned. "Do you want to see it, Mom, Harri?" They followed her up the stairs with Zach bringing up the rear.

"It's beautiful…in a morbid, sinister kind of way." Cayce stepped back to look at the painting from a distance. "Not exactly what I'd imagine you painting, but it does show your talent as an artist." She moved closer again. "You certainly caught the mood. How did you feel when you woke up from such a dream?"

"How do you think I felt? I went to sleep hoping to dream about Yu so I could paint her, and this is what intruded into my mind space." Piper gestured toward the painting. "I felt just as gloomy and dreary as the picture implies. I just wish I knew what it meant." Piper put her hands on her hips and continued to stare at the picture.

"Put it out of your mind, sweetie." Cayce waved her hand to signify dismissal of the dream. "When it's time, you'll be shown."

Zach stood by the door, watching the scene. He sensed the dream and the reproduction of it frightened Piper. He wanted to protect her, but he carried a secret that was becoming heavier to bear the more deeply he fell in love with her.

It all seems so perfect, but it's not. I've not been honest with her. How will she react when she finds out why I'm really here?

Put it out of your head, Zach. It's too early for confession, if it can ever come. You're no protector. You've proven that once already.

He turned away from the group and headed out the door, hurriedly retracing his steps to the parlor.

A few minutes later, everyone stood outside, shielding their eyes from the sun with their hands and looking up at the high-pitched roof of The Nugget.

"What are they doing?" Piper directed her question to Zach, who had rejoined the group after talking to Bill and Hank.

"They have to finish the roof. It never got done after Hank's roofer fell the other day. Those two young guys volunteered after Hank promised a bonus when it's completed." Zach pulled his sunglasses from his pocket but handed them to Piper, who was cupping her hand over her eyes. Then he pulled the bill of his cap back around to the front and pulled it down to shade his eyes. "Hank is making sure they're properly tied off this time."

After a few minutes of watching, Piper left the group and went to sit on the porch. When Zach joined her, she took off the sunglasses, folded them, and put them in his shirt pocket, patting his chest and letting her hand linger for a while as her eyes melted into his.

"Let's go inside and find something cold to drink." Zach looked at his watch. "Besides, it's almost time to celebrate our anniversary." He took Piper's hand and coaxed her out of her chair.

The kitchen became a scene from a sexy romance novel as Zach and Piper held on to each other, kissing as passionately as a couple who had been together for months rather than just one day. They were so wrapped up in each other they did not notice the dark shadow watching through the back window.

Sensing movement, Zach opened his eyes and saw what looked like a reflection in the window. He blinked, thinking his eyes were playing tricks on him, but when he stopped blinking, she was still there, staring at him. Even through her veil, her eyes made him uneasy; he was unable to pull his gaze from hers. Her eyes were light, too light, and had a magnetic effect on him. The figure grew bigger and seemed to be moving closer, and he thought for a second she would appear right in front of him in the room.

Piper pulled her lips away from him. "Zach? Is something wrong?"

Zach shook himself out of the reverie that was more like a nightmare in full daylight. Holding Piper in his arms, he turned their bodies to face the window.

"Look!" He pointed in the direction of the window, but when Piper looked, the reflection had disappeared.

"What? Was it Charlie?" Piper continued staring at

the window.

"No. It was a lady dressed in black, with a black veil over her face. I think it was Belle. She stared at us and then faded away when I told you to look." Zach pulled Piper closer as if he could protect her. "How eerie is that?"

The shadow made Zach uneasy. Deep down, he knew the figure was not a good spirit and wondered what she was up to. Even through her veil, he could see haunting, transparent eyes aimed at his as if she were trying to control him through her hypnotic stare. Zach had felt the same sense of uneasiness when showering in Belle's quarters, as if someone was watching, something that made him hurry. He knew he would be on guard, his senses on full alert, determined not to fall under Belle's hypnotic spell.

That afternoon, Piper packed up her art bag with easel and paints and headed toward the cemetery alone, since Zach had volunteered to run to the nearest hardware store to pick up new nail guns and air compressors for Hank. As Hank had told him, "For some strange reason, these things just stop working. I've never had this problem on any other job."

Hank's carpenters had to resort to the old hammer-and-nail method until Zach returned. He had tried to convince Piper to go with him, but she told him she really wanted to use the *plein-air* technique she had been trained to use in Europe. Her first project would be the beautiful Jesus statue her mom had shown her that afternoon. The mountains looming behind the statue would be the perfect complement to Jesus, and her mom had told her the best time, as far as the sun was concerned, would be late afternoon.

Her art bag was heavy, but Piper was accustomed to carrying it great distances after traipsing over the countryside in Europe. As she trudged up the valley, she felt sad looking at all the piles of logs and rotted wood, leftovers of the lives of miners and their families. One building in particular made her stop.

Piper crossed to the log remains, put her bag down, and stepped over rotted logs that had been burned. She pulled away some burned boards, hoping no rattlesnakes or other animals were hiding beneath, and discovered a large, rustic cross which, though singed, was still beautiful in its own way. She put the heavy cross over her shoulder and turned, ready to pick her way back through the burned timbers to her art bag.

"Get out!" A deep, demanding voice roared in her ear. Then something moved through her body, knocking her down. She fell on the rotted and burned logs, dropping the cross in the process.

"Ouch!" Piper pulled her knee up and examined the long scrape, at the same time looking around to see who or what had caused her to fall.

"Get out!" boomed the voice again, even louder, sending a wave of panic through Piper's body. At the same time, a strong breeze blew by her, knocking her hair loose and whipping it across her face. Then she felt a burning sensation on her arm. She held her arm up and noticed three long, red scratches running the full length of her arm, from elbow to wrist.

Maybe I scratched my arm when I fell or when I dropped the cross.

Piper rose to her feet and quickly retraced her steps away from the cabin ruins. As she headed up to the cemetery, Piper completely forgot about the cross.

When she reached her art bag, she remembered the cross and turned back, but hesitated, trying to decide if she really wanted to retrieve the cross.

The breeze turned to a wind, a wind that was isolated in the church ruins. She looked around, but no tree limbs or long-stemmed sage grass moved. A loud, popping noise close behind her made Piper cover her ears and convinced her to leave the cross and the ruins, at least for the time. Her nerves were on edge, but she turned up the canyon road, refusing to be deterred from her mission by the terrifying voice or the scratches.

When Piper arrived at the cemetery, she saw the magnificent Jesus standing watch over the departed and felt at ease again. Her mom had told her the story of the mass grave of aborted fetuses, and Piper had been sickened by it.

How could mothers kill their unborn children? Or did they even have a choice?

She looked around the cemetery and spotted the gleaming marble angel of Sara's grave. Making her way to it, she decided to paint the scene from the perspective of the precious little spirit Sara, whose soul should be with Jesus. Piper had been taught that all children who have not reached the age of accountability go to heaven. Her mom explained the existence of spirit children on earth as trapped energy or spirits that linger, often separated from their souls by either extreme happiness in the place where they had lived and their desire to stay longer, or perhaps from a sense of unfinished business. The little girl Chloe, whose spirit her mom and Harri had come in contact with at Spanish Oaks, Joshua's antebellum inn in South Mississippi, had left behind the energy that needed to be reunited with her mother. Once this was accomplished, Chloe had passed over, never to be seen or heard again.

Piper wasted no time once her easel was set up and her palette of paints laid out. As usual, she put a brush in her mouth and one behind her ear. She did not want to waste time cleaning a brush before changing paint colors, an effort to take advantage of her inspiration while it was at its height. Piper's emotions always ran high when she painted, and she became oblivious to anyone or anything going on around her. She also knew the sun would last but a couple of hours longer. She would not finish the painting that day, but she would have her outlines in place so she could work on it later, if she desired. More than likely, she would return each day at the same time so the light was always the same until the painting was finished.

Piper had the mountains outlined behind Jesus, the focal point just off to the right of the center of the canvas. Everything in the picture would draw the eye of the beholder to the statue. She knew this would be some of her best work, and several times she got behind Sara's grave and squatted down, getting the perspective of a seven-year-old girl looking up at the Savior.

Once when she was squatting on the ground, she felt someone watching her from the back of the cemetery. She turned quickly and saw a shadow dart behind a tree.

"Charlie? Charlie? Is that you?" She put the hand still holding the wet brush over her eyes and continued to look toward the tree. The first thing she saw was the brim of Charlie's forest ranger hat.

"Do you want to see what I'm doing? Come on over, Charlie." Piper waved the brush, directing Charlie to come over. "I'm Piper, Cayce's daughter. I met you last night. Remember? You really liked my friend Zach, and he liked you."

Piper watched as the whole head peeked around, and then the rest of Charlie emerged as he walked slowly toward her, his eyes on the ground.

When he got almost to her, Piper returned to her easel and motioned him to come closer. "Well, what do you think?" She stood back to give Charlie a clear view of the painting.

"Jesus good. Mountain good." Charlie dropped to his knees, sitting back on his heels, on the ground beside Piper's easel, and cocked his head to one side. "Clouds not good."

"Well, I have a lot more work to do before it's finished." Piper walked to the other side of the easel and stared up at the clouds. "What's wrong with the clouds, Charlie?"

"Clouds not white. Clouds blue. Bubbles in clouds." Charlie laughed. "Bubbles hide, but Charlie see." Charlie cocked his head again.

Piper looked at the clouds, trying to see what Charlie was seeing, and she saw it. "Oh, my goodness! You are so right. I see the blue bubbles." Piper took the brush from behind her ear and began mixing paints to add to the clouds in her picture. "There. Is that better?" She sat beside Charlie on her heels and cocked her head to the side just like he was doing so she could see what he was seeing.

He laughed again, and Piper laughed with him, her head still cocked to the side like her friend's.

"You two look just like Forrest and Forrest, Jr., sitting with your heads cocked like that." Zach had entered the cemetery from the back gate and walked up behind them.

"Charlie forest ranger, not forest." Charlie pulled his hat down farther on his ears to signal his identity and then covered his mouth, snickering at Zach's foolish statement. Zach and Piper smiled at each other, but soon Charlie's snickering turned to wild laughter, and Zach and Piper joined him.

Charlie and Zach stayed until Piper finished painting. She took the canvas off the easel and put it in a wet box to keep the paint from smearing. Once packed, she slung the strap to the back over her shoulder and moved toward Jesus.

"Let me carry that for you, Piper." Zach reached to take the bag, but Piper turned it away from him.

"I need to carry it, Zach. I'm used to walking with it, remember?"

"Oh, yeah. *Plein-air* technique." Zach put his arm around Piper's shoulder and walked beside her. He noticed Charlie didn't move.

"Are you coming with us, Charlie? No telling what Harri is cooking tonight."

"Charlie 'splore. Charlie night cat. Teesh say Charlie got cat eyes like Jezzie. Charlie see in dark." Charlie pointed toward his eyes.

"Where do you explore, Charlie?" Piper asked.

"Secret." Charlie put his finger to his lips as he whispered the answer.

"Be careful." Piper knew her warning was silly; Charlie had spent his whole life traipsing through these woods and mountains in both daytime and night. Charlie headed off into the woods without a wave or a look back, and Piper began the trek out of the cemetery with Zach by her side.

"Where do you think he goes?"

"I don't know." Zach put his finger to his lips and whispered, "Secret."

"He must have night vision like a cat to move around through the woods like he does. Teesh told Mom he doesn't even use a flashlight."

"He's got those really light-colored eyes, blue or maybe green. He doesn't look up much, so I don't know which color, not to mention having that hat pulled down so far it's impossible to see his eyes." Zach pushed the old rusted, rickety cemetery gate open and let Piper go through first.

"I read about a boy in China who had sky-blue eyes. His night vision was so good he could fill out a paper answering questions in total blackness. Doctors were always testing the kid to discover what made him able to see in the dark, but they just decided it was a fluke of nature. I doubt Charlie is like the Chinese boy, though. He probably just knows the area from living here all his life." Zach put his arm around Piper's shoulder again. "He's just like a blind person who uses his cane to get across busy intersections in cities and to find his way around his home, work, or any place that he's used to. Charlie is an amazing little fellow. I like him."

"And he obviously likes you. You should have seen his face light up when he heard your voice. But he's a forest ranger, not a forest." Piper laughed along with Zach, not at their new friend, but out of the simple joy of being around him.

Chapter Nineteen

The examination that had caused Billie so much grief and trepidation haunted her, demanding she devise a plan of escape. The next exam could prove to be her one chance at freedom.

She waited on her mattress for the camera light to go off. As soon as the menacing red eye blinked several times in succession signaling "lights out" and the onset of total darkness in her prison, she sat up and looked around, giving her eyes time to reset to nothingness. It would take a few moments for them to adjust, but she had noticed how she could see better after fifty-two days here; she had spent another week in captivity, marked by Exodus chapter eight and hours spent in night-time extreme exercising and strength training.

The totality of black gradually changed to shadows, and she felt more and more like a bat in a cave as she clung to her natural climbing wall, forcing herself to go higher each night, putting fear of falling behind her. Trembling at the thought of reaching higher on her rock wall with no rope, harness, or partner for belaying and security, she forced herself to think of a worse horror—the panic in Lisa's voice. This was all it took to make her stretch her body, her feet grasping for ledges remembered from her handholds of minutes before. Callouses had formed on the balls of her feet and on her fingertips from all the hard training, but this made her climbing easier.

Tonight, I'll reach the top.

She made the vow to herself, to her baby, and to Johnny.

The muscles in her arms and legs bulged as she strained to reach her goal. She was surprised at the strength she had gained since beginning her night-time routine. But reaching the top of the high rock wall was not her main goal. She was determined to escape.

The next day, as every day, she practiced yoga, but with a much deeper concentration than she had been taught in the classes she took at her local health gym. More than concentration was needed if she was to pull her plan off. She would have to put herself into a trancelike state where she could undergo the examination without flinching and without any display of consciousness. She had to make the two people with the masks think she was unconscious so she could implement her plan of escape. She still had to figure out a way to get rid of the drugged food without the Keeper knowing. In her subconscious, she again heard her Grammar.

Be careful, Billie. Be patient and wait. The answer will come.

Billie prayed and devoured the Bible, no longer just a means of counting days in captivity but a resource to give her the courage and the faith to save her life and the life of her baby. She began another of her long, private devotions, hoping to receive a "burning bush," a sign from God that assured her freedom would come.

She flipped through the Bible with her eyes closed tightly, seeking heavenly guidance, part of her daily ritual now, along with reading a chapter a day to keep up with days in captivity. Stopping on a page, she ran her finger down, and with her eyes still closed, allowed her finger to stop. Before opening her eyes, she begged God for an answer. Then she read the random passage in a whisper and smiled. She now knew she was doing the right thing and would escape.

The verses where her finger had stopped were numbers three and four in the thirty-fifth chapter of Isaiah.

"Strengthen ye the weak hands, and confirm the feeble knees. Say to them that are of a fearful heart, be strong, fear not; behold, your God will come with vengeance, even God with a recompense; he will come and save you."

As she read the passage to herself with only her lips moving, she felt something strange, the flutter of life in her newly protruding stomach.

It's a sign!

Billie cried and laughed at the same time, becoming louder with the recognition of the baby she was going to bring into the world. Her excitement was obvious; she was unabashed and unafraid. She refused to allow her captor to take away the joy of this moment.

The Keeper, who had been spying on her, questioned her excitement and laughter through his synthesized voice. Billie told him she had felt her baby move for the first time, and she continued to caress her stomach.

He berated her again, as if her excitement was a sin in itself, and blasted the scripture about whoredom and worldliness at her, but he could not stop her joy. He punished her by shutting off the lights early, leaving her in darkness for two extra hours during what should have been her late-afternoon daylight hours, daylight meaning the fluorescent lights in the ceiling.

Billie thought about using the punishment as an advantage and starting her exercise regiment early, but she was afraid the Keeper would change his mind and turn the lights back on and catch her climbing up the wall. Instead, she would get extra sleep and awaken later to train.

As she lay in the darkness, unable to sleep, she thought she heard a scratching sound coming from the wall behind her mattress. She eased her way toward the sound, being as stealthy and quiet as possible, looking like an animal stalking its prey as she crawled on her knees, her hands out in front for balance, her head and body low, no more than a foot above her mattress. She stopped and listened, turning her ears like radar so her sensitized hearing could zero in on the target.

Again she heard the sound, rock against rock, and then it stopped. Someone had opened a hole in the rocks. Billie was so close she could hear the person's breath coming in short, clipped spurts of air as if he or she had been holding it in.

Billie saw nothing, but she began feeling up the wall in the direction of the sound. Then she felt the edge of the hole where a small stone had been removed. She traced the edges of the hole on her side, keeping clear of the actual hole for fear of touching unknown eyes and scaring off her possible rescuer. The breach was about two inches in diameter. Her adrenaline was on high alert with the thought that someone who was not the Keeper knew she was here. With her face to the side of the hole, she whispered.

"Help me! Please help me!" Billie begged the eyes

behind the hole. She heard noise, footsteps backing away from the hole, and she put her mouth directly over the hole whispering louder.

"Don't go!" Her voice cracked as she softly pleaded. "Please don't leave me here to die!" Her plea turned to sobbing as she realized the peeper was gone. Crawling back to her mattress, she hugged herself and rocked and cried and rocked and cried.

But the intruder had not left the other side of the hole. Hearing a delicate sound emanating from the hole again, Billie forced herself to stop crying.

Be still and listen! Grammar admonished.

This time, she did not move toward the hole, but waited to see what would happen next. Then she heard it.

Plop!

Something had been pushed through the hole and had fallen onto the mattress at the end by the wall. Billie got onto her hands and knees and began feeling around under the hole. Her hand touched a small object, and she picked it up, passing it from her left hand to her right, tightening her fingers around it. In the dark, Billie smiled.

A knife! It's a pocketknife!

Quickly, she returned to the hole and put her mouth as close to it as she could.

"Thank you! Please don't leave me!"

But there was no reply. Then she heard the faint grating noise, and she knew the stone had been placed back in the hole. Billie clutched the pocketknife to her chest, holding it with both hands like the greatest treasure she had ever been given.

Be strong; fear not! God will save you!

Chapter Twenty

Cayce clicked off the satellite phone and threw it onto the counter, where it bounced twice before falling to the floor.

"He's not coming!"

Ignoring her sister's glare and the fallen phone, Cayce giant-stepped toward the walk-in freezer and scanned the shelves of ice cream.

"Oreos and crème…too sweet! Raspberry, granola crunch delight…too healthy! Chocolate vanilla swirl…definitely too Joshua! Ah-ha! Huckleberry cheesecake with chocolate chunks and pecans! Sinful and perfect!" Cayce grabbed a large serving spoon, threw the top of the container to the counter, and stomped out of the kitchen, her western boots making more noise than a bull in cleats on a gym floor.

Harri debated whether to follow, but she wanted to know what had caused the change of plans that put her sister in a state of fury. She reached into the refrigerator and pulled out a sugar-free, fat-free orange Jell-O, grabbed a small spoon befitting a demitasse instead of a regular-sized cup, and took short, dainty steps as she followed her sister to the front porch.

Cayce rode the rocking chair like she was in the Derby while taking huge bites of ice cream as if she hadn't eaten in weeks. She stomped her boots hard on the wood floor each time the chair returned her to a forward position. Her rocker didn't walk; it galloped, and she was continually scooting it back in place to keep from running into the porch rail. She was nowhere near the finish line. She didn't look up as Harri squeezed in front of her, careful not to be caught in the stampede, or pinned against the rail, and she took a seat on a settee as far away from Cayce as she could get and still be on the same end of the porch.

Cayce had so much ice cream on her mouth she looked like a milk ad, but she chose to add to it rather than wipe it off.

Harri sat quiet, taking tiny bites of her bland Jell-O, her mouth watering as she watched Cayce shovel in the ice cream. Finally, Harri could stand it no longer. She dropped her empty Jell-O carton on the floor and leapt from the settee.

"Give me that carton. You don't need to eat that whole thing, and I know you will if I don't stop you." Harri reached for it, but Cayce held it away from her.

"Get your own ice cream, Harri. There's a freezer full in there."

"I don't want ice cream. I want you to stop having a temper tantrum and tell me what's up with Cowboy Number One." Harri reached again and was quick enough to grab the carton away from her this time.

"Well, maybe I'll just have a bite." Harri walked back to her seat, digging deep in the carton to reach the ice cream with her small spoon.

She put the whole piled-up spoonful in her mouth quickly before any dropped off the delicate shovel. Cayce, with mouth open under a big scowl, watched her sister in disgust and then jumped out of the rocking chair, allowing it to jerk as it continued rocking, and stormed back inside. In less than a minute, she stomped out carrying another carton of ice cream.

"Red velvet cheesecake with swirls of real whipped cream! And don't even think about snatching this one, Sista, or I'll bite your hand off!" Cayce yelled the last part and clicked her teeth together in a biting gesture.

The sisters sat for a few minutes eating in silence except for the smacking of lips and the oohs and ahs of bingeing in action. Cayce was halfway through the new carton when Hank pulled up at the hitching post. He got out of the truck, laughing at the sight of the two.

After pulling out his handkerchief, he handed it to Cayce, who was still rocking so big she couldn't catch hold of the handkerchief. Hank put his boot under one rocker, stopping her in mid-rock, her body leaning back precariously with her boots dangling above the floor.

"I'll have to admit I like your red velvet lips, but from the looks of the way that carton is going down, you're going to be sick any minute." Hank took the carton and held out his hand for the spoon she held in a death grip.

"Shovel…please!" Hank kept his hand out.

Cayce reluctantly swapped the spoon for the handkerchief Hank offered as a trade. Taking a seat in the rocker next to her, he began eating what was left of the ice cream as she wiped her mouth.

"Let's see now…" Hank spoke with his mouth full. "From the look on your face, not to mention the out-of-control rocker and the fact that you've consumed more than half a carton of ice cream, I'd say you've talked to Joshua." Hank took another bite, keeping his gaze forward.

"Too right, dude!" Harri chirped in with her own

mouth so full the ice cream dribbled down her chin.

"Cayce, let your sister borrow that handkerchief, like a good sister." Hank still did not look at her as he put another big bite in his mouth.

"She can get her own," Cayce snarled at Harri, holding her hand up with pretend claws.

"What? Get my own cowboy?" Harri smarted off without cracking a smile or looking up. "Why can't I just have one of yours, Cayce?" She dug back into the carton after giving her chin a quick wipe with the back of her hand.

Hank almost choked on his bite of ice cream and began a belly-roll laugh.

"So you knew, huh?" Cayce shot daggers at Hank.

"Whoa, now!" Hank held his hand up, still holding the oversized spoon and trying to regain his composure. "I had nothing to do with it. Joshua just told me he had to travel to Mexico. Something about a construction project proposal."

"Yeah, well, he's had a lot of project proposals in the last few months." Cayce left the rocker and stormed into the hotel.

Hank looked at Harri, who just shrugged her shoulders as she continued consuming ice cream. Hank followed Cayce into the kitchen and found her busy washing her mouth and hands at the kitchen sink.

Cayce dried her face and hands on a paper towel and turned when she heard Hank coming through the door. She walked to him, took the ice cream carton and spoon, and returned to the sink, where she dumped the little bit remaining into the disposal and turned it on. She left it going for so long Hank walked beside her and flipped the switch off.

"Taking out your frustrations on the disposal?"

"No!" Cayce huffed, and then turned to face Hank, leaning sideways against the sink with her arms folded. "Maybe!" she added, sounding like she really meant, "What's it to you?"

Hank leaned against the sink beside her. "Well, I used to be partners in a big commercial construction company like Joshua's. When it ceased being fun, I sold my interest and came back to Idaho to ranch and start this small company. Big companies can be time-consuming and stressful, a deadly combination."

"It's not just Joshua. I'm not sure how *I* feel about *him* anymore," Cayce confessed. "He's seemed so distant in the last few months, and…well, I guess I have, too. He asked me to come out here to see if I could figure out what was going on with the paranormal activity, and then he doesn't show up. It's almost like he's afraid to come out here. I think he might be avoiding me, which is not a mature way to act, especially at our age." Cayce noticed Hank had lowered his eyes to the floor. "Did something happen when Joshua was out here?"

Hank stayed quiet for several seconds before responding. "He asked me not to tell you about this, Cayce. I feel like I'm betraying him."

"Please, Hank. I need to know what's going on—if it's me or something else. I'm a big girl. I can take it. Been here before." Cayce pleaded with her eyes.

"Okay. I'll tell you, but you're not going to like it, and maybe you won't believe it, either." Hank drew a breath.

"We didn't have the hotel this far along when Joshua was here, so Joshua set up an air mattress and a lawn chair and table in Absalom's unfinished room in Belle's quarters. You might like to know he had a picture of you on his table. Anyway, one day, he came out and seemed really different, like he had a lot on his mind. I asked him if anything was wrong, and he just shrugged."

"He wouldn't confide in you?"

"No. But he did ask me if I knew what happened to your picture. It had disappeared."

"Disappeared?" Cayce moved to a stool at the counter.

"That's what he said. Anyway, while Joshua was here, Belle was everywhere, kind of following Joshua around, and she wasn't wearing black or a veil. In fact, she pretty much looked and acted like—pardon my language—a whore." Hank took on a guilty look. "I really shouldn't be telling you this, Cayce. I am going to call Joshua when I leave here and tell him I told you, even if it means I might be kicked off the project."

"Don't tell me any more if you think it will jeopardize your job." Cayce was concerned for Hank and all the work he had done to restore Bar None, even in the face of paranormal sabotage. No way did she want his job at risk.

"No, I feel better I'm telling you, for some reason." Hank sat on a stool and faced Cayce.

"Joshua started acting really strange. He isolated himself in Absalom's room and didn't come out for three days. When he did come out, he looked like he had been through hell and back. He told me he had to leave. Said something about being possessed. He told me he wouldn't be back any time soon and gave me *carte blanche* to finish the project. Joshua also made me promise to watch out for you while you're here and not to let you or anyone stay in Belle's quarters. That is the real reason it isn't finished or furnished like the rest of the hotel." Hank opened his hands and shrugged. "That's all I can tell you."

"Basically, you're telling me Joshua fell for a ghost whore, Madam Belle, and Belle might be angry at me since I had a relationship with Joshua. It's pretty farfetched for anyone but me, but I have heard of it happening before." Cayce propped her elbows on the counter and rested her chin in her hands. "It really doesn't matter that much. I'm glad you told me, Hank." She touched Hank's arm, letting her hand linger. "I've known my relationship with Joshua was coming to an end for a while, not all his fault. Harri and I would have come anyway. Joshua will always be a good friend, if nothing more, and Bar None is a historical and paranormal treasure." Cayce left the stool and started toward the door, but then came back to Hank.

"Wait a minute. Joshua told you not to let anyone stay in Belle's quarters, but you and Zach shower there. Isn't that a little risky?" Her face was a combination of a frown and a smile.

"Truth?" Hank got an unusual look on his face.

"You've felt something, haven't you?" Cayce walked closer to Hank to gauge his reaction.

"No." Hank smiled and leaned close to Cayce's face. "But Belle has…if you catch my meaning." He laughed as he headed to the door, but had to sidestep as Harri bounded through holding her empty ice cream carton. Hank glanced back at Cayce, who stood with her hands on her hips and her mouth a flytrap of disbelief and shock.

"I can't believe you made me eat that. I'll have to walk ten miles to get those calories off." Harri headed to the disposal.

"I made you eat it?" Cayce diverted her attention to her sister, but continued to glance back at Hank, who was still smiling.

"Of course you did. I did you a favor by taking that away from you." Harri threw the container into the garbage and rinsed her hands under the faucet. "You can thank me later, after I finish throwing up. Yuck!" Harri hurried out of the kitchen, shaking her hands to dry them.

Cayce walked with Hank toward the porch. "I hope you warned Zach about Belle, since he showers in her quarters, too."

Hank smiled, as if enjoying Cayce's concern with the exploits of the resident prostitute. "I think Belle likes older men." Hank kept his eyes averted. "But you might want to warn Piper in case she's concerned for Zach."

Cayce decided it was time to change the subject. "How far are your horses, Hank? I could use a nice long ride…you know, to put things in proper perspective."

"How about I go load up, and I'll meet you back here in an hour." Hank turned toward the door.

With Hank's quick reaction, it was obvious to Cayce he was pleased, perhaps even excited, by her suggestion. She hoped she was not giving him any ideas. But then…maybe that was exactly what she was doing.

"But before I go, I need to leave something for you three ladies." Hank walked to his truck and brought out a large, heavy box. Cayce held the door open, and Hank took the box inside and placed it on the center table.

"These are wallpaper samples you three need to look at and decide which one should go in the parlor in Belle's living quarters. Joshua's orders." Hank noticed Cayce's frown and decided to rephrase his statement. "Sorry. I meant to say Joshua's request. Actually, you can go ahead and pick out wallpaper for the bedrooms, as well—Belle's room and Sara's. Joshua told me to pick for Absalom's room, but I'd just as soon you ladies pick that, as well." Hank took out his pocketknife and cut the tape loose and folded back the flaps. "I'm not really into flowers."

"Wow! These are beautiful!" Cayce had her head in the box and was pushing aside rolls of wallpaper samples when Harri reentered the room.

Cayce butted heads with Harri as they both began taking out rolls of mostly floral wallpaper, samples looking like they were left over from Victorian mansions.

"What's going on? Did I miss Christmas?" Piper and Zach came through the front door, and Piper immediately headed for her mom and aunt.

"Wallpaper samples for Belle's living quarters." Harri held up a roll covered in tiny blue flowers. "How beautiful!"

"And so authentic-looking!" Cayce brought out several rolls and lined them up on the center table.

Piper stopped at the roll with the tiny blue flowers. She picked the roll up, removed the cellophane, and rolled out a yard or so, staring at it as if mesmerized.

"This was in Sara's room." Piper made the statement matter of fact, never looking up at the others.

"What?" Piper asked as she looked up and noticed

the others staring at her. She rolled the paper back up and handed it to her aunt. "You don't believe me? How about I show you?" Piper headed for the stairs, leaving everyone gawking after her, but no one moved. "Here." Piper flipped through the sketch pad on her way back down the stairs. She laid the open pad down beside the blue-flowered wallpaper, and the whole group gathered around it, staring with mouths open.

The scene Piper had sketched and then colored with art pencils was the tea party with two little girls seated at a child's table, each drinking from a china teacup, pinkies held daintily up and crooked as the perfect little ladies of society. One little girl had long, golden ringlets pulled back from her face by a huge pink bow. The other little girl had her long, dark hair in waist-length pigtails that outlined a thin, pale face with bright blue eyes twinkling with forced happiness. The blonde girl wore a white cotton dress with little pink flowers embroidered on the round collar. The dark-haired girl wore a gown of soft cotton and lace, aqua blue like a reflection of her eyes. The background was a little girl's bedroom with a beautiful tall four-poster bed looking as if it had sprung from the midst of a garden of thousands of tiny blue flowers.

"Oh, my gosh! Are you thinking what I'm thinking?" Harri looked at Cayce.

"Probably so. It's Sara and Teesh on Sara's last day of life." Cayce turned to Piper. "Piper, when did you do this?"

"Actually, it was the last dream I sketched before leaving France. I distinctly remember thinking the little dark-haired girl was ill. She giggled, happy with her friend's visit, but it was a weak giggle." Piper picked up the sketch and looked at it closer. "I remember how tired she looked, but yet so happy. What a pleasant and unselfish child, like she was afraid of hurting her friend's feelings if she got back in bed where she needed to be."

"From what Teesh said, Sara was always more concerned with others than with herself. Thinking of Teesh's feelings would have been just like Sara." Cayce picked up the roll and handed it to Piper.

"It's unanimous." Piper looked at her mom and aunt, who nodded in agreement as Piper handed the roll to Hank. "This one is for Sara's room."

"See if you can figure out the rest of the rooms. I'll call the order in from my truck, and with luck, they'll send it out today. This is a company specializing in authentic reproductions of historical wallpaper. They have warehouses full of it."

"Piper, look at the rest of these samples and see if you have a sense for Belle's room, the parlor, and Absalom's room." Hank took out a felt pen and labeled Sara's roll.

Piper looked at each roll and began separating them as the group watched in awe.

"This with the red roses is definitely for Belle's bedroom." Piper put her finger to her lips as if in deep thought as her eyes darted from roll to roll.

"Yellow daisies is not exact, but is closer than anything in the box." She held the roll up to Hank, who had his Sharpie ready. "Belle's parlor."

"Black-eyed Susans…" Piper hesitated. "No… they're sunflowers. Definitely in Absalom's bedroom." Piper hesitated again. "Because they remind him of what sometimes grew in and around cotton fields in

Mississippi."

Cayce, Harri, and Hank stared at Piper, mouths open.

"I saw it in a dream, but it was an older African-American man, someone from Absalom's past...his father, I think...talking about a picture that once hung in his home. Not here...somewhere in a city. He was explaining how sunflowers attracted insects harmful to cotton plants." Piper paused, putting her finger to her top lip as if thinking. "I even remember what he called the sunflowers—a 'trap crop'—because they trapped insects. I never sketched that dream, but I never had it again. It seemed relatively unimportant compared to the other dreams I was having." Piper handed the roll to Hank and headed up the stairs without any further explanation.

Chapter Twenty-One

Cayce rode beside Hank in silence for the first thirty minutes. Her mind was in a state of confusion, not knowing whether she was distraught or relieved over the fact Joshua had canceled on her again. She missed the good-looking cowboy she had become so intimate with after the adventure in south Mississippi a year ago, but as the reverse side of the old saying goes, *Distance makes the heart go yonder*, and she thought the same thing had happened to Joshua. Now here she was with yet another cowboy, not unusual since she lived in the West, but she had not been attracted to anyone other than Joshua until now. There was something about Hank that felt right, the same kind of right she had felt with Joshua, but different...maybe even better.

Oh, well!

Cayce sighed aloud without realizing it.

There's too much paranormal work to be done to think about romance right now. And like I told Hank, Joshua will always be a good friend, just like Cody is even long after our divorce.

Cayce was jolted out of her thoughts by Hank abruptly stopping his horse and taking her mount by the bridle, forcing it to stop. He dismounted and threw his horse's reins on the ground, then pulled her reins completely out of her hands, and ground-tied her horse also before walking to the other side of her to stand looking up at her.

Cayce looked down at Hank. "What are we doing?"

Hank reached up and motioned Cayce from her saddle with his hands. With her hands on his shoulders and his hands around her waist, she dismounted, looking even more perplexed. Hank hung his hat over her saddle horn, pulled Cayce to him, and kissed her long and hard, knocking her hat off in the process. When he released her, she stood stunned, not moving.

Hank took his hat and put it back on, pulling it down to the customary two-finger-width between eyes and hat. Then he picked up Cayce's hat and placed it on her head, pushing her hair behind her ears like she'd had it before. He let his fingers linger on her cheeks, still saying nothing and staring into her eyes. She returned the stare with her lips still apart from the surprise kiss.

"Now! That's out of the way. Let's enjoy the rest of our ride in these gorgeous mountains and quit dilly-dallying around. In fact, let's enjoy the rest of our stay at Bar None and see where this goes. We're both too old not to take advantage of every feeling and every moment." Hank picked up Cayce effortlessly, set her back in the saddle, and handed her the reins. He then mounted. "Race you to the top!"

Both reached the top of the hill at the same time, but only because Hank slowed for Cayce to catch up with him, in both thoughts and actions.

"Wow! This is spectacular! Almost as pretty as my Beartooth Mountains in Montana." Cayce scanned the panorama of the Sawtooth Mountains before dismounting and taking a seat on a boulder overlooking the valley below.

"Mind if I join you?" Hank sat down on the other side, not waiting for an answer.

"Any more surprises?" Cayce smiled.

"No. At this point, the surprise is over and expectations have set in…I hope." Hank put his arm around Cayce, who leaned against him. "And you don't have to worry about Joshua. I called him when I went to get the horses and told him I was pursuing you."

"And did you get carte blanche for your pursuit as well as for your work on Bar None?" Cayce smiled, eager to hear his answer.

"He said he'd expected it to happen. He knows you too well. He told me to watch after you and not to let you get hurt. Said you were a special lady. He also told me to give you a kiss for him, but I declined. I told him all kisses would be mine and mine alone from now on." To prove his point, Hank kissed her long and thoroughly.

Cayce pulled herself out of the kiss. "You're not married, are you?" She looked at Hank. "With what my daughter went through in the last year, I feel I have to ask."

"No. Divorced for a long time, but not married. Not even any kids to tie me down, unfortunately. Completely unattached and have liked it that way, up until now." Hank pulled her close again. "Is there anything else you're worried about?"

"Just one thing. From now on, you take your showers in the hotel. Belle does not have carte blanche where you're concerned." Cayce gave Hank a serious look and then burst out laughing. "Now, please continue where you were."

And continue he did. Hank kissed her, a longer kiss this time, holding her face against his with his big hands, pressing his lips hard against hers and engulfing her whole mouth. He moved his hands and encircled her with his arms, pulling her tightly to him. Cayce lost her breath in Hank's passionate kiss, but even more importantly, she lost all thoughts of Joshua.

The debacle of her former romance ceased to be a source of distress and confusion.

Chapter Twenty-Two

"The wagon train trip is two days away. Will you be ready, Harri?" Cayce sat at the counter in the kitchen watching Harri trying to make biscuits with a sourdough starter she had gotten from Teesh.

"I just don't know about these sourdough biscuits. I've never had any luck with a starter unless I cheated and got some from someone else, like I did with this I got from Teesh." Harri added more flour to the starter, "feeding" it. She replenished what she'd used from the small crock Teesh had insisted she take.

"I can't believe Piper got that Mormon cookbook for me. I guess that's why I left it and bought Sally's instead. It has the sourdough biscuit recipe I'm trying today. It's almost exactly like Sally's recipe. If it turns out, I'll put it in the Bar None cookbook, giving credit to the original pioneer cook, of course. If it doesn't, then I'm going back to my non-starter sourdough biscuit or maybe my non-starter/non-sourdough biscuit recipe and use the old tried-and-true recipe I use in the Teacake."

"Just make biscuits like you ordinarily do. Harri's Best recipe, or non-starter/non-sourdough biscuits, cannot be beat. Nobody's going to know the difference." Cayce took another bite from the huckleberry scone, Harri's trademark in Bar None.

"Yes, but I'll know. It's okay for now, since I don't

have time to wait for starter to ferment, but Joshua wants it true to the period, and so do I, if it's going in my Bar None cookbook. And we both know Sally made sourdough biscuits for the miners. But I can tell you this—I don't plan on making enough to fill that huge dough bowl. We're judging a biscuit load by my butt, not Sally's. That baby—the dough bowl, not Sally's butt—is going in the Teacake for looks only." Harri nodded toward the dough bowl, now placed on top of a primitive walnut jelly cupboard. Harri frowned as she kneaded the dough again.

"I'm cooking this batch in the oven, but as soon as I get those Dutch ovens I bought from Lester cured, I'll be using them. Maybe your new cowboy will build a campfire for me so I can try them out before we hit the wagon train."

"It's that obvious, huh?" Cayce looked to see Harri's reaction.

"A little. I might have been snoring when you sneaked out of your room last night, but I was awake when I heard you come back to bed. And that giggle I heard followed by that wild 'yes' you thought you whispered when you got into bed told me you didn't go to the kitchen for a glass of milk or a bottle of water. No guess needed as to where you spent part of the night, especially the way you two kept looking at each other over dinner."

Harri rolled out the dough, ready to use her biscuit cutter to make each biscuit as exact in size as possible. "And no need to try to be discreet or pretend to Piper, either. She's already speculating, as if she's not trying to hide her own little bed-hopping excursions in the middle of the night—or day, for that matter."

224

"Are you feeling left out, Harri?" Cayce smiled as she walked behind her sister and put her plate in the dishwasher.

"Do I look like I feel deprived? My day will come, but I'm not ready yet. I'm kind of enjoying the single life God forced me into. What is it they say on Facebook? No longer in a relationship?"

"Don't know. I'm not into Facebook as yet. Piper can probably tell you if you really want to know."

Hank entered the kitchen, but did not go straight for the coffeepot as he usually did. Instead, he walked up behind Cayce, put his arms around her in a bear hug, and planted a big kiss on her cheek. Cayce, a look of surprise on her face, watched Hank as he made his way to the coffeepot.

"What?" Hank smiled. "Like I said, we're too old to dilly-dally." He stopped to give Cayce another quick kiss, this time on the lips, and headed out the kitchen door, coffee mug in hand.

"Mornin', Harri," he called without looking back as he headed through the door.

"Mornin', lover boy." Harri never looked up as she meticulously cut each biscuit.

****

"Cayce, why don't you go down and invite Teesh for dinner? I have beef stew with fried corn on the cob, and Mother's famous chocolate pie with 'm'rang,' as Charlie calls it, for dessert. And I want you to do me another favor and attach this picture to Teesh's bandana and leave a message for Charlie." Harri wiped her hands on her apron and reached for the picture lying on the counter. "I've even decided to invite Steve this time. I feel kind of bad for not inviting him before now,

225

but he doesn't seem to come around much anymore."

"I don't think we've offended Steve. He's just a loner, kind of like Charlie."

Cayce looked at the picture of a rich, dark chocolate pie with two-inch tall meringue, the picture a contribution from Piper's artistic ability.

"If this picture doesn't get Charlie to show up, nothing will." Harri turned back to the stove and took the lid off the huge cast-iron pot to give it two quick stirs with her wooden spoon. This was Cayce's cue to come and stick her nose as close to the stew as possible without singeing her nostrils.

"Hmm! Smells heavenly." Cayce picked up the picture and left. Zach and Piper had just pulled up to the front as she exited.

Cayce walked to Piper's side of the Jeep. "How about you two deliver a message to Teesh for me, and this one to Charlie."

"I already know what's cooking." Piper took the picture from her mom after getting out of the Jeep. "Zach and I will get the bandana from Teesh while delivering the invitation, and we'll tie the picture on the statue for Charlie. We're going for a jog back down the canyon road as soon as we change into running clothes. We can park at Teesh's and start our run there."

A few minutes later, Cayce watched as her daughter and her new boyfriend kicked up dust heading out of Bar None in the Jeep. She hoped Piper was doing the right thing. None of them really knew Zach, but they all liked him on first meeting. Still, she felt Zach was keeping something from Piper. There was a look of guilt in his eyes only a mother—especially one with Extra Sensory Perception where her daughter was concerned—could discern.

Cayce started up the steps to the hotel but turned, looking over at the saloon, where the construction noise had stopped. She smiled and decided to go and check on the progress, meaning the construction boss. For some reason, she had put off investigating the saloon. She had learned to trust her instincts, but now she thought it was time, helped by her newfound relationship with Hank.

Whoosh!

Something hit her hard, knocking her off the top step. She tried to catch herself on the second step, but was hit again, and her fall backward knocked the breath out of her. She lay on the ground, trying to get her breath back, unable to move.

"What the hell?" Hank was just coming out of the saloon and saw Cayce fall. He ran to her and bent down. "Are you all right, Cayce? What happened? Did you lose your footing?" He helped her to a sitting position.

"I…I…don't…know. Something…knocked me off …the steps!" She coughed, trying to get her breath back. "I'm okay, Hank." She tried to stand but sat back down, feeling a little dizzy. Hank lifted her and took her to the porch, where he set her in one of the rockers.

"You say something knocked you off the steps?" Hank looked around but saw nothing. "Was it that damned black fog again?"

"I don't think so. Whatever it was, it was invisible…a force of some kind." She looked past Hank, who squatted down beside her chair, and saw a shadow, there one second and then gone like a puff of air. In that split second, Cayce saw her.

"Belle! It was Belle! I just saw her there, on the porch of the saloon." Cayce pointed. "I'm sure it was her. Who, or what else, could it be? But why is she so angry with me?" Cayce shook her head in disbelief.

"Well, I can believe it. There's been some activity today. A two-by-four flew down the stairs but didn't hit anyone, and one of the workers came running down saying he heard a sound like a swarm of blowflies right at his head. He was sure it was the same fog that caused Will to fall off the roof, but he was too scared to turn around and look. The men couldn't work for the inability to look behind them as they're pounding nails in front of them. I sent the hands back to camp early, with pay, hoping no one will drag up. Finding help in these parts is tough for a normal job."

Cayce rose from her chair. "It's time I went into the saloon. I need to use the Gift to see if I can contact some of these spirits. It's the first step in getting them to settle down."

"Are you sure, Cayce?" Hank walked in front of her down the steps to make sure nothing knocked her down again.

"These are not all nice spirits like our little Sara, but I'm sure, Hank." Cayce stopped on the bottom step, put her hands on Hank's chest, and looked eye-level into his face. "And, Hank, you have to take a step back now. This is who I am and what I do." Cayce gave Hank a quick kiss. "Promise?"

Hank put his fingertips in his pocket and looked at Cayce, her face still next to his, looking like he was not ready for the quick kiss to be over.

"All right. Let's go. I'll try, but that's all I can promise. If I think you're in danger, I *will* protect you."

Hank opened the door to the saloon, and they both stepped inside. Everything was quiet, too quiet, and ominous. Cayce walked around, collecting vibes from the huge, open room while Hank stood at the door watching. Her footsteps echoed off the high ceilings of the expansive saloon.

A long bar against the back wall formed the focal point of the room, and Cayce was glad to see it had not been refinished. The past did not need to be covered up if her senses were to connect. She walked over and ran her hand along the full length of the massive bar, hoping the Way would find her. Then she did the same to the mirror behind the bar. She perched herself on one of the numerous bar stools and stared into the vintage beveled mirror, original to the saloon, according to Hank, and running the full length of the bar behind shelves that would eventually be filled with liquor and glasses for the many guests who would come. The mirror was missing many spots of silver, something adding to the treasured antiquity of the Nugget's decor.

As Cayce stared into one of the dark crevices in the otherwise-shiny reflective surface, she sensed movement. The shadowy cracks undulated like silver and black waves on a shining but turbulent sea as they transformed into boisterous miners still dirty from a long day in the diggings. The drunken men grabbed on to tiny, slant-eyed, smile-plastered figurines who looked like they would crack and disintegrate in the tight embraces of their crude dance partners as they were jerked around the dance floor.

Blackjack dealers, card sharks, and cheats, in striped or black collarless starched shirts, sported slicked back hair and waxed mustaches and competed for the attention, or the money, of the miners at the gambling tables. One he/she thing dressed in baggy men's pants and an oversized, dirty coat, dark hair cropped at the ears and covered by a beat-up man's felt hat, danced alone, her peg leg resounding like a horse's hoof on the wooden dance floor. Every past participant found life again in the silver tapestry behind the bar.

Cayce stared, trancelike, into the mirror, not noticing Hank had moved to the barstool beside her. He sat quietly, as he had promised.

The big, rounded bartender, his dark handlebar mustache out of place against his shiny, hairless head, slid a whiskey bottle down the slick bar top. The bottle passed right through Cayce's hands propped on the bar, but Cayce did not flinch as it passed through. The "it," who Cayce recognized as Peg, grabbed the bottle at the other end, turned it up, and guzzled it, letting some trickle down her ugly scarred chin, not without a chin hair or two. Peg, with her new dance partner the whiskey bottle, headed back to the dance floor.

The swinging doors swung wide open, and two men dressed in black held them there. They stared at the bar crowd from their posts at the door.

The miners grew silent, staring. Many hid their bottles behind them and pushed away from the petite girls as if their intentions had been innocent. The piano player stopped abruptly and moved behind the piano; the moneychangers stepped back from the tables, joining other groups of terrified onlookers; and the bartender slid down behind the bar, his bald head reflecting in the bottom of the mirror. Some miners dove through open windows, and those China figurines that could make it to the stairs fled upward, holding their frilly gowns high in their hands and scurrying like tiny, delicate mice racing to their dens.

Boom! Boom! Boom!

Foot-pounds? Or has the train left its phantom track and is hurtling out of control into The Nugget?

Cayce glued her gaze to the mirror, hypnotized, but without the terror of those living the scene.

They act like they know who or what is coming.

She continued to stare into the pocked mirror.

What can stop time in its…cracks?

Boom! Boom! Boom!

The two men moved farther inside and stretched the doors open as wide as possible as the footfalls stopped at the doors.

The biggest, burliest man Cayce had ever seen filled the doorway. He looked to be at least seven feet tall, with a bulky body to match, topped by a clean-shaven face offset by dark, disturbed eyes.

He thrust his way into The Nugget, his piercing gaze darting right, left, and center, capitalizing on the fear-stricken faces of the onlookers. The man was dressed in black from head to toe and dragged a heavy wooden cross, the upper end resting on his shoulder like Jesus going to Golgotha. Two more men in black marched behind him and then hurried to his side, taking the heavy burden from him and holding it against the wall in the saloon. The cross became a battle flag, the precursor to what was about to ensue. In a voice booming louder than his footsteps, he released his wrath on the roomful of sinners.

"No whoremonger nor unclean person hath any inheritance of God!"

His voice exploded like ignited dynamite cutting

through a mountain. He grabbed a long, black cat-o-nine-tails tucked in his waistband under his coat and swung it, as men and women screamed, covered their heads, and ducked, many stampeding toward back exits.

"'Neither fornicators, nor idolators, nor adulterers, nor thieves, nor covetous, nor drunkards, nor revelers shall inherit the kingdom of God!'"

With each sin announced, the man lashed out with the whip, barely missing many bystanders.

Pop! Pop! Pop!

Again he struck the floor with the whip, each piece of metal on the ends of the nine tails hitting at the same time, and then he turned it on an empty table.

Pop! Pop!

The table and two chairs disintegrated, and the crowd shrank farther away; a few risked passing the giant's helpers and hunkered down, scurrying through the swinging doors still propped open by men in black, who showed no expression as they allowed the miners to escape. The burly giant then turned his attention to the card tables and struck out at them.

Pop! Pop!

Two more tables broke apart, cards and money flying in every direction, but no one made a move to retrieve any of it. The giant stood where one table lay in pieces, his whip and his hands held high as he raised his eyes to heaven as if he were Jesus among the moneychangers in the temple at Jerusalem.

"For the love of money is the root of all evil..." His thunderous bass voice halted in mid-verse as his gaze wandered up the staircase.

Belle, beautiful beyond comparison with any woman in the establishment, was dressed lavishly in a red silk gown; her delicate white skin signified false purity under the bright saloon lights. With her shoulders held proudly back, she teased the supposed man of God with her cleavage.

She stopped midway down the stairs, and her gaze met the intruder's. Her long, dark hair was tousled, loose over one shoulder and hanging across the edge of her right breast. Her flawless face broke into a wide smile, and she tilted her head down, batting her eyelashes as she looked up in flirtation. Her left gloved hand rested on the stair rail, and her right hand hung loosely at her side, hidden in folds of red silk.

"Well, well, Reverend Abel Mather." Belle smiled a deceitful smile as she accentuated the word "Reverend." "What brings you to my establishment? Lusting for the good old days?"

"Watch your mouth, woman," the Reverend bellowed, snapping his whip as if cast as a violent Petruchio in Shakespeare's *Taming of the Shrew*. "Though thou clothest thyself with crimson, though thou deckest thee with ornaments of gold, though thou rentest they face with painting, in vain shalt thou make thyself fair; thy lovers will despise thee; they will seek thy life."

"You were my lover, Abel." Belle took a step down. "Do you despise me now?" She stopped. "Or do you dream of the way it used to be?" Belle droned the word "dream" as she smirked at Abel.

"Get behind me, Satan!" He snapped the whip again and took a step toward the stairs, his dark eyes burning like coals of rage in a firepit of hatred.

"What about your daughter? Was she Satan? Do you yet despise your own flesh even as she lies dead in her grave?"

"I…have…no…daugh…ter!" His face grimaced in anger as he drawled each syllable singularly; his eyes shot rays of loathing up the stairs. "You killed her when you brought her into your world of whoredom, Jezebel."

The madman gave a demonic yell as he took three giant steps toward Belle, his cat-o-nine held high, ready to lash out at the woman. The bartender hurried from behind the bar, ready to run to his boss's defense, but he was pushed back by the crowd parting like the Red Sea, giving the crusader-turned-murderer an open path to the madam.

Belle's smile never waned, and she showed no fear or thought of retreat as she waited for him to come closer. When he was no more than six feet from her, she brought her right hand from its hiding spot in her dress. She released the rail, bringing her left hand up to meet her right gloved hand, which held a Colt .45. With gun steady, she aimed straight at the Reverend's heart and pulled the trigger with no hesitation and no possibility of remorse. Belle's hands shot up with the recoil of the heavy pistol, but her smile broadened as her bullet hit dead center.

The Reverend's body shot backward, but he did not fall; his chest exploded and a dark-red ripple widened over his lapel. His hard eyes betrayed panic as he stared at Belle in disbelief. His whip fell and he placed his hand over his chest, the blood gushing between his fingers, covering his hand. His massive body crumpled to the floor, jarring the saloon like the aftershock of a strong earthquake.

His followers did not run to his side. The swinging

doors hit the walls hard as the other men in black fled through them without looking back at the stilled body of their master.

The clink of glasses hitting against each other cut the silence as the bartender filled the bar with glasses and bottles of the best whiskey.

"Drinks on the house!"

Miners cheered and then herded toward the bar and free drinks. Two miners stepped over the huge, bloody heap, hurrying to reach the bar before the glasses were all claimed. The piano player beat the piano in a festive tune, only giving one quick glance to the blood-soaked body lying in a mound only a few feet from him. At one point, he lifted his feet from the pedals without missing a beat as a river of blood ran under the piano toward the swinging doors, as if it, too, thought an escape was possible.

Belle turned and walked slowly back up the stairs, holding the tail of her red silk dress in her left hand and her Colt .45 in her right as young ladies peeked down from the top of the stairs, their tiny hands covering open mouths. They looked with small, dark, angled eyes from the bloody remains to the delicate madam without uttering a word or a scream.

Chapter Twenty-Three

Billie made it to the top of the wall twice in what seemed no time at all. But instead of climbing a third time, she turned herself around and around like she remembered doing as a child, intentionally making herself dizzy and losing her sense of direction. Putting her hands out, she felt around the walls until she felt a section of the wall not familiar to her. She closed her eyes as if she could add to the darkness, and felt of the rocks as high as she could reach, locating each rock outcropping large enough for a hand or foothold. Once the rock map was ingrained in her mind, she placed her hand and foot on rock ledges remembered, and up she climbed.

When she reached the highest point she had mentally mapped, she began feeling with each hand, locating new outcroppings and climbing higher, repeating this process until her arms grew tired. Slowly, she made her way back down the wall. By the time she reached the bottom, her muscles screamed with fatigue. After finding the table in the center of the room, she got her bearings and made her way to the mattress, where she collapsed in exhaustion.

Billie didn't know how long she slept, but she was awakened by a scratching noise. Her peeping friend was back. She rose onto her knees and put her ear close to the rocks. Soon, the rock was pulled from its hole, and she heard him or her breathing again. Not wanting to frighten the person away, Billie sat quiet and waited.

Thump!

Again, something had been pushed through the hole. Billie felt around beneath the hole and picked up a small, metal tube-like object, a small flashlight, a Maglite. Billie picked up the end of the mattress and shielded the flashlight so she could see if it worked without shining the light out into her cell. With one small twist, a stream of light shot out. Quickly, she turned it off.

Billie lowered her mattress and crawled back toward the hole. She felt for the hole, and after finding it, put her mouth close to it.

"Thank you." Billie whispered. She was surprised when she heard a strange male voice answer in a whisper.

"Welcome."

"What's your name?" Billie decided to see if she could get the voice, a he, to talk to her.

"Charlie." A moment of silence, and then he asked, "You?"

"Billie...my name is Billie." She waited, not wanting to scare him off. "Can you help me get out of here, Charlie? I'm really scared." Billie spoke in a cracked whisper, on the verge of crying, both out of fear and hope, but all she heard was silence.

"Billie? Charlie not know Billie."

Billie thought by the way Charlie talked he was mentally slow, but it didn't matter. He had already helped her with the knife and now the Maglite.

"Get help, Charlie. Please tell someone you trust...a friend. Bring them here."

"Secret." Charlie was talking at the hole from a distance now.

"Please, Charlie. I'm going to have a baby, and I need to live; my baby needs to live." Billie sobbed softly. "I'll die if you don't help." More silence...longer this time and Billie thought Charlie was gone.

"Charlie go."

And just like that, Charlie placed the rock back in the hole and left Billie with her tears, her fears, and darkness.

After weeping for a few minutes, Billie sat up and shook herself out of her self-pity. Reaching under the mattress, she found the small hole she had made in it with the knife Charlie had left her before. She stuffed the Maglite far up inside the mattress next to the knife, making sure to pull the cotton stuffing around the objects and back toward the opening. Then, placing her hand gently on her stomach, she curled into a fetal position.

Be strong; fear not! God will save you! And I'll help. Just show me the way.

Chapter Twenty-Four

Piper and Zach had been running for forty-five minutes, and once their rhythms synchronized, they talked without panting all the way down the winding road. They left the Jeep at Teesh's as planned, after delivering the invitation to her and leaving the picture tied with the bandana around one of the children's necks on the Jesus statue. Piper remarked she hoped Charlie would find it in time for her aunt Harri's fantastic stew, and especially the "Charlie Chocolate Chocolate Pie," as Harri now referred to another of her signature desserts. She'd made the "m'rang" extra thick just for Charlie.

Zach stopped to get a rock out of his shoe. "Your mom and Harri are exceptional people, Piper. I can't get over all those pies Harri baked just so Hank could take them to the crew at their camp."

"You can't get those pies out of your mind, can you?" Piper smiled down at Zach as he retied his shoe.

"I'll have to admit, my stomach is rumbling at the thought of a big slice of Harri's pie, not to mention the stew. It smelled wonderful. But what's with fried corn on the cob? Isn't that taking something healthy and making it unhealthy?" Zach started running again slowly. "Not that I'm going to refuse it, mind you. I haven't tasted anything Harri's cooked yet that wasn't to die for."

Just as they rounded a curve, Piper turned to Zach, her nose held tight with her right hand. "Speaking of 'to die for,' what is that smell?" Piper let go of her nose and pulled her T-shirt up over her nose and mouth.

"Damn! That's bad, isn't it?" Zach followed Piper's example and pulled his shirt over his nose. "Let's move over to the other side of the road. I think the smell is coming from your side."

"Let's run faster and see if we can hurry and get by it." Piper sprinted, almost pushing Zach into the ditch on the other side in an attempt to get away from the odor. "I think we're getting closer, not farther away. Maybe we need to turn around and go back. It's probably a deer carcass, or some kind of road kill." Piper's speech sounded both nasal and smothered. She had her nose and mouth in her T-shirt with her nose pinched shut.

"Well, I think I see where it's coming from. See those buzzards circling over there?" Zach pointed with his free hand to a small hill about a hundred feet from the road.

"That's too far away for road kill. Wonder what it is." Piper stared in the direction of the scavengers, two of which had now landed and were picking at something.

As they got even with the birds, Piper stopped. Her gaze lingered on the spot where the buzzards sat.

"Zach, that looks like clothing. You don't think…"

Zach stared in the direction of the birds and lifted his sunglasses, propping them on his cap with the hand not covering his nose. "I see what you mean. I have to check it out, but if it is a human, he or she is too far gone for us to help now. Stay here. It will be more unbearable up close." Zach took off his T-shirt, stretched it as long as he could get it, and tied it around his nose and mouth. Before he could stop her, Piper had copied his move, leaving herself in her halter sports bra.

"Tie this, Zach; tight, please." Piper turned her back, holding the ends of her T-shirt out for Zach.

"Are you ready? I assume you're going with me." Zach's voice sounded muffled in the T-shirt. Piper nodded her head in agreement, not wanting to risk opening her mouth even under the T-shirt. The two left the road and climbed over boulders to where the buzzards were now on full alert, watching the intruders approach.

When they got within thirty feet of the decomposition, Zach picked up several stones and threw them at the buzzards and all took flight, cursing Zach in vulture profanity. The birds circled overhead, ready to light and finish their feast.

"Holy shit! It's definitely a body, Piper. We better not bother it or go any closer. We have to call the sheriff's office. It looks like the body's been dragged a good piece. See that black boot farther up? And the body has pieces of black leather, maybe a jacket, but it's been torn to shreds, probably from animals." Zach put his arm out to stop her.

"Piper, I don't want you to go any closer. I'm going to circle around the main part where it looks like the animals have really been aggressive and try to get up there where that boot is." He looked at Piper. For once, she seemed to be listening to him.

"Actually, I'm feeling a little nauseated." Piper's eyes watered above her T-shirt mask, and she wiped each eye with the tail of the shirt. "I think I'll go back to the road. Maybe somebody will come by, and I can tell them to call the sheriff's office."

"Good idea. I won't be long, and I'll be careful not to disturb anything."

Zach turned and circled the site, coming up the hill from the main part—or parts—of the body. He did not want Piper to see how anxious he was as he made sure the body was male and not female. His heart pounded into his throat, not from exertion, but from fear.

The boot looked like a man's black lace-up boot, the kind a motorcyclist would wear, but he had to look farther and make sure there was not a female body in the area. When he took a closer look at the boot, he heaved. A decomposing foot filled the boot and was covered in maggots, indicating the flesh had been there for a while. But there was no way he could determine when the person was killed. The body was not decomposed much, but it could have been buried and then dragged from its burial site. Zach needed to know if another body had been buried with the motorcyclist. He hoped and prayed the man was alone in death.

Piper watched Zach disappear over the hill. She wished she could have stayed to help him, but she just could not take the close proximity to the only human remains she had ever seen. Minutes seemed like hours, and she wished Zach would hurry and return. She paced, mostly in circles in the road, and then she spotted a boulder beside the road. She sat on it, pulling her feet up on the rock while holding her shirt even tighter over her nose and mouth and burying her face into her knees.

Come on, somebody! Anybody, except the murderer who did this!

She stretched her neck to see down the road but saw nothing but miles and miles of curved dirt road. Wondering where Zach was, she almost called out to him when she saw something shining on another boulder just to the right of where she sat. Leaving her rock perch, she bent over and picked up the shiny object lying on its side in a small crevice in the rock. A few inches from it, she found another of the same object. Clutching the small items tightly in her right hand, she returned to her perch. She stared at the objects in her right hand.

Buttons. No, not buttons…snaps.

She rolled the snaps over and over in her hand, looking at them closely.

Snaps from a cheap western shirt, the kind Dad hated and never wore. He referred to men who wore western shirts with snaps instead of buttons as drugstore cowboys.

Piper was deep in thought when Zach came over the hill. Before he got close to her, he stopped, pushed his T-shirt down around his neck, and heaved.

"Zach, are you all right?" Piper stood, dropped the snaps, and ran toward Zach.

"No! Stay there, Piper!" Zach was still leaning over. "I'll be okay. Just give me a minute." Piper did as she was told, and in a couple of minutes, Zach walked toward her, wiping his eyes and mouth on the tail of his shirt. Then he pulled the T-shirt mask back around to the front and covered his mouth and nose again.

"I should have gone with you, Zach. It must have been awful." Piper put her arm around his waist.

"The worst thing I've ever seen." Zach wiped his eyes on his shirt again. "It's a guy, looks like a motorcyclist, by the leather jacket and boots. Found bits and pieces of denim, too—blue jeans, I guess. I didn't get close enough to really see the body, or what was left of it, but I found where it had been dug out of a shallow grave and dragged down to where most of the remains are. There was no sign of another body as far as I could see, so I guess he was alone. There were animal tracks all around the gravesite. It looked like whoever buried him placed rocks on top to keep the animals from getting to him. Obviously, it didn't work."

"I wonder how long ago he was killed. I assume he was murdered; he didn't bury himself."

"No way of telling. It's just now beginning to get warm up here, and it can still be below freezing at night. Cold temperature and being buried, even in a shallow grave, would slow decomposition. The authorities will be able to tell, and from the looks of him, there's enough left to get DNA, but probably not fingerprints. Looked like de-gloving has already happened."

"De-gloving?" Piper asked, never having heard the term.

"After a few days, the outer skin sloughs off the hands, and if it's not caught in time, no fingerprints can be deciphered. If you can catch it early, you can soak the skin to soften it, then stretch it over your own hands, over rubber gloves, of course, and take a fingerprint. It's pretty amazing."

"And you know this how?" Piper cocked her head to one side and stared at Zach.

"I watch CSI." Zach said it matter-of-factly, trying to lighten the mood but without success. "Actually, I know someone in forensics with the FBI who works at the Anthropology Research Facility, ARF, or The Body Farm, as it's known. It's part of the University of Tennessee Medical Center. They actually place bodies, cadavers, in an open forested area in East Tennessee and study decomposition under different situations. It hclps law enforcement determine time of death, among other things, about cases involving decomposed bodies."

"Sounds like a disgusting and nasty job." Piper cringed at the thought.

"After seeing this, I have a lot more respect for my friend the forensics expert." Zach turned away from Piper, and she thought he was going to throw up again.

"Man, I'll never get that smell out of my head, even though it's not like I thought it would be. Kind of a sickening, sour/sweet, pungent smell."

"Yep, that pretty much describes it. I know I'm wearing this T-shirt over my face until we can leave here." Piper looked down at her halter bra. "Thank goodness this sports bra is pink. Maybe if someone comes by, they won't realize what I'm wearing, or not wearing."

"I see dust on the road. Maybe we're in luck." Zach moved to the other side of the road. Piper crossed and stood beside him, prepared to flag the driver down.

"Piper, you need to ride up to Teesh's cabin with whoever this is and get the Jeep and go call the sheriff. I'm staying here to watch the site until the authorities get here. I don't want any tampering, and once we tell this person on the road, the word will spread."

A man in an old blue pickup pulled over after seeing Zach waving his hands for him to stop. Piper had put her T-shirt back on just before the man got to them, and now had her hand cupped over her mouth and nose.

The man reached across the seat and rolled his window down on the passenger side.

"Howdy!" He leaned way across the seat and yelled out the window. "Need a ride?"

Piper and Zach both recognized the man at the same time.

"Lester, thank goodness you came along. Remember us from the other day at your antique shop? I'm Piper, and this is Zach." Piper leaned into the truck that smelled old, dirty, and oily, a pleasant reprieve from the smell outside.

"Well, I'll be darned. I sure do. What you two doing way down Difficult Road?"

Zach opened the truck door. "Could you give Piper a ride up to Teesh's cabin, Lester? She can fill you in on what's going on. She needs to get back to Bar None and call the sheriff's office."

Lester gave the two a questioning look. "The ghosts on a rampage or something?" Lester tried to make a joke, but Zach could see concern on his face. "Hop in, young lady. I just happen to be heading to Teesh's anyway. You can tell me what all the hullabaloo is about on the way."

****

When Piper told Lester what she and Zach had discovered, Lester acted stunned.

"Ain't been no murders around these parts in decades. I can't even remember the last one. Must be some of them Hell's Angels or something, some outside no-gooder! Dang it! No telling who'll show up now." Lester gripped the steering wheel tighter. "I guess I'll have to tell Teesh, but I shore do hate to. She'll be real uneasy knowing there's been a murder just down the road, especially knowing it's gonna bring in a bunch of outsiders—news media and all that." Lester shook his head. "They'll be bugging her for information and history, something she only likes to share with friends like your mother and your aunt and you two."

"Maybe she'll come stay with us at Bar None until the sheriff's department can come up with some answers." Piper looked at Lester.

"Ain't likely. Teesh is not afraid of much, and she'd never leave her cabin. Besides, she's a pretty good shot with that old Colt .45 of hers. At least, she used to be."

A few minutes later, Lester pulled up in front of Teesh's cabin. Piper got out and headed for the Jeep. "I need to get to Bar None and call the sheriff on the satellite phone. I'll let you be the bearer of bad news to Teesh."

****

Piper waited with Zach. When the sheriff and his team got to the site, Zach walked with them to show them where the grave had been and then returned to Piper.

"There's nothing else for us to do, Piper. The sheriff said he'd let us know what he finds out. We might as well head back to Bar None and take about a two-hour shower. I don't know about you, but I'm burning these clothes I've got on."

"I promise this will all wash out, with enough bleach shot into the laundry. Besides, I didn't bring another pair of running shoes. As far as washing out memories—especially that smell? Not likely. I think we'll have that forever." Piper sighed.

Piper and Zach bypassed all questions and headed for the showers. Zach did not take the time to go to Belle's quarters but hit the communal showers with Piper. They took their toothbrushes into their shower stalls and scrubbed their teeth while showering as if the pungent smell had sunk into their taste buds. Piper thought her mouth would be raw after the scrubbing she gave it. She also put shampoo up her nostrils, to alleviate the smell that seemed to linger, and then suffered a sneezing attack.

"Thank goodness for coconut-scented shampoo. You want to use it, Zach?"

"Can I come in and get it?" Zach laughed.

"Uh, no! Not with my mom downstairs, thank you very much!" Piper put the lid on tight and handed the shampoo over top of the shower stall to Zach.

"Oh, yeah! Much better. This is one time I don't mind smelling like a woman. It's got to beat the generic, near-nothing smell of my travel shampoo."

Zach finished first and wrapped himself in one of the huge luxury towels provided by the hotel. He waited for Piper and handed her a towel after she shut the shower off. Before she could finish wrapping herself in the towel, Zach joined her in the dressing area of the stall. Taking both towels and placing them on the wooden seat, he grabbed her to him, kissing and caressing her, lingering on his favorite parts.

"I just need one more thing to erase the unpleasantness of this afternoon."

Piper smiled and returned Zach's embrace.

A few minutes later, the two left the showers, each covered in towels and smiles.

Chapter Twenty-Five

"I just can't believe Charlie would pass up my chocolate pie. I wonder what that little guy is up to." Harri had left the table and looked out the window again. "Actually, we haven't seen him since the ordeal with the black fog the other night. You think it was too much for him, Teesh?"

"Oh, don't worry about Charlie. He'll stay gone for days and days sometimes. Don't know where he goes. He likes to wander." Teesh took another bite of the chocolate pie. "This pie is wonderful, Harri. I will need the recipe, but I guess it will be included in your cookbook, right?"

"Oh, yes. Everything you taste while I'm here will be in there." Harri gathered up dishes and headed to the kitchen. Cayce, Piper, and Zach stacked the rest of the dishes and followed Harri, who stopped at the kitchen door.

"I think we're all avoiding talking about something that needs talking about. As soon as we get this table squared away, let's have coffee in the parlor and talk about the body Zach and Piper found."

"You're right, Harri. We'll leave the stew and everything on the stove for Hank. He should be here shortly, and hopefully he will have a report from the sheriff's office. He said he was stopping by there on his way from Idaho Falls." Cayce followed Harri.

Shortly after everyone finished coffee, Hank entered.

"We saved you dinner, Hank. It's on the stove."

"Thanks, but I want to tell you what I found out first." Hank hung his hat on the coat tree at the entrance and took his place on the settee by Cayce. Everyone's eyes focused on him.

"You know the flyers you and Harri got on your way to Bar None, Cayce?"

"You mean the young couple missing from Montana?" Cayce kept her eyes on Hank.

"The sheriff is pretty sure the body belonged to Johnny Stinson, the young man who owned the motorcycle. The pieces of clothing found and the boots all match what he was wearing in the picture the girl texted back to her mother."

"What about the girl, Billie Townsley?" Zach leaned up in his chair, intent on hearing Hank's answer.

Cayce and Harri glanced at each other. Each one knew what the other was thinking.

"The sheriff said they combed the area, and there was no sign of the girl's body or any of her clothing or personal effects."

"So what does he think happened to her, to Billie?" Zach now clasped his hands together tightly, almost in a death grip, unaware that Cayce and Harri were closely watching his reaction.

"The sheriff wouldn't speculate."

Zach turned to Cayce. "Do you still have that flyer you picked up? We all need to look at the picture closely so we can get the girl's picture in our heads. Hopefully, we won't be identifying a body, but the boy's body was awfully close to Bar None. I told the sheriff we would be on the lookout, especially since we're going on the wagon train trip up into the high country day after tomorrow."

"I have the flyer in my suitcase." Harri stood and headed for the stairs. "I'll be right back."

Zach acted nervous, rubbing his hands on his thighs.

"Something wrong, Zach?" Piper put her arm around Zach's waist, giving him a squeeze. "I mean, other than finding Johnny Stinson's body, as if that isn't enough to give us both nightmares the rest of our lives."

"Yep, I'm fine. Just think I need a little fresh air." Zach left the hotel and went out on the front porch. Piper followed him and found him leaning against a porch post, fingertips in pockets, gazing at the moon as it peeked over the mountains. He turned and saw her coming toward him and smiled, opening his arms to her. They stood embracing for a few seconds before Zach lifted Piper's chin and kissed her. They were in the middle of a deep kiss when Cayce opened the screen door.

"Sorry to interrupt, but you two need to come in and etch Billie's picture in your minds."

"Okay. We'll be there in a minute, Mom."

Cayce looked at the two young people and wondered whether Piper had the same question on her mind she and Harri did.

How did Zach know the girl's name was Billie Townsley?

Cayce had purposely not brought up the subject of the girl's disappearance, not wanting to put a damper on her own daughter's visit. She closed the door and rejoined the group.

"No, I know I've never seen her around here, but then, I don't get out much." Teesh passed the picture to Steve, who took his glasses out of his pocket and scrutinized the picture.

"She's a pretty little thing, ain't she, with that long blonde hair? I know I ain't seen her. Would remember her for sure if I had of." Steve passed it to Hank.

"I know these flyers are all over this part of Idaho. I've seen them at every gas station and café around, even in the valley." Hank took another hard look at the girl.

Cayce's shoulders relaxed the tension she hadn't realized was there.

Ah, that could be how Zach knew the girl's name. He ran that errand for Hank the other day and filled the Jeep up at the little gas station where the surly teenage boy works.

Zach and Piper came back into the room, and Hank handed the flyer to Piper, who studied the picture. "Wow! She's so young and beautiful. This says she just graduated high school." She shook her head. "To think, she had her whole life ahead of her, and then this." Piper reached to hand the flyer to Zach.

"Has!" Zach sharply corrected Piper, and then softened his tone. "Think positive, Piper. Billie *has* her whole life ahead of her. Nobody's found a body yet, so we don't need to put any negative energy out there." Zach took the flyer from Piper and took a quick glance and then gave it back to Hank.

Piper eyed Zach. "Negative energy? When did you get so New Age?"

"Me?" Zach pointed to himself. "Oh, no. I'm not New Age. I just like to be positive. If this was my little sister or someone in my family, I'd want everyone thinking positive and looking for a living being, not a corpse." Zach stood. "Can we change this gruesome topic? I'd really like to get this whole scene from today out of my mind before I go to bed tonight."

"I think that's a good idea. I for one am going into the kitchen and cut myself another piece of pie." Piper took off toward the kitchen. "Anyone else want a piece?" She shrugged her shoulders after everyone declined her offer and headed into the kitchen alone.

"There is one more thing I need to show you that the sheriff gave me." Hank reached into his pocket and pulled out a folded piece of notepad. "The sheriff found this stamped on the boy's body, under his shirt, right over his heart. The sheriff had no idea what it meant, and neither do I. It's not a tattoo; at least, it's not permanent. The sheriff said one of the lines was kind of smeared, probably by body fluids." Hank spread the notepad out and showed the group the drawing.

"It looks like a diamond, but the ends are rounded, not pointed." Cayce outlined the shape. "That's definitely a cross in the middle—not just straight lines, but a thick cross with no shading inside the rounded lines, like some of the crosses you see on necklaces."

"What's this at the top of the diamond?" Zach asked. "It looks like an upside-down hook or something."

"I have no idea, and neither did the sheriff. He asked me not to talk about this. He wants the information withheld from the media."

"You think it's some kind of satanic cult responsible for this?"

"No idea, Harri. But I know it would behoove us

all, especially you ladies, to stick close to Bar None, or stay with a group." Hank folded the notepad and put it back into his pocket and then directed his gaze to Zach. "Zach, you're in charge of Piper. Don't let her go running or go away from the hotel to paint or anything, at least not by herself."

"Not a problem!" Zach offered with a big grin.

"Now we can change the subject," Hank announced, but the group fell silent. Piper re-entered with two cups of coffee and handed one to Zach.

"Thanks, babe. Did you leave any pie?" Zach set his coffee down and pulled his shirtsleeve over his hand to wipe off a bit of chocolate Piper had missed on her top lip.

"There's plenty left for Charlie or any of you who wish to indulge in seconds as I did. And I might add it was every bit as delicious as the first piece, but just a tiny bit smaller." Piper held two fingers up to show an inch of smallness.

"Speaking of Charlie, Teesh and Steve, when did you see him last? I'm concerned since he didn't show up for my chocolate pie." Harri looked at Teesh.

"The last time I saw Charlie was the night we ate chocolate gravy. Lester brought me some money today to get Charlie some new boots and some other items, so after I run into town tomorrow, I'll be hanging the bandana up again. He'll show up eventually, looking for any pie left over." Teesh laughed, and did not seem concerned at Charlie's absence.

"I'm trying to think when I seen him last." Steve combed his beard with his hand. "Actually, I seen him day before yesterday…no, it was yesterday morning real early. He come by and traded a little dust for a

Maglite I had. You know…one of them little flashlights? I was gonna put new batteries in it for him, but he didn't give me time. He took it and run off."

"I've never known Charlie to use a flashlight. He says he can see in the dark, you know. I tell him his eyes are like Jezzie's." Teesh chuckled. "He gets a kick out of that. Loves that old cat of mine. They're kindred spirits, those two."

When there was a lull in the group conversation, Hank brought up Cayce's experience in the saloon. She was reluctant to tell of her encounter with the Reverend but wanted to get Teesh's take on it. She began with being pushed down the hotel steps by Belle.

"Mom, you didn't tell me! You don't need to even think about going in that saloon anymore. Belle must not like you." Piper glanced at Hank. "She's probably jealous of you and Hank."

Hank almost choked on his coffee.

"Whoa, now!" Hank wiped his mouth on the back of his hand. "Let's don't go there! I'm just trying to come to grips with what I'm feeling for your mom. I don't need a madam interfering, especially one that's been dead since 1928." Hank put his coffee down and took Cayce's hand. "Go ahead, Cayce. Tell them what happened in the saloon."

Cayce had them all spellbound as she told the rest of her story. She added extra drama as she recounted the Reverend's murder scene, and then hit the group, including Hank, with her own theory.

"I think the black fog is the spirit, or demon, of Reverend Abel Mather, an overzealous frontier preacher who hated Belle because his daughter followed in Belle's footsteps." Cayce tried to gauge everyone's reaction, especially Teesh's.

"Teesh, do you remember Reverend Mather?" Everyone's eyes turned to Teesh.

"No, but I remember my grandparents talking about him. Abel Mather was a hell-fire-and-brimstone preacher, as they called it. Grandpa used to tell me how my daddy would hide his face under Grandpa's suit coat in church he was so scared of the preacher. Grandpa said no one in town liked the man, but there was no other church, so they all endured for a while. I'm not sure how Reverend Mather died. Another church, a Presbyterian, was built, and my family and most of the town folks always went to it."

"I'm sure I could find information about it in your old newspapers, Teesh. Do you mind if I come and have a look tomorrow?"

"Not at all. In fact, you can bring any of them, or all of them you want, here to the hotel and browse to your heart's content. I know you'll take care of them."

"I'll pick them up, if that's all right," Zach offered. "I need to be doing some research for my book on Bar None. I've gotten sidetracked since I've been here." Zach put his arm around Piper and gave her a hug.

After Teesh and Steve left, Hank and Cayce finished cleaning up the kitchen, insisting Harri had done more than enough. Harri did not argue.

"Great! I think I'll turn in early. I'm exhausted from being in the kitchen all day."

"Hank and I are going to the baths when we finish here. I think Piper and Zach are going, too. You sure you don't want to join us?"

"Why? Do you need a chaperone?" Harri gave her sister her most sarcastic smirk. "Goodnight," she called over her shoulder as she headed for the stairs, not giving Cayce time to think of an equally sarcastic answer.

****

Steve walked faster than usual to his cabin. It had been hard sitting there so nonchalant, listening to the talk of the boy's murder. He had to get the word out, and fast. As soon as he entered his cabin, he locked the door behind him, something he rarely did, and made sure the curtains were all pulled tight, even on the back windows, so not even the tiniest movement could show through. He left the lantern low, leaving barely enough light for him to maneuver through the cabin.

At the back corner, he scooted the old battered chest aside just enough to get behind it, where a small door was concealed by camouflaging it like the rough lumber of the cabin walls. Inside the door was a small landing and a set of stairs, also made from rough lumber. He had to scrunch up and duck to go through the tiny door, and once in, he closed the door behind him, bolting it shut. The secretive man turned on a battery-operated lamp located at the top of the stairs before descending the small, steep, narrow stairs, going sideways one step at a time.

The underground room was as big as the cabin upstairs. Its walls and ceiling were covered in thick soundproofing material. Shelves of books lined the walls, and a high-priced computer sat on a table in front of the shelves. Another generator sat beside the table, and he immediately started it up. It made little noise. Without him hitting a switch, a bright ceiling light came on, and the computer made a noise that let him know he was connected to the outside world. Steve wasted no time as he sat in the desk chair typing out his message with the skill and speed of a well-educated man.

****

The moonlight undulated through the wavy old salvaged glass window of the bathhouse, its reflection adding a heavenly amber color to the already romantic waters.

What makes this water medicinal at the moment is the man beside me; he's good for my heart. Can Hank be the one? I guess only time will tell. I thought Joshua might be the one I'd grow old with, but that didn't pan out. 'Pan out'—a good term for what's happening in this old gold town.

As if sharing her thoughts, Hank pulled Cayce to him. With his arms around her, he was oblivious to her daughter and Zach on the other side of the baths in the shadows, probably making out—something he wanted to do but wouldn't.

There'll be plenty of time for that, I hope.

Hank was content to wait, especially since Cayce seemed to share his feelings.

Cayce cuddled close to Hank, feeling totally content. She refused to glance toward her daughter and Zach, but then something strange happened.

First, a harp played dreamy background music to the sound of a lazy, rippling stream, conjuring up a mental scene of clear water cascading over giant rocks with lush green ferns and evergreens forming the backdrop. Then the lights flickered as if someone or something was playing with the switch. The lights grew dimmer and then bright, repeating the process as the music continued to play.

"What's going on?" Piper left the shadows and moved closer to her mother and Hank. Zach trailed behind her, holding her hand.

"The switch is over by the door, or I should say 'switches.' They're side by side and only require the slightest touch to turn the music on and off or to dim the lights and brighten them," Cayce answered as they all turned and looked toward the door.

"So who's operating them?" Just as Piper finished her question, a soft giggle could be heard in the direction they were all looking.

"I guess we know now." Cayce smiled. "Did you all hear what I heard?"

"If you mean that sweet little giggle, I know I heard it." Piper smiled. "Sara, is that you playing with our lights?"

As if in answer to her question, the light grew brighter.

"If it's really you, make the lights dimmer." Once again, in answer to Piper's question, the lights dimmed. She looked at her mother, and Cayce nodded her head, giving Piper the go-ahead to ask questions.

"Is this fun, Sara? Do you like this question-and-answer game? If you want us to ask you some more questions, turn the light brighter."

The lights grew brighter.

"Are you alone, Sara? If you are alone, dim the lights."

The lights stayed the same.

"If someone is with you, dim the lights." Hank asked for the change this time.

The lights dimmed.

"Are the blue bubbles with you, Sara? If they are, turn the lights brighter."

The lights brightened in answer to Piper's question.

Cayce and the others watched, totally captivated by Sara, and felt this game could provide the answers to many questions.

"Sara, do you know you are a spirit, and that you are no longer alive like we are? If you know this, dim the lights."

There was a pause as if Sara was thinking, or did not want to answer, and then the lights dimmed.

"Are there others who are no longer alive who are sometimes with you, other than the blue bubbles? If there are others who are sometimes with you, make the lights brighter."

The lights brightened in answer to the question.

"Does the black fog scare you, Sara? If you are afraid of the black fog, dim the lights."

Sara was quick to respond to the question, but it was a different response. The lights dimmed and brightened several times in rapid succession as if the little girl was frantic to let her new friends know she did not like the black fog, or that the fog was a threat to her.

"Do Charlie and the blue bubbles always protect you from the black fog? Dim the lights if Charlie and the bubbles protect you."

The lights dimmed.

Piper looked at her mom, and as if she had read her mind, Cayce nodded her head "yes" and smiled at her daughter.

"Sara, we know you love the statue of Jesus. If you could pass on and go to Jesus in heaven, would you like that? If you would like to go to Jesus, make the lights brighter."

Once again, the lights brightened and dimmed in rapid succession letting them know she very much wanted to be with Jesus.

"You can go, Sara. Jesus wants you with Him. Is there a reason why you don't go with Jesus?" The lights dimmed slowly as if the little girl was letting Piper know she was sad.

"Are you waiting on someone to go with you?" Cayce asked. "If you are waiting on someone, brighten the lights." The lights brightened.

"I'm going to say some names of people I know you love. When I say the name of the person you're waiting on, dim the lights." Cayce kept her eyes focused on the area where the light switches were and called out names.

"Teesh, or Virginia as you knew her…Absalom… your grandmother Belle…" The lights dimmed but only slightly with the mention of Belle, so Cayce continued. "Your mother, Salina, who you never really knew…Charlie." Immediately, the lights flickered from brighter to dimmer and then repeated the process.

"You love Charlie, don't you, Sara? So you're waiting until Charlie can go with you to be with Jesus? If you're waiting for Charlie, make the lights really bright."

The light filled the bathhouse, making it almost as bright as daylight. The rippling water music stopped and changed. Bach's "Minuet in G" played softly, but with a lighthearted beat. Hank closed his eyes and hugged Cayce tight.

Then came the most unusual and loveliest spectacle the group had ever seen. The couples clung to the sides of the bath as they gazed upward. Blue clouds danced overhead like swirls of full satin and silk gowns worn by the ladies of old, waltzing around a ballroom. In the midst, aqua-blue ribbons attached to a pearly white wisp moved with grace. It was magic!

The group continued to watch in awe as the clouds separated and darted above their heads like a giant mass of blue bubbles blown by angel children. Then the bubbles formed clouds again and danced around their little angel for several more minutes. The music softened as the lights dimmed. The bubbles and Sara faded, disappearing completely, and the group knew Sara had left them.

****

Despite her tiredness, Harri tossed and turned, unable to sleep. Finally, she got up and went to the kitchen for a glass of milk and a little sliver of pie that turned out to be a big sliver of pie. She picked up the Mormon cookbook and became engrossed in it, and after a seizure of yawning, she decided to try bed one more time.

As she put her dishes in the dishwasher, she felt someone's drilling gaze on her back. Reluctant to turn around for fear the Reverend would be looking down at her, she walked to the window, pretending to look out, hoping to catch a reflection in the glass of anyone standing behind her.

As she pulled the curtain back, she saw the figure of a small woman dressed in black standing by the counter. Her face was covered in a black veil. Harri continued to watch, frozen, as Belle came closer to her.

Harri could feel her heart in her throat, and knew she had to turn around before Belle got to her. The madam's eyes burned through the veil, and Harri could feel her anger, or perhaps her envy, because she was alive and Belle was not. The spirit floated like a mist without actually taking a step and was only three feet away now.

Harri jerked herself around, prepared to face Belle and her fury, but the veiled madam had vanished. A heavy piece of paper fluttered down from nowhere and landed on the floor where Belle had stood. The paper was a small lithograph of Belle and an African-American man who looked to be in his early fifties. Harri scrutinized the photo, and even though it had faded with age, she could see what Belle was telling her. Now Harri had to decide whether to show the portrait to Cayce or not.

A door banging upstairs jolted Harri out of her thoughts. She tucked the photograph into her pajama pocket and ran halfway up the stairs. The slamming door came from her end of the hall. Once again Harri's heart pounded, and she wondered whether she should wait for Cayce before going any farther. Then she smelled it—an aroma so strong she had to cover her nose with the tail of her pajama top or risk asphyxiation.

"You won't believe what just happened in the bathhouse, Harri!" Cayce yelled in excitement as she burst through the front door, almost giving Harri a heart attack. Cayce had a towel wrapped around her as she joined her sister on the stairs. She stopped and put her nose in the air and sniffed.

"Good grief!" Cayce pulled the towel over her nose and spoke through it. "I think these flower garden walls have sprung to life. That smell would be nice if it was toned down a notch, like to about nine percent of its present strength." She looked up at Harri. "Is that your perfume? It smells like it. It can't be mine, because I don't have any." Cayce coughed through the towel. "Dadgum! That's caustic!"

"If it is my perfume, then somebody sprayed it like furniture polish!" Harri forgot her fear and put her legs in high gear, rushing to check on the expensive bottle of perfume she had left on her dressing table.

When she burst through her bedroom door with Cayce on her heels, her makeup was strewn all over her dresser, and her perfume bottle was empty. Harri held the bottle up to the light and shook it, but there was not enough in the bottom to even reach the long tube attached to the spray top. She rushed to the window and raised it all the way up, shivering as the cold mountain air rushed around her and through the room. Cayce ran into her adjoining room and came back clad in thick sweats and heavy socks, a stocking cap pulled tight over her wet hair. Cayce threw Harri a hooded sweatshirt, and she immediately put it on over her pajamas.

"I can't believe this!" Harri's jaw tightened as she cinched back her anger. After a big, deep exhale, she asked, "Do you think Sara did this? She's never messed with my stuff in such a destructive manner." She looked around to see if anything else was out of sorts.

"Not Sara. She's been entertaining us in the bathhouse. I'll tell you all about it as soon as I can breathe again." Cayce had her nose covered with her shirtsleeve.

Harri noticed the open wardrobe door. Her little black dress she always brought along "just in case," whatever that meant, was wadded up in the bottom as if a frustrated fat person had held the petite dress up to her plus-size body. It had been taken off the satin hanger Harri always packed just for the dress, and the hanger had been thrown on top of it. One of Harri's expensive Italian stilettos lay on its side on the floor and was sprung apart as if the ghost of Sally, the three-hundred-pound-plus sourdough biscuit maker, had wedged her fat foot into it.

"This is ridiculous! No way sweet little Sara would do this, but who did? It couldn't be Belle. I know her feet are small, and she'd take better care than that of expensive perfume. Besides, Belle just visited me in the kitchen." A loud cackle echoed down the stairs. Harri and Cayce looked at each other.

"Peg!" Cayce and Harri spoke at the same time.

"That explains the one stretched-out high shoe. Peg's other foot *is* a stiletto, heel only." Harri rushed out of her bedroom, gunning for the ghost. Cayce followed on her sister's heels; Harri chasing a ghost was something she didn't dare miss.

"Exactly what do you plan to do when you catch her, Harri, as if you could? She's halfway to the mine by now." Cayce pointed to the front door standing wide open. "Look at the bright side. At least she won't smell like tobacco and whiskey for at least a few days—make that weeks." Cayce began laughing and couldn't stop, standing on the stairs, holding her sides. Harri stormed back up to her room, gathered her makeup, locked it in her suitcase, and shoved the suitcase under the bed.

"I'm not locking this from you, Sara," Harri announced to the empty room. "If you want to play with my stuff, you just let me know. I'll hear you giggle and bring it out for you." When she turned back, Cayce was looking down at her sister's dresser, her mouth wide open.

"Where did this come from? You must have a secret admirer. Maybe it's from Abel Mather." Cayce held up a beautiful gold hand mirror.

"Not funny! Cayce, give me that!" Harri grabbed the mirror from Cayce and moved it from hand to hand, admiring it. "Did you feel how heavy this is? I need two hands to hold it. It looks like gold." Harri eyed it closer, running her fingers over the edge. "I don't believe this!"

"What?" Cayce looked closer at the mirror in her sister's hands.

"Just a minute." Harri opened the middle dresser drawer and pulled out the hairbrush she and Cayce had found in Peg's cabin and put it next to the mirror. "It's a matched set."

Harri turned the mirror over and over in her hands, admiring every detail. The mirror's edge was wrapped in wide ornate patterns of leafy swirls, fleur de lis, and plumes that looked as if they had been plucked from the tail of a royal peacock. Each intricate pattern added delicate detail to the already luxurious item. The fancy edging was attached to a twisted gold rope outlining the silver reflective oval, showing its antiquity, value, and intrigue. All of the ornamentation was of the purest gold, making the large hand mirror worth a fortune.

Harri held the antique mirror with two hands, looking at her reflection. As she looked deep into the pocked silvering, her reflection faded, and another appeared, a beautiful young woman with a smooth face, her dark eyes cisterns of sadness that made Harri instantly melancholy. She placed the mirror face down on the dresser, realizing that Peg, whom she had just lambasted, had presented her with another unique and expensive treasure.

Chapter Twenty-Six

Billie awoke to the sound of the small automatic door being opened and knew she had overslept. Her breakfast had arrived. She took the cardboard tray and set it on the table. Then she sat, folding her hands in prayer like she had been trained to do from the first day. She finally forced herself to eat for the sake of her baby. She waited for the booming voice of the Keeper to begin his daily prayer and sermon about her sinful condition, a distorted and terrifying sound she loathed and dreaded each morning, but today was different. The voice was spoken through a synthesizer, but it was the soft voice of a female. She read the same scripture, but it was without the meanness and wrath of the devil Keeper. When she finished, Billie looked up toward the camera.

"You're not the Keeper. Who are you?"

"No, I'm not the Keeper. But I am of his Fold." The woman hesitated as if realizing she had said too much. "No more talking, please."

"The Fold? What is that, and who is the Keeper?" Billie figured the woman would not answer, and was surprised when she did.

"The Keeper is the good shepherd; the good shepherd giveth his life for the sheep. He knows the sheep, and the sheep know him." She paused for a few seconds. "And other sheep I have, which are not of this fold; them also I must bring, and they shall hear my voice; and there shall be one fold, and one shepherd. John 10." The voice paused for several seconds. "I must go now."

"Wait! Please don't go!" But there was no answer. Billie was alone again. Still, she somehow felt this new voice held compassion where none existed with the Keeper. In her mind, she began to devise a new plan.

Billie reached for her oatmeal, anxious to see if the bitter taste of drugs was there. It contained no bitterness. This was not her day to be examined, and she was secretly glad, not ready for her daring escape attempt. She would get one chance and one chance only, and felt she needed more time to plan and train. Her mattress contained the only aids she would have— the pocketknife and the Maglite.

The woman's voice was the same at lunch and again at dinner, and she was the same one who read scripture and prayed for forgiveness of Billie's sin before turning off the lights that night. Billie risked one more question at dinner, even though the woman had told her she could only read scripture to her and was not allowed to converse.

"When will the Keeper be back? I need to talk to the Keeper. What if I have complications with my baby?" It was a long shot, but with the new plan forming in her mind, Billie decided to risk it. The long seconds of silence following her question made her believe the woman would not answer.

"The Keeper will be gone for a while, but you are in good hands. I can help you. I have helped deliver many babies, even ones who come too early and don't make it into this sinful world. Do not worry." There was a pause before the woman spoke again. "Are you feeling any pain, Billie?"

"Only fluttering, but I don't know what I should be feeling. I'm scared."

"You feel your baby. Do not be afraid. If you yell for me, I will hear you." And with that, the member of the Fold was gone.

Billie took out her Bible and turned to the concordance and looked up the word "fold."

An enclosure for sheep.

Billie then looked up John 10 and read the full chapter to herself.

The Keeper thinks he is a protector of the sheep, whatever that means. His fold must be his followers. I wonder how many followers the Keeper has.

Billie closed the Bible and lay back down on her mattress.

I don't feel like the sheep; I'm not being protected.

Feeling the flutter in her stomach, Billie caressed her baby as she always did. The lights were turned off in her cell, and Billie prepared herself for training.

As she climbed the wall that night, she devised her plan—a bold plan, but one that might just work if she could pull it off before the Keeper came back. When she lay back on her mattress ready to rest after an extra-long training session, she stuck her fingers into the hole under her mattress and moved the knife and the Maglite closer to the hole, ready to be grasped in a hurry.

As she did every night now, she moved her lips, mouthing her words of comfort.

Be strong; fear not! God will save you!

Chapter Twenty-Seven

Piper dreamed again of the gloomy cabin in the burned forest, a repeated dream even though she had sketched and painted it thinking this would prevent its recurrence. But this time, the dream continued and changed scenes without any transition or spooky prelude music like movies used to indicate something horrifying was about to happen. It was her worst nightmare, the one she had not told her mom or Zach about—another situation she had sketched hurriedly after dreaming it, hoping to ward off a repeat.

She was no longer looking at the drab cabin in the burned-out forest but found she was underground, feeling her way along a dark cave or tunnel. She trembled in terror but could not shake herself out of the nightmare. A small beam of light appeared as if lighting her way, intentionally coaxing her down a different path. But after she started down the new tunnel, the light disappeared, leaving her in blackness again. She stopped and closed her eyes tightly, trying to get her eyes adjusted to the dark. When she started walking again, Piper heard a girl moaning just ahead.

She hastened her step, heading toward the sound and walking faster than she should in the dark. She heard the moan again, softer but closer, and hurried forward, barely touching the wall as she moved. The moaning stopped, but the urgency to reach the girl and help her had not.

A few more feet and I'll reach her, whoever she is. I have to help her!

Suddenly, the ground dropped from beneath her! She plummeted, landing with a thud and knocking the breath from her lungs. She landed on something softer than the ground. Pain raced through her body. Piper panted, waiting until she got her breath back, and then felt under her, moving her aching body quickly to the side. It was a body—a small person, a girl, and she lay on her stomach. Piper felt all over the girl's body until she found her hand. She put her own hand around the girl's wrist, feeling for a pulse.

No pulse!

Piper felt for the girl's head and put her ear to her mouth.

She's not breathing!

The girl's body was still pliable, so there might be a chance to save her. Piper needed to turn the girl over and apply CPR. As she turned her over, something fell to the ground. She grasped it, something small. *A Maglite!*

She twisted the end of the flashlight, and it cast a beam of light around the deep hole she and the girl now shared.

Piper screamed; her voice echoed off the rock walls of the tight enclosure, bouncing back into her terror-filled subconscious.

Chapter Twenty-Eight

When Piper came in, her aunt and mom were in the kitchen gathering up what would be needed for the wagon train trip the next day. Piper had been up for hours but had not come downstairs. Her gut, her Gift, told her the horrible nightmare was important, and she had to get it on paper quickly while all the gory details were vivid in her mind, even though she had sketched it quickly once before. This time, the dream had been much clearer, so she added details hidden from her the first time the nightmare occurred. As she had looked at the finished sketch, she knew there was one more detail to add. She closed her eyes, getting the marking in her memory, and had finished the drawing.

"Need any help?" Piper looked around at the work in progress in the kitchen.

"Always. You can tape those boxes and pack these dry goods." Her mom looked past Piper. "Where's Zach?"

"He went with Hank to get the horses. Hank wants to ride up the trail we'll be following tomorrow to make sure the sites are ready for camping." Piper rubbed her hands together and smiled. "I can't wait! This will be so much fun…like the old days at the ranch, huh, Mom?"

"So true, but I don't remember having outhouses all along the way."

"Wow! What a luxury!" Harri drawled in sarcasm.

She stopped and looked at Cayce. "You were serious about that battery-operated hair dryer and curling iron, weren't you?"

Cayce laughed. "Curling iron, yes. Blow dryer, no. But I've got an extra western hat you can borrow."

"Never mind. I'll just wad my hair up under one of your baseball caps and look like Peg. But I'm taking my swimsuit and hitting every hot springs pool we come to. Agreed?"

"Agreed." Cayce held out her hand to Harri, who sealed the deal with a good firm shake. "But I don't think you could look like Peg if you were playing her on Broadway."

"I just hope Hank gets me the extra help he promised for cooking and cleaning up. I'm used to quite a bit of help in the Teacake, you know."

"We'll help. I told you Zach and I both will help." Piper packed the boxes. "About the ride up today, I'm going. How about you, Mom?"

"Yep! You know I'm not going to be left behind. And I'm planning on taking a fly rod and my vintage creel I absolutely love, dear, thoughtful daughter. Maybe we'll bring back some more trout for you to cook, Harri."

"I'm taking my new Winston, too. I've never gotten a chance to use it. Hank says there are some streams full of brookies and cutthroat in the high country. Zach wants to use his vintage Hardy, too."

"I'm taking my gold pan…that is, when we take the wagons up. I'm hoping there's something more lucrative than trout in those mountain streams." Harri rubbed her hands together.

"Fly fishing, panning for gold—it should be fun."

Cayce walked into the pantry and brought out a big bag of flour and a container of shortening. "Why don't you go today, Harri? You can stand one afternoon astride a horse."

"Yeah. Right." Harri bowed her legs and walked slowly to the pantry. "Not on your life, Sista. Actually, Teesh is coming over and we're going through her old newspapers to see if we can find any information about the"—she made the universal gesture for quotation marks—"black fog. I've got us some leftover stew and biscuits ready to heat up, and I'm hoping Charlie will come by and eat pie with us."

"Teesh told you to stop worrying, Harri." Cayce headed back to the pantry. "Boy, you sure did an about-face about the Peeping Tom, or Boo Radley, as you referred to him."

"Yeah. I really like Charlie. He's such a good soul. I feel blessed to know him." Harri took out the vintage Dutch ovens. "Look at these. All cleaned up and cured to perfection. I'm adding my method of curing cast iron to the cookbook."

"I think Charlie has taken a special liking to you and your chocolate factory, Harri," Piper added. "And Sara sure does love him, as well as Teesh."

"Yeah, but Teesh is a little vague about Charlie's family, especially Lester. She changes the subject or gives a partial story every time I ask her about Lester's relationship, or lack of one, with Charlie. And Lester is Charlie's financial guardian. What's up with that?"

"I'm sure Teesh has Charlie's interest at heart. She really loves that little man." Harri picked up a giant bag of marshmallows and threw it to Cayce, who put it in the box and picked up the tape, ready to close the box.

275

"Oh, wait! Before you close that box, I have something very important to add." Harri walked into the parlor, and Piper heard her open the small coat closet, a recent addition by the front door.

"Here you go. An absolute must for camping, if you're taking marshmallows, that is."

"Coat hangers?" Piper asked. "What do we need with coat hangers on a camping trip?"

"I'll show you, dear niece." Harri unwound the twisted wire from around the hook. Cayce smiled.

"Once I get this straightened out, it will be perfect for roasting marshmallows." Harri held her breath and bit her lip in an attempt to get the tough tight wire separated from the hook. She stopped and grabbed the hook to twist it away from the rest of the wire.

"We could just trim green sticks to a point like Dad used to do," Piper offered. "I think it would be easier."

"Boy, this is a lot harder than it used to be. They just don't make coat hangers like they used to." Harri grunted and shook her fingers. "Here, you're a strong rancher woman. You try it."

As soon as Cayce took the coat hanger, she stopped and stared at it. She pulled the other end of the hanger, making it elongated, and twisted the hook downward, inside the shape she had created.

"Look familiar?" As she held the hanger up, Harri stared with her mouth open.

Piper had no clue what was so exciting about a bent hanger and lost interest, going to look out the window. "They're here!" She took off for the parlor as her mom handed the hanger to her aunt, and then they both followed Piper.

Her aunt muttered, "So much for helping."

276

When Piper looked back, her aunt shrugged, holding up the hanger shape, staring at it.

****

Cayce and Piper finished saddling their horses before Hank and Zach got the packhorse loaded.

"You girls didn't waste any time," Zach commented as he saddled his horse.

"It has been months since I've ridden. I can't wait, Zach. I'll always be a cowgirl at heart, even though I might be an urban cowgirl sometimes." Piper mounted her horse and rode it around the yard. Soon, Cayce, Zach, and Hank joined her.

Harri came out on the porch, Teesh following, each with a glass of iced tea in hand.

"Guess you don't know what time you'll be getting back?" Harri asked.

"Nope. Don't wait supper on us, Harri." Cayce looked up to see Zach and Piper loping up the canyon trail. "We'll grab a sandwich when we get back." Cayce kicked her horse and headed after the two.

"I've got my satellite phone, Harri, if you need us for any reason." Hank mounted his horse and headed after Cayce.

****

Harri and Teesh pored over the volumes of old newspapers, having decided to search just the period up to 1928. The stacks of the *Bar None Sentry* rose to a height hiding the two of them.

"I'm not sure we needed every volume of the newspaper, but I know Zach is interested in the town when it was in its heyday. Cayce and I are more interested in it from the beginning of the early twentieth century. Looks like Zach emptied your cellar."

"It's fine, Harri. I haven't had this much interest in the newspaper since the museum came to look."

Harri told Teesh about Cayce and the others having the question game with Sara the night before in the bathhouse and how Sara was terrified of the black fog. Teesh did not think the Reverend Mather had lived during her and Sara's lifetime, and since Belle died in 1928, the Reverend had to have died prior to that time if Cayce's paranormal experience in the saloon was true, and Harri sensed it was.

"Cayce and I have looked the cemetery over, and we never found the grave of Abel Mather. I wonder if he was buried somewhere else."

"I doubt it. More than likely, his tombstone has disintegrated and his grave is no longer marked. That happened to a lot of the graves in the old cemetery."

"Okay, Teesh, you start with the issues from the early nineteen hundreds, and I'll take the first few years the paper was in business."

An hour passed with neither finding anything about the Reverend's death. Harri frequently walked to the window and looked out, hoping to see Charlie making his way toward the hotel. Teesh watched her and smiled.

"Now, you stop worrying about Charlie, Harri. He will be just fine. If the pie is gone, you'll just have to make another one, and I know you will. I believe Charlie has found some really good friends, and you're at the top of his list, Miss Harri of Harri's Chocolate Factory." Teesh chuckled, and Harri smiled as she walked back to the table.

"Now, back to the search for the Reverend Abel Mather." Harri flipped through another volume.

****

I loathe Absalom's lover. A snarl covered Belle's face under her veil as she stared at the two women below. *But Abel Mather makes my teeth gnash. I'll help the lover's sister and the old woman find out about Abel if it will send him to hell faster.*

****

Another hour passed without the two finding anything about the black fog. The historians were in the kitchen eating stew when they heard a loud bang. They both hurried back into the parlor and found one of the volumes had fallen from the table, or had been pushed and lay open on the floor. Harri left it open and put the volume in front of Teesh, who began scanning the page.

"Here it is, Harri! It's the story of the shooting in The Nugget." Teesh pushed the volume over in front of Harri, who read the article aloud from it.

September 12, 1915. The Reverend Abel Mather was shot and killed in The Nugget Saloon after a brief altercation with customers. The Reverend is said to have gone temporarily insane and wielded his whip at several bystanders and then threatened The Nugget's owner, Belle Ezell. Miss Ezell is reported to have pulled a Colt .45 and shot the Reverend dead.

One miner stated, "The preacher done went plum damn crazy and was acting like Satan had holt of him. He was lashing out at ever'body who got 'twixt him and Belle."

The sheriff declared Miss Ezell innocent of any crime since all witnesses supported her claim to self-defense. No trial will be held. A graveside service will be held at the cemetery due to the burning of the Church of the Good Shepherd, Reverend Mather's church. One of the pastor's fold, Hyrum Smith, will officiate. Burial will follow at Bar None Cemetery.

"Well, that's that. Now we know what Cayce saw in the saloon really happened, and I'd say she's right about the Reverend being the black fog. What do you think, Teesh?"

"I'd have to agree. I guess that's why the church was never rebuilt after it mysteriously burned down." Teesh glanced up at the second floor, where Belle was sometimes seen as an apparition. Then she continued. "Thank you, Belle, for showing us this article. Now, if you can show us how to eliminate that nasty black fog, maybe Bar None and you can have some peace. If you want it, that is."

Harri glanced up at where Teesh was looking and thought she saw a shadow move down the hallway. She redirected her attention to Teesh.

"I know the church was never rebuilt. It has always looked just as it looks today, but more churches were established when the town was in its boom time. They all shut down when the town started dying. What few Christians remained held meetings in their homes."

"I wonder why the townspeople let such a man kill their little church. I saw a picture of the log church in an earlier volume, and it was a beautiful little church. Hank says Joshua plans to rebuild it. Do you know the history of the old church, Teesh?"

"Well, I bet we can find it. Let's go back to some of those early newspapers, about 1880." Teesh moved volumes aside. Harri helped when she saw Teesh struggling with the heavy volumes.

"Here we go, Harri. It has to be in this volume. See here? This is the wedding picture of Absalom and Yu in

1878. I think she gave birth a couple of years later. It says here, Absalom had the log church built for his and Yu's wedding. I guess he wanted his new wife to be converted to Christianity. Don't know what she would have been as a Chinese immigrant. Maybe Buddhist?"

"Probably Buddhist. See if her baby girl is listed in the obituaries. Cayce and I couldn't read the headstones where Absalom, Yu, and Tamara are buried."

Teesh went through the rest of the volume and then started in another one. Soon, she tapped Harri on the arm and pointed to the obituary. "Yep, here it is. Tamara Lin Duluth, infant daughter of Mr. and Mrs. Absalom Duluth, died August 2, 1880, and was buried in the Bar None Cemetery."

Harri flipped forward a few more pages and found Yu's obituary. "How tragic! Yu died three months after her daughter. Absalom had it all and lost it all in three months' time."

"Life is never long enough, it seems; although in my case, I think I might be overdue." Teesh chuckled again. "No complaints, mind you."

Harri and Teesh continued to look through the volumes, not sure exactly what they were looking for but driven to continue. Harri closed her eyes and ran her finger down the big stack they had not yet gotten to, and stopped at one near the bottom.

"Let's see if the Way finds me." Harri flipped through the volume, turned a page, and then flipped back.

"Oh, my! This is terrible, Teesh! I feel so bad." Harri continued to scan the article while Teesh waited patiently. Harri looked up with tears in her eyes. You'll have to read it, Teesh. I don't think I can." Harri put the page in front of Teesh, and she read aloud while Harri cried.

December 12, 1918

Cave-In Claims Life of Local Miner

Bar None was hit by tragedy Sunday afternoon when a cave-in occurred in the Duluth Mine, near the Bar None entrance. It was said some of the town's children were playing in the mineshaft without their parents' knowledge just before the tragedy occurred. The cave-in began as a rumble, and two of the children ran out, but two others were trapped by falling rock. The two children who escaped ran for help to the cabin of Peg Leg Annie Coleman. Peg sent the children for more help while she headed into the mineshaft.

Peg cleared enough of the rocks and timbers away for the two trapped children to get free, but another timber began to sway, threatening to trap them all. Peg put her back to the timber and yelled for the children to run to the entrance. Peg, with strength unheard of for a woman, held the timber for several minutes, making sure the children had time to get out, and then was trapped herself when the whole east tunnel collapsed.

Mine owner Absalom Duluth and his partner Belle Ezell expressed sympathy for the town's loss and called Peg a hero. Rescuers attempted to recover her body, but the cave-in was just too big an undertaking. Her body was not recovered. No known next of kin were available for notification.

Harri grew so upset she excused herself for a minute. She went to her room and continued weeping. Part of her sadness was feeling guilty for the way she had made jokes about Peg. Harri spoke out loud in hopes Peg was listening.

"Please forgive me for being so unkind to you, Peg. I had no idea you were a hero, but that shouldn't matter. My parents taught me to be kind to everyone, and I have not been kind to you. Look at what you gave me as an offer of friendship, and I gave you nothing but a tongue lashing for wasting an unimportant bottle of perfume." Harri picked up the mirror. "These beautiful gifts will be part of a monument to you, so you will be remembered not as Peg Leg Annie, but as Annie Coleman, a dear, sweet lady who gave her own life to save two children. I'll see to it your cabin is rebuilt and your beautiful possessions are returned to it."

Harri looked in the mirror and again saw the reflection of the beautiful young woman she had seen before. The woman smiled at her and nodded her head.

****

Hank stopped his group at the first campsite and ground-tied his horse, wrapping the rope to the packhorse on his saddle horn. The rest of the group halted by him.

"Wow! It's beautiful up here. The tourists will love this." Piper walked to the edge of the hill to get a better view of the valley below. "So where do we go from here, Hank?" Piper yelled over her shoulder just as Zach walked up beside her. She moved close as he put his arm around her waist. "Is this not fantastic, Zach?"

"Awesome," Zach said, gazing at her.

Piper looked at him and noticed him staring at her. "Oh, you!" She nudged Zach with her shoulder.

"We're going to follow that razorback along there and make our way halfway up that peak," Hank yelled to Piper, pointing out the direction they were going. "The men were supposed to build another outhouse and campsite there. We plan to make that one by the first night." Hank remounted, and Cayce did the same, pulling her horse up beside Hank.

"You two coming?" Hank called back as he and Cayce rode off.

Piper and Zach mounted up, putting their horses in a lope to catch up to their leader.

"I hope we have a little time at the next campsite. I brought my sketchpad." Piper patted her saddlebag.

"I think Hank is pretty anxious to see if his crew did what they were supposed to do. He's in boss mode. Guess we'll know for sure tomorrow when we bring the wagons up."

"How many wagons are we bringing, Zach?"

"Hank said just two the first trip. When Joshua opens up Bar None to the tourist trade, he wants at least five wagons, always a spare or two in case any break down." Zach pulled his horse to a stop and threw his leg over the saddle horn. Piper stopped beside him.

"As they say in the movies, 'wha'sup?'"

"Nothing other than the fact I can't wait any longer to kiss you. Lean over here, beautiful." And kiss they did, almost falling off their horses, which became antsy with waiting.

It took two hours of hard riding to get to the next campsite, much faster than the wagons would go. Several times, Zach and Piper lingered and then had to gallop to catch up.

"We're almost there. Just over this hill and we should see the campsite. It's right by a creek where we can rest and water the horses. I stopped in town and picked up some sub sandwiches and even put some drinks on ice. Maybe you three will get to wet a fly in the creek."

"You should have told me. Harri and I could have packed a lunch."

"You and your sister have done enough. It was my turn." Hank kicked his horse into a gallop, and the others followed as they sped up the hill to the campsite.

As they topped the hill, Hank quickly handed Cayce the rope to the packhorse and kicked his horse into a dead-out run. When he reached the site, he leapt from his horse, not giving it time to come to a complete stop, threw the reins down, and ran toward the creek.

"What the hell?"

Chapter Twenty-Nine

"It's ruined! The whole damn campsite has been destroyed." Hank picked up an empty gasoline can and threw it as far as he could, frustration obvious. "They even burned the outhouse. Harri won't be happy about that." He took off walking away from the site.

Cayce had to run to catch up with him. When she got to him, he was squatted down on the ground digging in the burned pile.

"The timbers from the outhouse are still a little warm. I'd say this was done in the last couple of days." Hank left the pile and walked around looking at the ground. "Look here, Cayce. Four-wheeler tracks. How the hell did they get four-wheelers in here?" Hank looked off into the distance. "But I guess the way they're making that machinery nowadays, four-wheelers can go anywhere horses can, maybe more."

"So much for the wagon trip tomorrow." Cayce put her arm around Hank's shoulder and gave him a comforting back rub. "What now?"

"I didn't intend for us to go all the way to the last camp, but I've got to see if it's destroyed." Hank stood and looked at Cayce. "You guys better ride back to Bar None. This will be an all-nighter. I've got sleeping bags and emergency gear on the pack horse, but it will get really cold in these mountains come night."

"Ooh! We might need to zip our sleeping bags

together for warmth." Cayce tried to lighten Hank's mood, and the smile he gave her showed it was working.

Piper and Zach dismounted, looking bewildered.

"What happened, Hank?" Zach asked, turning in a complete circle, looking at the destruction.

"I don't know, but I'm going to find out."

Hank told Zach and Piper to go back to the hotel and received the same reaction he had gotten from Cayce.

"Okay, but if we get there and catch the criminals in action, it could prove dangerous. I've got a pistol and a rifle with me. Zach, do you know how to shoot?"

"Hunted all my life. Grew up in the Wasatch Mountains of Utah. I'm a pretty good shot, at least for deer, elk, and moose."

"Wait a minute! Don't underestimate the women in this group. Piper and I both are good shots, thanks to Cody McCallister and life on a Montana ranch."

"You were the next one I was going to ask, sweetheart. Okay, let's head up, but first, we need to call your sister and tell her what we're doing."

****

Charlie made his way through the long mineshaft as speedily as possible, having used his own secret entrance to the mine, the one his dad had shown him. Charlie did not like Peg's entrance.

Charlie not like Peg. Peg scare Charlie.

He couldn't get the sound of Billie's plea for help out of his mind. Charlie tended to dwell on things, but this was worse than normal.

Billie have baby. Charlie help Billie. Charlie help baby. Charlie get bestest friend.

287

Charlie had already wasted time by going all the way through the mineshaft to get Janie, but Lester saw him sneak out behind the trees planted to hide the mine's entrance in the mountain behind the antique shop.

"I told you never to come through the mountain, Charlie!" Lester yelled at Charlie like he always did, but this time Charlie did not run away.

"Charlie need Janie! Charlie need Janie!" The little man screamed back at Lester, coming closer than he'd ever been to the only person alive he hated.

"Well, you won't get Janie. She ain't here and won't be back for days. I wouldn't let you see her no-how. Now get yourself back through that mountain, and don't you ever come here again, or I'll blow up the entrance so you can't get through." Lester picked up a big stick and came toward Charlie with the stick raised in the air. "Scat, boy, before I really lose my temper."

Charlie turned and ran back through the mine like the black fog was chasing after him. His heart was pounding, but he kept running. It took hours to go back through the tunnel, but he kept going. He did not like the entrance he had to go through next, and never used it. Peg was always standing guard. As he approached the boarded opening covered with No Trespassing signs, he molded himself against the mine's wall, slinking toward the entrance as quietly as Jezzie about to pounce on an unsuspecting chipmunk.

"Boo!" Peg screeched into Charlie's ear, causing him to yell and take off as if someone had hit him with a cattle prod. Charlie ran right through the rotting boards, knocking them in every direction, and never looked back as he raced down the road toward the hotel and another friend who might help Billie's baby.

Peg's high-pitched cackle echoed down the canyon behind him.

****

Although she was not hungry, Billie ate her lunch. She was ready to carry out the plan to save herself and her baby. If the plan worked, this would be her last day held captive by the Keeper. That morning, when she closed her eyes and searched the Bible for guidance, she hit on Joshua 1:9.

"Be strong and of good courage; be not afraid, neither be you dismayed; for the Lord your God is with you wherever you go."

Be not afraid; God is with you. Be not afraid; God is with you.

The phrase became another mental chant, a primer for her adrenaline and her faith, and a tranquilizer for her palpitating heart and frayed nerves. She had slept little the night before, anxious to see if the Keeper was still gone, and felt rewarded when she heard the female member of the Fold's synthesized voice that morning and again at lunch.

Billie knew the woman was watching through the camera, but she had learned to be very discreet as she hid the little container of ketchup in her hand, the same thing she had done two times before, sneaking the ketchup off the tray without the watcher seeing her. She hoped the woman would not notice the empty plastic container was not on the tray she had placed on the depository.

Immediately going to her mattress to lie down as the tray was removed from the revolving shelf, she stuck the ketchup under her mattress with the other two containers and curled into a fetal position.

I have to wait until the time is right.

****

It was almost dark when Hank and his group reached the third campsite. He breathed a sigh of relief as he saw the outhouse still standing and the rest of the campsite untouched. He'd figured it, too, would have been destroyed, another act of sabotage, but from the living, not the departed.

"We can camp here in the open, or we can go up a little farther to an old shell of a cabin I found the first day I was up here. It would provide a little more coverage against the cold, and the fireplace to the cabin is still standing." Hank looked at his companions. "Group decision."

"I say go to the old cabin," Piper quickly replied. She already had her down jacket out of her saddlebag. Packing it had been a last-minute emergency order by her mother, a battle Piper fought but was now thankful she had lost.

"Agreed," her mom added.

"Guess the women have decided for us, Hank. I'm good with it," Zach added.

The four mounted their horses and punched them into high gear, anxious to get to the cabin, but when they got within sight of it, Piper came to a sudden stop and leaned up in her saddle, staring. Zach stopped his horse and turned back to see why she had stopped.

"That's it!" Piper pointed.

"That's what, Piper?" Zach looked in the direction Piper was staring.

"The cabin from my dream." Piper moved her leg

and reached into her saddlebag and pulled out her sketchpad. She flipped through the pages and handed the pad to Zach. Soon, they were joined by Hank and her mom.

"What's wrong?" her mother asked.

"Well, I'll be damned! You're right." Zach passed the sketchpad to her mom, who held it where Hank could see it, too.

"It looks exactly like the sketch and the painting, now that I think about it," her mom observed. "The Way has led us here, but why?"

The four slowed their horses as they headed up the path through the blackened section of trees, a path that looked like a scene from a horror movie rather than a pristine mountain wilderness. The thawing berms of dirty snow helped the scene little, adding to its gloom-and-doom image. Piper felt she was being transported back to her nightmare and kept her horse as close to Zach as possible. Zach, as if sensing her uneasiness, reached over and took her hand.

A few minutes later, Hank creaked open the charred door to the cabin. Her mom was right behind him, followed by Piper and Zach.

The roof was partially gone, as were some of the walls in the cabin, but the fireplace appeared solid. A stack of firewood stood to the side of the hearth, and it looked as if someone had built a fire at some point in the last few weeks. A little snow still stood in the dark corners where the roof was intact, letting the cabin's visitors know they were in for a very cold night. Hank took a stick propped against the chimney and spread the ashes left in the fireplace. "Look around and see if you see any kindling to start a fire."

"I think I saw some on what's left of the porch." Zach and Piper headed for the door.

As Hank pushed the ashes, he found a piece of flannel cloth that had not burned.

"Look here, Cayce." Hank lifted the cloth with his stick. "Wonder why someone burned clothing in the fireplace?"

Cayce came to Hank's side and stared at the piece of cloth, about four inches at the widest spot. She surprised Hank by lifting it off the stick and giving it a good shake to remove the ashes. Her eyes widened and she took on a look of astonishment mixed with alarm.

"Red-and-black plaid. I think this is more than a coincidence."

"What do you have there, Mom?" Piper asked, walking up beside her mom and laying down her armload of kindling. Cayce handed the cloth to Piper.

Hank poked around in the ashes again.

"Here's something else." He used his fingers this time and pulled out something small. "It looks like part of a western snap off a shirt." Hank wiped it off on his jeans.

"Let me see." Piper looked fully alert now and took the snap from Hank. "It's just like the two I found on the road where we found Johnny's body." Piper scrutinized it closely. "See here? This little melted wad was plastic that was supposed to look like pearl."

"What snaps, Piper?" Zach placed more kindling on top of Piper's pile. "You didn't show me any snaps you found." Zach looked at the object in Piper's hand.

"I didn't think it was anything, and you started throwing up right after that. Guess I just dropped them and forgot. I bet they're still there." Piper looked at

Cayce. Hank saw the interest and concern on her face.

"I think you're right about the Way finding us, Mom. I want to hear about your experience at that outhouse."

"Let's unload the packhorse and take care of the animals first. And we better get this fire going. It's about to be dark and cold." Hank headed to the door, trailed by Zach. "You can tell us around the fire."

After Hank got the fire going, they all huddled around it, and Cayce related the story of her experience touching the bloodstain at the outhouse in the wilderness.

"I couldn't see the man's face who hit the boy with the tire iron, but I know the shirt showing between his hooded jacket and gloves was plaid like this." Cayce held up the piece of cloth again.

"And I know the snap is like the one I saw at the crime scene." Piper looked at the others. "And I also know I've been to this cabin before…in my dreams."

"Let's see that sketch again, Piper." Zach took the pad and flipped through to find the cabin scene. As he turned through the pages, he stopped on a sketch he had not seen before.

"What's this? Some kind of a church service?" He pointed to a group of people sitting on benches. All had their Bibles open. They were looking up at a big man standing before them with his arms outstretched like he was talking to God. His face was covered in a hood, reminding Piper of the Ku Klux Klan she had studied about in her college American history class. The hood didn't seem to bother the man's congregation.

Zach continued to look at the church scene with Piper. "I don't believe this!"

"What?" Piper leaned closer to see what he was seeing.

"Take a good look at the woman here. Does she look familiar to you?"

Piper took the sketchpad. Her mouth flew open. "It can't be! Is it?"

Hank spoke up. "You two are killing us over here. Care to share?"

"It looks like Janie, Lester's granddaughter from the antique shop. I can only see a little of her side profile, but the hair and the glasses are the same. I'm sure it's her."

"Yep. Me, too," Zach added. "Remember how strange she acted when she saw you, Piper? Are you sure this was a dream? Maybe she saw you there."

"Not possible, Zach. I had this dream and sketched it when I was still in France. This one wasn't scary, so I dismissed it."

"You know, there is something called teleportation." Zach began to explain. "Remember, my background is psychology, but also know I don't believe all the theories and just plain notions some people in the field come up with, including dream teleportation.

"It's the belief a person can actually transport their body to another place during dreaming. For example, say you dream you're at this religious meeting." Zach pointed to the sketch. "And somehow you communicate with Janie, who is physically sitting in the meeting. Janie sees you, whether in her mind or through hallucination. That's about as far as I can go with this possible scenario. I won't ask if it makes sense, because it doesn't make sense to me, but I might become a believer if this pans out like I think it will."

"Well, I must have seen her, but I don't know how she could have seen me. Remember, I told you she looked vaguely familiar?"

"I do remember that, and now we know or think we know maybe she had seen you before…just not in the real sense of the word."

"Janie was not there the day Harri and I stopped, so I can't help you with this one. I've never seen her, or vice versa. Do you recognize any others in the scene?" Cayce moved to sit beside her daughter and looked at the sketch with her. "That is the spookiest-looking preacher I've ever seen, not counting Abel Mathers, alias the black fog."

"No, but then, I didn't recognize Janie until Zach recognized her." Piper looked at the sketchpad again. "The men are all too distorted to tell much about them."

Cayce reached for the sketchpad. "Do you mind if I look through your sketchpad, Piper? There might be something else in here you need to share with us." She flipped through each page and came to Piper's most recent sketch, the one she had just done that morning.

"Whoa! Now this is a nightmare! You better tell us about this one." Her mom handed the sketchpad to Piper, but she didn't look at it. She knew which one it was.

"This was the second time I sketched this dream and the second time I dreamed it, but this time—last night, to be more explicit—the details were more vivid and more horrific. I had been up a while when I came down this morning, re-sketching and adding the new details of the more lucid dream." Piper looked at Zach to see if he was impressed with her psychological terminology.

He smiled. "Let me see that sketch, Piper." As Zach looked at the sketch, his face turned pale. He handed the pad back to Piper and headed to the door, not stopping until he was some distance from the cabin.

Piper followed him. "What's wrong, Zach? And don't say, 'nothing.' Something has been bothering you, and I think it's more than finding Johnny Stinson's body."

Zach turned to face Piper. His eyes glistened, and his face was full of sadness and distress. "Just give me a minute, Piper, and I'll come in and talk to all of you. But I want to be composed when I do."

Chapter Thirty

Harri was about to turn away from the window when she saw Charlie running toward the hotel. Her face brightened as she turned to Teesh and headed to the door. "Charlie's here."

Harri threw the door open with a big smile on her face, but her smile changed quickly as she saw the desperation and fear on Charlie's face. He did not hesitate this time but bombarded his way in through the open door.

"Harri, come! Help Billie!" Charlie took Harri by the hand and tried to drag her to the door.

"Wait, Charlie! You're not making sense." Harri stopped Charlie, who began to jump up and down and shake his hands.

Teesh hurried to his side and hugged him. "It's okay, Charlie. Calm down and tell us what's wrong."

Charlie pulled loose from Teesh and began again. "Harri come! Help Billie and baby! Billie scared!"

Harri looked at Teesh and headed for the flyer that was still in the parlor. She opened it and showed it to Charlie. "Is this Billie, Charlie?" Harri pointed to the girl on the back of the motorcycle.

"Billie got no hair! Billie in dark! Billie scared!"

"But is this Billie, Charlie?"

"Billie!" Charlie pointed to the girl on the bike. "Billie got no hair! Billie scared!"

Harri grabbed her jacket and headed out the door behind Charlie. "Wait, Charlie! We need a flashlight if Billie's in the dark." Harri grabbed a big flashlight out of a kitchen drawer and ran after Charlie. "Where are we going?" Harri yelled to Charlie once she stepped off the porch.

"Peg's mine!" Charlie headed down the road, but turned back and ran up to Harri when she moved too slowly. "Charlie not scared. Help Billie and baby. Harri come! Help Billie!" Again, Charlie grabbed Harri's hand and pulled her toward the entrance to the mine.

"Teesh, hit redial on the satellite phone. It will call Hank back. Then call the sheriff," Harri yelled to Teesh, who stood on the porch wringing her hands and watching as Harri ran after Charlie.

****

The Keeper was careful to drive the speed limit only because of the bloodied tools he was carrying in the back of the now dark green SUV. The email he had received was very alarming, and he knew it was time to move the rescue operation to a new location.

I was careless. I should never have buried the body so close to the mission, but I was afraid of getting caught. My faith was not strong enough in that weak moment.

Not much farther and I'll be able to get off the main highway.

He picked up the satellite phone and dialed. "Is everything all right at the mission?…There's trouble. Be on high alert.…No, I can't tell you any more right now. I will be there in another hour or so."

****

Zach regained his composure but dreaded going

into the cabin. It was confession time, and with the new development, he felt helpless. He was a failure, and he had broken a promise to a person who had been important to him.

Piper turned and looked at Zach when he opened the door. She gave him a smile of reassurance, something he needed from her. He had fallen in love with this green-eyed girl and thought she felt the same about him, but he knew he was about to put their relationship in jeopardy.

Piper patted the bench beside her, and Zach came over and sat. As he rubbed his hands on his thighs, everyone tried to ignore him to make him feel more at ease. Piper slipped her arm through his, sensing he needed support.

"I know I owe you all an explanation, but this is very complicated." Zach turned to face Piper. "It's really hard to tell you, Piper. I'm afraid you'll never trust me again." He turned to face Cayce and Hank. "I guess it's no secret to any of you I've fallen in love with Piper." He looked back at Piper. "I've not been honest with you, Piper. I told you I was unattached, and I was telling the truth, to a degree."

Piper removed her arm from Zach's and gave him a look of disbelief.

"Where is this going, Zach? I'm not liking what I'm hearing." Piper stood and moved to the wall beside the fireplace. "I was feeling so bad for you. I thought perhaps Billie was your little sister and you recognized her from the sketch I did of the dream."

"Let me explain, Piper, but you're not going to like what I tell you." Zach stood. "You sit down. I think this will be easier if I stand."

Piper took Zach's seat on the low bench, pulled her knees up to her chest, and rested her chin in her hands. She did not look at him as he spoke.

"Several months ago, I was in a relationship with a girl. She was a graduate student at BYU." Zach dropped his gaze, focusing on the floor. "Yes, what you're thinking is correct. She was one of my students. I knew it was wrong, but she was beautiful and swept me off my feet, so to speak, and we were both impulsive. From the start, she was a lot more serious about me than I was about her, but we moved in together. I finally realized I didn't care enough about her to stay in the relationship and risk losing my job, so I told her I was moving out. She was pretty upset, but we split under amiable terms."

Zach leaned against the wall. "A month went by, and I didn't see her or talk to her. Then one day, I got a call. She told me she was pregnant with my child. I was shocked. She had told me she was taking birth control when we lived together. At first, I didn't believe her, so she emailed me a copy of her doctor's report. She was eleven weeks, so I knew the baby was mine."

Cayce moved to sit by Piper. She picked up her daughter's hand and held it tightly. Piper did not let go and finally looked up at Zach.

"I went to see her and told her I would take care of her and the baby, and that we could get married. I promised to be a good father and husband, if that was what she wanted." Zach's voice cracked. He cleared his throat and changed his stance while looking at Piper, afraid of her reaction. She met his gaze only briefly, and he felt he had lost her forever.

"She hugged me and told me that was all she

wanted to hear and she would be in touch with me later. I never heard from her again. I went to see her parents, and they told me she had left Utah and was going to have an abortion. I'm Mormon, though not as active as I should be, and I don't believe in abortion unless there's a threat to the mother's health, or the mother was raped, pretty much the stance the church takes. I tried to find her to stop her. I looked everywhere, but it was like she had disappeared off the face of the earth."

"You're obviously not talking about Billie, since your girl was a graduate student." Piper made eye contact with Zach and this time did not turn her gaze away from him.

"No. Her name was Denise Mansfield, the first girl to go missing in this area." Zach redirected his focus to Cayce. "I promise I'm not the kind of man to shirk my responsibilities, Cayce. I took a sabbatical to search for Denise. I've been in touch with my friend in the FBI, and he told me they had indications she might have been kidnapped outside an abortion clinic in Boise, information not released to the news media. A homeless guy in a building across the street from the clinic saw a man watching the clinic through binoculars. The man didn't see the homeless guy. When the man left, he got in a black SUV and followed Denise's car. The clinic was the last place she was seen before she disappeared. Her car has never been found, but the black rig has been spotted in this area."

"So the whole story about researching Bar None was a lie."

"Not totally, Piper. I am researching ghost towns for my book. But I did pick Bar None because it was a remote location in the area where the vehicle was last seen about a month and a half ago, about the time Billie and Johnny disappeared. The FBI believes the missing girls are all somehow connected to this black SUV."

"So how did you recognize Denise in my sketch? Other than Billie and the girl beside her, who looked to have been dead for days, all that was in the pit was another decomposed body."

"I don't want to look at that sketch again, but I need to show you. Can you get it, Piper?"

Piper went to her pack and took out the sketchpad and turned to the gruesome sketch. "Are you sure you want to do this, Zach? You don't have to. I believe your story."

"I need to look at it again…just to be sure."

Piper handed the sketch to Zach and stood beside him as he looked at it.

"Even with the decomposition, the facial features look like Denise, and she had auburn hair, although it was never that short. But the real identifying factor is her hand. Look at her hand, propped against the wall." Zach pointed to the girl's hand. It was becoming skeletal, but some skin was still intact. "Denise was born with her index finger on her left hand half the length it should have been. If you look at your sketch, you'll see it in the drawing."

"I remember sketching that and thought I'd made a mistake. I closed my eyes several times while sketching, and some details almost sketched themselves. Her hand bones are a good example of the power in detail given to me by my Gift."

Zach continued to stare at the sketch. "Oh, my gosh! Look here, at this scar on this girl's head. No, it's not a scar. It's like a brand. Where did we see this?

Hank, look."

Hank left his seat to see what Zach had found. As soon as he looked at the brand, he reached in his pocket and pulled out the small piece of paper with the diagram he had gotten from the sheriff's office. "Yep, it's the same. I bet if we could see the back of the other two girls' heads, we would find the same brand. That monster!" Hank handed the diagram to Cayce, who also compared it to the sketch.

"It's the same. You didn't recognize this when you were sketching this morning, Piper?" Cayce showed the diagram to Piper.

"I've never seen this before. When did you show this to everybody, Hank?"

"Last night when we were all in the hotel lobby."

"Wait a minute. That was when you went in the kitchen for that second piece of pie, Piper. You didn't see this, and we forgot to show it to you." Zach handed the piece of paper back to Hank. "It doesn't matter. We still don't know what it means, but with what we know, the abortion clinic abduction of Denise and possibly the other girls, and the cross in the middle of this peculiar diamond shape, I'd say we've got some extremist religious and/or anti-abortion group we're dealing with. In fact, my FBI buddy mentioned it as a possibility, but he never mentioned any group names."

"Like that book I had to read in high school, *The Scarlet Letter*. These poor girls were branded for their sin." Piper shook her head. "Let's hope the abductor at least had the decency to sedate them before he branded them."

Just as everyone was trying to come to terms with Zach's disclosure, Hank's satellite phone rang. Hank walked outside with the phone, but Zach could hear his voice getting louder and sounding panic-stricken. He burst back through the door and yelled for everyone to saddle up.

Everyone hurried outside and threw their blankets and saddles onto the horses while Hank filled them in on what Teesh had told him on the phone.

"Charlie is leading Harri to Billie somewhere in the mine tunnels. That mine has tunnels running all through the mountain, but there is an entrance not far from here. I just hope we can still get through it. The mine has had a lot of cave-ins in that section, so we have to be careful. There are plenty of flashlights in the saddlebags on the packhorse. Zach, let's get the guns and ammunition, and Cayce and Piper, you find the flashlights. We've got to hurry. Charlie and Harri are in more danger than they know."

Zach held out his hand. "Give me the satellite phone, Hank. I need to call Frank, my FBI friend, and get them involved. I'll catch up with you."

****

Billie felt under her mattress for the hole. Being as discreet as possible, she removed the pocketknife and then the flashlight, putting each one under the edge of the mattress. Next, she took out the ketchup containers already opened. She was lying on her stomach but flipped to her side, her back to the camera. She smeared the ketchup on the front of her paper dress and put some between her legs just in case the woman looked before Billie could grab her. Billie felt strong, her adrenaline at the highest level it had ever been.

Be not afraid; God is with you. Be not afraid; God is with you.

Billie began flailing around on the mattress and groaning as if in severe pain.

"Oh…oh! Something's wrong! Help me!" She grabbed her stomach and bowed up, intentionally letting her gown ride up so the fake blood would show. Then she looked down at her dress and screamed.

"I'm bleeding! Oh, God, I'm bleeding! Please help me!"

The synthesized voice came over the speaker. The woman's voice had panic in it. "What's wrong, Billie? Where do you hurt?"

Billie rolled into a fetal position facing the camera. "Everywhere! I'm bleeding! My baby! Help me! Please!"

"I'll be right there, Billie. You will be all right!"

A few seconds later, Billie heard keys rattling at the door she had never seen opened since being held captive. Billie screamed again, writhing in pretend pain and whimpering as she held her stomach with her knees up. Just under her mattress was the knife with the blade open and ready for her to use if she needed it.

A small lady who looked to be in her forties entered the room and practically ran to Billie on the mattress. She knelt beside the girl, who continued to cry and yell.

The woman peeked under Billie's dress and saw the red on her upper thighs and on her dress. "You're bleeding, Billie! You need to come with me. It looks like you're miscarrying." She stood and held her hand out to Billie. "You have to stand and lean on me. I need to get you to the delivery room before you hemorrhage."

Billie reached for the woman's hand, but pulled her

down onto the mattress. Quickly, before the woman could realize she had been fooled, Billie had flung her over on her stomach and was sitting astride her, holding her hands behind her back. When the woman began to struggle, Billie pulled the knife from under the mattress and held it to her throat.

"Be still and very quiet, or I will cut your throat."

The woman was no match for Billie's strength and did as she was told.

The knife was very sharp, and with quick slices, using only one hand, holding the woman tight against the mattress with the other hand, Billie cut strips of mattress ticking. She tied the woman's hands behind her back, but not before removing the woman's jacket. Billie cut the tail off the woman's skirt and made a tight gag for her mouth. Then she pulled her to her feet and dragged her over to the shower area beneath the camera.

Billie used the other ticking strips to bind the woman's feet together, but not before removing her tennis shoes. These, she slipped on. They were snug, but she knew she could run faster with shoes than barefooted. She then pulled the woman behind the toilet, as close to the back corner as possible, and tied her to the pedestal with long strips of mattress ticking as well as strips of material from her skirt.

Billie grabbed the flashlight from under the mattress and put the woman's jacket on over her paper dress as she headed for the cell door. The woman had left the key in the lock. Billie pushed the door shut and locked it with the key. She stuffed the key chain, which held two keys, into her jacket pocket and ran through the tunnel lit down each side with track lights.

She had no idea where she was going but burst through the big door at the end of the tunnel, only to find she was again in darkness. When she tried to go back through the door, she discovered it had locked behind her. Quickly, she pulled out the keys and tried each one, but neither of them worked.

"Damn! She must have more keys on her that I didn't see!" Billie cursed in a whisper, and then felt guilty knowing God was hearing her. She looked up in the endless dark and said, "Sorry!" Then she began running again.

A tiny bit of light shone in the tunnel, coming from a few spotty, battery-operated lights, the kind that her dad put along their sidewalk that would automatically come on in the dark. She would save the flashlight batteries for the pitch dark she knew she would be in eventually, remembering she could see nothing through the hole Charlie had peeked through.

She stopped for a moment to get her bearings.

My cell would be that way.

She pointed to her left.

That means Charlie was behind the wall just there.

Billie took off running again in the direction she thought Charlie had been, but came to a solid rock wall. She was forced to turn the flashlight on to find another way out. The light was bright, and Billie was thankful to the peeper for his gift. She folded the pocketknife and put it in her right-hand pocket. Luckily, the pocket had a zipper so she could secure it, with no risk of it falling out. Casting the light all around, she saw a small opening a few yards ahead.

There!

Billie ran toward the opening.

Now she was in total darkness. She cast the light up ahead and ran at full speed.

Thank you, Lord, for making me cheer and run track even though I would rather have been sneaking out with Johnny.

Soon Billie came to a juncture and had to stop. Once again, she tried to get her bearings in order to make a decision as to which opening to take. She took the one on the left, but soon came to a dead end. Backtracking, she took the one to the right and found a track of some kind, like a small railroad track.

This is some kind of old mineshaft, probably a gold mine. These tracks were used to haul out ore. If I follow the tracks, eventually I'll reach outside.

Once again, she ran, keeping the light pointed just ahead of her on the track. She was glad for the woman's tennis shoes. The tracks and the loose rocks fallen from the walls and ceiling would have hurt or cut her feet and slowed her down.

Be not afraid; God is with you. Be not afraid; God is with you.

She was panting now but refused to slow down. She had to get out of the tunnel she knew was part of a mineshaft. The flashlight flickered, and Billie gasped as she ran.

Please don't go out on me, batteries! Please!

Billie flashed the light ahead as far as she could see and then turned it off to save the batteries. Just ahead lay a downed timber covered in rocks, and she had to remove some of the rocks to get through.

Billie worked fast and soon made a hole big enough to slip through. The track was no longer in front of her, and she knew the cave-in must have hidden the main tunnel. She was in a side tunnel and slowed some, unsure of her footing. She didn't know how long she had been running, but it seemed an eternity.

And God said, "Let there be light;" and God saw the light that it was good.

Billie repeated the verse from Genesis in her mind, over and over as she ran, but no light appeared. Once again, she took the flashlight out and shined it ahead. Again she ran without the light on, but this time, she was not so lucky. She had not seen the big rock lying to the side, and she tripped over it, taking a nasty spill on her knees and hands.

She knew her knees were cut and bleeding, but she couldn't take the time to whimper.

I'm not a baby; I'm having a baby. Help me, Jesus!

Running blind through the tunnel now more like a cave, she decided not to turn the light on but to trust her instincts and her faith. She dragged her right hand down the tunnel wall and felt outcroppings of rocks like the walls in her cell. She stopped when she felt the wall curve. Then, and only then, did she turn on her Maglite.

Rock outcroppings went as high as she could see on the tunnel walls, and she felt it must be some type of underground opening. It was not closed in like the tunnel but was like Blanchard Caverns in Arkansas, where her mom had taken her when she was a child.

She began to tire and slowed her pace. Her breaths had become rapid, and she felt nauseous breathing in the musty, stale air. She wished she had grabbed the remainder of her ration of water, but there had been no time to think. She only hoped the Keeper would not return to find she had escaped. He probably knew the tunnels, but she was only running on faith and the promise God was with her.

When I get out of here, I'll never miss church, and neither will my child.

She started to turn her flashlight on when she heard something. She stood still and listened. Water dripped somewhere above her, but there was something else.

Voices!

Someone was in the tunnel.

Billie stuck the flashlight in her pocket with the knife and re-zipped it. Then she took off the tennis shoes, tied the strings together, and tied them around her neck where the shoes could dangle behind her and out of her way.

Now let's see if all that rock-climbing training will pay off.

Billie felt for rock ledges and put her hands and feet in place. It was a slow climb, and she could hear the voices getting closer. She put them out of her mind and continued up, knowing she had to be careful and surefooted. Without light, she had to feel her way as high as she dared go, hand over hand, foot over foot, until she sensed her nearness to the top of the cave wall. The voices grew loud, two men talking, and then a light appeared. Fortunately, she had a good hand and foot hold and felt she could hide suspended like a bat until the men passed. She could only hope they were friendly.

"I ain't never been this far in the tunnel before. I don't like it...kind of claustreephobic, or whatever that word is."

"Claustrophobic, you moron! Just keep going. We still have a ways to go to get to the cells and the chapel. The Keeper said he would meet us and the rest of the

Fold there."

"I still don't see how come we couldn't just go the usual route. Don't nobody know nothing about the Fold. The Keeper's too smart for that."

"Obviously not, or we wouldn't be trudging through here like moles. Just keep quiet and walk. I don't like trying to make conversation with a person who talks like he was raised by a pack of wolves…no, make that marmots. Wolves are too smart for you."

"I've heard you talk, and you don't sound no better, Mr. Big Shot, so keep your smart-ellic remarks to yourself."

"The colloquialism is *smart alec*, in reference to Alec Hoag, a notorious criminal from the 1800s. My speech is pretense…for the sake of the lambs and the Fold, and you know it. I am a medical doctor, in case you've forgotten, not a mountain bumpkin. Yours is pure ignorance. Now keep quiet and keep moving. The sooner we're out of here, the better."

"How come the Keeper killed that motorcycle boy? I thought the Fold don't believe in killing. Seems to me killing a boy is same as killing an unborn child."

"Thinking is not your strong suit, Lester, so be quiet and walk."

Tears stung her eyes as she clung to the rocks and heard the men's conversation. Now she knew.

The Keeper killed Johnny because Johnny wanted me to have an abortion. The Keeper must have been there and saw us come out of the clinic. It's the only way he could have known.

Billie thought back to that day and remembered a long, black SUV had pulled out behind them when they left the clinic. She had not noticed it following them, but she had seen it again at the service station where they stopped for gas. She'd thought nothing of it at the time.

Slowly, she climbed back down the wall, hoping she would not have to climb again. Her legs and arms were trembling from holding on so tightly. After removing the tennis shoes from her neck, she quickly put them on, tying them tight. Again she ran, this time in the direction from which the men had come.

****

Harri had a hard time keeping up with Charlie and was amazed at how fast he could move through the darkness of the mine. He was too far ahead, and she couldn't see him in her flashlight beam. They had been running for a long time and getting nowhere, and she wondered whether her little friend was sure of the trail.

This must be the secret place where he goes.

Suddenly, Charlie came running back toward her. He grabbed the flashlight and turned it off and took Harri by the hand, pulling her back in the direction they had come. After only a few feet, Charlie yanked her into a side tunnel and stopped, shoving her close to the wall and pulling her down into a crouching position. He put his hand over her mouth, and Harri knew she needed to be quiet and still. Then she heard voices. Two men were coming up the main tunnel. She saw light and heard mumbling but could not make out what they were saying. As they got closer, she could feel Charlie trembling. The man in the back stumbled and cursed.

"Walk behind me, Lester, before you make us both fall."

Now Harri knew why Charlie was afraid. Teesh had said Charlie did not like Lester even though he was

312

Charlie's financial guardian. Harri thought she recognized the other voice as Steve's, but it sounded different, more polished.

We've trusted the wrong people. So who else will end up as part of this nightmare? Teesh? Hank? Zach?

Harri put it all out of her mind when Charlie tugged at her hand. They were off to the races again. A short time later, Charlie led her into another short side tunnel. Again, he placed his hand over her mouth. She waited beside him and heard him making a soft scratching noise. A small circle of light shot through a hole in the tunnel wall. Charlie had his eye to the hole, and then moved back and pushed Harri toward the hole. Harri could see movement in the lighted room and heard a man's booming voice. She moved her ear to the hole so she could hear what they were saying.

"Billie escaped. I don't know how she came up with a knife, but she did. I sent Janie to the infirmary to settle down. She's an emotional wreck and a liability."

"Don't you go gettin' no ideas about doing harm to Janie like you done to that boy! She's a good member of the Fold and helped you and the doc here save a lot of lambs. She was a lamb herself, you know, and she's my granddaughter. And don't you forget it!" Lester sounded angry.

"No one is going to harm Janie, Lester, so be quiet! We need to find the girl before she gets out. Are you sure you didn't see her in the tunnel? I don't know how you could have missed her."

"No. She was not in the tunnel." Steve was speaking, but not like the Steve they all knew. Harri put her eye to the hole again to make sure it was Steve.

"Perhaps she was hiding in one of the offshoot

dead ends. We didn't know we needed to be looking for an escapee."

"Let's get going. I'm going to get the electric eye lights to the pit ready. If she gets close to the entrance, she'll fall right in like the others. It's our last chance to stop her."

"Others? Wait a minute, Keeper. I don't know nothin' 'bout no pit. I ain't helpin' harm no girl!" Lester was yelling and backing up with his hands raised.

Harri could now see one of the men, a very big man, but he had a mask on.

He must be my age or older, and he thinks he's the Lone Ranger.

Lester looked from the Keeper to the other man. Harri had to restrain a gasp when she saw a fist come up and strike the old man hard, knocking him down. A man with white hair and beard bent over Lester and hit him again, knocking him out this time.

Steve!

Harri knew they had to act fast. She reached for Charlie and pulled him out of the offshoot, as the man who called himself the Keeper had referred to it. When they were far enough away not to be heard, Harri stopped Charlie and whispered in his ear.

"Where's the pit, Charlie?"

"Charlie not like pit!" Charlie was speaking too loudly, and Harri covered his mouth, holding her hand tight.

"Charlie not like pit!" Charlie repeated in a whisper.

"We have to go to the pit, Charlie, to save Billie and the baby." Harri whispered, taking Charlie's arm.

"Take me there, Charlie. Please! We have to hurry to save Billie."

"Billie scared! Charlie run like wind." Charlie began running again, holding Harri's hand.

Harri ran with her eyes closed, as if she could make it any darker or less scary, and prayed she wouldn't trip. She could not risk turning on the light; the Keeper and Steve would be coming behind them soon. Charlie took her so fast she felt like a kite on a string, and Charlie was controlling the string.

Chapter Thirty-One

Hank led the group into the mine entrance. "Be careful, and watch your footing! Try not to touch any of these old timbers. This ancient shaft has seen better days." Hank shined his flashlight ahead and noticed some of the timbers swaying as if ready to fall at any minute.

"I think Piper and Cayce should go back, Hank. This is too dangerous. If the mine caves in, no one will be able to find us."

"I'm in for the duration, Zach, and I know Mom is, too. Are you getting any feelings, Mom?"

"Just cold and damp and an adrenaline rush—same as all of you—and you're right, Piper. I'm in for the long haul. Besides, the horses are outside. Someone will find them eventually, and Teesh knows where we are, and probably Bill and the sheriff, too, by now." Cayce walked fast, but glanced at her daughter to try to get a sense of what she was feeling. "What about you, Piper? Any feelings?"

"Yes. Extreme panic, but I don't know if it's mine, Billie's, or…" She glanced at Zach and paused. "The others'." She moved up beside Zach and took his hand. He smiled at her and squeezed her hand.

Hank stopped and listened.

"What is it, Hank?" Cayce moved to stand beside him.

"Just the creaking of these old timbers." In just seconds, he started again, this time jogging.

****

Charlie moved faster, and Harri panted, trying to catch up. Finally, she stopped, bent over, and rested her hands on her knees.

"Let me…catch…my breath…Charlie," she was whispering through her huffs. Charlie must have realized she was not behind him and backtracked.

He squatted down beside her, reached over, and touched her hand.

"Harri okay?" he asked in the sweetest deep whisper she had ever heard.

"Yes…just out of shape." She stood and touched his arm. "Let's go, but a little slower, please."

****

Billie was running for her life, their life, and her adrenaline kicked in again. She ran like a blind person, like Grammar, without the aid of a cane or time to pick her footing, and afraid to risk the flashlight. Just when she thought her heart would explode, she saw a glimmer of light, a glimmer of hope, and knew she must be getting close to the mine's entrance. She hoped and prayed she would not run into any other members of the Fold, especially not the Keeper himself. The light was faint, not enough for her to see her path, but enough to make her go faster as she headed toward it.

And God said, "Let there be light; and God saw the light that it was good."

The light ahead flickered before going out, but she ran on. Then, the ground dropped from beneath her; her body hurtled through open space, out of control. There was only enough time for one quick scream before she hit bottom, landing on her side.

Excruciating pain shot through her. She wanted her flashlight, but it was hard to move. Finally, she rolled over onto her stomach and willed herself to get to her knees, but she could not pull her legs under her. Her head hurt, and so did the rest of her body. She found it difficult to breathe. When her breath did return, she used her right hand, the only one she could feel, and felt of her stomach. Her baby fluttered, letting her know she or he was still alive. It was then Billie noticed an unbearable stench. She covered her nose and mouth with her right hand and lay a few minutes deciding what to do.

She moved her hand from her face and took short breaths, trying not to take in any more of the smell than she had to, and stretched out her right arm. She felt around and stopped when she touched something partially beneath her, the something that had cushioned her fall. It was hard, but she could also feel something soft like clothing. Having no other choice, she pulled out the Maglite. She had to know where she was and what her options were, assuming there were any, and she had to know if what she had felt beneath and beside her was what she feared it was.

The Maglite gave several weak flickers before dying, but in the quick spurts of light, she saw the most horrific sight of her eighteen years. Deep-socketed eyes set in drying, dark flesh stared at her as if still begging for help, and Billie knew she had found Lisa. She gasped, and her own eyes rolled back in her head as darkness and loss of hope engulfed her.

****

As Harri followed Charlie, he led her around a

curve that seemed to be taking them back in the opposite direction.

This must be a side tunnel. I hope Charlie knows where we're going.

Harri heard cracking and popping and realized the old timbers in the mine were not sturdy in this section. She hoped they would not need to be rescued—or worse, recovered. She trembled and then put her fears out of her mind, ready to concentrate on the young girl, Billie. Charlie slowed, and Harri felt many loose rocks in their path, fallen from the walls of the tunnel.

Soon, she saw a faint light up ahead. Charlie slowed to a creep and put his arms out as if to prevent Harri from running past him, something highly unlikely as she breathed deeply, recovering from Charlie's speed.

If I get out of here, I'm starting a whole new fitness regime, a tougher one than I did before. I will get back in shape like I was a year ago…or maybe more fit! No more chocolate pie and brownies for you, Harri. Well, maybe just a little piece of pie every once in a while.

Charlie stopped and reached for Harri's flashlight. She knew the light was for her benefit; Charlie could see like Jezzie with his cat eyes.

He turned the flashlight on and shined it at the ground in front of him, and Harri saw a hole four or five feet in diameter just in front of them. Charlie seemed reluctant to move to the side of the hole, so Harri took the flashlight from his hand and moved to the edge, being careful not to get too close.

"The pit," she whispered, and Charlie moved carefully to her side, still refusing to look into the hole. Harri turned the beam downward—and wanted to scream, but restrained herself. At the bottom of the deep pit, she could see two bodies—one that was partly skeletal, and the other that looked much fresher, in an early process of decomposition. But what Harri was most intent on was the body lying partially on top of the others. She thought she heard a sound, a soft moan.

"Billie! Billie!" Harri called.

Charlie looked in the hole now and called down. "Billie! Charlie bring friend!"

Slowly, the girl lifted her head and followed the beam of light upward.

"Help…me!" She begged in a soft, weak voice, and then closed her eyes again.

Before Harri had time to figure out how to get to Billie, she heard voices in the tunnel behind them. There was nowhere to run. The hole consumed the passageway. The only way out was back through the tunnel.

"Charlie, you have to get help!" she whispered. "Can you jump across the pit?"

Harri could see Charlie nodding his head. Charlie pushed Harri gently to the side and backed up several feet. Then he took off in a sprint. Harri held the beam where he could see better, or so she could see if he made it.

Harri could not believe how fast the little man's legs moved. When he reached the pit, he never faltered as he sailed across the opening like a wild buck jumping a fence. Harri held her breath until Charlie cleared the hole, landing on the other side with a foot or two to spare.

"Run, Charlie! Run!" Harri whispered as loud as she dared, and run he did. Harri's heart was racing, and she turned her flashlight off. She headed back through the tunnel to find an indentation where she might hide, but knew it was a long shot. She held tight to the big, heavy, metal flashlight, her only possible weapon. The voices were close, and her only choice now was to melt herself against the tunnel wall and wait.

I may go down, but I'm taking at least one of them with me with this big flashlight…if I can reach the top of those big monsters, that is.

****

Charlie heard voices ahead, but he did not stop. He hoped the bad people were behind him. But regardless, he had to get to the tunnel entrance he knew was close to the summer cabin where he and his dad had lived until his dad died. The cabin had burned a few years ago when lightning struck a tree nearby, and Charlie only visited the cabin now, living full time up the valley from Bar None in the old log winter cabin his dad had built before Charlie was born.

As Charlie got closer to the voices, he recognized them as more of his friends. His legs moved faster, and he began to call.

"Zach! Hank! Billie need help!"

All four friends heard Charlie's voice at the same time. Hank and Zach left Cayce and Piper behind as they sprinted in the direction of Charlie's panic-filled voice.

"Harri and Billie need help!" Charlie yelled as he took off running back the way he'd come.

Chapter Thirty-Two

A large helicopter landed in front of the hotel, kicking up so much dust Teesh had to hurry inside and shut the door. Before the propellers had stopped, several cars pulled up, filled with law enforcement agents. Teesh stepped back out but had to shield her eyes from the glaring lights of the helicopter. She motioned for the sheriff and one of his deputies to come inside. Soon, two FBI agents in full SWAT gear entered also.

The sheriff had a map spread out on the table by the time the FBI got inside.

"This is a map of the Duluth mine. I grabbed it out of the archives, knowing we'd need it. That old mine is extremely dangerous, more so the farther in you get, and any of the timbers could go at any time."

The FBI team began studying the map. Soon, four more agents joined them, including the helicopter pilot. The head agent pointed to different entrances to the mine and directed teams to different locations.

"Tell me what my deputies and I can do to help."

Once informed, the sheriff ordered his deputies to the entrance behind the antique shop and to another entry farther back in the mountain, accessible by a logging road. The FBI divvied up the entrances in the wilderness areas, and two of them headed toward Peg's entrance. In just minutes, the helicopter took off again.

Teesh watched it all in the darkness that had fallen and hoped everything would be all right and the girl Billie would be found alive and safe. She also prayed Charlie and Harri would not be harmed. She felt guilty for not having told what she knew about Janie and Lester and hoped it would not have been helpful information that could have prevented some of this. Knowing it was now just a matter of time before she would have to disclose the whole story, she went back inside and got her big black purse off the sofa. She reached inside and pulled out a very old journal, took it to the table, and began reading it after she had prayed silently for her friends.

****

Harri held her breath. The voices were close. She had the element of surprise on her side and could at least knock out one of her opponents. Deep down, though, she knew she was no match for the two big men, one of whom was Steve.

My first impression of him was right on. I should have trusted my instincts. I hope he's in the front so I can get in one good lick on him.

Harri stood still, her weapon held high, ready to hit whoever came first. She'd aim as close to between the eyes as possible. Then out of nowhere, a thick, black shadow covered her like a black drape, pinning Harri against the black tunnel wall and camouflaging her from the beam of the men's flashlight. The drape smelled of tobacco and whiskey, and an overwhelming scent of expensive perfume. Harri thought this was definitely not the Reverend Abel Mather. She listened as the two men passed right by without seeing her.

Only when the men were out of sight and hearing

did the shadow move. Harri turned her flashlight on and shined it back down the tunnel, away from the Keeper and Steve. The shadow moved in front of her beam and headed around the corner.

Harri chose to follow the shadow rather than the men, feeling it a better option—especially since the shadow had saved her from capture. She kept the light on low beam and close to the ground and continued back through the tunnel. The timbers creaked and groaned, causing her to pick up her pace.

When she reached a juncture and did not know which tunnel to take, the shadow appeared briefly, and Harri obediently followed. She heard a sound up ahead, like scurrying, and wondered whether a bear or a cougar had found its way into the tunnel.

So which do I prefer? Being brutalized by the Keeper and Steve? Falling into the pit to decompose with the others? Or being eaten by a bear?

Her mental images were interrupted by the appearance of two men—or were they monsters?—moving fast in her direction. Too late she realized they had long guns aimed at her.

Harri started to scream, but something moved toward the men. Her friendly neighborhood shadow knocked the guns out of their hands.

"What the hell?" the leader yelled.

"Stop! FBI!" The man had pulled his handgun from his side holster.

"No! Don't shoot! My name is Harriet Wellington, and I come in peace!"

I come in peace? I sound like I'm addressing aliens. I'll take the Keeper over aliens any day...I think.

Harri dropped her flashlight and held up her hands.

The two agents ran to her. "Are you Harri?"

"Yes. My friend Charlie is up ahead, trying to get help. There's a young lady trapped in a deep pit in the tunnel, and two very bad guys are heading toward her."

"Keep going straight ahead. You'll come to the entrance. Other agents will be waiting for you there." The agent picked up the flashlight and handed it to Harri as they gathered the assault weapons that had been mysteriously knocked out of their hands. Then the two took off toward the pit.

Harri felt some relief, but she would not feel totally at ease until she saw Charlie and Billie safely outside the pit and the tunnel. She also hoped the agents kicked some serious butt when they reached the Keeper and Steve.

Harri saw the shadow a couple more times and smiled, knowing the shadow had made the men drop their weapons. It seemed to be protecting her.

She reached the cellblock first. A wide, heavy door had been propped open, and she could see a lighted room full of people up ahead. She hoped the men she'd met had a radio and had told these agents she "came in peace."

Before she went through the doors, she looked behind her. The shadow was gone, but just down the tunnel she heard a female laugh, a familiar cackle that was not mean-spirited.

"Thank you, Peg!" Harri whispered. "Remember, if you want some fashion advice, come see me at the hotel before I leave. Our little secret." Peg gave her biggest laugh, showed herself for a second, and limped off down the tunnel.

****

Charlie led Hank and the others straight to the pit. Hank shined his flashlight down and saw Billie, but the girl was still.

Piper was first to join him. "She's alive, Hank. I know she's alive. Get me down to her, and I'll give her CPR. It's what I'm supposed to do!" Piper looked to her mom for support.

"As much as I hate to see my daughter in that pit, I think she's right. Piper is trained in CPR, and she was shown."

"I'll go with you, Piper."

"No. Denise is down there, too, Zach."

"I know. But I can't help Denise. My concern is you, Piper. Please let me be with you."

"I don't know how we'll get either of you down there." Hank looked around, but did not see a rope or anything that would reach to the bottom.

"Charlie help!" Charlie pulled everyone back away from the pit, backed up, and ran toward the pit, leaping over it easily. In seconds, he had disappeared. When he returned a few minutes later, he had a rope curled over his shoulder.

"Forest ranger rope." Charlie pulled his old hat down tighter, threw the rope across the pit to Hank, but stayed on the other side. Charlie beamed with pride and puffed out his chest, and his friends knew that, in his mind, he was a forest ranger like his dad.

Hank tied the rope around his waist and gave the other end to Zach. "Are you two sure you want to do this?"

"Yes. I need to go first, Zach, and start CPR on Billie as soon as possible."

Zach knew not to argue. He helped Piper tie the

rope around her waist, then held it tight and let Piper gradually down into the hole. As soon as she reached the bottom, she untied the rope, knelt beside Billie, and felt her pulse.

"I can't feel anything, but it could just be weak. I'm starting CPR." Piper turned Billie over on her back, and just like in her dream, the Maglite rolled out of the girl's hand.

Zach was by her side in no time, and Hank and Cayce watched from above. Cayce shone the flashlight on Billie.

Zach watched for any sign of life, focusing on the living and not the dead around him, keeping his back to Denise. He did not want to look at her.

He put his fingers on Billie's wrist, hoping to get a pulse, and looked up and smiled at Piper when she gave him a quick glance. "I'm getting a pulse, Piper. Keep going."

Billie coughed and opened her eyes. She looked up and saw a beautiful young woman with golden curls and light eyes smiling down at her. Rays of amber light surrounded the young woman as if she were heaven sent.

"Are you an angel?" Billie asked. "Am I in heaven? I see the light. Is my baby here with me?"

"You're alive, Billie. You and your baby are alive. We're going to get you out of here and take you home." Piper reached for Zach's hand while holding Billie's head in her lap.

But before the three could be helped from the pit, voices were heard in the tunnel. Hank and Cayce motioned for Charlie to jump back across, but he shook his head and headed in the direction of the voices.

"The pit is right up here. If Billie's still alive, I'll shoot her, Steve. If you have a problem with that, go back now. We can't risk her talking. When we leave, we'll explode the mine and they'll never find her or the others. The lambs and the Fold will be safe."

The Keeper began whistling his battle song.

Billie scared! Charlie help!

The little man stopped at one of the oldest, weakest timbers and put his back to it, keeping his face toward the voices. He pushed against the timber, using all the strength in his little body. He could feel the timber shaking loose. Rocks, small rocks, pelted him, and he put his hands over his head to protect his old hat while continuing to push on the timber. As the voices got closer, Charlie pushed harder. A black shadow moved to his side, but he was not afraid. Charlie pushed, and the shadow helped. The timber swayed, and the rocks plummeted down. The tunnel rumbled. The Keeper and Steve saw Charlie and ran toward the pit and safety.

"Billie scared! Charlie not scared!" Charlie screamed at the men as he ran head-on toward them. He beat his chest and gave a deep-throated yell like Tarzan and charged into the big men, head-butting them, knocking them both into a heap on the mine floor.

The tunnel shook violently, the old timber gave way, and Charlie, the hero, and the two bad men were buried under an avalanche of timbers, rocks, and boulders.

Tears streamed down Cayce's face as she realized what had happened. Hank took her hand and squeezed it, but only briefly.

"Mom, what's going on? What was that noise? Where's Charlie?"

Cayce couldn't answer for a few seconds as she swallowed to prevent her voice from shaking. There was more to do. "It's okay, Piper. We're going to get you and Billie out. Are you ready, Zach?"

Cayce heard noises behind them and turned to see several men in SWAT gear racing through the tunnel.

"FBI!" the leader yelled.

Piper heard the FBI agent and squeezed Zach's hand tighter. Holding tightly to Piper's hand, Zach turned to face Denise, his eyes full of tears and compassion.

"I'm taking you home, Denise, to your parents. And then I'm going to find our baby."

Chapter Thirty-Three

Cole Springs Hotel was a somber scene in the days following the mine disaster and the horrors left by the Keeper and his fold. Charlie was gone, but he'd left a hero's legacy and stories to be told for years to come.

Teesh visited Cayce, Harri, and Piper often during those days. She was not dealing well with Charlie's death. On the fourth day, the day the emergency crew had said they should be able to reach Charlie's body in the mine cave-in, Teesh arrived early, wanting to be there when the little man she had loved so dearly would be brought home to Bar None. An ambulance, a respectful formality, and a hearse were both waiting.

Harri had made iced tea and served them all in the parlor. In the middle of the tray was a big plate of Chocolate Factory Brownies, in honor of Charlie. Hank and Zach were not helping the emergency crew today, thinking they needed to be with Teesh, Piper, Cayce, and Harri when Charlie was brought out.

Everyone ate a brownie in his honor. Harri had cut them in bite-size squares, knowing it would be hard for any of them to eat. When they finished, Teesh took out the journal she had brought on the day of the catastrophe, meaning to share it at that time. No one in the group knew what Teesh wanted to share with them, but they were all eager to hear.

"It's story time, my friends. But before I tell you a story, I have something for Zach. This is a journal given to Grandmother by Marissa. Marissa was the daughter of Reverend Mather. Marissa worked for Belle and was also my grandmother's best friend, even after she went to work for Belle as a cook, not a prostitute.

"I'm not going to ruin the surprises you will find in this journal, Zach. You should read it for yourself, and it will add to your history of Bar None. Marissa gives you quite a bit of information about Belle and Absalom, as well. You can share it with the group once you've read it. My mother passed it on to me and said I was sworn to secrecy like she had been. I swore I wouldn't tell what is in here, but I didn't promise her no one else would. I think it will help some of the spirits to reach peace." Teesh handed the journal to Zach, who thanked her by giving her a kiss on the cheek and promising to take good care of it.

"But now for my story. It's not *Charlie and the Chocolate Factory*, but it is a story that needs to be told." Teesh locked her fingers in front of her and began.

"My baby sister, Irene, was a beautiful young woman who could have had any man in the area as a husband, but, like so many, she chose the wrong man and she married too young. She married Lester, a religious fanatic and an overprotective and domineering man who treated his wife more like a prisoner than a wife, trying to protect her from the sins of the world. He wanted children more than anything, but Irene did not want to bring children into her unhappy marriage. All she wanted was to run away from Lester, which she attempted to do many times. Papa tried to get Lester to let Irene return home to him and Mother, but Lester refused.

"Then Irene became pregnant. Her mind was already slipping away, and Lester's treatment of her finished her off." Teesh took a sip of tea and looked at her audience. They all seemed to be hanging on her every word, so she continued without pausing again.

"One day, Lester came home from work and found Irene trying to abort her baby with a wire coat hanger."

Cayce gasped. Now she knew why the Keeper used the stretched-out coat hanger as a symbol and a brand, a modern-day scarlet letter for the young women he felt had committed the unforgivable sin. Cayce looked at the others and knew they, too, had connected the coat hanger's meaning with the symbol.

"I know that is gruesome, but please don't judge my sister. She was in a miserable state of mind by this time. Lester took her to the hospital, and they were able to save the baby. Lester had Irene watched around the clock until my niece, Katherine, was born a few months later.

"When Katherine was six years old, Irene had to be institutionalized. She had attempted suicide three times, and Lester feared she would kill herself and Katherine. Lester used the same over-protectiveness with Katherine, and it worked until she was twenty. That was when she became smitten with a handsome young man new to the area. Katherine became pregnant and tried to run off with her lover, but Lester caught her and would not allow her to marry this worldly young man who had caused her to commit the ultimate sin." Teesh took a swallow of tea before continuing.

"Katherine gave birth to twins, a boy and a girl, but from the start, Lester knew something was wrong with the baby boy. Not only did he look different, it was obvious his mind would not be normal. Shortly after giving birth, Katherine became despondent, extremely depressed, and hanged herself, leaving Lester to care for his two grandchildren." Teesh used her napkin to wipe a tear from the corner of her eye.

"Being the religious zealot he was, Lester immediately blamed the father of the babies, saying it was his sin that had caused Katherine's suicide and the defect in the baby boy. Lester wrapped up the infant, took him to his biological father's cabin here in the valley, and presented him as the curse the man deserved." Teesh stopped, giving her audience time to collect their thoughts. "Need I tell you more?"

"Charlie. He was your great-nephew—Katherine's son and Irene's grandson." Piper summarized what they all knew.

"Yes, and his grandfather giving him to his daddy was the best thing that could ever have happened for Charlie. His daddy loved him unconditionally and called him his blessing, not a curse. And Charlie adored his daddy, the forest ranger. They were inseparable, and Newton, Charlie's daddy, taught him to be independent. That's why Charlie was able to live on his own and to take care of himself all these years after his father died."

"Well, I think that calls for another brownie." Harri gave each one another small brownie.

Piper held up her tea glass and proposed a toast to Charlie. They all stood with their glasses held high. "Here's to you, Charlie, not a forest, but the best forest ranger ever, and our hero. We love you, Charlie."

"Hear, hear!" They clinked glasses and smiled and ate their brownies, savoring each bite for Charlie Chocolate.

****

Three days later, Charlie's funeral was held at the cemetery, outside in nature, beneath the mountains in Charlie's world. Jesus loomed over the crowd; his arms outstretched, encompassing them all. It was the largest group of mourners seen at the tiny cemetery for at least a century. Some came out of curiosity and others were part of the news media. Several people spoke, including Harri, Zach, and Teesh, but the one that brought tears to their eyes spoke while wearing handcuffs. With Teesh's insistence, the sheriff brought Janie to bid her twin brother goodbye. Janie began by apologizing to the crowd for her part in these terrible crimes.

"I dedicated my life to protecting the lambs. Charlie and I were lambs, and I believed we were saved by my grandfather, Lester, but he was not the good man I thought he was." Janie made eye contact with the audience as she spoke. "I found out I had a twin brother when I was ten years old, after finding a picture of us taken with our mother when we were just babies. When I was older, my grandfather told me my mother, Katherine, had tried to abort us as babies just as her mother had done, causing Charlie to have a mental defect. My grandfather blamed our biological father, whom I never met. Now, I don't know if the story my grandfather told me was the truth or if he used it to convince me to join the Fold." Janie reached up with her handcuffed hands and placed them over her heart. She sobbed at this point and had to stop for a minute to regain her composure.

"I thought I was helping the young mothers. The Keeper told the Fold he had released the girls after they gave birth, while their babies had been placed in loving homes. I had no knowledge the girls had been allowed to perish in the pit, not until Billie escaped. But Charlie knew. He kept trying to get me to go into the tunnels with him, but I was too afraid. He kept saying he needed to show me something bad, but he wouldn't tell me what. How I wish now I had gone with my brother. Perhaps I could have saved the lives of those young girls." Janie looked down in shame before continuing.

"Charlie and I met often in the old burned-out cabin in the high country. We had to stop meeting there when I saw the Keeper and Steve coming from the cabin one day. Charlie and I hid in the forest until they were gone. We met at the cemetery after that." Janie's face changed, and she smiled.

"I gave Charlie haircuts and used to leave packages for him with Teesh, packages that always included my huckleberry fudge, his favorite. My brother and I loved each other unconditionally, but because of our grandfather, we were never allowed to visit openly. The few times he caught us, he beat me. I would yell for Charlie to run, but it did not stop me from meeting Charlie every chance I got. Charlie even found his way through the mineshaft in the woods behind the antique shop, and we would meet there until our grandfather caught us one day. He beat Charlie, too, that day, and every time he could catch him anywhere." Janie laughed and cried when she used Charlie's voice to say, "Charlie run like wind!"

****

The crowd of mourners showed open compassion for Janie. Many, including Cayce, Harri, Teesh, and Piper had requested in writing that the courts be lenient with her, but they all knew she would be charged with kidnapping, at a minimum.

Janie was not allowed to remain for the burial; she was whisked away by a sheriff's deputy. The mourners and spectators watched Janie's exit with tear-filled eyes.

Charlie was buried next to Sara, in a wooden coffin made from the trees of the forest he and his dad loved.

Burying Charlie by Sara was Teesh's decision. "He wouldn't want to be buried in a strange place like Idaho Falls, where his father is buried."

They each put a handful of dirt on top of Charlie's coffin. Charlie was buried in the everyday clothes he loved—his old, holey boots ready to run the streets of gold, and of course his forest ranger hat, always his security blanket, pulled tightly down almost over his eyes, making his ears stick out.

A reception was held in the hotel after Charlie's funeral, and the whole crowd of mourners stayed to enjoy a feast of "ever'thang chocolate."

****

The sheriff came by the hotel the next day with information for both Hank and Zach. The body of the man who called himself the Keeper, the last one recovered, had been pulled from the cave-in.

"So who was he?" Hank asked.

Cayce stood beside Hank, anxious to hear the identity of the murderer.

"William Hargill. He had only been in this area the last two years, but no one suspected him of being a criminal, least of all a murderer."

"You've got to be kidding." Hank shook his head in disbelief. "So that's why he never came around to find out what was going on here the last few days."

"Did you know him?" Cayce asked.

"William Hargill, better known as Bill, my job foreman. No wonder Belle and Reverend Mather couldn't scare him off. He had too much at stake here, other than his good-paying day job, not to mention being as mean, or meaner, than the ghosts-in-residence."

"I've got some information for Zach, too," the sheriff announced. "Is he around?"

"He and Piper are down at the cemetery, putting fresh wildflowers on Charlie's grave."

"Good, I'll run this down to him. He seemed pretty anxious to get this information."

****

That night, the group ate their last meal at Bar None together. Hank would stay on to finish the restoration of Bar None for Joshua, who would be in Mexico for an undetermined period of time. Teesh, of course, would be staying, and would act as consultant to make sure "Hank gets it right," as she said, speaking of the rebirth of Bar None. Cayce and Harri would be leaving the next day for a long ride back to Montana in Hawk, where Harri would fly out in a few days back to her city and The Teacake. Harri had already begun the Kegel exercises in preparation for the bumpy ride in Hawk. Zach had business, as he called it, to attend to the next day, and had asked Piper to accompany him.

The meal ended with biscuits and chocolate gravy, a fitting conclusion to their adventure in Bar None.

Later, while having coffee in the parlor, Zach decided it was time to share more information with his new friends.

"I finished reading the journal last night, and thought I'd share a little history with you." He smiled at Piper, and she nodded, signifying she already knew what he had found.

"First of all, Absalom and Yu's baby girl, Tamara, did not die in childbirth."

Cayce and Harri gasped in disbelief. Teesh smiled with approval.

"Belle was jealous of Yu with Absalom, so when Yu had her baby, Belle switched the infant with the stillborn baby girl Marissa had given birth to the day before, a baby conceived by her being raped by her own father, Abel Mather. Marissa had taken refuge with Belle, a different story from what Abel told. Isn't that ironic? Belle helped Marissa and yet ruined the lives of so many innocent young Chinese girls." Zach shook his head in disbelief.

"So true, but is that not an awesome ending to such a tragedy?" Harri was intrigued with this change of events and could hardly contain herself. "Wait 'til I get back. I need more coffee."

Harri returned a few minutes later with the pot and refilled everyone's cups. She set the empty pot on the table and hurriedly took her seat, pointing her index fingers at Zach.

"Okay, Zach. Hit it!"

"To thank Belle for her help, Marissa agreed to take Yu's baby to San Francisco. Marissa was a wet nurse for the baby. She was supposed to deliver Tamara to a crib, a whorehouse that raised baby girls, Chinese baby girls, for the prostitute trade, but when Marissa saw the deplorable conditions in the crib, she couldn't do it. Besides, she had grown to love the baby after weeks of traveling across country with her."

"Marissa left the city with Tamara, not knowing what to do. She knew she could not take the child back to Bar None and could never tell Belle she had not followed her orders. Marissa met a Mormon couple on the train on her way back to Bar None and gave the baby to them. The couple had been childless for the fifteen years of their marriage and felt they were meant to meet Marissa on this train. Marissa convinced the couple to name the baby Lin after her birth mother, and the couple agreed, but named her Marissa Lin, feeling their child should also be named for the brave woman who saved her.

"They kept in touch with Marissa for years, giving her updates on their daughter, the only child the couple ever had. Marissa returned to Bar None and continued to work for Belle. Marissa established a close relationship with Absalom as a friend and confidante, but she never told Absalom his and Yu's child lived, something she regretted until the day she died, which was after a short illness in August 1915.

"Marissa Lin lived a happy life, married, and had many children of her own. I'm sure Yu's and Absalom's bloodline continues today. I plan to check on this as soon as I have access to the Internet again."

"Remarkable!" Harri stood and cupped her hands around her mouth and yelled up to the second floor, "Did you hear that, Belle? Yu lives on, with many descendants, and it's all your doing."

When the group settled down after laughing at Harri, Zach continued.

"But that's not all." Zach turned to Piper. "You remember when you picked that wallpaper for Absalom's bedroom and said Absalom's father liked sunflowers because they grew in cotton fields in Mississippi?"

"I remember. I dreamed it. And the wallpaper is being hung in Absalom's bedroom tomorrow. Right, Hank?" Piper looked at Hank.

"Right, and all the rest of it you picked, too. I really think you ladies need to stay around to see the finished product." Hank looked beside him at Cayce and put his hand on her knee.

"Oh, I'm coming back, and real soon. You can bet on that." Cayce bumped Hank with her shoulder.

"Okay, back to Mississippi." Zach paused, giving everyone time to refocus. "I've already told you about the close relationship Marissa had with Absalom. She wrote in her journal about a conversation she had with Absalom one night when he was very drunk and emotional. He told her he was from the North and how he had to run away as a young man because he killed his stepbrother." Zach took a long pause.

The group looked flabbergasted, and Harri urged Zach to continue. "Get to the nitty gritty, Zach. You're killing me."

"All right, Harri. Here goes. Absalom's stepbrother was no good; he drank too much and was mean to everybody, including his own mother. He raped his own half-sister when she was only thirteen years old. Absalom saw his little sister Chloe crying, and went after the stepbrother, fought with him, and killed him. Absalom's father sent his son west with enough cash to start fresh and told him to change his name and never to tell anyone who he was and never to return home. He was afraid his son would not get a fair trial. Okay, are you ready for Absalom's real name?"

"Zach, I'm warning you!" Harri waved her closed fist at Zach, giving him a frown.

"Okay. Enough suspense. It was Caleb Devaux, Junior." Zach paused to let it all sink in.

"Whoa! Say it ain't so!" Harri began to clap. "Woohoo, Cayce! I guess you're gonna have to call Cowboy One after all, or is he Two now, and tell him the Way found him and presented some more family history on a silver—no, make that a gold—platter!" Harri elongated the word "gold."

"Of course. It all makes sense; Absalom, son of David in the Bible, book of Second Samuel, I think, committed fratricide, meaning brother-killer. Absalom killed his brother Amnon for raping Absalom's sister, Tamar." Cayce rolled out a hand as she called out each name. "Tamar…Tamara, the closest to his real-life sister, at least in trauma, as he dared get without naming her. Absalom was Joshua's own blood relative, and Joshua doesn't even know it. And Caleb, Senior, named his little girl Chloe after his niece, who disappeared as a child from Spanish Oaks in south Mississippi."

"Well, that explains it!" Harri jumped to her feet and headed for the stairs at a full run while everyone stared at her. "Don't say anything until I get back."

Harri ran into her bedroom and ransacked her dresser drawer until she found the pajama top. She reached into the pocket, pulled out the lithograph, and was headed back downstairs when she heard the family picture fall behind her. Thinking she had jarred it when she got her pajama top out, she hurried back to set the picture upright. The hard back of the frame had slipped, and a corner from a piece of paper was sticking out.

Carefully, Harri removed the back. An old, folded, yellowed piece of newspaper fell out. Harri carefully unfolded it and found the same family photograph. Under it was an article about a fire in a hotel in Bozeman, Montana, that claimed three members of a family—the husband and two children, a boy and a girl. The mother and father had both tried to rescue their children but were unable to get them out in time. The father and the two children perished in the fire. The only surviving member of the family was the mother, Anne Marie Coleman, who was severely burned on the face and hands.

****

In just a couple of minutes, Harri ran back down the stairs, her eyes full of tears she tried to wipe away with her sleeve. In her hand, she clutched a photograph and the newspaper article.

"Here, Cayce, I have something for you. Belle gave it to me, but I think she meant for you to have it. It might explain why she was so angry at you." Harri handed Cayce the lithograph. "It's a little faded, but I think you will recognize the man with Belle in this photograph."

Cayce stared at the picture. "It's Joshua!" Cayce brought the picture closer to her eyes. "But it can't be Joshua unless he's reincarnated." She turned the picture over to see if anything was written on the back. "No, it's not Joshua. It's his long-lost cousin, Caleb, Junior, also known as Absalom."

Cayce passed the photograph around so everyone could look at it. "But if I thought Absalom, alias Caleb, Junior, was Joshua, chances are Belle thought Joshua was Absalom, or pretended Joshua was Absalom, when he was here." Cayce looked at Hank. "That explains a lot."

"But does it change anything, Cayce?" Hank had a look of desperation on his face.

"Not one bit." She grabbed Hank's hand and gave it a reassuring squeeze that caused Hank to smile.

"Are we ready to continue now?" Zach looked at Cayce and Hank, who nodded, but Harri was first to speak.

"Since Marissa was the one most hurt by her devil father, Abel Mather, did she mention anything in her journal about her father's church, something that might help us send him away from Bar None? You know—a one-way ticket on the Grim Reaper's Rapid Transit?" Harri was thinking about Belle helping Teesh and her to find the article about his death at Belle's hands.

"No, but there is a drawing on the last page of the journal I'm sure means something. It has haunted me ever since I saw it. It's a wooden cross, and there's a Bible verse under it, written in large script as if Marissa needed to make an important point. Here, I'll show all of you." Zach picked up the journal and turned to the last page and passed it so the rest of the group could see it.

"That's it! The cross I found in the old church! I tried to take it, but when I picked it up, an awful voice told me to get out. It was so terrifying, I left the burned ruins in a hurry and never went back for the cross."

Piper rubbed her knees, as if feeling the bruises of that day.

Cayce ran her fingers over the cross and read the Bible verse aloud. "Romans 12:19. Avenge not yourselves, but rather give place unto wrath: for it is written, Vengeance is mine; I will repay, saith the Lord."

"I think I understand now why the evil Abel Mather has targeted Belle, the restoration attempts of Bar None—especially Belle's establishment—and also Sara and the blue bubbles." Cayce looked at her audience to see if they were following her thoughts, but they all stared at her, their eyes full of questions.

"Belle, Sara, all prostitutes, and even the unborn fetuses aborted by Belle's girls, all symbolized Marissa and her stillborn infant, Abel's own child conceived by his weakness and cruelty. In Abel's twisted and dark mind, he felt he had to rid himself and the world of everyone and everything connected to Belle and Marissa, his way of retaliation for those he blamed for his own transgressions. His pretending to be sent by God rather than the devil, his real master, was his own way of scapegoating and covering up his sins."

She sat up straight. "I have to go to the old church and retrieve the cross Piper found." She closed the journal and handed it back to Zach.

"Are you finished now, Zach? Dude, you laid some bombshells on us, thanks to Teesh!" Harri patted Zach on the back and gave Teesh a big hug.

"Actually, I'm not finished, but this has nothing to do with the history of Bar None." Zach was all smiles, and reached for Piper's hand, giving it a great big squeeze.

"The FBI searched Steve's cabin as well as the homes of the other members of the Fold, and it seems Steve, alias Dr. Stephen White, who performed all the deliveries and examinations for the Keeper for years, had a secret room under his cabin. It was filled with medical books and other things. The FBI confiscated Steve's computer and found all the information pertaining to young women abducted, both in Idaho and other areas of the West, and the children they bore. They also found records of who adopted these children after the mothers mysteriously disappeared." Zach paused and watched the *And so…?* expressions on Harri's and Cayce's faces. Then he blurted it out in one gigantic breath.

"I'm a father! I have a baby boy. Children's Services has him in protective custody. They found him in a halfway house operated by the Fold, a place where they kept babies awaiting adoption. I'm going to see him tomorrow in Boise and get the paperwork and blood work started to establish he is mine so I can bring him home with me. Piper is going with me." Zach smiled his biggest smile at the girl beside him as his friends congratulated him with hugs and handshakes.

Cayce left the group and headed to the front porch. It was late afternoon, and she knew what she had to do. She stepped down on the first step, but turned when she heard the door open and footsteps behind her.

"Surely, you don't think you're going to that old church by yourself?" Hank walked over and joined Cayce on the steps, putting his arm around her. Behind him stood Piper, Zach, and Harri. Cayce turned and smiled, appreciative for the support of her family and friends.

When they got to the church, Piper looked for the cross, but it had been moved from where she'd dropped it in the front of the church.

"It's okay, Piper. I'm sure it's back in the ruins, hidden under the debris. The Way will deliver it to me." Cayce looked at the group but directed her next words to Hank.

"None of you are to come in, regardless of what you see or hear. Follow me if I leave the church, but don't come close. I will be fine. Do you understand, Hank?"

"Yes, ma'am," Hank replied.

"Piper, Harri, Zach?"

They all nodded in agreement, and Cayce stepped over rotting and burned logs and what was left of the flooring. She stopped in front of what would have been the pulpit where the demon preacher hurled hellfire and brimstone at his mesmerized congregation. A dark mist formed in front of her.

A deep, petrifying voice boomed, "Get out!"

Cayce ignored the voice, walked to the back corner, and moved boards and logs until she saw the rustic cross beneath. She lifted the cross and stood silent, watching, as the old church transformed back to the way it had stood over a hundred years ago.

Absalom walked into the church and stopped in front of a beautiful altar engraved with the Biblical words, "Believe on the Lord Jesus Christ, and thou shalt be saved, Acts 16:31."

Cayce knew, immediately, Absalom had built the altar and carved the words with his own skillful hands.

Absalom was carrying the cross he had carved for Yu, the same one he had passed on to Marissa for comfort during her own trials and discontentment. He'd carved it from one long piece of wood, red cedar like the kind that grew in the South, with deep red wavy lines running along its full length. A beautiful burl formed the midsection where a carved rendition of Christ could have been attached but was not. Absalom had been taught Jesus was resurrected, and therefore he refused to place a carving of the Savior's body on the cross.

As he openly cried, Cayce read his thoughts. He was seeing his beautiful wife Yu dressed in a white wedding gown, her long train laid out perfectly behind her. She held a bouquet of wildflowers, and she turned and smiled at her husband-to-be through her white veil.

Absalom carried something else besides the cross. Cayce heard sloshing—a jug of kerosene. The emotionally distraught man yelled at the pulpit.

"This church will not be desecrated by you or any of your followers any longer, Abel Mather. Your funeral will not be held here. I will destroy the church I built, leaving only memories of Christians and of my beautiful wife Yu. And I leave the cross I gave to your lovely, innocent daughter Marissa, whom you violated just as my brother violated my sister." He propped the cross against the altar with new words he had just carved, promising vengeance.

"Rest in peace, sweet Marissa." He whispered the words, pausing at the end with his eyes closed as if praying, or, perhaps, remembering. Then he lifted his eyes to the ceiling and heaven beyond and continued speaking in hushed words, his eyes and heart overflowing. "You have been avenged."

Absalom's whole demeanor changed. His voice

blasted from deep in his throat, and he yelled in an angry, violent voice, shaking his fist in the air.

"Burn in hell, Abel Mather!" After igniting the kerosene he had sprinkled, Absalom turned and left the church, refusing to look back.

Flames shot up all around Cayce, but she felt no heat. She picked up the cross, Marissa's cross, left by Absalom to burn with the church, taking with it the sadness of Yu, Marissa, Absalom, and all those Christians whose church had been desecrated by a demon who pretended to be a follower of God.

As she left the church with the tarnished cross, the black fog screamed at her, demanding she stop. The loud, swarming mass surrounded Cayce, but she was not to be deterred. Holding the cross tightly to her chest with both hands, she left the blazing ruins and headed down the dirt road toward the cemetery.

The others followed only a few feet behind her, at Hank's insistence, with Hank taking the position closest, just in case.

She walked through the cemetery as if in a trance, each step instinctively measured and sure, passing the monument of Jesus and the mass grave of aborted fetuses, passing Sara's grave and Charlie's grave, and all the graves of other former residents of Bar None. She saw Belle, dressed in her mourning clothes, standing near the back of the cemetery, and headed toward her. The black mass circled Cayce, growing larger and louder, drumming hundreds of invisible wings in satanic warning, but she ignored it.

When she reached the shadow, Belle held her hand out and dropped something to the ground. Cayce stopped and laid the cross at Belle's feet and picked up what the madam had dropped. She pulled the drawstring of the small leather pouch open. The bag was filled with gold dust like Charlie had hurled at the black fog the night he saved Sara and the blue bubbles. Cayce scattered all the dust over the ground that showed no indication it had ever been a grave, and hurriedly moved back, sensing what was coming next.

Lightning shot across the clear skies, its jagged energy striking the gravesite and the black fog that hovered over it. The ground rumbled and shook as the demon screeched in suffering and fear, writhing and twisting like a giant snake in its death agony. The ground pulled the beast toward it like a magnet, causing it to burrow itself into the grave like a crazed tornado. The black fog vanished.

Cayce locked gazes with Belle, but there was no smile or sign of any emotion from either of the women. Cayce turned to walk away, but turned back when she heard something drop to the ground behind her. There at her feet was the small, framed snapshot Joshua had taken of her several months ago, the picture that had disappeared from his room in Belle's quarters. Cayce picked the photograph up and put it in her pocket.

"Thank you," she whispered to the silent and empty space where Belle had stood. Then she turned and walked out of the cemetery with her followers close on her heels. Hank moved to her side and took her hand. As the group passed by on the road outside the rusting, fallen fence outlining the history of Bar None, they stopped and looked back to the distant spot where Cayce had left Belle and the black fog. The cross stood like the monument it was meant to be, a talisman sending the demon to eternal damnation.

Chapter Thirty-Four

That night, the moon was full and the stars were out by the millions. Harri, Cayce, Hank, Piper, and Zach walked to the old cemetery, wanting to share their last night together in Bar None with Charlie. Teesh drove the old green Studebaker, still with Charlie's last shine on it, to join the gathering of friends.

Teesh sat on the base of Jesus's statue, and the rest of the group sat on the ground in His golden radiance created by the moon.

Yu was no longer visible. Zach and Piper had been to the cemetery earlier that day, and Zach had delivered the special information to Yu, just in case she was listening. Yu Lin, Beautiful Jade, had found the peace to move on, knowing her baby girl had lived a long, happy life.

All of their eyes focused toward the brilliantly shining white angel tombstone that now marked the spot where two earthly angels rested. The friends sat silent, waiting, hoping for one last visit with Charlie and Sara. Then it happened.

First, the sky filled with celestial clouds backlit by rays of light that could only be heaven-sent. A passageway opened in the midst of the clouds, shining like a Milky Way of sparkling gold dust. They all watched, mesmerized, hoping for a manifestation of translucent figures. Harri abruptly stood and pointed toward the path, her gaze widening.

A black shadow limped up the glittering trail. The dark figure was a hag dressed in men's clothing, an old black hat pulled low to conceal the scars of a mother who had tried to save her children but failed, only to save the children of others later. At the top of the path, beneath the clouds, stood a handsome man with his arms outstretched. A lovely young girl stood by his side, an angelic glow surrounding her like a full-bodied halo. A small, tow-headed boy in short pants, white shirt, and suspenders held to his daddy's knee. His free hand opened and closed, opened and closed toward the woman approaching, and his dimples deepened as his smile filled his face.

The figure's peg leg made her walking cumbersome, but she continued to climb slowly upward, her head held higher with each step. Halfway up her sparkling course, her darkness began melting away, beginning at the ground and moving up her stooped body.

First, her peg leg and her miner's brogan boot disappeared, leaving her with two small feet covered by shiny black, women's lace-up shoes. Her pace quickened as her men's clothing transformed into a long, full, gray skirt with a white lacy bodice tucked neatly in at her trim waistline. The old hat vanished, uncovering beautiful long, brown hair that hung in big curls down her back. She reached out and placed her hand in the strong hand of her husband as her children joined them, and all encircled the mother in a family embrace. The woman turned and looked down with the smooth, flawless face of a beautiful young woman. Her face erupted in a jubilant smile aimed at Harri.

"Goodbye, Anne Marie!" Harri called out, smiling at her friend. She gave a farewell wave as Annie and her family turned and disappeared into the cloudy mist.

Next, the blue bubbles appeared as if propelled from the monument of Jesus. They bounced close together, like a cast of hundreds of tiny blue dancers waltzing to Bach's "Minuet in G," heavenly music played by an orchestra of angelic musicians. The bubbles dipped down, beckoning to Sara and Charlie, and began to swirl faster as they escorted the two new angels upward.

The sky exploded with long sparks of brilliance emanating in all directions like festive, muted fireworks. The sparks beckoned to the bubbles, and they merged again, undulating to the silent strings of angel harps. A meteor shower of aqua blue rose higher and higher; waves oscillated on a magical sea of blue clouds and stars. The onlookers strained their necks and shaded their eyes so they could see into heaven's dazzling beacon.

The bubbles parted, allowing earth's angels to continue up their gold-strewn course alone, but before they reached the end, the two best friends, Charlie and Sara, turned, holding hands, and smiled down at the people they loved.

Two star-wrapped objects floated gingerly down, glistening against the mountain's silhouette, sailing and dipping in long waving motions, caught in the mountain breeze like feathers from angel wings. The old brown hat, a forest ranger's hat, its security no longer needed, glided slowly and gently down to land at the feet of Jesus in front of Teesh. A delicate blue ribbon followed, spinning gracefully like a tiny ballerina, and curled itself softly on top of the hat.

Cayce, her eyes full of tears and her heart overflowing with joy, stood and began singing and the others joined her:

Jesus loves me, this I know,
For the Bible tells me so,
Little ones to Him belong,
They are weak, but he is strong.
Yes, Jesus loves me.
Yes, Jesus loves me.
Yes, Jesus loves me.
The Bible tells me so.

A word about the author…

Dr. Sue Clifton is a retired principal, fly fisher, paranormal investigator, and published author. Dr. Sue, as she is known, can't remember a time when she did not write, beginning with two plays published at sixteen. Her writing career was placed on hold while she traveled the world with her husband Woody in his career, as well as with her own career as a teacher and administrator in Mississippi, Alaska, New Zealand, and on the Northern Cheyenne Reservation in Montana.

Dr. Sue appeared in October 2015 in A&E's five-part series for television *Cursed: The Bell Witch* and was also featured in *USA Today* in articles about her nonfiction book which included the truth about the Bell Witch Legend as told through clairvoyant Angel Leigh.

Dr. Sue now travels and writes with her sister Nyoka Beer in search of places and material for their new series "Sisters of the Way" with The Wild Rose Press.

Dr. Sue divides her time between Montana and Mississippi and loves all things vintage. With her vintage camper "Delta Blue," Dr. Sue attends events of the national outdoor women's group Sisters on the Fly.

Dr. Sue is the author of twelve books: seven novels in series with The Wild Rose Press, Inc.; and two nonfiction books, two paranormal mysteries, and a children's book elsewhere. Dr. Sue supports Casting for Recovery (CFR), a national organization providing fly fishing retreats for women with breast cancer. A portion of her profits from all book sales goes to CFR.

Visit Dr. Sue at www.drsueclifton.com
and at Novels by Dr. Sue Clifton on Facebook.

Thank you for purchasing
this publication of The Wild Rose Press, Inc.

For questions or more information
contact us at
info@thewildrosepress.com.

The Wild Rose Press, Inc.
www.thewildrosepress.com

To visit with authors of
The Wild Rose Press, Inc.
join our yahoo loop at
http://groups.yahoo.com/group/thewildrosepress/